For my daughter-in-law, Megan Kelley Small, with love.

Bedazzled

Also by Bertrice Small:

The Kadin
Love Wild and Fair
Adora
Unconquered
Beloved
Enchantress Mine
Blaze Wyndham
The Spitfire
A Moment in Time
To Love Again
Love, Remember Me
The Love Slave
Hellion
Betrayed
Deceived
The Innocent

"The O'Malley Saga"

Skye O'Malley
All The Sweet Tomorrows
A Love For All Time
This Heart of Mine
Lost Love Found
Wild Jasmine

"Skye's Legacy"

Darling Jasmine
Bedazzled

BERTRICE SMALL

Bedazzled

KENSINGTON BOOKS
http://www.kensingtonbooks.com

KENSINGTON BOOKS are published by

Kensington Publishing Corp.
850 Third Avenue
New York, NY 10022

ISBN 1-57566-432-1

First Printing: July, 1999
10 9 8 7 6 5 4 3 2 1

Printed in the United States of America

Prologue

LONDON, 1616

"*Is he dead, Mother?*" The boy peered closely and curiously at the body slumped in the dark-blue tapestry chair.

The woman held a small looking glass attached to the gilt cord about her waist up to the man's nostrils. The mirror remained clear, not the faintest hint of breath upon it. "He is dead, my son," she replied matter-of-factly. Then, reaching into the bosom of her gown, she drew forth a dagger with a beautifully carved and bejeweled handle. She looked at the weapon a moment, admiring its artistry, regretting it would be lost to them. Handing it to the boy, she commanded, "Put it into his heart as I have shown you."

The boy stared down at the blade in his hands. "I always wanted this dagger," he mused. "Why must it be this dagger, Mother? I shall not be allowed to have it now, shall I? It isn't fair!"

"We have been over this several times, my son," the woman said quietly. "This weapon is known to belong to your older brother. As he and Lord Jeffers have had a very public falling out over Lady Clinton, when this dagger is found in Lord Jeffers's heart, it will be assumed that your brother killed him." She smiled. "You do want to be your father's heir, *caro mio,* don't you? How much nicer to be his heir than just his second son. There is little satisfaction in being a second son."

"I suppose so," the boy said, and he sighed. "Will they hang Dev for this murder, Mother?"

"If they catch him," the woman replied. "But hopefully they won't. I really don't want your elder brother's death on my conscience. I just want *my* darling little boy to be his father's heir. It isn't our fault that your father was married, had a son, and was widowed before I wed him."

"But if they don't hang my brother, then how can I be our father's heir? What if Dev proves his innocence?"

"Your brother will have no chance to prove his innocence, dearest," his mother explained patiently. "We have been over this before. Your brother is rash, and he will be convinced to flee England before he can even be arrested. He will never dare to come back with the threat of execution hanging over him. Now push the dagger into Lord Jeffers's heart, dearest." She lightly touched his hand encouragingly.

The boy did as his mother had bid him, twisting the blade with some pleasure, she noted, not particularly shocked. The woman took the goblet from which her victim had been drinking, splashing the remaining contents into the fireplace, where they hissed briefly, then died away. Using her own handkerchief, she wiped the goblet free of the residue of finely ground glass and hair—the items she had used to kill her prey. Then she poured fresh wine from the decanter into the goblet, and replaced it upon the table opposite a second goblet, which she tipped over to give the appearance of both anger and haste on the part of the victim. "There," she said, well satisfied with her efforts.

Her son was growing fretful. "Can we leave now, Mother?" The boy whined impatiently.

She nodded. Taking his hand, the pair slipped unnoticed from the house that Lord Jeffers had rented when he was in residence in London. His valet, the only servant Lord Jeffers employed, had been given the night off. The woman had made certain, using one of her own serving girls, that he would not return until dawn. Even now, as she and her son mounted their horses—which had been hidden in the alley belonging to their victim's house—and rode quickly back to their own elegant abode, the woman knew her stepson would have been informed already of Lord Jeffers's demise, and encouraged to escape lest he be blamed for the crime.

Of course the young man would argue—he always did—and attempt to reason with the family's majordomo, but poor desperate Rogers would convince him, for he loved the young man whom he had known his entire life as he would a son. Rogers was old now. His weakening mind could easily be confused. The woman had coolly informed him, just before she and her son had left the house that evening, that Lord Jeffers would be found murdered in the morning with the young master's dagger in his heart. If Rogers did not forewarn the young man, he would surely be arrested, convicted, and hung for the crime. After all, was not the quarrel between the two men over that strumpet, Lady Clinton, public knowledge? Lord Jeffers had no other known enemies.

"But, my lady, how could you know such a thing?" the old man had quavered. Then he shuddered when she smiled knowingly at him. He was not so old that he didn't realize she knew because she planned to commit the murder herself. He had always suspected she was a dangerous woman, but as a servant he was helpless to her will. His master was at court with the king. There was no way he could get a message to him in time. Besides, would his lord believe such a tale?

Rogers had always known that her ladyship was jealous of the young master's position. He knew she coveted it for her own son, but he had never imagined she would kill for her child. Still, she was giving the elder son a fair chance to escape with his life, even if he would lose everything else he held dear. She would have the young master's inheritance for her own.

He bowed stiffly. "I will see my lord makes a good escape, your ladyship."

The woman nodded. "I knew that I could count upon you," she said. Then she added, "You have always been a careful man, Rogers. Is it not comforting to at least know he will be safe, *and* that you will have a comfortable old age?"

"Yes, my lady," he had replied impassively, "I am grateful for your kindness." But when she had gone, he had run up the staircase of the house faster than he had ever imagined he could at his age, delivered the bad news to his young master, and then convinced him, not without great difficulty, to flee for his own safety. Less than a year later, Rogers had died quietly in his sleep. The truth of Lord Jeffers's death went with him.

Part I

ENGLAND, 1625–1626

Chapter

"Welcome to France, madame," the duc de St. Laurent said to his mother-in-law as he handed her from her great traveling coach.

"*Merci*, monseigneur," Catriona Stewart-Hepburn said, curtseying stiffly, her famous leaf-green eyes making contact with the duc's but a moment and then peering beyond him anxiously.

James Leslie, the duke of Glenkirk, stepped quickly forward, a smile on his handsome face, his arms open to enfold his mother into his warm embrace.

"Jemmie!" she cried out, her eyes filling with tears even as his arms closed about her, and he kissed her soft cheek. "My bairn!"

Glenkirk laughed, and then he hugged his mother. "Hardly a bairn, madame. Nae at my age." He stepped back, and gazed upon her. " 'Tis good to see you, madame. When we learned that you would be coming, we brought over our entire brood so you could finally meet your grandchildren, some of whom are already half grown."

"And your wife, Jemmie," his mother said. "You have been married more than a decade, and I have never met her."

"Jasmine has been so busy having our bairns that I couldna let her travel. She was nae a lass when I married her after all." He tucked her hand in his arm. "Come, and let us go into the château.

They are all awaiting you, my wife and family, and my sister, and her children."

"Jean-Claude," Lady Stewart-Hepburn said, turning to her son-in-law, " 'tis really quite good of you to have us all."

"The château is large," the duc de St. Laurent replied cordially, "and a few more children makes little difference."

His mother-in-law raised an eyebrow, and then she laughed. James Leslie had three sons of his own, plus two stepdaughters and two stepsons. Seven in all, and it was hardly a trifle especially when added to her daughter and son-in-law's six children. Her youngest child, her daughter, Francesca, had married her dashing French duke fourteen years ago when she was sixteen, and had lived happily with him ever since. Shortly afterward her beloved second husband, Francis Stewart-Hepburn, had grown suddenly ill, and died. But he had lived to see both of his daughters settled. Francesca with her Jean-Claude, and Jean, or Gianna as she was known, the wife of the marchese di San Ridolfi. Their son, Ian, was another matter, and had yet to settle down.

"How is Jeannie?" the duke of Glenkirk asked his mother as they entered the house.

"So Italian that you would never fathom that she was a Scot," his mother answered him.

"And Ian? What mischief is he up to these days?"

"We must speak on Ian," came the terse reply.

They entered a bright salon where the family awaited them.

"*Grandmère! Grandmère!*" Francesca's children rushed forth to surround her, demanding her attention as they welcomed her.

"Welcome, Mama," the duchesse de St. Laurent said as she kissed her parent. "I thank God that you have come safely to us."

"The trip is long, and it is tedious, Francesca," her mother replied, "but not dangerous." How beautiful she was, Cat thought. She has *his* wonderful auburn hair, and my eyes. When she smiles, I see *him*. She acknowledged Francesca's children, the four boys and two little girls, greeting each by name. Then, looking across the salon, Lady Stewart-Hepburn saw that her eldest son had joined a beautiful woman with night-dark hair and spectacular jewelry.

Seeing the direction of her gaze, the duke of Glenkirk led his wife forward. "Madame, my wife, Jasmine Leslie."

Jasmine curtsied gracefully. "Welcome to France, madame. I am pleased that we finally meet."

"As am I," the older woman said, kissing her daughter-in-law on both of her smooth cheeks. Then she stepped back a pace. "You are very beautiful, Jasmine Leslie, and quite different from the wife I chose for Jemmie when he was young."

"I hope I compare favorably, madame," Jasmine answered.

Lady Stewart-Hepburn laughed. "Isabelle was a sweet child, but a moon to your sun, my dear. Now, I want to meet my grandchildren! *All of them!* I consider your bairns mine, too, as my Jemmie has been father to them longer than their own sires, eh?"

For a brief moment, Jasmine was speechless, and her turquoise eyes grew misty. Then, recovering herself, she beckoned her offspring forward. She was truly touched that Jemmie's mother could be so generous.

"Madame, may I present my eldest child, Lady India Lindley."

The young girl curtsied prettily.

"And my eldest son, Henry Lindley, the marquis of Westleigh. My second daughter, Lady Fortune Lindley. My son, Charles Frederick Stuart, the duke of Lundy."

While the girls curtsied, the young boys bowed.

Lady Stewart-Hepburn acknowledged them graciously, saying to the eleven-and-a-half-year-old duke of Lundy, "We are distantly related, my lord, on your late father's side."

"My grandfather spoke of you once," the young duke replied. "He said you were the most beautiful woman in all of Scotland. I see he did not lie, madame."

His stepgrandmother burst out laughing. "God help us all, my lord, but you are surely a true Stuart!" She wondered what this boy would say if he knew that the now-deceased old man who had been his grandfather had once been an unstoppable satyr who had destroyed her first marriage.

"And these are Jemmie's bairns," Jasmine was continuing. "Our eldest, Patrick, then Adam, and Duncan. We had a little lass, but lost her almost two years ago. She caught measles and died a month after my dearest grandmother. She was named for that lady, and for Janet Leslie. Janet Skye."

"I remember my great-grandmother, Janet," Cat told Jasmine. "We called her *Mam.* She was a very formidable woman."

"As was my grandmother," Jasmine replied.

"Is it true you were once in a harem?" India Lindley suddenly burst out.

Cat turned to look at the girl. She was easily on the brink of womanhood, and every bit as beautiful as her mother with black hair and the most wonderful golden eyes. "Yes," she answered. "I was in the harem of the sultan's grande vizir."

"Which sultan?" India persisted.

"There is only one sultan," Cat said. "The Ottoman."

"Was it exciting or awful?" India's eyes were alight with unbridled curiosity.

"Both," Cat told her.

"India!" Jasmine was mortified by her daughter's outrageous behavior, but then, India was so damned headstrong, and always had been.

"My mother was raised in a harem," India volunteered.

"Was she?" Now it was Cat's turn to be intrigued.

"My father was the Grande Mughal of India," Jasmine explained. "My mother was English. She is married to the earl of BrocCairn."

"I remember your mother," Cat replied. "Velvet is her name. She stayed with us at Hermitage years ago. You don't really look like her, do you?"

"I have some of her features, but I am mostly a mixture of my maternal grandmother and my father," Jasmine answered.

That would indeed account for the slightly Oriental tilt of Jasmine's unusual turquoise eyes and the faint golden tint of her skin, Lady Stewart-Hepburn thought. She let her gaze wander to the pert India. The girl had skin like milky porcelain and a faint blue sheen to her midnight-colored hair, but where had she gotten those eyes? They were like a cat's. Gold, not amber, and with tiny flecks of black in them. The older woman settled herself into a chair by the fire. France in April was a chilly place. The fuss of her arrival had died about her. Her children and their mates had ensconced themselves about her on a settee, a chair, and a stool. Her grandchildren were amusing themselves.

"How old is India?" she asked.

"She will be seventeen at the end of June," Jasmine said, suspecting what her mother-in-law would next ask. She was not disappointed.

"And she is not married?"

Jasmine shook her head.

"Betrothed?"

"Nay, madame."

"You had best see to it soon then," came the pithy observation. "The wench is ripe for bedding. Close to overripe, and susceptible to trouble, I would wager."

James Leslie laughed at his mother's words. "India has nae yet met a man to attract her attention, Mother. I want my girls to wed for love. I did, and I hae never been happier."

"Mam had me betrothed to your father at four, and we married but moments before your birth when I was barely sixteen," Lady Stewart-Hepburn noted. "Love was not a consideration in making the match, although I came to care for your father."

"*But you loved Lord Bothwell unconditionally,*" the duke of Glenkirk reminded his parent. "Besides, yer first marriage took place forty-seven years ago. Times have changed since then, Mother."

"And you would allow your stepdaughter to make an unsuitable match in the name of love?" Cat was surprised to find she was appalled. *I am obviously growing old,* she thought.

Jasmine interposed herself between her husband and his mother in the conversation. "India will never choose unwisely, madame, for she is most proud, and extremely aware of her heritage. She is the grandchild of a great monarch, and her father's family was an old and very noble one. It pleases her that my stepfather, and her stepfather, both have ties to the royal family. She adored my grandmother, Madame Skye, and was weened upon the tales of her adventures, and her relationship with Great Bess. When the time comes, India will pick the right man."

"Have you had no offers for her?" Cat was curious.

"Several, but they did nae please India. In most cases, she felt the families involved were simply looking to her fortune, and nae to her," the duke of Glenkirk told his mother. "She was correct. India can be very astute."

"A girl in love for the first time is not always careful or wise," Cat cautioned.

"Well, as no one has yet caught India's fancy, I do not believe we have cause for worry," Jasmine replied.

The Leslies of Glenkirk had come to France to represent their country at the proxy marriage of the new king, Charles I, to the French princess, Henrietta Marie. King James had sickened, and died unexpectedly on the twenty-seventh of March. The marriage negotiations had already been concluded, although there was some difficulty about the princess's religion. Charles Stuart had no time to argue with his government. He was suddenly king, and without an heir. While he did not feel he could depart his country to personally celebrate his marriage with his father newly deceased, he felt strongly that the marriage must go forward immediately, and his queen be brought to England.

The marriage, which originally was to have been celebrated in June, was now moved forward to the first of May so Charles's enemies in the parliament would not have time to marshall their forces, and delay or prevent the match. The duke of Buckingham was to have acted as the king's proxy at the June celebration, but now he had to remain in England to attend the old king's funeral, which was set for the end of April, for it was not unusual for a king to lie in state several weeks. Instead, the duc de Chevreuse would act as the English king's proxy. Chevreuse was related to both the French royal house and the English, through their mutual ancestor, the duc de Guise. He was therefore a suitable choice, and acceptable to both sides.

Most of the English court remained in England, but Charles had asked the duke of Glenkirk and his family to attend his wedding.

It would be a far more pleasant occasion than poor old Jamie's funeral, the duke conceded to his wife, and if his sister, the duchesse de St. Laurent, would ask their mother to come from Naples for a visit, Jasmine and the children could at least meet Catriona Hay Leslie Stewart-Hepburn.

The young king's reason was more personal. James Leslie himself was distantly related to Charles, and his stepson, little Charles Frederick Stuart, was the new monarch's nephew, although he had been born on the wrong side of the blanket. Such accidents of birth did not matter to the Stuarts except where the succession was concerned. They had always welcomed, recognized, and considered their bastards legitimate members of their clan. The king wanted some of his family blood at his wedding ceremony, and the Leslies of Glenkirk would acquit themselves, and therefore the Stuarts, quite well. They were also not important enough to be missed at the official mourning ceremonies since they only rarely came to court.

The St. Laurent château was in the countryside two hours from Paris. The Leslies had been included on the guest list for the signing of the marriage contract and the betrothal ceremony on the twenty-eighth of April, as well as the wedding on May first. They would attend with the five oldest children. The St. Laurents, Lady Stewart-Hepburn, and the two youngest Leslie children would come for the wedding only. The Lindley children, and their Stuart half-brother had been too young to participate in King James's court when Queen Anne had been alive. She had died the year India was eleven. The queen had adored fêtes and masques. She had loved art, music, and dancing. Her dour husband had tolerated her follies, as he called them, for love of his Annie. Once the queen had died, however, James's court became less entertaining. It was hoped that the new French queen would enliven Charles Stuart's court even as the late Anne of Denmark had enlivened the court of James Stuart.

Glenkirk and his family were astounded, even openly awed, by the elegant magnificence of the Louvre palace. There was absolutely nothing like it in England. They were met by the two royal English ambassadors, the earl of Carlisle and Viscount Kensington, who quickly escorted them to King Louis's chamber where the signing would take place. First, however, the proper protocol had to be followed. The two ambassadors handed the contract to the king and his lord chancellor to read. This done, the king signified his acceptance of the terms previously agreed upon, and only then was the princess summoned to her brother's presence.

Henrietta-Marie arrived, escorted by the queen mother, Marie di Medici, and the ladies of the court. The princess was garbed in a gown of cloth-of-gold and silver, embroidered all over with golden fleurs-de-lys, and encrusted with diamonds, rubies, emeralds, and sapphires. Once the bride had taken her place, the bridegroom's proxy was called. The duc de Chevreuse came into the king's chamber wearing a black-striped suit covered with diamonds. He bowed first to the king and then the princess. Then the duc presented his letter of authority to the king, bowing once again. Accepting it, Louis XIII handed it to the chancellor, and then signed the marriage contract. Other signatories were Henrietta-Marie, Marie di Medici, the French queen, Anne of Austria, the duc de Chevreuse, and the two English ambassadors.

The contract duly signed and witnessed, the formal religious betrothal was performed in the king's chambers by the princess's godfather, Cardinal de la Rochefoucauld, the duc de Chevreuse answering for the king of England. The ceremony over, the princess retired to the Carmelite convent in Faubourg St. Jacques to rest and pray until her wedding on the first of May, and the guests departed, the duke of Glenkirk and his family returning to Château St. Laurent.

On Henry Lindley's sixteenth birthday, which happened to be the thirtieth of April, the Glenkirk party, the St. Laurents, and Lady Stewart-Hepburn traveled to Paris for the royal wedding. It was better, the duc said, to go the day before rather than waiting until the first, but the roads were clogged anyway with all the traffic making its way into the city for the celebration. By chance, James's brother-in-law had a small house on the same tiny street as did Jasmine's French relations, who would not be coming for the wedding. The de Savilles lived in the Loire region, many miles from Paris, and while of noble stock, they were not important. Besides, it was springtime, and their famous vineyards at Archambault needed tending more than they needed to be in the capital for the princess's wedding to the English king, so they gladly loaned their little house to their relations.

The wedding day dawned gray and cloudy. By ten o'clock in the morning it was raining. Nonetheless, crowds had begun gathering outside of the great square before Notre-Dame the previous evening. Now the square was overflowing with people eager to see the wedding. The archbishop of Paris had gotten into a terrible row with the Cardinal de la Rochefoucauld. It was the cardinal who had been chosen to perform the wedding ceremony, despite the fact that the cathedral was the archbishop's province. The royal family had brushed aside the archbishop's protests as if he had been no more than a bothersome insect. Furious, the archbishop had retired to his country estates, not to return until after the wedding. He could not, however aggravated he might be, deny the princess the use of his palace, which was close by the cathedral, and so at two o'clock that afternoon in the pouring rain, Henrietta-Marie departed her apartments in the Louvre for the archbishop's residence in order to dress.

Fortunately a special gallery had been constructed from the door of the archbishop's palace to the door of the cathedral. It was raised eight feet above the square and set upon pillars, the lower half of which were wrapped in waxed cloth, and the upper half in purple satin embroidered with gold fleurs-de-lys. At the west door of the cathedral was a raised platform which was sheltered by a canopy of cloth-of-gold that had been waxed to prevent the rain from penetrating it. At six o'clock in the evening, the bridal procession began streaming out of the archbishop's palace, moving down the open-sided gallery toward the cathedral.

The bridal party was led by one hundred of the king's Swiss Guards. The first two rows were a mixture of drummers and soldiers with blue and gold flags. Following the guards came a party of musicians. Twelve played upon oboes. There were eight drummers who were followed by the ten state trumpeters playing a fanfare. Following the royal musicians was the grand master of ceremonies behind whom strode knights of the Order of the Holy Ghost in jeweled capes. Next came seven royal heralds in crimson-and-gold-striped tabards.

The bridegroom's representative, the duc de Chevreuse, was proceeded by three ranking noblemen. He was garbed in a black velvet suit, slashed to show its cloth-of-gold lining. On his head was a velvet cap sporting a magnificent diamond that glittered despite the dullness of the late afternoon. Behind him were the earl of Carlisle and Viscount Kensington in suits of cloth-of-silver.

The populace standing in the pouring rain on either side of the gallery struggled against each other, attempting to get the best glimpse of the wedding party and the court. Cries of "God bless the king" and "Good fortune to the princess" were heard by those moving along the gallery toward the platform and the cathedral. Most of the guests would pass through the raised, canopied flooring, and take their places within the cathedral. Only certain chosen ones would remain upon the dais to see the ceremony performed. Because the king of England was considered a Protestant, it was necessary to perform the wedding ceremony before the doors of the cathedral, but as all weddings had once been performed in this manner, little was thought of the arrangement. Afterward, a mass would be celebrated within Notre-Dame.

Among the chosen to view the wedding, India Lindley stood shivering as she drew her cloak about her. She should have worn her rabbit-lined cape, but it was not nearly as fashionable as the one she was wearing. She looked at the French courtiers in their magnificent clothing. She had never seen anything like it. It was utterly spectacular, and she felt like someone's poor country relation. Her mother, of course, had fabulous jewelry which covered a multitude of fashion sins, but she and Fortune looked positively dowdy even in comparison to the bosomless eleven-year-old Catherine-Marie St. Laurent, whose claret-colored silk and cloth-of-gold gown was delicious.

"Here comes the bride," Fortune singsonged next to her. Fortune was enjoying every moment of this colorful and marvelous show. It didn't matter to her that her mother and sister looked like a pair of burgher's daughters.

India focused her eyes upon Henrietta-Marie, who was escorted by both of her brothers, King Louis XIII, resplendent in cloth-of-gold and silver, and Prince Gaston, elegant in sky blue silk and cloth-of-gold. The petite sixteen-year-old bride was dressed in an incredible gown of heavy cream-colored silk embroidered all over with gold fleurs-de-lys, pearls, and diamonds. The dress was so encrusted with gold and diamonds that it glittered as she walked. On her dark hair was a delicate gold-filigreed crown, from whose center spire dripped a huge pearl pendant that caused the watching crowds to gasp.

"I have better," murmured the duchess of Glenkirk, and her mother-in-law restrained her laughter.

Behind the bride and her brothers came the queen mother, Marie di Medici, wearing, as always, her black widow's garb, but dripping with diamonds in recognition of the occasion. Finally came France's queen, Anne of Austria, in a gown of cloth-of-silver and gold tissue, sewn all over with sapphires and pearls, leading the French court. The few English guests had already been brought to the raised and canopied dais to await the arrival of the bridal party now come.

The cardinal performed the wedding ceremony, and then the bride, her family, and the French court were escorted into the cathedral for the celebration of the Mass. Inside, the cathedral was filled with other invited guests: members of the parliament, other politicians, and civic officials, garbed formally for this occasion in ermine-trimmed crimson velvet robes. The walls of the cathedral were hung with fine tapestries, and the bridal party was seated upon another canopied, raised dais. Having settled the bride upon a small throne, the duc de Chevreuse departed her side to escort the two English ambassadors and the few English guests to the archbishop's palace for they would not attend the Mass.

"Ridiculous!" Jasmine muttered beneath her breath.

"*Be silent!*" James Leslie said softly, but sharply. While he agreed with his wife that this prejudice between Roman and Anglican, Anglican and Protestant, was absurd, it was a fact they had to live with, and to involve one's self in the sectarian fray was to make enemies. It was better to remain neutral. Lady Stewart-Hepburn nodded her approval of her son's wisdom.

"Did you see the gowns?" India said excitedly to her mother. "I have never seen such clothing!"

"A bridal gown should be beautiful," Jasmine replied.

"Nay, not the bridal gown," India responded. "It is lovely, of course, but it is the gowns worn by the women of the French court that I am envious of, Mama. Your jewels, naturally, always overshadow anything you may wear, but Fortune and I look like two little sparrows compared to the French ladies. Why, even flat-chested Catherine-Marie outshines us. It is most embarrassing! We are here to represent our king, and we look like two serving wenches!"

"What's wrong with our gowns?" Fortune asked her elder sister. "I think we look quite nice. I do like Queen Anne's short hair, though. Can I cut my hair like that, Mama?"

"No," Jasmine said. "Your hair is beautiful, child. Why would you cut it? If this Spanish queen of France would cut and frizz her own hair, it is because her hair is not as fine as yours, Fortune."

"Nor as red," Fortune grumbled.

"I am going to have an entire new wardrobe made when I get home to England," India said. "I shall dazzle King Charles's court, Mama, with my French fashions and their vibrant colors. Our countrymen wear such dull colors. Pale blue, rose, brown, and black. And, Mama, you have so much jewelry. Would you not let me have some of it, *please?*"

"She is certainly not shy about asking for what she wants, is she?" Cat said to her son. "She has been, I imagine, quite a handful to raise, Jemmie, eh?"

The duke of Glenkirk smiled. "She is nae worse, Mother, than any other girl," he told her. "She hae always been an obedient lass."

"Give her what she wants, and then find her a good husband," was his parent's advice. "She will not be obedient much longer, I think."

"I agree with your mother," Jasmine said. "There is a wild streak in India that I have never really recognized before. Perhaps I have not wanted to see it because it reminds me of my brother, Salim. But suddenly I see familiar traits in India, and I remember that my father indulged Salim, even when his disobedience was unforgivable. And yet our father forgave him. Drunkenness, lechery, theft. *Even murder.* There was only one thing my father would not forgive him."

Curious, Lady Stewart-Hepburn asked, "What?"

"Salim desired me as a man desires a woman. My father could not countenance it, and I was married to my first husband, Prince Javid Khan. Salim had him murdered, and knowing he was near death, my father smuggled me out of India. When I was India's age I was about to be wed to my second husband, who was India's father."

"Then you must find a husband for India," Cat said. "It is obvious it is time for her to be settled before she causes a scandal. I wish I knew a suitable match for her in Naples."

"Oh, no!" Jasmine cried. "I should not want her so far away from us. Like my grandmother, I want my family about me, and we have all our family in England and Scotland, madame. All but my Uncle Ewan O'Flaherty, who lives in Ireland. And, you, madame, who remain in the kingdom of Naples. Jemmie has told me of your, ah, *difficulty* with the late king, but now that James Stuart is dead and buried, would you not consider coming home to Scotland again? There is a place for you at Glenkirk always."

"Bless you, my dear Jasmine," Cat said, her voice thick with emotion, "but my beloved Bothwell is buried in Naples, at the foot of our villa's garden, and that is where I will lie one day, beside him in death as I was in life. Besides, my old bones are too used to the warmth of the south to tolerate the damp and chill of Scotland any longer."

"Your great-grandmother returned home from a warm climate," the duke said quietly.

"I am not Janet Leslie," Cat said as quietly.

Outside the salon where they were waiting, a canon boomed.

"It would appear the Mass is finally over," the earl of Carlisle noted dryly.

"Took long enough," Viscount Kensington responded. "Do these Catholics really think God is going to overlook their fornications and other mischief just because they spend so much time in church on their knees? Well, let's hope this little queen we've gotten proves as fecund as her old mother."

"Come to the windows," the earl called to them. "The rain has finally stopped, and there are fireworks being shot off."

They stood watching as the rockets soared into the skies, bursting red or green, gold or blue sparkles against the darkness. The wedding party and its guests made their way to the archbishop's palace where a banquet was to be held in the great hall, which had been newly decorated for the occasion with tapestries from the Louvre.

A banquet table stretched from one end of the hall to the other. The king had been placed in its center beneath yet another embroidered cloth-of-gold canopy. To his right sat his mother. To his left, his sister, England's new queen. The proxy bridegroom was placed on Henrietta's other side. The bride was served by a high-ranking nobleman, her old friend from childhood, Baron Bassompierre, and two French marshals.

When the meal had at last ended, all the guilds of Paris paraded before the new queen, and her brother's Swiss Guards performed an intricate drill. At eleven o'clock, the exhausted bride retired back to the Louvre. For the rest of the week, all Paris rejoiced, and celebrated the marriage that united England and France. There were balls and banquets so numerous it was difficult to get to them all. The finest, however, was given by the Queen Mother in her new and magnificent Luxembourg Palace.

Then, suddenly, George Villiers, the duke of Buckingham, arrived in France. He had come, he announced grandly, to escort England's new queen home. Buckingham was very tall, and extremely handsome. His dark eyes when fixed upon a woman made her feel she was the only woman in the world. His wife was devoted to him, and while he was considered a terrible flirt, Lady Villiers had no cause for jealousy. Buckingham had such beautiful features that the late King James had given him the nickname of Steenie, because the old monarch said George Villiers had the face of St. Stephen, who had been noted for his beauty.

The French queen was openly admiring of the Englishman. The French male courtiers hated him on sight, for they considered Villiers arrogant. It was their opinion he behaved as if he were a king himself, and they could barely tolerate his presence. Their wives disagreed, sending the duke languishing looks each time he came their way; smiling invitingly, sighing over his chestnut curls, his exquisitely barbered mustache and little pointed beard. The queen and the other ladies of the court were always delighted to have the English duke among their company. He swept into their midst one afternoon wearing a suit of silver-gray silk, and gold tissue. The suit was sewn all over with pearls, but the pearls were forever dropping off, and rolling across the floor. As servants scrambled to retrieve the gems, the duke of Buckingham waved them away with a smile. The pearls were naught but trifles, he told them, implying there were plenty more where they came from. Keep them, he said.

"You have done it quite deliberately," the duchess of Glenkirk scolded George Villiers. "These pearls are sewn too loosely so, of course, they will drop off. You are intent on annoying these poor French. What a wicked creature you are, Steenie!" They had known each other ever since Villiers's very early days at King James's court.

The dark eyes twinkled. An elegant eyebrow arched mischievously, and then he smiled at her, but he said not a word.

At last, on the twenty-third of May, the new queen of England's great cavalcade finally departed Paris. It was made up of the several hundred people who would accompany Henrietta-Marie, including, besides the lords and ladies who were to make up her household, a large number of servants: cooks, grooms, a surgeon, an apothecary, a tailor, an embroiderer, a perfumer, a clockmaker, eleven musicians, Mathurine, her Fool, and twenty-four priests, including a bishop.

The king had an attack of the quinsy. His throat was so enflamed that he could barely speak. He bid his sister farewell at Compiegne, and returned to Paris to recuperate. At Amiens, Marie di Medici developed a fever. After a few days, it became obvious that Henrietta-Marie would have to leave her mother and travel onward with her great train by herself. Charles was already sending impatient messages to France requesting his bride come forthwith. Finally, they reached Boulogne where twenty ships were waiting to take the new queen and her retinue to England. There was also a party of English ladies and gentlemen who had come to greet the new queen, but while Henrietta-Marie was polite, she showed little warmth toward these members of her new court. They were Protestants, and must be avoided as much as possible, her foolish spiritual advisors warned her, little caring if she made a good impression on her new subjects as long as her soul was safe.

The duke of Glenkirk and his family had taken their leave of the young queen in Paris. They would see her in England, but it was not necessary that they be part of the great company traveling with Henrietta-Marie to her husband. They returned to the château with the St. Laurents so they might have a few more days with Lady Stewart-Hepburn, who would be spending the summer in France with her youngest daughter.

James Leslie tried hard to get his mother to return home to Scotland with them. "You dinna even know this Stuart king, Mother, and his parents, your last link wi the royal Stuarts, are both gone now. Come home wi us to Scotland. There is always a place for you at Glenkirk."

Catriona Hay Leslie Stewart-Hepburn shook her head. She had been a dazzling beauty in her youth, and while time had aged her, she was still a stunning woman. Her honey-blond hair had turned a snowy white, just faintly tinted with gold. Her leaf-green eyes, however, had not changed. They were as clear and beautiful as they had always been. Now they fixed themselves on him. "Jemmie," she said, "you are my eldest child, and I love you dearly, but I will not leave Bothwell, as I have already told Jasmine. Besides, as I have also said, my old bones are too used to the sunshine and the warmth of the south. Going home to Scotland would take ten years off my life. While I miss Francis, I am not all that anxious to join him yet. I enjoy my grandchildren too much, I fear." She laughed, and patted his hand. "You have done very well all these years without me."

"Do you not miss your children?" he queried her. "My brothers and my sisters hae given you grandchildren, too, Mother."

"And all have at one time or another come to Naples with their families to see me," she responded. "They do not need me, either, Jemmie. A woman raises her bairns, and then no matter how much she loves them, she must let them go on to live their own lives. A mother and father are like the sun around which their children move. Then one day it all changes. The bairns are grown, and become like the sun themselves, which means the parents must take a lesser position in their lives. There is no tragedy in this, for a mother wants her bairns to flourish and lead their own lives. They go on, *and we go on.* I loved all my bairns, but you were not my only life.

"Soon Jasmine's three eldest will be ready to leave the loving nest you and she have built for them. You must let them go, Jemmie, as I let you, and your brothers, and sisters go. And you must let *me* go, my son. While you may not realize it, you did so years ago when I left Scotland, and you became head of the Leslies of Glenkirk. Seeing me after so long a time has but made you nostalgic."

"I dinna realize how much I hae missed you, Mother, until now," James Leslie said. "Will you nae return to Scotland ever?"

"You know I will never leave him," she replied.

"He would like it if he were buried in the soil of his native land," the duke of Glenkirk said slowly. Then he chuckled. "I'll wager he was awaiting Cousin Jamie at heaven's gate, and Queen Anne with him. She always liked Bothwell, Mother, didn't she?"

Cat nodded. "All the women liked Francis," she recalled with a small smile, "but if he were awaiting Jamie at heaven's gate, surely the king thought he had been sent in the opposite direction from which he anticipated, although seeing his Annie might have reassured him." She laughed, and then grew pensive again. "Aye, he would like to have been laid to rest in his native land, Jemmie."

"Do you think he would object to being planted in Leslie soil?" the duke inquired of his mother.

"On the grounds of the old abbey," Cat said softly. "Could you, Jemmie?"

"Did we nae once hoax the royal Stuarts, Mother?" the duke answered her. "You and I together?"

"You would not think it disloyal to your father's memory?"

"My father is nae buried at Glenkirk," the duke said. His mother did not know it, of course, for she had been gone from Scotland, but the duke's father, the fifth earl of Glenkirk, had not been lost at sea as had been reported, before the king ordered him declared dead. Actually, he had been captured by the Spanish, and gone exploring with them in the New World, where he had made himself a new life.

The duke had learned of it almost twenty-five years ago when his father appeared suddenly at Glenkirk to make amends for his long absence. He was extremely relieved to learn he might go on with his new life, and return to the young woman who awaited him in a place called St. Augustine. James Leslie had never seen his father again, although every few years a missive would arrive filled with news of his adventures, and the half-siblings his new wife had borne him. "My father was a good Scotsman, Mother, and if it had been possible, he would have been buried at Glenkirk himself. I dinna believe he would object to you and Bothwell being there. He owes you that much," the duke said meaningfully, and then, "Besides, who will know it but us?"

"Then one day we shall come home to Scotland together, he and I," Lady Stewart-Hepburn said, and suddenly her eyes were filled with tears, which slid down her beautiful face even as she attempted to prevent them. "Ahhh," she said softly, "we had such grand times, he and I, as we rode beneath the border moon." Then, catching hold of her emotions, she said, "We will travel in a single coffin. That way there will be no questions. Just the duke of Glenkirk's old mother returning to be buried in her native soil. And no one shall ever know where Bothwell's grave is, Jemmie, for even in Naples there are those who believed those scurrilous tales of witchcraft and magic Cousin Jamie and his Protestants spread about Francis. There are some who come to take soil from his grave, believing it has powers. I must keep a watch there all the time, or they would surely steal his body away to use in their vile rites."

"I dinna think I will get you home too soon, Mother," the duke said, seeking to lighten the moment.

"No," she replied with a small laugh. Then she hugged him. "Thank you, Jemmie, for your generosity."

"I hae always enjoyed sharing secrets wi you, Mother," he chuckled. "Only Jasmine shall know besides we two."

"Agreed," she answered him. "I will miss you."

"And I you," he told her. And then the duke of Glenkirk took his mother for a final stroll in his sister's gardens.

Chapter 2

"Such extravagance!" the countess of Alcester said, in very disapproving tones. She turned to her niece. "You are spoiling the chit, Jasmine, by allowing her to have such a wardrobe. Every fortune hunter at court will descend upon you when India parades herself in this splendor."

"Am I so witless, Great-aunt," India defended herself, "that I cannot separate truth from fiction? I have turned down half a dozen matches in Scotland for the very reason I knew it was my fortune that attracted the gentlemen in question and not me. Fine clothes will do little, if anything, to dull my perception of men."

"Your tongue is too quick for a girl of respectable upbringing," the countess snapped. India was too damned headstrong, even as her mother had been. *Even as my mother was,* Willow, Lady Edwardes, countess of Alcester, thought irritably. *Thank heavens my daughters have all been obedient girls, and my granddaughters, too, although perhaps one or two of them bear watching.* "If you will take my advice, Jasmine, although I suspect you will not, you and James will make a good match for India and cease this nonsense and outrageous expense." Then, heaving her bulk from the chair in which she had been sitting, Lady Edwardes shook out her own dark skirts. "I do not like London anymore," she grumbled, "and no one should live here at this time of year. It is too warm, and much too damp, but what could we do? We had to come to London to greet the new queen."

"I think the queen is very pretty," India noted.

"All young girls are pretty," her great-aunt said, "and this one no more or less than many, but there will be difficulty over her religion, mark my words. And if all those French with her persist in their rude habits, the king will do well to send them away." She moved toward the door. "I am going back to your uncle's house now," she announced. "I will see you all in the morning when we go to court, and I hope, Jasmine, that your daughter will be suitably garbed like a proper young Englishwoman, and not decked out like some foreigner." The countess of Alcester stamped through the open door, which a servant held for her, her skirts swinging indignantly as she went.

"Fat old cow!" India muttered when the door had shut again.

"She has just forgotten what it is like to be young," Jasmine told her daughter, although personally she agreed with her daughter's assessment. Aunt Willow had always been prim and proper. It was as if she strove to be entirely and totally different from her own mother, a lady of passion and colorful character. It often made her seem joyless and didactic. "Your great-aunt is correct in one thing, however, India," Jasmine said. "Tomorrow you will wear one of your less spectacular gowns to court to greet the queen. It would not do to outshine Her Majesty when she is undoubtedly striving to make a good impression upon her new subjects. She will be feeling strange, and, I suspect, not just a little frightened in her new land."

"Like when you came to England?" India said.

Jasmine nodded. "At least the queen can go home again if she wants to visit France. Once I left India there was no going back."

"Do you ever regret leaving?" her eldest child asked.

Jasmine shook her head. "No. My life there was at an end. My fate was here with your father, and later in Scotland with your stepfather, my darling Jemmie. You must never fight your fate, India, even if it is not the fate you believe you would choose."

"My fate isn't very interesting, Mama," India said. "I will have to choose a husband very soon, or risk being an old maid. I will settle down, and have children as you, and Grandmother Velvet, and my great-grandmother, Madame Skye, did. There is no excitement or surprises in such a fate. It is all quite ordinary, I fear."

"Neither Madame Skye, nor my mother, nor I led dull lives in our youth, India," Jasmine reminded her daughter, "although I do hope you will not face quite all the excitement we did. I am not certain you could cope with it, being so gently raised."

"Grandmother Velvet was gently raised, and she managed to survive her adventures," India reminded her mother.

"It was a different time," Jasmine said softly, thinking her English born and bred daughter did not know the half of it.

"Come, and help me choose what I will wear tomorrow, Mama," India said. "And we must choose something for Fortune. She will wait until the last minute, and somehow manage to look like nobody's child, embarrassing us all. Fortune's appearance matters little to her, I fear."

The duchess of Glenkirk laughed aloud at her eldest child's assessment of her younger sister. It was so accurate. India cared very much how she looked, and how she appeared before the world. Her hair was always properly coiffed, her gown fresh, her nails neatly trimmed. Fortune, on the other hand, was an unrepentant hoyden whose red hair was always flying and tangled as Fortune dashed impulsively through life, her skirts muddied and more than likely a smudge upon her pale cheek. The duchess's mother said that Fortune would change when she got older, but Fortune would be fifteen in just a few weeks and showed no signs of maturation. How on earth could she and Rowan Lindley have spawned two such different daughters? "Let us choose your sister's gown first," Jasmine suggested, knowing it would take India forever to settle upon her own garb.

India nodded her agreement. "The main problem will be to find something clean," she said, "but I suppose Nelly does her best to keep up with our wild Fortune." Then India laughed. "No one can make me angrier than Fortune, Mama. She does not seem to care at all, but I do love her!"

"I know you do," the duchess replied, and then together the two hurried upstairs to seek out a wardrobe, India's elegant new silk skirts rustling as they went.

Impressed by the exquisite clothing she had seen at the French court, India Lindley had returned from France determined to have a new gown, nay, a dozen new gowns fashioned in the same manner, of the finest materials, sewn all over with jewels and gold thread, with fine brocade petticoats that would show through the gown's front opening. She thought the farthingales and bell-shaped skirts of her great-grandmother, grandmother, and mother's day far more elegant than the skirts of today that fell to the floor in simple folds, with the fullness toward the back. It was somehow sloppy, India thought, but it was the fashion now. Opulent fabrics, India thought, would take the curse from this less elegant mode.

India had therefore raided the O'Malley-Small trading company warehouses where there were incredible fabrics stored that her mother had brought from her homeland nearly twenty years ago. There was so much fine stuff that India knew even if she and her sister were completely outfitted in dozens of new gowns each, there would still be enough of the beautiful materials left over. She had picked carefully, colors and fabrics that would flatter her skin. Then she had personally overseen the making of the garments, which were far richer than those normally worn now in England. Satisfied that her gowns were every bit as good as those that would be worn by the queen and her French ladies, India looked forward to going to court.

The king and queen had been remarried at St. Augustine's Abbey in Canterbury, and had then made their way to London, coming into the city by barge as there was plague about. It was not the official state entry that Henrietta-Marie had expected. Still, the young queen waved at the crowds through the open window of the vessel as they stood there along the Thames bank in the wind and rain to greet her. The king was more sedate, waving regally, his face somber. Afterward, however, the queen had retired to rest from her long journey. It was just now at the end of June that she felt ready to attend the formal proclamation of her marriage.

The ceremony took place in the Great Hall of Whitehall Palace. The king and his queen sat upon their thrones while the marriage contract was read aloud to the assembled dignitaries and the court. Looking about her, India was quite satisfied that she was the best dressed Englishwoman in the hall. Fortune, of course, had rolled her eyes as India had been laced into a small corset, but India knew it was worth it, for her small breasts swelled discreetly over the low, square neckline of her gown, pushed up by the corset. The gown itself was of claret-red silk with a wide, ivory lace collar that extended low on the shoulder. The sleeves reached the elbow, and showed ivory-and-gold brocade through their slashes that matched the tantalizing glimpse of petticoat through the gown's skirt opening. The duchess had refused to allow her daughter to wear her own famous rubies, believing pearls more suitable to the occasion. India's hair was as fashionable as her gown, her dark locks being fixed into a flat, coiled knot at the back, with a single lovelock tied with a gold ribbon draping itself teasingly by her left ear.

"Damn me if that ain't the most beautiful girl I've ever seen," Adrian Leigh, Viscount Twyford, said to his friend, Lord John Summers.

"Too rich for your blood," Lord Summers replied dryly.

"You know who she is, Johnny? And why should I not aspire to such a magnificent creature?"

"Because she is the stepdaughter of the duke of Glenkirk, *and* the sister of the marquis of Westleigh. A virgin, and an heiress far beyond your reach. You don't want to marry, Twyford. You want to seduce. Seduce that beauty, and you'll end up very dead. Whatever they have planned for Lady India Lindley, it isn't you."

"I'll be earl of Oxton one day, Johnny," Viscount Twyford replied, "and what a countess she would make! India? 'Tis an odd name."

"The duchess of Glenkirk, the girl's mother, is from that land, I am told, although her mother is English or Scots, I'm not sure which. I do know they are a wealthy family, and somehow distantly related to the king's family. Lady Lindley's half-brother, the duke of Lundy, is also the king's nephew. Wrong side of the blanket, of course, but you know these Stuarts, Adrian."

"The women are obviously hot-blooded," Viscount Twyford noted, his blue eyes fixed on India.

"Be careful, Adrian," his friend teased. "If your mama should find out you have an interest in such a suitable girl she will be quite piqued. I know how she dotes on you. It is said she will never give you over into the care of another woman."

"My mother would do well to remain at Oxton Hall, looking after my father. He has not been well in recent years," Twyford said sourly.

"She's still a handsome woman," Lord Summers remarked.

"She concentrates on remaining so," the viscount replied. "It is her sole interest. That, *and certain men*. She will not prevent me from marrying, Johnny, when I find the right girl, and I believe I have. It is my duty to have an heir. I know it would please my father." He fixed his eyes on his companion. "I must be introduced to Lady India Lindley, Johnny. Do you know any of the family?"

"I have an acquaintance with her brother, Henry Lindley, the marquis of Westleigh. My little estate borders his holdings at Cadby. If he is here, I suppose I might presume upon him. He has a good nature." Lord Summers swept the Great Hall with his mild gaze. "Ahh, there he is! With his stepfather, the duke. Come along, Adrian. This is as good a chance as we'll get, I think."

The two men made their way across the large chamber which was filled to overflowing with the court. The marriage contract having been read, the king had gone into a nearby chamber to dine, and the queen had retired to her apartments. This left the courtiers to mill about, visiting and gossiping with and about each other.

When they had reached the area where the duke of Glenkirk stood speaking with his stepson, Lord Summers stopped, and waited to catch Henry Lindley's eye, saying when he did, "I came to pay my respects, my lord, and to introduce you to my friend, Viscount Twyford, who, having seen your sister, Lady India, tells me he will perish if you do not introduce them." Lord Summers grinned in friendly fashion at the marquis of Westleigh, who was three years his junior.

"Introduce me to these gentlemen, Henry," the duke of Glenkirk said. He took in the measure of the two young men before them.

"Lord John Summers, Father. His estate borders mine. We have sometimes hunted together when I have been at Cadby," Henry Lindley said. "And this is his friend, Viscount Twyford."

"Do you have a name, young man?" the duke of Glenkirk demanded.

"Adrian Leigh, sir. I am the earl of Oxton's son, and heir." He bowed to James Leslie and the young marquis.

"And you wish to meet my stepdaughter, sir? To what purpose?" the duke inquired fiercely.

A tinkle of laughter greeted his words as the duchess of Glenkirk, overhearing, turned and took her husband's arm. "Do not be such a ninny, Jemmie. Viscount Twyford would appear to me to be a fairly respectable young man, and India is a beautiful young girl. To what purpose indeed." She laughed again, then said, "Henry, take both these gentlemen and introduce them to India." Then she lightly touched Adrian Leigh's arm. "You are respectable, sir, are you not?"

"Aye, madame, I am," he said boyishly.

"Then go along with my son, my lord," Jasmine instructed him.

The trio hurried across the hall again, this time headed for India, who stood with another young girl chattering. She smiled at her brother's approach, holding out her hand to him.

"Henry." She quickly looked at her brother's two companions, and then directly at her brother.

"Mama says I may introduce these gentlemen to you, India."

"But I recognize Lord Summers," India said, smiling prettily at him. "You hunt with Henry at Cadby, don't you?"

"I did not know you had seen me, mistress, as we have never been formally introduced until now," Lord Summers said, bowing to India.

"How could I fail to notice so handsome a gentleman," India said coquettishly, tossing her head just slightly.

"God's blood!" the girl next to her swore.,

"*Fortune!*" India looked scandalized. "She is my younger sister, and has never been out in society before," India excused her sibling. "She will never, I fear, behave properly."

"Is flirting outrageously with a man you've just met proper?" Fortune demanded.

India flushed. "I am not flirting! I was being polite."

Fortune snorted.

Henry Lindley laughed. "Sisters," he said, effectively dismissing them both as silly creatures. "India, if you are quite through being indignant I will introduce you to Viscount Twyford, who for some reason has insisted upon making your acquaintance. The word *beautiful* did pass his lips when he spoke of you."

India Lindley turned her golden eyes upon Adrian Leigh. She held out her hand. "How do you do, my lord," she murmured.

"Much better now that we have met, my lady," he returned, taking her slender, elegant little hand and kissing it.

Fortune rolled her eyes comically. "Henry, I am suddenly nauseous. Will you escort me away from this sickening sweetness?"

India did not hear her. She had the presence of mind to withdraw her hand from Viscount Twyford's grasp, but she was already intrigued by him.

"*Zut alors, India! Un Anglais avec charme,*" a voice declared, and an outrageously beautifully dressed young man turned from the throng. Taking up India's hand, so recently released by Viscount Twyford, he kissed it gallantly. "*Bonjour, ma belle cousine.*"

"René! Oh, René, you have grown up, haven't you?" India's gaze swept over the handsome Frenchman. He was quite gorgeous.

"*Oui, chérie, je suis un homme.*"

"Speak English, René! You are in England now, and not France," India scolded him. "And you do speak better English than most English speak French, Cousin. How good it is to see you again!" She turned again to Lord Summers and Viscount Twyford. "This is the chevalier St. Justine, my cousin. René, Lord John Summers, and Adrian Leigh, Viscount Twyford. René, I didn't know you were coming with the queen from France. I didn't see you in Paris," Jasmine said. "Why are you here?"

"One of Her Majesty's gentlemen of honor fell ill at the last moment, and as I had just come up from Archambault to Paris on estate business, and stopped at the Louvre to pay my respects to King Louis, it seems I was in the right spot at the right time. It's quite an accolade for the family that I was chosen, *chérie.*"

"*And just how are you related?*" the viscount asked, not simply curious, but strangely jealous. She called him cousin, but exactly how close were they? The froggie was perhaps too handsome, too suave.

Lord Summers, the chevalier, and young Henry Lindley all recognized the suspicion in Adrian Leigh's tone. It was an incredible presumption on his part to voice such an inquiry, but India seemed totally unaware.

"René's great-grandmother and my great-grandfather were brother and sister," she answered the viscount. "I spent part of my childhood in France. René and I were playmates. René! Do you recognize Henry all grown up. And there is Fortune over there with Mama."

The chevalier bowed to the marquis. "My lord, it is good to see you again as well. Now, however, I shall go and pay my respects to your parents, and Lady Fortune, eh?"

"I'll come with you," India said, tucking her hand through his arm. "Mama will be so surprised, René. Henry . . ." She called to her brother. "You come, too." Then, smiling at the other two gentlemen, she moved off across the Great Hall with her escorts.

"You have an admirer, *ma petite,*" René St. Justine noted mischievously as they walked.

"A bit bold for my taste," Henry Lindley replied. "There is something I have heard about the family that is not savory, but I cannot think what it is right now."

"I do hope you are not going to be one of those overly protective brothers, Henry," India said sharply. "Remember that I am older than you are. I thought Viscount Twyford rather charming, and he is handsome."

"You are ten months older than I am, India," her brother reminded her. " 'Tis hardly a generation. The earl of Oxton! *Yes! Now I remember!* The earl's eldest son was implicated in the murder of a rival in love, and fled England. He disappeared, and has never been heard of again. The earl fell into a deep decline, and has not appeared publicly since it happened. Your swain is his younger half-brother, India, son of the second wife, who is said to take her lovers from among her servants and tenants. Charming, indeed! I'm surprised a fellow as decent as Summers would associate with such a man. I hardly think Viscount Twyford suitable for you, Sister."

"You cannot blame the viscount for the behavior of either his elder half-brother or his mother, Henry. How unfair of you!" India cried. "I like him, and if he wishes to pay me his addresses, I shall welcome them. Say anything to Father about his unfortunate relations, and Father will know about that little housemaid at Greenwood you have been fucking in dark hallways. Didn't think I knew, did you?"

"God's blood!" her brother swore. *"How did you know?"*

"Are all men that noisy when they fuck?" India wondered aloud.

The chevalier burst out laughing. "India, you have not changed, little cousin. I am so glad!" Then he paused a moment and said, "But Henry is correct in one sense, *chérie.* A man is rarely unlike his family in his behavior. Besides, you can do better than a mere viscount. You are the daughter of a marquis, the stepdaughter of a duke. You have a marquis for a brother and a duke for a brother, and that little duke is the king's own nephew. Aye, *chérie,* you can do much better than a provincial little viscount."

"I shall do as I please," India answered him, and he laughed once more. "I am not just well connected, but rich as well, René, and when you are rich, you can do as you please," she told him.

"Within the law," her brother reminded her disapprovingly.

While the queen struggled to find her way within this new court she had been married into, and her French household and the English court jockeyed for dominance, the younger, less important members of her train, led by the chevalier St. Justine, and the younger English courtiers became friendly. None of them cared for power. They simply wanted to have fun. It was summer. The weather was pleasant, and new to court, most of them found it exciting. Filled with youthful exuberance, they involved themselves in hunting and picnics, boating, tennis, and archery contests from dawn till dusk. Then they danced the night away, or took part in little masques. Often the young queen joined them, for like her late mother-in-law, Anne of Denmark, she loved such merriment. The king, however, who had enjoyed his mother's revels in his youth, was now weighed down by his office, and not often amused.

"I want to go to Queen's Malvern," Lady Fortune Lindley complained to her mother one warm and muggy morning. "Why must we remain here with the court? We have never followed the court. Soon summer will be at an end, and we shall be returning to Glenkirk, Mama."

"Your sister has entered society, and if we are ever to find her a husband, Fortune, we must remain with the court. Right now, all the eligible young men are here," Jasmine explained to her middle daughter.

"If India wants to remain here, fine!" Fortune said, "but can't the rest of us go up to Queen's Malvern? It isn't just me. We all want to go, isn't that so, Henry?"

"I should be at Cadby," her brother agreed, nodding.

Jasmine looked to her children. "Charlie?" she said.

"I have paid my respects to my uncle, Mama, and been presented to the queen," Charles Frederick Stuart, the duke of Lundy replied. "It is not necessary for me to show myself at court again until the coronation, which my uncle, the king, says will be next winter."

The duchess of Glenkirk peered questioningly at her three Leslie sons.

"We would rather be in the country, Mama," said Patrick, speaking for himself and his two younger brothers, Adam and Duncan.

"I suppose that we could send the seven of you to Queen's Malvern," Jasmine said thoughtfully, "and your father and I could remain here to chaperone India, but you would have to behave yourselves if I did," she warned them.

"Adali is at Queen's Malvern, Mama," Fortune reminded her parent. "You know Adali would not let us run wild. If anything, he is sterner with us than you and Papa."

"Well," Jasmine considered, nibbling on her lower lip.

"And I will help him oversee the boys," Fortune pressed gently.

"And I will be at Cadby, Mama," Henry reminded her. "It would just be our younger brothers and the baby for Adali to monitor. Fortune will spend her days riding, and she cannot get into trouble just riding."

"I see no reason for your father to object," Jasmine decided. "Very well, you may all go up to Queen's Malvern."

"Yaaaaay!" her offspring cheered.

"When?" Fortune pressed.

"Tomorrow, if you can pack yourselves up by then," her mother replied, and Fortune's siblings cheered lustily once again.

"What is this all about?" India demanded to know, coming into the family hall where they were all seated. She was dressed for riding in a deep blue velvet skirt, and a jacket trimmed in silver.

"We are going to Queen's Malvern . . ." Fortune began.

India shrieked. "Nay! We cannot! I do not want to go up to the country. It is boring, and then before we know it we shall have to return to Scotland. *Ohhh!* I shall never see Adrian again!" She turned on her sister. "This is all your doing, Fortune! You are simply jealous because the gentlemen are attracted to me, and not attracted to you and your carroty hair! *Ohhh!* I hate you! I shall never forgive you! I shall die if I cannot remain with the court!" She flung herself into a chair.

"If you ask me, she should be sent home to Glenkirk right now," muttered Henry Lindley, darkly.

"You are not going to Queen's Malvern, India," her mother said. "I intended to let you remain here with your father and me, but now I wonder if Henry isn't perhaps right. Apologize to your sister this moment! And I was not aware that Viscount Twyford had caught your fancy. He is not at all suitable for a girl of your breeding and wealth."

Henry Lindley quickly shook his head at India, denying any betrayal of her secrets.

"But I like Adrian, Mama. He is charming, and he is very amusing. *And he likes me,*" India finished smugly.

"Has he said so?" Jasmine asked her daughter.

"Gracious, no!" India replied. "But René says it is so."

"Fortune is awaiting your apology," Jasmine said quietly.

India quickly hugged her sister. "I'm sorry," she said. "You know I didn't mean it, Fortune."

"If this is what an interest in men does to a person," Fortune answered, "I hope I shall never seek to attract a gentleman's attention." Then, picking up her skirts, she hurried from the hall, saying as she went, "I have to pack if we are to be ready by the morrow. Come, laddies!"

Her brothers scrambled to their feet and dashed after Fortune.

"Why don't you and Papa go with them?" India said innocently.

Jasmine laughed. "Because you must have a chaperone."

"But I'm seventeen!" India protested.

"*Just,*" her mother reminded her.

"In Grandmother Velvet's day girls younger than I came to court," India grumbled. "I don't understand why I can't stay alone."

"In your grandmother's day, the girls at court your age were either maids-of-honor serving old Queen Bess, married, or in the charge of a parent or older relative, and, like you, seeking husbands of good name, good repute, and suitable fortunes. This is not, however, your grandmother's day. A young woman of good family is properly supervised by her family lest society receive the incorrect impression that she is either not valued, or that her behavior is loose."

"You are *sooo* old-fashioned," India muttered.

"If I am," her mother replied serenely, "I shall remain so, and until you have left my home for your husband's home, you will obey me. You will also not give me cause to regret that I have allowed you to remain with the court when I should far prefer to go home to Queen's Malvern myself with your sister and brothers. I am quite capable of changing my mind, India. Now, tell me about

Viscount Twyford. Does he seek to pay his addresses to you? He really is not suitable, you know."

"*Why not?*" India was curious as to what her mother had heard.

"His father's family is a respectable one," Jasmine said. "They are Glocestershire people. I am sure you know about his brother, Deverall. It was quite a scandal, and such things do not die."

"Deverall Leigh murdered a rival," India said.

"So it was said, and the fact that he fled England did nothing to erase that impression. Many, however, did not believe it. Deverall Leigh was an honorable young man, but still it was his knife found in the victim's chest, and he ran away. A convenience for his stepmother, and her son, Adrian. No one saw or heard the murder of Lord Jeffers. His serving man was away that night, and there was no one else in the house. And, of course, there was the knife. Deverall Leigh can never return to England without facing the hangman's rope, for there is no one to attest to his innocence, if indeed he is innocent. I had heard that his father had disowned him. What choice did the poor man have? So your friend, Adrian, will one day be the earl of Oxton, and sooner than later if the rumors are to be believed," Jasmine finished.

"But why do you hold Adrian to account for his brother's behavior, Mama? You have said the Leighs are a respectable family," India replied.

"I said his *father's* family was respectable. His mother, however, is another thing. She is a foreigner. Her family is not the equal of her husband's. She is said to take lovers. Men of low station. Her husband is a broken man. Some say her behavior is as much to blame as the alleged behavior of Deverall Leigh. This young man who has caught your fancy is *her* son. *Raised by her.* What kind of man can he be? The acorn, India, does not fall far from the oak. Besides, the Leighs are not a family of wealth, and you have always sought to avoid those young men who were fortune hunters. What makes you think Adrian Leigh is not?"

"Because he is obviously interested in *me,* Mama! The others were always asking about my lands, and my other holdings, and what kind of income I had from my inheritance. Adrian never asks such things."

"Then possibly he is different, India, but he is still not suitable," Jasmine responded. "Still, as long as his behavior is correct toward you, I see no reason you should not continue to enjoy his company." *Better she think I have no violent objection to this young man,* Jasmine thought. *I do not want to drive her into his arms. He is clever, this Adrian Leigh. He has to know that India is very, very wealthy. It has never been a secret. He is willing to wait, and see just how wealthy she is until he has her securely netted. A dangerous opponent, I fear. Damnation! Why could not the perfect man come along, and sweep India off her feet? Jemmie's mother was right. My daughter is ripe for the taking, and a girl in love for the first time is not always prudent.*

James Leslie stood with his wife the following day, waving the majority of their children farewell as they set out with their servants for Queen's Malvern. "I should just as soon go wi them," he said dourly, but he understood the importance of their remaining. Come autumn, though, they would return north whether it pleased India or not. And he agreed with his wife that they would allow India a certain measure of freedom, for nothing was more embarrassing to a young girl than to be obviously overseen.

India danced that same evening away, in a magnificent gown of peacock-blue silk with a silver lace collar, the bodice of which was embroidered all over with pearls and diamante. She wore pearls in her dark hair, and her lovelock was tied with a silver ribbon studded with twinkling crystals. About her slender throat was a choker of creamy baroque pearls. She was flushed with pleasure, and her creamy cheeks were rosy.

"You are the most beautiful girl in the entire world," Adrian Leigh told her passionately, his sapphire-blue eyes glittering.

"I know," India replied, and then she laughed at his surprise. "Do you want me to demure, and giggle like some little ninny?" she teased.

"No," he said, surprising her. "I want to steal you away and make love to you for hours on end. Would you like that, my India?"

"As a virgin, I have no idea whether I would like it or not," India replied pertly, "and I am not *your* India. Even when I am married, I shall belong to no one but myself, Adrian. The women in my family have always been both independent of spirit, and independent in their own wealth. I see no reason to change such a fine custom, do you?"

"I would change nothing about you," he told her fervently. "I adore you just as you are, India." He bent his blond head, and brushed her lips impulsively with his.

India tossed her head, half avoiding him. "I have not given you permission to kiss me," she said, tweaking the fabric of his sky-blue silk doublet.

"I should be a poor suitor if I meekly waited for your permission," he said, pulling her into an alcove and pinioning her against the wall. The blue eyes stared down into her gold ones. "You are ripe for kissing, India, and I vow that no lips but mine shall ever touch yours," Adrian Leigh said, his mouth fully touching hers for the first time.

Warm. Firm. Not at all unpleasant, India thought. Her heart raced madly with her first kiss. Her stomach felt as if the bottom had suddenly fallen out of it.

Then he took his lips away, smiling down at her. "Did you like it, India?" he asked her.

She nodded.

"You have nothing to say to me?" he said.

"Again," she commanded him. "I want to see if it's as nice the second time as it was the first."

Adrian Leigh laughed. "Very well," he acquiesced, and kissed her a second kiss, encouraged this time when her own lips pressed back against his. He raised his head up. "That's it, India. Kiss me back." Then he kissed her a third time, and India's arms slipped about his neck. Her little round breasts pressed against him.

"Tsk! Tsk! Tsk! I think that is quite enough, *chérie,*" India heard her cousin, the chevalier St. Justine, say with a feigned sigh of exasperation.

Guiltily India pulled away from the viscount. "*René!*"

He drew her blushing from the alcove. "You must have a care for your good name, *chérie,* even if Monsieur le viscount does not."

"My intentions are honorable, Chevalier," Adrian Leigh protested.

"If they are indeed, Viscount," René St. Justine said, "you surely know better than to take a well-bred virgin into a dark alcove and enflame her innocent passions with kisses."

"René!" India was mortified. "I am not a child, damn it!"

"The gentleman knows what I am saying, India, even if you do not understand," he replied. "Now, come and dance with me, Cousin." He led her off, leaving Viscount Twyford standing in the semidarkness. India was certainly well guarded, Adrian Leigh thought to himself, but he meant to have her for his wife. Much to his surprise, those unschooled little kisses she had returned his kisses with had aroused him.

"Was it your first kiss, *chérie?*" René inquired, curiously.

"I will be so glad when I do not have to answer to my family for my every action," India muttered as they walked together. "How did you know we were there, René?" India was torn between irritation and outright anger.

"I saw him push you into the alcove, and when you did not emerge as quickly as you should have, I came to rescue you," he told her. "If I saw it, India, then others certainly did. You are not a girl of easy virtue, *Cousine,* but if you allow gentlemen to take you into dark places, you will gain a reputation whether you want one or not. Your viscount sought to put you at a disadvantage, I fear, and you are too innocent of the world to understand that. Now, however, you do, eh?"

"Why does everyone think Adrian is bad?" India asked him.

"Perhaps not bad," the chevalier said thoughtfully, "but he is, mayhap, opportunistic. To catch an heiress such as Lady India Lindley would be quite a coup for him."

"But I haven't said I wanted to marry him, René, nor has he even mentioned the subject," India replied.

"He does not have to, *chérie.* If he sullies your good name, then no one else will have you despite your wealth and your beauty. You would fall into his lap like a ripe fruit, *ma petite.* I do not think you want anyone to manipulate you like that, India, eh?" René St. Justine's brown eyes were questioning. Bending, he kissed her cheek.

"But I do like him, René," India said. "Still, you are correct in realizing that I don't like being beguiled into an untenable position. So, I suppose the answer is not to allow gentlemen to put you in dark corners." She laughed. "I thought I was so grown up, René. It seems I am not. I am glad I have you for my guardian angel. Henry has gone to the country with my siblings. Court did not suit them at all."

"Alas, *chérie,* I shall only be with you for a little while longer. The gentleman whose place I took has recovered, and will be coming from Paris soon; and I am needed at home. I may be a chevalier of France, but I am also the finest wine maker at Archambault. I must return to France in time for the harvest, and you will be returning to Scotland."

"The king wants Papa here for the coronation," India said. "I hope I shall be allowed to come from Glenkirk then."

"If you behave, and do not give your mama and papa any difficulty, *chérie,* I suspect they will allow you to come," René said, his eyes twinkling, a small smile upon his lips. "But you must be very, *very* good, eh?"

India laughed. "I will be, Cousin," she promised him, "because in a few weeks' time I shall go north, and unless I can come to court this winter, I shan't ever see Adrian again. Then I shall die an old maid, eh?" she mimicked him teasingly.

"*Non, non!*" the chevalier protested. "You shall not die an old maid, *chérie!* Somewhere in this world is a wonderful man just waiting to make you happy. You will find him, India. Never fear. You will find each other. This I know!"

Chapter

3

George Villiers, the duke of Buckingham, had come to court as a young man. He had found favor with old King James, worked his way up the social ladder from the second son of a knight to a dukedom, and married an earl's daughter, Lady Katherine Manners. But James Stuart was old, and having gained his favor, George Villiers set out to win over the king's only surviving son and heir, Charles. In this endeavor he was successful, and now George Villiers was, next to King Charles, the most powerful man in England.

Wealth and power had bred in him the desire for more wealth and power. In the young queen he sensed a rival, and so he set out to destroy any small influence she might gain with her equally young husband. His tactic with King James had been to subtly create a conflict between the old man and his son. When the disagreement was full blown, the king's beloved Steenie would step in and mediate between king and prince. It was clever, and neither James Stuart, or Charles Stuart ever realized they were being cunningly maneuvered by the wickedly adroit Villiers.

The duke attempted to work the same tactic on the queen, but Henrietta was far more clever than her husband, and quite used to such court intrigue. She resisted George Villiers strongly, and he, fearful of losing his position, set out to destroy her marriage to Charles Stuart by deliberately fostering misunderstanding between the two. Henrietta could not complain to her husband, for, like his father before him, Charles was of the firm belief George Villiers was his true and best friend.

Both king and queen had been virgins on their wedding night, for Charles was far too prim to have taken a mistress or tumbled a servant girl in a dark stable. As neither his father nor Buckingham wanted any other influence in Charles's life, they had discouraged his involvement with women. The young couple dared to speak to no one about this painful experience. They stumbled along in their physical relationship; the sixteen-year-old queen shy of her equally shy but demanding husband who had been told by Villiers that what the man wanted was what God approved of, for man was superior. Villiers then convinced Charles that his wife's shyness was a refusal of his wishes, and an attempt to gain the upper hand. Things went from bad to worse.

"Whoever heard of a name like Henri-etta?" Villiers said one day to the king. "It's so *foreign.* The queen is English now, and really ought to have a good English name. Perhaps we could call her Queen Henry."

Henrietta, of course, as the duke had anticipated, fell into a terrible rage upon hearing the suggestion. "*Mon nom est Henrietta!*" she screamed. "*Henri? La Reine Henri? C'est impossible! Non! Non! Non! Je suis Henrietta!*"

Charles found her passionate Gallic outburst distasteful. "We will speak when you are calmer, madame," he said coldly. Then his gaze swept the queen's chamber. "All these *monsieurs,*" he said in reference to his wife's French attendants both male and female. "They really must go, madame. It is time you were served by your own people."

"These are my own people," the queen answered him sharply.

"These persons are French, madame. You are England's queen, and should be served by good Englishmen and -women," the king replied, his tone equally sharp.

"It was agreed," Henrietta said, struggling to remain calm, "that I should have the right to choose my own household, sir."

"It was not agreed that they should *all* be French," the king snapped. Buckingham has sought a place for his sister, the countess of Denbigh, within your household, and yet you have been adamant in your refusal, madame. I like it not."

"The comtesse is a Protestant, sir," the queen said. "You cannot expect me to be served by a Protestant."

"*I* am a Protestant, madame," the king replied. "It did not stop you from marrying me, nor will it stop you from having my heirs one day, and they will be Protestant." He glared at her.

"Marie, Your Majesty," said Madame St. George, who had been the queen's governess, and now sought to turn the argument back to the original, and less volatile ground. "If the queen's name, Henrietta, seems unsuitable for a queen of England, would not Marie, Mary, Queen Mary, be better? I know Your Majesty is not so petty that he would insist upon calling the queen by any other name but her own in private, but Queen Mary would be her official title, *if it would please Your Majesty.*" She curtsied. "Mary is English, is it not? And it is my mistress's second Christian name."

"It seems a good compromise," the king said, pleased to have gotten his way, and not wishing any further outburst from his wife, who nodded mutely in agreement.

The duke of Buckingham was equally pleased, but for a different reason. The English had long memories, and they had not forgotten Bloody Mary Tudor, the last Roman Catholic English queen who had persecuted the Protestants. She had not been popular, and neither would this Queen Mary be. He chuckled to himself, well pleased.

When parliament opened, the queen was not present, for her confessor, Bishop de Mende, had somehow gotten the idea that a Church of England religious ceremony was central to the occasion. The king was furious. The parliament was offended, and granted the king only a seventh of the monies he needed. He adjourned the session, and moved his household to Hampton Court, for the plague was still rife in London.

Buckingham continued to undermine the queen, advising her that her clothing was far too lavish, and unsuitable for an

Englishwoman. Her hairstyle was too foreign. Her temper too quick. He advised her that she should be more amenable to her husband, or Charles would send her back to France. Then he attempted once again to gain a place in her household for not just his sister, but his wife, and his niece as well. The queen was outraged, and this time did complain to her husband. In response, Charles went hunting to avoid the uproar, and while he was gone, the countess of Denbigh held a public religious service in the royal household. The queen and her people interrupted it, not once, but twice, trekking through the hall chattering and laughing, their dogs in their wake, as if nothing unusual were taking place. Buckingham dutifully reported this to the king, making certain Charles's anger was well roused.

The king was indeed outraged, but not at Lady Denbigh for deliberately baiting the queen. His anger was directed solely at his wife, whom he decided to punish by sending her entire retinue of French back to Paris. Now Buckingham realized he had gone too far. He did not wish to be responsible for endangering the alliance between England and France, which this marriage represented.

In Paris, King Louis and his mother had heard of the discord between the recently married couple. They were not at all pleased, and decided to send an envoy to investigate. Buckingham quickly persuaded the king to allow the queen's household to remain for the time being.

The plague having finally subsided, the coronation was set for February second. At Glenkirk, James Leslie grumbled loudly at having to make the trek from the eastern highlands of Scotland down to London at the midpoint of the winter. The snows were deep. The trip would be cold, and take forever. They would have to leave immediately after Twelfth Night.

"I dinna intend taking all of you bairns," he said to his assembled family.

"I am perfectly happy to remain home," Fortune Lindley said.

"Henry, Charlie, and Patrick shall go, because the first two are English, and the last my heir," the duke of Glenkirk said.

India held her breath, and threw a beseeching glance at her mother. Adrian Leigh had been permitted to correspond with her, and had kept her apprised of all the gossip, and the coronation plans.

"I think India should go, too," Jasmine finally said.

"Why?" James Leslie demanded.

"Because she is Rowan's firstborn, and an English noblewoman of an old and respected family, who certainly should see her king crowned," Jasmine said quietly. "Besides, this is an excellent opportunity for us to look over the young men from suitable families. Many will be at the coronation who do not as a rule come to court. It is a wonderful chance for her. Besides, it will please me to have my daughter with me, Jemmie."

"Verra well," he said grudgingly, "but I dinna want to see that fancy young viscount hanging about India." He looked directly at his stepdaughter. "He's nae for you, mistress. Do you understand me, India? I hae been patient allowing him to write to you once a month, but you will nae wed such a fellow. This time I would see other suitors at our door. Ye dinna hae your cousin, René, to hide behind any longer. Did you nae know I knew 'twas young Leigh who you were so anxious to be wi, and nae the chevalier?"

India bit back the quick retort on her lips, and hung her head in a contrite fashion. She would damn well do what she wanted to do, but she would wait to get to England before she made that announcement. "Yes, Papa," she said meekly, "and thank you for allowing me to go."

"And ye'll pick a husband, India," James Leslie told his stepdaughter. "Either down in England, or here in Scotland, lassie. You'll be eighteen this June, and you canna wait any longer."

"Mama was only eighteen when I was born," India noted.

"But she hae already hae two husbands," he said. "And, besides, it takes time to make a bairn and birth it."

"I want to love the man I marry," India told him.

"I'll nae force you to the altar, lassie." James Leslie said, "but you must be more tractable and practical in this matter."

"I will try, Papa," India promised him.

* * *

"What a little liar you are," Fortune mocked her sister afterward when they were alone in their chamber. "You want to marry Adrian Leigh, India. I know you do! And he would like to marry you, although I do not think he loves you. Just your wealth."

"Of course he loves me," India said angrily to her sister. "He has told me so in his letters, Fortune."

Fortune shook her head. "I do not understand you, India. You have always been so careful where fortune hunters are concerned, yet now you become clay in the hands of this viscount. What is the matter with you?"

"You don't understand," India began.

"I know I don't," Fortune agreed, "but I do want to, India. You are my sister and I love you. We are only two years apart, and while we are very different, it doesn't mean I don't care what happens to you, because I do. Adrian Leigh writes you in a manner I do not believe he should be writing you. He behaves as if you were formally betrothed."

"You haven't read my letters, have you?" India was outraged.

"Of course I've read them," Fortune said matter-of factly. "You don't hide them very well, India. If Mama didn't trust you, she probably would have read them, too, and then you should not be going to England for the coronation. This Adrian Leigh is very bold, sister."

"He kissed me," India said. "The first time René caught us, and scolded me roundly. After that we were more careful. Ohhh, Fortune, I cannot imagine my life without him! Papa simply has to change his mind about Adrian. I cannot bear to think of marrying anyone but him."

"But why?" Fortune was entirely perplexed. Certainly Adrian Leigh wasn't any more handsome than their brothers. His prose to India was just plain silly—her lips were two turtledoves—and his spelling was utterly atrocious. What in the name of all heaven was so special about him that India was behaving like a little ninny?

"I cannot explain," India said helplessly. "He is just too wonderful, Fortune, and I love him. You will understand one day."

Fortune shook her head. "You had best be careful, sister," she warned her sibling. "If you don't choose a husband, and you know it cannot be your swain, Papa will choose one for you. Parents still do, you know. It is their right. Mama and Papa have been very lenient with us."

"*It must be Adrian,*" India replied stubbornly.

Fortune shook her head again. "We shall have no peace in this house, I am thinking, until you are safely married, India."

"To Adrian," came the reply, and Fortune laughed.

"I hope to never have a daughter like you," she said.

The duke and duchess of Glenkirk departed Scotland on the seventh of January, arriving at their house in London, Greenwood, on the thirtieth of the month. There was barely time for their clothing to be unpacked and pressed. Waiting for them upon their arrival was Viscount Twyford, filled with news. James Leslie was not pleased to see the young man, but listened politely.

The queen, it seemed, would not be at the coronation. Once again she had taken the counsel of her religious advisors, ignoring the pleas of both her mother and her brother, the king of France, who wanted her crowned with her husband. Henrietta, however, had been convinced by Bishop de Mende that the Protestant archbishop of Canterbury could not possibly place the crown of England upon her Roman Catholic head. Only he, a French Catholic bishop, could.

As that was completely unacceptable to the English, the queen would not be crowned at all; nor would she be in the abbey when her husband was. Of course the queen's behavior was outrageous. The duke of Buckingham was openly irate at what he claimed was an insult to England's church, and to Charles himself. The entire court was talking about it, Adrian Leigh told them, all the while throwing languishing glances at India, who kept sneaking peeks at him from beneath her dark lashes.

Adrian Leigh's mother had, to his annoyance, come up to London for the coronation. When she learned from her son that India would also be there, she began to advise him, and while he was no longer fond of her as he had been when he was a boy, he had to admit she was a wretchedly clever woman.

"Her stepfather will not even discuss the matter of marriage with me," Viscount Twyford told his mother. "I attempted to bring it up today when I went to Greenwood to welcome them back to London. I asked if we might speak privately, but he held up that big hand of his and said there was nothing I had to say to him that would possibly be of interest to him. How the hell can I ask for the girl's hand if he won't let me? India says he disapproves of our family because of the Lord Jeffers murder, *and* because of your poor reputation. Why the hell must you consort with men of such low station, madame? If you must take a lover, could it at least be one of noble blood? Could you not at least be discreet?"

"Blue blood runs cold," MariElena Leigh replied dryly. "Besides, Adrian, my lovers are not your concern."

MariElena Leigh was still a beautiful woman with smooth white skin, dark hair, and large, exciting dark eyes. Reaching out with very long, slender fingers, she plucked a sweetmeat from the plate before her and popped it into her mouth, the pointed tip of her pink tongue catching a drizzle of honey from the corner of her sensuous mouth.

"When the scandals you create endanger my marrying one of the wealthiest virgins in England, madame, they most certainly do concern me," he told her angrily.

"You cannot erase what has been, Adrian," she said. "If her family objects to you, you must take another tact, my dearest. I am surprised you have not considered it. Does the girl love you?"

"She believes she does," he said thoughtfully, "but I am the only man ever to kiss her, or try to court her. She is inexperienced, and has been very sheltered by her family. They have allowed her to refuse the eligible suitors who have come courting her. And why? She believes they were only after her wealth. I, on the other hand, have never mentioned her wealth. Although I am told by those who know that she is an heiress of considerable property."

"A fat dowry could help us to rebuild Oxton Court," his mother said slowly. "*Do you love her?* Could you be happy with this girl?"

"She is perhaps a trifle too independent for my taste, but her wealth makes it possible to overlook her behavior. Besides, once we are married, and I have control over India, I will see she changes her ways. The women in her family are very fecund, and several children should take a great deal of the spunk out of her." He laughed. "I will enjoy having her in my bed. Aye, madame, I could be content with Lady India Lindley and her wealth."

"Then you are going to have to reach out and take what you want, my son," his mother said. She licked the sweetness from her fingers.

"What do you mean?" he demanded. "Her stepfather will not even speak to me except when forced to do so, madame."

"Adrian, if you do not take this girl while you have the chance to take her, I can guarantee you that the duke of Glenkirk will see you do not get another chance at her. Convince her to elope with you. Even if you are caught before you can marry her, her reputation will be totally ruined. No one else will want her, and you will win by default," the countess of Oxton said to her son.

"I don't want to get caught," he replied. "I want to wed her, and bed her before her family can intervene. If we were stopped before I could accomplish those two things, the duke is quite capable of dragging India back to Scotland and marrying her off to some highlander who would know nothing of the scandal; and finding his bride a virgin, would be satisfied with the match. I must take her someplace that they are unlikely to look for us at first. *But where?*"

"Take her to Napoli, to my brother's house," his mother suggested. "Your uncle Giovanni will welcome you at Villa di Carlo. You can marry the girl, and bed her to your heart's content The Leslies of Glenkirk are unlikely to seek you there, for how could they know of it? When she has given you a son, then bring her home to England. Her family will be forced to welcome you then, Adrian."

For the first time in many years, Adrian Leigh embraced his

beautiful mother. "You are so damnably clever, madame!" he said. "You have always looked after my best interests. It is perfect!"

She shook him off gracefully. "You must convince the girl, Adrian, and, believe me, it will not be easy." She sat back in her chair, and, reaching for her goblet sipped the wine he had earlier poured them.

"Why not? She loves me," he declared with the enthusiasm of his youth. Picking up his own goblet, he swallowed the cool red wine thirstily until the goblet was empty.

"She loves her family, too," the countess of Oxton replied wisely. "She will be torn between you both. You will have to make her choose you over them, my son, or you have not a chance, despite her feelings."

"But how, Mother?"

"We must make certain that the duke and his family continue in their coldness toward you despite your charm and good manners. The sweeter you appear, and the chillier their reception, particularly if it is in Lady India's presence, will only help but make the girl take your side. Do not at any time criticize her family, my dearest. Defend them, saying if you had a beautiful daughter, you would want to protect her, too, from what you believed was an unsuitable match. Remind her what a fine old family the Leighs are. Say things like 'We are not wealthy or powerful people like your family, but we are honorable and noble.' That, too, will make her take your part. You will appear to be a worthy and virtuous young man, held unfairly responsible for the wicked behavior of your elder brother, and your flighty mother, neither of whom you approve of, and would disown if it would not break your poor old father's heart."

Adrian Leigh laughed, genuinely amused by his mother's cunning. "You are absolutely diabolical," he said. "Again I say it is a perfect plan, Mother, and I thank you." He leaned from his own chair and kissed her cheek.

"If she proves too reluctant, Adrian, you must make love to her in order to convince her. I do not mean you should deflower the girl, but I assume, from what you have told me, that you have only traded kisses with her so far. Caress her breasts. First through the fabric of her gown, and then, if you can, slip your hand into her bodice and gently fondle her. Be certain not to frighten her, however, else you lose your advantage with her."

"I should like that," he said softly. "She has the most tempting little breasts I have ever seen."

The countess of Oxton smiled at her son knowingly. He was a great deal more like her than he was willing to admit. His wife would not be unhappy with him as she had been with her son's father, the cold bastard.

The king was crowned in Westminster Abbey on Candlemas Day, February 2, 1626. The queen watched the procession from a window in the gatehouse of Whitehall Palace. The king wore a white satin suit, but, overall, the coronation was an austere event as the royal treasury was almost bare. Only the generosity of several wealthy families, prevailed upon by the duke of Buckingham, made it possible for there to be a celebratory feast afterward. The duke and duchess of Glenkirk had kept a sharp eye on India, whose behavior was demure in the great abbey. Afterward, when they entered the banquet hall at Whitehall, however, India managed to give her parents the slip, and find her way to Adrian Leigh, who greeted her warmly.

Helpless to stop her without causing a scene, James Leslie nonetheless saw where she went. Back at Greenwood House that evening, he paced the family hall angrily. "She hae deliberately disobeyed us, Jasmine, and I for one hae had enough of her willfulness. We will leave for Scotland at the beginning of the week."

"What good will that do?" his wife asked. "India will correspond with young Leigh, and we will be returning to England come summer."

"There will be nae more letters! By summer India will be either betrothed or, better yet, married," James Leslie replied firmly. "Since India will nae choose a suitable match for herself, we will choose one for her."

"Ohh, Jemmie!" his wife murmured. "I don't like to do that to India. I want her to love the man she marries."

"Your father chose Prince Jamal, your first husband, for you. You dinna know him until you married him, and yet you were happy," the duke reminded his wife. "Your grandparents chose Rowan Lindley, India's father, as your second husband, and you grew to love him, didn't you? So much so that you almost died when he was killed. King James chose me as your third husband, and we have nae been unhappy, hae we? I know you love me, darling Jasmine, and I certainly love you. India is behaving in a childish manner. She hae deliberately fixated herself upon an unsuitable man, and refuses to look elsewhere, because she thinks if she continues in her stubbornness she will, as she hae many times before, get her own way. But this time it is nae about a gown or a puppy. This is India's life, and I will nae hae her miserable for the rest of it because she chose the wrong man. I owe that to her father."

"Have you any ideas for an appropriate match?" Jasmine asked.

"Well, I would hae you ask your aunt Willow about eligible young Englishmen, and I know both Angus Drummond and Ian MacCrae hae unmarried sons. They would be more than favorable to a match wi our daughter. Both the Drummonds and the MacCraes are solid families. Nae great titles, but educated, and nae fanatical where religion is concerned. Still, your aunt may know of some suitable young noblemen, and India, being English by birth, might prefer to live in England near her two brothers, Henry and Charlie, and your family."

"I suppose it is the only way," Jasmine said reluctantly. Her husband might be taking a firm approach, but he certainly wasn't being unreasonable, she thought. India, of course, would rage and howl, but they had no other choice. Her mother-in-law had been right when she had suggested that India was ripe for bedding. Before the girl caused a scandal with the wrong man, they were going to have to marry her off to someone more eligible.

"By summer we'll hae a wedding," the duke decided firmly. "Then you and I will hae to consider what to do about Fortune, for she will be sixteen in July, and should also be wed."

"I had thought to take her to Ireland," Jasmine said. "I had always intended giving her MacGuire's Ford and its lands. I think she should therefore have an Irish, or Anglo-Irish husband, Jemmie."

"Excellent!" he agreed. "*We* will take Fortune to Ireland this summer. Henry will go to Cadby, Charlie to Queen's Malvern. Patrick will remain at Glenkirk in my stead, and the other two lads may either go down to England, or remain at Glenkirk. Then it is settled, my love?"

Jasmine nodded. "It is all for the best," she agreed. "It is past time we established the girls, but I hate to lose them. The time has gone so quickly. Just yesterday they were little lasses, running barefoot through the vineyards at Belle Fleurs. Do you remember the first summer we brought them to Glenkirk and they swam naked in the loch? I remember how they splashed and giggled, refusing to come out of the water even when their lips were blue with the icy, icy cold." Her eyes grew moist. "Where did my little girls go, Jemmie? Where did they go?"

He put a comforting arm about her. He had no answer to such a question.

In a dark corner of the family hall India had listened to her parents so cruelly deciding her fate. Now she sidled carefully from her hiding place and slipped into the hallway of the house, bumping into her sister, Fortune, as she exited.

"You've been eavesdropping!" Fortune accused her.

"*Be quiet!*" India hissed. "Mama and Papa will hear you. I didn't mean to eavesdrop. I was in the hall when they came in, and they didn't see me, so I hid in a dark place, and listened. You won't believe what I heard! Some of it concerns you. Come on!" She half dragged her younger sibling up the stairs to the bedchamber they shared. Closing the door behind her, she announced dramatically, "We are to be married!"

"*What!*" Fortune squeaked. "Have they relented about your viscount? And what do you mean by *we?*" She plunked herself down upon the bed. "Speak up, India!"

"They won't let me marry Adrian, and they intend to pick a husband for me. Either some son of one of Papa's uncouth friends, or someone our old dragon of a Great-aunt Willow thinks is suitable. Papa says I'm to be married by summer. Then Henry is to go to his seat at Cadby, and Charlie to Queen's Malvern."

"What about me?" Fortune pressed. "You said *we* were to be married. I don't know anyone I want to marry."

"They're taking you to Ireland this summer. Mama says she's giving you MacGuire's Ford and its lands. I suppose you're getting it because you were born there. She hasn't been back to Ireland since our father was murdered before you were born. They are going to look for an Irish, or Anglo-Irish, husband for you. You will be married probably before summer's end. Well, little sister, what do you think of that?"

Fortune was strangely silent for a long moment and then she said, "There are three thousand acres belonging to MacGuire's Ford. It's a goodly estate to have. I wonder if the horses will be included as part of my dowry. I'll get a fine husband with all of that."

India was astounded by her sister's reaction. She had fully expected Fortune to rebel even as she was rebelling. "Don't you care that you are going to be married to some stranger?" she demanded.

Fortune turned her turquoise eyes on her sister. "A woman, particularly women of our class and wealth, must be married, India. I have absolutely no experience with men, and so I think I shall rely upon our parents to pick my husband. They will not force either one of us into a bad match. I imagine I'll be given a choice, and can choose the man I prefer myself. If you were not so pigheaded you would not be in the difficulty that you are in now. Mama and Papa made no secret that Adrian Leigh was not for you. They said it plainly, but you will have your way, or die trying, won't you, sister? Well, this time you will not get your way, and I think you had best accept that. It's past time we were both married."

"I will marry the man I love!" India snapped.

"Don't be such a fool, India!" Fortune snapped back.

"You will not tell Mama and Papa that I overheard them?" came India's reply.

"Of course not," Fortune said. "It's months away." Then she grew thoughtful. "I wonder what he will be like. I shall enjoy having my own home, although I shall miss the family. We will all be scattered now, won't we?" Fortune was a practical girl, if a bit wild.

India was no longer listening to her sister, however. She somehow had to find Adrian, and tell him of these latest developments that threatened to part them. He would know what to do. Leaving Fortune, she hurried back downstairs to the writing room, penning a message to Viscount Twyford, and then, sealing it with wax, she pressed her signet ring hard into the soft substance. Slipping from the room, she let herself out into the garden and ran down the lawns to the riverside.

"Oi!" she called to a passing werryman, who, seeing her wave and hearing her call, rowed over to the Greenwood quai.

"Aye, lady? Where does ye want to go?"

India handed him the packet, along with a coin. "Take this to Whitehall. Give it to the royal boatmaster and tell him it is to be delivered immediately to Viscount Twyford, the earl of Oxton's heir. You're to wait for him. Do you understand? You are to bring Viscount Twyford back here."

The werryman felt the weight of the coin in his hand. He didn't have to look at it to know it was double, probably triple, in legal fare. "Yes, m'lady," he said, pulling at his forelock respectfully. Then, pushing cockle away from the quai, he rowed away. It never occurred to him to keep her coin, and throw the missive in the rapids beneath London Bridge, for he was an honest man. Besides, the gentry had a way of repaying dishonesty.

India watched him go, relieved. It was going to be all right. She and Adrian would figure out what to do together. Picking up her skirts, she hurried back up to the house, realizing as she ran that she was cold. In her haste she had forgotten her cape, but it didn't matter. Nothing mattered but her future with Adrian Leigh.

Chapter

4

Greenwood House was silent at the midnight hour when India heard the rattle of pebbles at her window. Slipping from the bed she shared with Fortune, she hurried across the chilly floor, and, swinging the casement open, peered out. Seeing Adrian Leigh standing in the moonlight, she called softly to him, "I will come down." Then, pulling the window shut, she caught up her cape and headed toward the bedroom door. Fortune murmured softly and turned in the bed, stopping her sister for a moment to make certain that her sibling was not awakening. Satisfied she slept, India eased herself through the door, and, pulling her cloak about her, ran quickly down the staircase, through the hallway, and into the library. Pushing open one of the large windows, she summoned her swain to her.

"*Adrian! Here!*" She beckoned to the shadowy figure.

The viscount climbed through the open window, drawing it shut behind him. Then, pulling India into his arms, he kissed her.

Startled, and breathless, she gently extracted herself from his embrace, laughing nervously. "Adrian! For shame! I have not asked you here for the purpose of dalliance." She was flushed, and her heart was beating rather more quickly than before. He was so bold, she thought.

"No, sweeting? I am disappointed," he teased her. "Then, pray, m'lady, why have you summoned me?" He took up her hand and kissed the fingers on it.

"Ohh, Adrian, I do not know what to do," she cried softly, and did not protest when he pulled her back into his arms and began to stroke her dark hair.

"What is it poppet?" he encouraged her. "Tell me, and I will endeavor to make it better." He kissed the top of her head. She was so trusting and sweet and rich. He knew she was his for the taking.

"We will be returning home next week. Papa says since I will not choose a *suitable* man to marry, then he and Mama must pick a match for me. But I don't want to marry some stranger! Oh, what are we to do, Adrian? They are going to separate us forever," India sobbed softly. "If they take me home to Glenkirk, I will never see you again! Oh, I know it is bold of me to say it, but I couldn't bear it if we were parted from one another! I will die. I know I will."

"I cannot let you do that," he said as softly, thinking that his soon-to-be father-in-law had just provided him with the very opportunity he required to steal Lady India Lindley away from her overly protective family. When his mother had suggested it, he hadn't thought it would be this easy.

"But Adrian!" She gazed up into his face, and he thought she was really quite beautiful. "What can we do?"

"Your father has left us with no choice, my darling," he told her in a calm and most sensible voice. "We must run away and get married before they can take you back to Scotland, India."

Now she looked up at him, and found herself very torn. He was so handsome with his long, straight nose, and his silky blond hair. His sapphire-blue eyes seemed to look at her with such love and devotion. "Ohhh, Adrian! I do not know. It seems so impetuous a thing to do."

"Ah, India! Do you not love me?" he asked her in a hurt tone.

"Oh, yes, Adrian! I do love you!" Then she blushed furiously, for she had never said such a thing to him before.

"And I love you, my darling," he quickly reassured her, knowing such a declaration from her lips required a similar devotion on his part.

"But I love my family, too," she said, worrying her lower lip with her top teeth in her concern.

"You do not have to stop loving them, my darling, just because you love me," he told her, "but is it really just of them to keep us apart when we love each other? I know that my mother and my half-brother have brought shame upon the Leighs of Oxton Court, but I am my father's son first and foremost, India. We are an old and noble family. Is it fair of your father to hold me responsible for Deverall and Mama's bad behavior? I think the duke of Glenkirk a better man than that, my love. Still, he is a father protecting a beloved daughter, and I do understand how he feels even if I think him wrong. If we are married, then you and I settle the entire matter by controlling our own destiny. I know our actions will anger your parents at first, but when they see how happy we are, they will forgive us. I know it."

"But where could we go, Adrian, that they would not follow?" India asked, snuggling against him. She felt so safe now.

"We must leave the country," he ventured, waiting to see what India's reaction would be to that.

"*Leave the country?*" She was more than startled by his suggestion.

"There is no other option, India. Where can we hide in England, my love? Your family is large, and scattered all about the whole country. And we certainly cannot go north, can we?" He chuckled, and kissed her on the tip of her nose.

"We cannot go to France, either," she informed him, joining in with his train of thought. "We have family there."

"We could go to Naples," he suggested.

"*Naples?* Why Naples, Adrian?" His hand was caressing her back now, and it was really quite pleasant.

"My uncle, the Conde di Carlo, lives in Naples," he said. "We could go to him, and be married there. Then we could remain with my uncle until we had our first child. If we returned home with our son, your father could not annul our union, sweeting."

"My father's mother lives in Naples," India said. "Lady Stewart-

Hepburn. Papa's sister is the marchesa di San Ridolfi. What if we ran into them, Adrian? Then Papa would know where we were!"

"We will be wed privately, my love, and remain safely within the walls of my uncle's estate. Have you ever met these ladies, India?"

"My stepgrandmama, last summer in France, but not the marchesa," she answered him. A wave of doubt washed over her. It seemed so rash an action to take, running away and marrying.

"Perhaps you do not love me enough, India, to dare such a bold course," he subtly taunted her, seeing the indecision on her face.

"Ohh, but I do!" she cried.

"No, I think not," he replied sorrowfully, goading her further.

"But I do, Adrian! I swear I do!" India insisted.

"Then say you will pledge yourself body and soul to me as my wife, sweetheart," he said, his voice holding just a hint of pleading. "Say you will marry me and be my wife and bear my children! *Say it!*" But before she might speak, he was kissing her passionately, his lips hot and hungry upon hers; the hand that had been caressing her back was now sliding beneath her cloak, moving to caress her bosom lightly.

India's head was spinning with delight. Her lips parted slightly beneath his, and she drew her perfumed breath into her own mouth. When his hand slipped into her nightgown bodice to cup a single breast, she gasped with surprise. No one had ever touched her breasts before! The warmth of his palm was intoxicating, and when his thumb and his forefinger gently pinched her thrusting nipple, she almost swooned, falling back against his arm with a soft moan of distinct pleasure. If this was love, it was wonderful!

Lifting his head from her, he begged, "Say you will marry me, my darling. Can you not sense how I long for you? How much I love you, my precious India? *Say it! Say it, or I will fling myself into the river this very night, for I cannot live without you!*"

"*Yes. Oh, yes,*" she breathed.

Immediately he removed his hand, dipping his head to kiss the swell of her bosom over her gown. "Your virtue is a precious jewel to me, my love," he told her solemnly. "I must cease our loveplay lest I lose control of my passions and shame us both. We have a lifetime before us in which we may pleasure each other, but not until we have married."

"Oh, Adrian, I do love you!" she told him, wishing he were not quite so noble at this moment in time. She had liked his caress, and his kisses. Her entire body seemed more alive now than it had ever been, but the wet stickiness between her legs in that secret place was confusing. She didn't know what it was, and she certainly couldn't ask Mama now.

"Do you know exactly what day your family plans to depart for Scotland?" he asked her in practical tones. "I must find a ship sailing for Naples. I suspect we do not have much time."

"In three or four days' time at the most," India replied. "He has not given the order for our possessions to be packed up yet."

"I will go to the docks in the morning and find us a vessel," he told her. "There will be someone sailing for the Mediterranean soon."

"Go to the O'Malley-Small Trading Company docks," India advised. "I will not sail on any other ship but one of theirs. If we trust ourselves to strangers, we could end up murdered for our possessions and thrown overboard, Adrian. Sea travel can be dangerous, but the O'Malley-Small ships belong to my family, and we will be safe."

"But will these people not recognize you, India?"

"Not if I board the ship in disguise, Adrian," she told him, feeling quite clever. "You shall be a son of the conde di Carlo, and I your elderly great-aunt, Lady Monypenny, newly widowed and childless, returning home to Naples, my girlhood home, after many years, in order to die. You have been sent by your father, my nephew, to escort me. This will allow us to purchase two cabins without arousing suspicion. I shall keep to my cabin during the voyage so my disguise may not be penetrated by anyone else on board. Am I not cunning, my sweet lord?" She grinned mischievously at him.

"Indeed," he agreed, a bit surprised by her resourcefulness. Perhaps India's mind was a little too skillful at deception, he considered, but then he remembered how rich she was, and how beautiful, and how well she had responded to his roving hands. She was tamable. All women were tamable under the right circumstances, and he would not be a harsh master.

"You must go now," she told him. "Come tomorrow night, and use the same signal to call me. Our plans must be finalized by then."

Giving India a quick kiss, the viscount opened the casement window and stepped through it into the night. "Until tomorrow, my love," he told her, and then he was gone into the darkness.

India sighed as she latched the window shut. He was so wonderful, her Adrian, and soon they would be man and wife. How sensitive he was! Not only did he sympathize with Papa, who was being totally unreasonable and difficult, but his carefulness and concern for her person and her innocence showed her that he was a man of excellent character. Her parents were wrong about Adrian. He was the perfect man for her. Leaving the library, she crept back up the staircase to her bedchamber, and slipped easily into bed next to her sister, who was now snoring. She thought she would be too excited to sleep remembering the events of the last hour, but India was soon slumbering as heavily as Fortune.

In the morning she feigned a headache, and kept to her bed until half the morning had gone by, sipping smoky black tea that her mother had brought her to ease the alleged throbbing in her temples.

"We thought we might spend the afternoon at court," Jasmine told her daughter. "Do you feel well enough to come?"

India sighed deeply. "I think not, Mama," she said. "The pain is easing, but a trip upon the cold and damp river will but bring it back. We are not leaving London tomorrow, are we? I will get another chance to bid their majesties farewell, won't I?"

"Your father has decided we will depart on Tuesday," the duchess told her daughter. "It is only Saturday. You will have the opportunity to say good-bye to the king and queen, India."

"Then I think I shall remain within the house today," India replied. "I should be fine by the morrow."

"Would you mind if we went to Whitehall?" Jasmine asked.

"Henry and Charlie have already made some important contacts, and perhaps I shall find a lovely gentleman for you, my daughter."

India smiled wanly. "There is no one for me but Adrian, Mama."

"Oh, my darling girl," Jasmine said, "you must put him from your mind. He is entirely unsuitable, and your father will not hear of it. Jemmie has tried so hard to raise you as Rowan Lindley would have, India, and I know Rowan would agree with Jemmie about your viscount. Put it aside, my daughter, for you will not be happy until you do."

India sighed. "I will try, Mama," she murmured.

"That is all I ask of you for now," Jasmine replied.

When the Leslies had departed for Whitehall, taking Fortune with them as well, India arose and began to pack her own little trunks. Neither she nor Fortune had been allowed to bring servants on this trip. The house was quiet, and practically servantless, for the duke had not bothered to hire extra help on this visit, and only the small permanent staff that lived at Greenwood was in residence. There were five of them. The majordomo, the housekeeper, the laundress, the cook, and the stableman. India now took an armful of laundry to the laundress.

"We are leaving on Tuesday," she said. "I want to travel with clean undergarments, Dolly. Would you mind doing these today? I'm sure Mama and Fortune will want their things done, too, and this way we will not overburden you by piling everything on you at once."

"Of course, m'lady, and most kind of you," the laundress answered.

India hurried to the library, and, opening the false panel where her parents hid their valuables when they were in London, she put her hand into the dark cavity. The chamois bag of coins her father always took when they traveled was quite plump. The duke obviously had already been to the goldsmith's bank in preparation for their return trip. India smiled to herself, and withdrew her hand, closing the panel. She fully intended taking that bag with her when she left with Adrian. It would be a down payment on her dowry.

She would wager after he paid their fare he would have little left and be glad for her foresight. Her father's gold would keep them quite comfortably for the next year. She returned to her own bedchamber.

Her family had not returned by the midnight hour when Adrian Leigh once again tossed pebbles at her window. India flung open the casement and, looking down, said, "You must be careful. My family have not yet returned from Whitehall, and will be coming by the river. What news, my darling lord? I dare not come down. I can see the river better from here, and you must be gone before they return."

"You were right, my clever poppet," he told her. "The *Royal Charles,* the O'Malley-Small Trading Company's newest cargo and passenger vessel, departs for the Mediterranean on the morning tide Monday, and it will stop at Naples. I have booked us two cabins as you instructed, and we must be aboard by five o'clock in the morning at the latest."

"Who is its captain?" she asked.

"Thomas Southwood," he replied.

"My cousin," she said thoughtfully. "But as he has not seen me in many years, I expect we will be safe. Especially as I shall be disguised as old Lady Monypenny. Come for me at four o'clock in the morning. I shall bring two small trunks and my jewelry, so do not come in a small werry. You have done admirably, my darling." India blew him a kiss. "Go now before we are caught. I love you, Adrian!" She drew the window shut, her heart soaring. Just a few more days and they would make good their escape! She climbed into bed, and was already sleeping by the time her family returned home.

The next day was Sunday, and they attended religious services at Whitehall Palace. The king preferred the more Catholic Anglican service despite the grumblings from the many Puritans in his court.

"Go and have your own services then," he ordered the more outspoken of them. "Do none of you remember that I am pledged to be as tolerant as I may? You do not like England's church, and you do not like the queen's faith. Go then, and hold your own candleless plain services with no outward show of faith but your droning voices."

Coming from the king's chapel, they saw Adrian Leigh exiting the queen's chapel.

"And there is another reason you cannot wed with that fellow," James Leslie said, his hand reaching out to prevent India from joining her chosen swain. "He is a practicing member of Rome's church, and that is a dangerous thing to be here right now in England as we all know."

"The Leslies of Glenkirk were once Roman Catholics, and so was Mama," India replied pertly. "Did not old Queen Elizabeth once say there is but one Lord Jesus Christ. The rest is all trifles?"

"Everyone was once a member of the Roman church," the duke said patiently, "but times have changed now. While I do not believe God gives a damn how we worship him, as long as we do, and are respectful, we must be prudent, India. This family, and your mother's family have survived by being careful. We do not involve ourselves in politics, or religious bickering. We keep our own counsel and pay the taxes levied on us without complaint. Nonetheless, it would be unwise, even if Viscount Twyford were a suitable match for you, *which he is not*, for you to wed a practicing member of the Roman church at this time. It is foolish to draw attention to yourself, for if you do, you will find that many people are easily envious of a wealthy and beautiful young girl such as yourself. Such people will strive to harm you."

India pulled angrily away from her father. "This is my last day at court," she said. "Let me do what I want, and associate with whom I choose, Papa. I am seventeen, and I am not some wee lass who needs to be told what to do. If you will take me from the man I love and force me to wed someone of *your* choice, at least Adrian and I have had this one last day together!" Then with an angry swish of her garnet-colored velvet skirts, she was gone.

"Let her go," Jasmine advised her husband. "She is a sensible girl, and will make peace with the situation if you do not irritate her any further, Jemmie. She must sort out her feelings by herself."

"Why is it I want to turn her over my knee and whack her bottom with my slipper?" the duke asked his wife.

Jasmine laughed softly. "Because she has gone and grown up on you, Jemmie," she teased him. "No father likes to see it happen to his daughter. Not only that, she prefers another man over you these days. What a betrayal to your heart!" She pulled him down, and kissed his cheek. "But I will always love you, my lord duke, and I will not leave you for anyone but death, and then reluctantly."

He chuckled. "Oh, my darling Jasmine," he told her, "it is good that you are wiser than I. Come, and let us enjoy the day. We will bid our friends and family farewell, and be gone from this place. There is too much strife here, I regret, with Buckingham deciding the queen is his enemy and the French king sending a diplomat to sort out what the hell is going on that our king, and his pretty little queen, cannot get along. And the Puritans are gaining more influence and power every day. They will be trouble, mark my words. There is nothing worse than someone who truly believes his way is the only way and everyone must conform, or be punished, or perish. I shall be glad to be back in my highlands at Glenkirk. I do not think I will come to London again. By the way, have you spoken to your aunt Willow yet about some young men for India. I want her married as soon as possible. Let her be her husband's problem. We have one more daughter and five lads to settle before our job is done," he concluded with a chortle.

"Do you honestly believe that marrying them off absolves us of our parental responsibilities?" Jasmine asked. "I do not care how old they get, they will always be our children, and we will always care what happens to them, Jemmie Leslie!"

"But they'll be out of the house," he reminded her cheerfully.

They spent their day making their farewells, and James Leslie was pleased to see India awaiting them at the riverside quai without Viscount Twyford in tow when they were ready to depart. It was just dusk when they reached Greenwood House. Once inside, India asked her brothers to bring down her trunks and place them in the front hall.

"But, dearest," her mother said, "we are not going until Tuesday morning. There is no hurry."

"Papa is always saying that I am tardy, and that I keep everyone waiting and make them late being behind with my packing. I decided this time to be ready before all of you. I even had the laundress do my laundry yesterday so she would not be overburdened. I want to see my trunks here in the hall, Mama." Then she giggled charmingly. "It may be the only time in my life I am ahead of Papa's schedule."

"Well, go and get your sister's trunks," James Leslie commanded his sons. "If she is ready now, she deserves the credit for it, and we shall all look admiringly upon her trunks here tomorrow as we pack our own clothing for our departure."

India smiled sweetly at her father as her brothers brought down her luggage. "I was very rude to you today, Papa. I apologize for my discourteousness, but I do not ask your pardon for loving Adrian, even if you won't let us marry. I think you are being very unfair. You will not even give him a chance, but hold him responsible for the bad behavior of his mother and half-brother. It is wrong, Papa, and I am ashamed that you would do such a thing. You have always been a fair-minded man until now." She curtsied.

The duke gritted his teeth and held his temper. "You know that I love you, India. You must accept that I know what is best for you. I only want you happy, *and damn it,* I will see that you are in spite of yourself!" He caught himself. "First love is always the most poignant, but it is not necessarily the most lasting. I want a lasting love for you. You have always trusted me, India. Why will you not trust me in this matter? You are my daughter, and I don't want you hurt."

"If you do not let me marry Adrian, I will be unhappy the rest of my life," India announced dramatically.

"Since you two cannot agree on this point," Jasmine said, interjecting herself between her eldest child and her husband, "I think it best we do not discuss it again tonight. India, you have done a fine job of getting ready, and since you are, you will help your sister and me to pack our own possessions tomorrow. Now, go to your room, my child, and rest. You know how difficult it is to rest along the road, and we have a very, very long journey ahead of us," Jasmine concluded.

Kissing her parents, India moved serenely up the staircase and entered her bedchamber. She had given her father one last chance, and she had hoped against hope that he would change his mind and then they wouldn't have to run away. She sighed. Adrian had been right all along. Her father was not giving them any other choice. Well, this time tomorrow they would be well at sea and on their way to Italy, and all her parents would know from the note she was leaving them was that she and Adrian had gone off to marry and they would not come back until they had.

"Why do you bait Papa that way?" Fortune demanded, entering the room. "He is not being unreasonable. Your viscount really isn't right for you, India, but you are always so insistent upon having your own way."

"Papa has never said he disapproved of Adrian, only his family," India retorted.

"A man is his family," Fortune replied. "You packed early so you could sneak off tomorrow, and spend time with your swain, didn't you? Mama saw right through you, and now you'll have to help us," she teased her elder sister. "I am very fussy about how my things are packed. It will take you all day between us, I fear."

"If you are not careful," India threatened her sister, "I'll take all your clothing and throw it out the window!"

"Ha! Ha!" Fortune taunted, and, picking up a pillow, whacked India with it.

Within moments, the two were engaged in a pillow fight that ended with them both collapsing into gales of laughter upon the bed.

"I shall miss you, little sister," India said.

"*Miss me?*" Fortune looked puzzled.

"When Father marries me off to his dark stranger in a few months' time," India quickly said. "God's boots! Do you realize our childhood is just about at an end? By this time next year we could be both great with child!" She stuffed one of the pillows beneath her skirts and paraded about the room. "Ohhh, I hope it's a son for my dear lord."

Fortune giggled. "Why do men always want sons?" she wondered aloud.

"Well, our real father didn't get one first," India said. "He got me before he got Henry, and then he got you after he died."

"Do you remember our real father at all?" Fortune ask wistfully.

India sighed deeply. "I have one tiny memory of this great, big, golden laughing man lifting me up in front of him on his horse and riding me about, but that is all. It really isn't much, is it?"

"It's more than Henry and I have," Fortune answered her. "Our real father wasn't even alive when I was born, but I do remember Prince Henry a little bit. He was handsome, and could never take his eyes off Mama. Just imagine if he had been allowed to marry Mama. Then our Charlie would be king now instead of his uncle Charles."

"Mama was considered unsuitable," India said. She had been older than Fortune, and remembered more.

"Just like Adrian is unsuitable for you," Fortune responded.

"I am going to bed," India announced, ending the discussion.

The two sisters washed themselves, put on their nightgowns, and climbed into bed. Across the room the fire burned brightly, warming the bedchamber. India blew out the candle and settled down. If she did not wake up in time, Adrian had promised to throw pebbles at the windowpane again. As her trunks were in the hall by the front door, it would only take her a little while to dress and go down to join him. She wasn't certain she would sleep, but she did, Fortune snuggled close next to her, making her familiar little sleep noises.

India awoke suddenly in the darkness. The clock in the hallway struck three times. She lay quietly for several minutes and then arose carefully, wincing as her feet touched the icy floor boards. Padding across the chamber, India added some coal to the fire, and it soon after sprang to life again. The clock chimed the quarter hour. She dressed slowly in a black velvet gown, a starched white ruff about her neck. On her feet she wore dark walking boots. In the attics she had found a mourning veil she would wear with her dark gloves and long dark cape. While she dressed, the clock in the hall chimed the half hour, and now was chiming three-quarters of the hour. India stuffed her jewelry pouch in her beaver muff and slipped quietly from the room.

She tiptoed down the staircase, moved as silently as she could through the hallway and entered the library. Going to the panel, behind which her father hid the valuables, she opened it and thrust her hand inside. Immediately her fingers made contact with the chamois bag. Pulling it out, she opened it, making certain that it was filled with gold coins. Satisfied, she pushed it into her muff with her jewelry and closed the panel. Now she hurried out into the main hallway of the house again, and, going to the front door, she slowly, and not without some difficulty, drew the bolts securing the entrance aside. She did not have to wait long.

There came a gentle scratching at the door, and India opened it immediately, allowing Viscount Twyford into the house with another man. He immediately picked up one of India's trunks and headed back down to the river.

"Take the other trunk," India instructed Adrian. "I want to rebolt the door so no one notices the door unlocked in the morning and raises an alarm too soon. I'll go out the library window, my love, and join you in but a moment."

The viscount took up the second trunk and India shut the door behind him, sliding the bolts back into place. She then retraced her steps to the library and exited through one of the casement windows, pushing it shut behind her. It was unlikely anyone would notice the window was unlatched if it gave the appearance of being closed tightly. Then, without a backward glance, she hurried down the lawns to the quai where her transport awaited her. As he helped her into the boat, she had only a momentary pang, but then her heart soared. They were free!

"Lift your veil, madame, so I may be certain it's you, and not your papa hiding beneath the gauze," he teased her.

India raised the silk fabric. " 'Tis I, my love," she said.

The werry moved quickly down the river into the Pool, and was rowed directly to a dock at the O'Malley-Small Trading Company. Adrian Leigh climbed from the small vessel and helped India onto the dock. Leading her to a sturdy gangway before a great sailing ship, he helped her to board. India moved slowly and heavily in her guise as an elderly widow. Beneath her veiling she might have been anyone.

"Ahh, Signore di Carlo," a cultured voice spoke, "you are right on time, sir. And this will be your aunt? My condolences, madame, on your great loss."

"Monypenny was old. He lived a good life," came a gravelly voice from beneath the veils. "You are one of Lynmouth's lads, aren't you?"

"Aye, madame, I am his fourth son," Captain Thomas Southwood replied. "Geoff is the heir. John is a churchman, and Charles is married to an heiress. I, however, prefer the sea as a wife. She's less troublesome, and asks little of a man."

"Heh! Heh!" came the snicker from beneath the veils. "Then you are like your grandmother, who, I am told, was a pirate."

"A base canard, madame." Captain Southwood was smiling. "Now, my steward will show you to your cabin." He bowed.

"What was all that chatter?" Adrian Leigh asked nervously when they were alone again. "You will give us away before we have even escaped."

"I am supposed to be a garrulous old lady, and as such it is highly possible that I would know his family. It has put him off guard, Adrian. He doesn't imagine for one moment that I'm not the old lady I am supposed to be."

The *Royal Charles* moved out into the Pool precisely on schedule, and made its way majestically down the Thames with the outgoing tide toward the sea. India remained in her cabin once she entered it. She stood by the small porthole that looked out on the deck, and beyond it, the river. They passed by Greenwich, and the shipyards at Tilbury. The mid-February day was gray, although not stormy. India had thought when they had left Greenwood that she detected the faintest hint of spring in the air. How long would it be before she enjoyed another English spring and summer again? She felt the deep roll of their vessel as the Thames entered the Channel, realizing with singular clarity of mind that her course was set. She could not go back, and for the first time in her life India Lindley wondered if she had really done the right thing. Shivering, she drew her fur-lined cloak about her tightly.

Chapter 5

The *Royal Charles* was a serious cargo vessel. It had left England with a load of wool and Cornish tinware in its deep holes. The ship made its way down the English Channel past Land's End, and plotted a course across the Bay of Biscay. At Bordeaux it took on a consignment of red wine. It then sailed around Cape Finsterre, putting in at Lisbon, where it took on a cargo of hides. Hugging the coast for a time, it moved around Cape St. Vincent and into the Gulf of Cadiz, stopping at the city of Cadiz to take on baskets of oranges and lemons. They sailed through the Straits of Gibraltar, docking at Málaga to onload barrels of sherry. It was here that the other passengers, two Spanish wine merchants, debarked. They would next put into Marseilles to offload the wine and take on salted fish, and then sail on to Naples, Adrian informed India, having obtained his information from the captain.

India had not come out of her cabin since they had left London, except for short walks on the deck at night, well muffled in her veils. She was in deepest mourning, Adrian had explained to Captain Southwood, and preferred her solitude. She found the sea soothing.

Tom Southwood laughed. "We are fortunate to have had fine weather so far, Signore di Carlo, or Lady Monypenny would find the sea not quite so salubrious. I am sorry, however, that she will not take her meals with us. I found her a rather amusing old lady, outspoken and much like my late grandmother, Lady de Marisco."

"Alas," Adrian replied, "while my aunt's spirit is soothed by the sea, her stomach is a bit more delicate, I fear."

The weather had grown quite warm. They were in the narrowest part of the Mediterranean, Adrian told India. She was skittish, and would not allow him much time in her cabin or her company these days. He worried that she was regretting her actions, but India said nothing to that effect and so he believed her just nervous of travel. They would return overland when the day came, he decided, but for a quick cruise across the Channel.

They were several days out of Marseilles when the passenger steward sought out Tom Southwood. "Captain, may I speak with ye a moment?" The steward stood in the door of the main cabin.

"Come in, Knox. What is the problem?"

"Well, Captain, 'tis the lady . . . the one who is getting off in Naples. Ain't she supposed to be an old lady, sir?"

"Aye." Now, what was this all about? Tom Southwood thought.

"Well, Captain, she ain't an old lady. She's a young lady." Knox looked very uncomfortable. "I was going by her cabin this afternoon, and I seen her sitting on her bunk, brushing her hair. I stopped because I was so surprised that an old lady would have such fine tresses. Then she turned her head slightly . . . she didn't see me, sir . . . and it weren't an old lady's face. It was a beautiful young girl, Captain!"

"Damnation!" Tom Southwood swore, irritated. What the hell was going on? And he would certainly have to find out before they put into another port. A young lady. A Signore di Carlo who spoke accentless English. He had said he was schooled in England. *An elopement!* It was the only, and the logical, answer. Signore di Carlo was running off with someone's daughter. But whose? And what was Captain Tom Southwood to do about it? "Come with me," he said to Knox, and, leaving his cabin, made for the passenger deck. Knocking on the faux Lady Monypenny's cabin door, he entered without waiting for her permission to do so. A young girl jumped up from the bunk where she had been reading and gave a startled gasp. "Jesus Christ!" Tom Southwood swore again. "India Lindley!"

"I'm sorry, Captain, but you have mistaken me for someone else," India said in her plumiest tones.

"India, you are somewhat grown since the last time I saw you," Tom Southwood said grimly, "but you have your mother's look about you, and that fetching little mole she sports between your nostril and your upper lip, *and* you are wearing the Lindley signet ring your mother gave you. Now, what is this all about, and why are you masquerading as an old lady? Although I believe I know the answer to my own question."

"Then you need nothing from me, Tom," India said angrily.

"Is he your Italian tutor, this Signore di Carlo?" the captain demanded of her. "You're eloping, aren't you, and you chose my ship to do it on? I had heard you had grown into a little hellion, but I never thought you would cause a scandal like this! If anyone finds out what you have done, you will be ruined. No decent man will have you."

"But Adrian *is* a decent man!" India cried out, defending her love. "He isn't my Italian tutor, Cousin Tom. He is Viscount Twyford, the earl of Oxton's heir. We were eloping to his uncle's house in Naples to be married because Papa would not be reasonable. I love him, and he loves me! I chose your ship because I knew we would be safe, and I came aboard in disguise for obvious reasons."

"Knox, move Lady Lindley's things to my cabin, and see that her gentleman is confined to his quarters for the duration of the trip," Captain Southwood said.

"Tom! You cannot be so cruel," India sobbed.

"Cousin," he told her sternly, "if we are fortunate, there will be one of our company's vessels in Marseilles going west to England. If there is, I intend putting you on it, and seeing that you are returned home to your parents. If there is not, you will remain aboard my ship and return home with me. As for your swain, he has paid his passage to Naples, and he shall disembark there, *but without you!*"

"Noooo!" she wailed. "*No!*"

Grasping her lightly by the arm, Tom Southwood literally dragged his young cousin from her cabin to his. As they passed the cabin housing Adrian Leigh, they could hear him pounding on the door in furious frustration. Shoving India into the day room of the great stern quarters that were his, Tom Southwood said, "I will speak with your viscount, and explain to him that things have changed, India. You are going home, young lady!"

"I hate you, Thomas Southwood!" India shouted, and she flung a wine carafe at him. *"I hate you!"*

He ducked, and, beating a hasty retreat, exited his cabin, locking the door behind him. Now he returned to the passenger deck and let himself into Viscount Twyford's cabin. The young man leapt up from the bunk upon which he had been sitting. "Well, my lord, you are found out," Captain Southwood said grimly. "The game is up, and you will be put off in Naples. My cousin, India, however, will be sent home. You will be confined to your cabin until we reach your destination."

"You have no right . . ." Adrian began pompously, only to be cut off.

"Aye, my lord, I have every right. As captain of the *Royal Charles*, I am the master of this small seagoing domain upon which you currently reside. You do not have the duke of Glenkirk's permission to marry his daughter. You have cajoled and lured an innocent young girl away from the safety of her family. You are a cad, my lord. Now I will leave you to consider the seriousness of what you have done. I think it will be a long time before you dare to show your face in England. We are a large family, my lord, and we protect our own. I pray to God this has remained a private matter, and that India's reputation is yet intact. Do you understand me?"

"May I at least say farewell to India?" Viscount Twyford asked.

"You have said all to my cousin that you should, and probably a great deal more," Captain Southwood replied. "And do not bother trying to speak with India through the cabin walls. I have moved her to my quarters. She, too, will be confined even as you are, until she leaves this vessel. Now I will bid you good day, sir."

Thomas Southwood then found his first mate, Mr. Bolton, and explained to him what had happened.

" 'Tis a right bad coil, sir," Mr. Bolton said, shaking his head. "There's advantages to being a bachelor, I'm thinking. Pray the lord the lass hasn't ruined herself with a scandal."

India was so angry with her cousin that she refused to eat that evening. "I shall starve myself to death," she told him dramatically. "You shall return to England with my withered body in a coffin, and then Papa shall kill you!"

Thomas Southwood swallowed back his laughter. He had a younger sister, Laura, who at India's age had also been given to similar histrionics. "Suit yourself," he said mildly, "but this fish is really quite delicious. It was fresh-caught by Knox earlier today, and the artichokes came aboard at Cadiz. Would you like a fresh orange? They are very sweet."

"Go to hell!" India spat angrily, her hand inching toward a pewter goblet, a dangerous look in her eye.

He was quickly on his feet, and before she might throw anything at him, he dragged her up from her chair and across the cabin. "You may sleep in my bed, India, and I shall take Knox's trundle out here." He pushed her into his smaller sleeping cabin, locking the door behind her. "There is water for bathing and drinking, my dear," he called to her, and then returned to the table to finish his meal while she shrieked at him from her prison.

In the morning it was Knox who opened the door to let her out. "Captain says you may have the run of his quarters during the day, m'lady," the steward said pleasantly. "Can I get you anything to eat? Some fruit, perhaps?"

"No, thank you," India said politely. "Where is my cousin?"

"Captain don't sleep more than four, five hours, m'lady. He be up on deck, and has been since before dawn," Knox said. "Well, if I can't be of any service to you, I'll go tend to the young gentleman."

"Knox! Wait! Will you take a message to Viscount Twyford for me?" India pleaded. "I will make it worth your while."

The steward shook his head despairingly, edging toward the door, for he knew of India's penchant for throwing things. "I'm sorry, m'lady, but you know I cannot." Then he was out the door before she could argue with him, or pitch a missile at him.

India heard the sound of the key turning in the lock once again, and almost snarled in angry despair. She had not come this far to be denied. Setting herself in the window seat of the cabin's great window, she looked out. No escape here. The window looked onto the sea itself, and, peering down through the glass, she could see there was no ledge. The little sleeping cabin had no access to the deck. Only the door in this cabin itself had entree to the main deck. But she would find a way. *She would!* And she was certain that her beloved Adrian was also seeking a means of escape. Perhaps when they got to Marseilles, and her interfering cousin attempted to transfer her to another ship, she could escape them. And while they were looking for her she would sneak back on board and help Adrian. Then they would travel on overland to Naples. She wasn't going to be stopped now.

"*Sail ho!*"

She heard the call out on the deck. Looking out the great window, India could see another vessel in the distance.

"Put on more sail!" came the command.

India could hear the creaking of winches as additional canvas was raised, but the ship didn't seem to be gaining any speed. She looked back out the window again. The other ship was gaining on them rather quickly. It was a narrow, sleek vessel with scarlet-and-gold-striped sails. She turned as the cabin door opened and her cousin entered, a worried look upon his handsome face.

"Be quiet and listen," he told her. "In a few minutes we are going to be boarded by pirates from one of the Barbary States."

India paled, and gasped. "Can't we escape them?" she asked.

"Under ordinary circumstances, yes, but the bloody wind is dying on us, and without the wind we can't outrun them. Now hear me very carefully, India, for what I am going to say may save your life. My grandmother was once in a similar situation. If you are asked to convert to Islam, agree and save your life. Don't be a little fool and refuse. We need no martyrs in this family. Agreeing means you will be given, or sold, to a highly placed man, and not thrown into the common slave bagnio where you would be raped and forced into whoredom."

"But can't we be ransomed?" she asked him, horrified.

"Neither of us is important enough, Cousin," he told her. "One day I may be able to get a message home, and then perhaps . . " He stopped, and looked at her. "You may not be able to go back then."

"Ohhh, Tom!" India cried. "Not to see Mama or Papa ever again?"

"This family has a history of troublesome and adventuresome women, who usually end up surviving quite nicely, India. Listen, learn, and for God's sake remember that from the moment of your capture you are no longer the duke of Glenkirk's daughter but nothing more than a beautiful slave. You will be at the mercy of your master, whoever he will be. Keep your temper in check, Cousin, and a civil tongue in your head, or you could find that tongue yanked out. The Barbary pirates are fierce men."

"I would rather be dead than submit!" India cried dramatically.

Tom Southwood grasped his young cousin by the arms, and shook her hard. "Don't be an idiot, India," he said, and then, releasing her, he was gone out the door again. To her despair she heard the key turning in the lock. Did he never forget?

The corsair ship drew skillfully alongside the *Royal Charles*. She could now see the reason for its speed. While the ship had sails, it was also propelled by banks of oars, which had given it a great advantage over the larger merchant vessel, caught in a dying wind. India wished she could be out on the deck. What was her cousin doing? Was he going to fight?

"The crew stand ready to defend the ship, sir," Mr. Bolton said.

Tom Southwood shook his head. "Resistance would be futile," he told his first mate, who had already known it. "Look at their guns. Besides, I want the ship intact. Eventually we're going to steal it back, Francis Bolton." He chuckled. "You've told the crew what I said?"

"Aye, sir, but two of them is Irish papists, and half a dozen are hard-nosed Puritans. The sailmaker is a Jew, and the cook says he don't believe in anything. They won't convert," the first mate replied.

"Well, I've warned them, and hopefully enough of the lads will so we can sail this ship home one day," the young captain replied. "Heads up, Bolton, here they come!" He stood straight, his green eyes sweeping over the corsair's vessel. It was the largest of the galley class, with twenty . . . -four, -five, -six, -eight . . . benches of oars. Each bench would hold four or five men. This particular ship had an enclosure over the stern, which meant it carried janissaries. The rest of the deck was open to the sky. There was a large fixed cannon located on a low deck area, and several swivel guns sat amidships.

Then a large, tall man was standing before him. He spoke accentless French. "I am Aruj Agha, a captain in the royal Ottoman janissary Corps, based in El Sinut, and sailing under the command of its dey. Who are you, sir?"

"Captain Thomas Southwood, out of London, commanding the *Royal Charles*, under the aegis of the O'Malley-Small Trading Company. We are usually allowed unmolested in these waters, Aruj Agha. Why have you stopped us? Did you not see the pendant we fly?"

"It means nothing to me, sir," came the polite reply. "Whatever meaning it might have had once, it obviously no longer has that meaning. You and your ship are fair game, and now belong to the dey of El Sinut. What cargo do you carry?"

"Wool, Cornish tinware, hides, fruit, and barrels of sherry," was the response. "I also have two passengers, both of whom can be ransomed. One is the son of the earl of Oxton, and the other, who happens to be my own cousin, is the daughter of the duke of Glenkirk. Her younger brother is King Charles's bastard nephew. Her father will pay a fortune to regain her custody. I was taking her to visit her grandmother in Naples."

"If you are familiar with our world, Captain Southwood, then you know the rules on captives. I hope for your cousin's sake that she is an ugly little girl."

Thomas Southwood grimaced, and Aruj Agha laughed.

"No? Well, then, you had best let me see her," he said.

"I have locked her in the main cabin as I feared for her safety, sir. Please follow me."

"Very wise," Aruj Agha agreed. "We'll be taking your ship in tow, and so you, your passengers, and a few of your crew may remain until we reach our destination. I shall put my own men aboard to sail this vessel. We are three days out of El Sinut."

"And the rest of my crew?"

"They'll come aboard my galley, to be put in chains, of course. The dey will decide their fate once we arrive," Aruj Agha said.

Tom Southwood was not surprised. It was to be expected. The dey would give the men a chance to convert to Islam, and those who did would sail aboard his ships. Those who did not would be sold, go to the dey's ships as galley slaves, or go to the mines. It was a well known and common practice. Reaching the main cabin, he unlocked the door, calling to India as he did, "Cousin, it is I."

She stood in the center of the cabin, a sword in her hand. "You gave up without a fight," she accused him.

"We are a merchant ship, India. The corsair has guns," he explained. "Where the hell did you get that sword? Put it down. *Now!*"

"I cannot. I must uphold the family's honor, Tom, which you have so easily besmirched. I found the sword beneath your bunk. I will not give up without a fight," India declared.

Aruj Agha looked admiringly at India. The girl was a dazzling beauty. She wore a dark claret-colored velvet skirt and a man's full shirt. A large black leather belt surrounded her tiny waist. Her long, dark curls were loose, and her eyes flashed fire. She was utterly magnificent!

"*En garde, infidèle!*" India taunted, waving her weapon at him.

"*Jesu!*" Tom Southwood swore helplessly. How could he have forgotten the weapon beneath his bed?

Aruj Agha, however, burst out laughing. "Come, my beauty," he cajoled her with a friendly grin. "Your cousin did the right thing. It would have pained me to have to blow this lovely ship to pieces and kill all aboard. You will not be harmed. Indeed, I foresee a wonderful life ahead of you as the favorite in your master's harem.

Give me the sword." He held out his hand. India slashed wildly at it. Fortunately, the agha pulled his hand back swiftly, receiving only a glancing blow that nonetheless opened a small ribbon of blood across his fingertips.

Then India leapt forward, flaying at Aruj Agha wildly. The janissary captain was no longer in a mood to coax the girl. He met her attack, yanking the weapon from her hand and shoving her rudely to the floor, where he held her down with his booted foot. Tom Southwood never moved a muscle. He knew that the agha would not seriously harm India. She had too much value as a captive, but if she didn't learn the place she held in this strange new world, she was going to get herself killed.

"Tom! Are you going to let him do this to me?" India shrieked. "Help me!" She squirmed beneath her captor's boot.

"I warned you, India," he told her in their own tongue. "Now, shut up before he has you whipped, and don't say he wouldn't because he would. That is how recalcitrant slaves are dealt with here. I hope by now you realize the danger you are in." He turned to the jannissary, speaking French once more. "I have told her to behave herself, Aruj Agha, but she has always been very spoiled. I cannot guarantee she will listen."

"I've handled wild mares before, Captain. I am ashamed to have been taken off guard by a mere, unskilled girl. She is a virgin, of course. They are always more skittish in an unfamiliar situation." He looked down at India. "Are you prepared to be a bit more docile, my beauty." He lifted his foot from the small of her back and pulled her up.

"Go to the devil!" India spat at him. "I'll kill you given half the chance. I'll be no man's slave, damn you!"

Aruj Agha chuckled. "A spirited filly is always the finest," he announced. "Is she always this sweet-natured, Captain?"

"I'm afraid so," Tom Southwood replied.

"Where is Adrian?" India demanded of her cousin. "If they have harmed him, they will pay dearly!"

"*Shut up, India!*" he cautioned her. "You will only make it worse for your friend. He may be ransomed if this dey is generous of heart and greedy of spirit. Now, just do as you are told, Cousin."

"If he can be ransomed, why can't I?" she insisted.

"Because you are a beautiful virgin, and more valuable as a concubine. These people cannot imagine any father paying what you would otherwise fetch on the block, when, having been captured by pirates, you will be considered spoiled by our own people. Now, India, just be quiet and do as you are told. With Aruj Agha's permission, I will come and see you later." He concluded the last sentence in French so the janissary captain could understand him.

"Of course," Aruj Agha replied. "We want the girl content. Fear spoils a woman's beauty."

The two men exited the cabin, locking India in once again. Outside the door she could hear the orderly sounds of activity as the majority of the *Royal Charles* seamen were transferred onto the pirate galley where they would be shackled. The voices outside her door were now foreign, and indistinguishable but for an occasional English voice. She was frantic for Adrian's safety, and Tom had told her nothing. Her head was throbbing, and she had bruised her hip when Aruj Agha had thrown her to the floor. India suddenly felt like crying.

She heard the sound of the key, and the door opened again to admit Knox, the steward. "Captain wanted me to tell ye what is happening, m'lady, and bring you something to eat. Ye ain't touched a morsel since last night, and that ain't good. You've got to keep up yer strength."

"Where is Adrian?" India asked the steward desperately, and a tear rolled down her cheek.

"Now, don't you go fretting, m'lady, about the young gentleman," Knox told her, feeling a little sorry for the girl now. "He's locked in his cabin same as you. Captain says he might get ransomed. All the rest of the crew but for the captain, me, Mr. Bolton, the first mate, Mr. James, the second mate, and Will, the cook, has been sent over to the galley. We got a bunch of them heathen crewmen aboard us now." He set down the tray he was carrying and peeled the napkin back.

India looked wanly at his offering, and sighed. "I don't think I can eat a morsel," she said.

"If ye eats every bit of this meal up, m'lady, I'll carry a message to yer young gentleman," he bribed her. "Cook killed and roasted the last of the chickens today, and made some fresh bread. There's an artichoke, some grapes, and I've sectioned an orange for ye. Now, you eat it up. When I takes the gentleman his tray, I'll take yer message to him as well. All right?"

India sniffled, but began to pick at the food the steward had brought her. She took a nibble, and then another, and discovered to her surprise that she was actually hungry despite her low spirits. She quickly stripped the meat from the chicken wing, chewing it vigorously and swallowing it down. "Is there any cheese?" she asked the steward.

"Beneath the bread, m'lady," he answered her, masking a smile. The poor lass had not eaten in a day. Of course she was hungry. She had best eat now, for God only knew what kind of heathen food they would be offered when they reached port. *I'm getting too old for this kind of adventure,* Knox thought to himself. *If I ever get back to England, I'll find myself a nice widow with a bit put aside, and settle us in a cottage down in Devon, with a view of the sea from the windows, which will be more than enough for me. If I gets back.*

When India had finished all the food on the tray, Knox picked it up to go, asking, "What shall I tell the young gentleman, m'lady?"

"Say I love him," India began, "and that I'm praying for our deliverance. Tell him I wouldn't consider it amiss if he would pray for all aboard the *Royal Charles,* too. And he should find a way for us to escape!" India concluded.

"Yes, m'lady," Knox replied, thinking he would certainly leave off the last part of her message to Adrian Leigh. They didn't need the young milord trying to be heroic and getting himself killed. Not that Knox thought the young man heroic. He was rather more of an opportunist, taking his chances when they appeared favorable. Still, a little caution never hurt.

Alone again, India sat in the window seat once more viewing the empty sea. The sun was beginning to set in the west, almost directly in front of her. Above, the sky was a clear sharp blue, streaked with wispy pink clouds. The western horizon was flame, and purple and gold, with just the faintest edging of pale green. As the sky darkened, a single bright blue crystal star appeared in the early night sky. India sighed. It was so utterly beautiful. She wondered if Adrian was watching the sunset, too, and did he think of her as she thought of him? The sound of the door being opened caused her to turn her head from the window. She expected to see her cousin, but it was Aruj Agha instead. India stiffened.

"Do not be concerned, my beauty," he said in a reassuring voice. "You will not be harmed in my care. Let me light a lamp. It is dark in here." He drew the oil lamp down, and lit it with a small wick from the lamp he carried. "Remain in your place, my beauty, and let us talk. Do you understand what has happened this day?"

"You and your bandits have pirated our ship," India said sharply.

He chuckled, amused by her continued spirit. "It is my right to capture your vessel, girl," he told her. "These waters are under the control of that most gracious servant of Allah—may he be blessed forever—Murad, the fourth of that name. He is but a young lad, but we hope he will one day be a great sultan. As an infidel ship, you are fair game, my beauty."

"Who are you?" India asked, curious. "Are you a Turk?"

"I am a Bosnian, my beauty. It is part of the Ottoman Empire, but in Europe. I was conscripted into the corps of janissaries when I was eight years old. It was a great honor for my family. My uncle had been a janissary. I was educated by the corps, and nurtured by the corps. I worked my way up through the corps until I attained the rank of *agha*—captain, you would call it in your tongue," he told her.

"What will happen to me?" India asked. "My cousin says I will be a slave now. I am not a slave! I am the daughter of the duke of Glenkirk. Two of my brothers are dukes, and one a marquis. I am an heiress of great wealth, and related by blood to England's king."

Aruj Agha's brown eyes twinkled, and he stroked his russet beard thoughtfully. " 'Tis a most impressive pedigree, my beauty, but it does not change the facts. Your cousin told you the truth."

India jumped down from the window seat, and stamped her foot. "My family will pay you a fabulous ransom for my safe return. I could pay you the ransom myself. Don't you understand, Arug Agha? *I am rich!* Why, I own two trading ships: the *Star of India,* and the *Prince of Kashmir.* They are on the East Indies run, bringing spices, silks, and jewels to England each year. All that in addition to a great inheritance left me."

"I have listened to you carefully, my beauty, now you must listen to me. I do not have the right to make any decision regarding your fate. You, this ship, and everything on it, men and cargo alike, now belong to the dey of El Sinut, who rules in the sultan's name here. It is he who will make the decision concerning your fate. It is my job to bring you all safely into the harbor of El Sinut, and with Allah's help, guidance, and blessing, I will." He arose. "Now, I will bid you good night. You need have no fears, my beauty. You are quite safe."

"My cousin?" she asked.

"I will allow him to come and see you in the morning," the agha told her. Then, with a bow, he departed the cabin, locking it behind him.

India paced the room. This was impossible. *And none of it would have happened if you had heeded your parents,* a little voice in her head said. "God's nightshirt!" she swore, but the little voice was right, and she knew it. If she had listened to her family instead of allowing her foolish heart to rule her, she would be safe at home in Scotland, and not the captive of Barbary pirates. Her family wouldn't force her to marry someone she didn't really love. They could try, but in the end she would have gotten her way if she had just been a bit more patient, India decided. And as much as she loved Adrian, he had been wrong to cajole her into the elopement. Just look what had happened to them!

And *he* would more than likely be ransomed, but everyone seemed to be very sure that she wouldn't be. There was a stigma attached to a girl finding herself in this position. Still, her great-grandmother, and her grandmother, as well as her aunt Valentina, had found themselves in similar situations and come home to lead respectable lives. But that had been years ago. Times were different then, and people certainly more reasonable and open-minded. Now, if it were known that Lady India Lindley had been captured by Barbary pirates, it would cause a scandal of great proportions, and no decent man would offer for her. And if Adrian was sent home ahead of her, and she later returned, why even he wouldn't wed her! "God's boots!" India muttered. What a headstrong damned little fool she had been!

What in the name of heaven was she going to do? How could she save herself? Could she convince this dey to ransom her along with Adrian? It seemed her only option. The only other course open to her was to kill herself, and India knew she didn't have the courage to do that. Besides, if the truth were known, she didn't want to die anyway. But what if this dey fellow decided to keep her? India smiled grimly. She would be the most difficult, the most impossible, the most awful creature he had ever known; and he would certainly send her home, having concluded that a ransom was a better bargain than an uncooperative and raging girl. She was not about to be any man's slave! It was a totally unacceptable concept. She would not tolerate it!

She curled back into the window seat. The sky was dark now, and there was a thin new crescent of a moon reflecting itself delicately into the black sea. Around it, the stars were bright. Was her sister looking at that same moon? Fortune, who was so accepting of their parents' decision to find her a husband in Ireland, so content to settle herself at MacGuire's Ford, and be mistress of her own lands. *How much easier it would have been for all of us*, India thought, *if I had been more like Fortune.* Yet her sister could certainly not be called docile. Fortune was anything but meek and mild; but she was of a far more practical bent of mind than her elder sibling.

How long will it be before I see my sister and brothers again; and our parents too, India wondered. "Damn it, I miss them!" she half whispered to the empty cabin. "I have been so foolish. I will certainly never be this foolish again." She sighed, and continued looking out upon the sea, watching the wake of their vessel, just faintly silvered, as the *Royal Charles* sailed inexorably on toward El Sinut.

Part II

EL SINUT, 1626–1628

Chapter 6

"Would you like to come on deck as we enter the harbor?" Aruj Agha asked India on the morning they arrived in El Sinut. "Do you have a long, enveloping cape, my beauty?"

"I have two. The black wool with the fur lining I wore aboard in England, and a turquoise blue silk with a cream brocade lining," India told him. "That one has a hood."

"And is more suitable to our climate," Aruj Agha said. "But I will need something to veil your features from public view as well."

India rifled through her trunks, finally pulling forth a large, lace-edged handkerchief which she held up. "Will this do? And why does my face have to be hidden? Are you afraid someone will recognize me, and you will be forced to let me go?"

"No," he said with a smile. She was a persistent wench, he thought. "In our society respectable women cover both their hair and their faces from public scrutiny. Such delicate discretion allows a woman a greater measure of freedom without being accosted by bold men in the streets. Women who allow themselves to be seen are obviously women of low repute attempting to sell their favors." He helped her on with her long cape. "If you wish to appear in public in El Sinut, or anywhere else in the sultan's domain, you must be cloaked and veiled." He drew her hood up over her head. "We must affix the veil. Do you have any small pins?"

"In my jewel case," India said. "Will my jewelry be taken from me, Aruj Agha? It was all given to me by members of my family."

"I will intercede with the dey for you," he said, "but it is his decision, my beauty. You must understand that." He carefully pinned the white cloth across India's beautiful face, concealing everything but her golden eyes and dark brows. Standing back, he appeared satisfied. "Now we are ready," he told her with a broad smile. "I do believe that I could have a career as a lady's tiring woman, my beauty."

India giggled in spite of herself, and allowed him to lead her out onto the deck. The air was hot and dry. Ahead of them the great galley, its striped sails blowing gently in the slight breeze, rowed into an enclosed harbor, drawing its prey behind it. The harbor entrance was flanked by two square-towered lighthouses.

"They mark the ingress," Aruj Agha told her, "and are also responsible for the great chain that for now rests beneath the surface of the waters, but in emergencies can be raised to block entry to the port."

"They have a similar device across the Golden Horn in Istanbul," Tom Southwood remarked, looking about the anchorage carefully. There were at least three more big galleys, as well as galleots, brigantines, frigates, and small fellucas which could accommodate only three to five benches with one oarsman each, as opposed to the galley that had taken them in tow, and had twenty-eight benches with two oars for each bench, and four to five men on each oar. This was a busy and formidable anchorage. It would not, he now realized, be as simple as he had thought to take back the *Royal Charles* and escape, but as an honorable man, he had no choice but to eventually try.

India wasn't in the least interested in the harbor, its vessels, or its operations. It was this place, El Sinut, that fascinated her. It was a city like none she had ever before seen. The buildings were all white, and the hot midmorning sun glaring off them was almost blinding. They were not all of one height and most seemed to be terraced, each succeeding story set just slightly back of the one below. In what appeared to be the center of the city was a large building, the dome of which was overlaid in gold leaf, and glittered brightly.

"Is that your dey's palace?" India asked Aruj Agha.

"No," he told her, "that is the grande mosque of El Sinut."

"What is a mosque?" she inquired.

"It is what we call our holy place, like your churches," he explained to her. "Do you see the four towers surrounding the dome? They are called minarets. Six times each day the imans, our priests, ascend the minarets, and call the people to prayer."

"You pray six times each day?" India said, incredulous.

"We are devout people," he replied.

"What is going to happen now, Aruj Agha?" India questioned him as their ship was made fast to a dock.

"Why, we will go up to the dey's palace. It is there." He pointed.

Following the direction of his finger, India saw a large cluster of buildings on a low hill just below the grande mosque. They were as faceless and anonymous as all the other buildings in the city.

"A litter will be brought for you," he said, answering what was obviously to be her next question.

"And the others?" she wondered aloud. "My cousin? Viscount Twyford? Will they go, too?"

"They will walk behind us, my beauty," he responded. "I must now see to the arrangement," he told her. "I will leave you in the company of your cousin." Aruj Agha moved away from them, all business now.

"I am afraid," India suddenly said, looking up at Tom Southwood.

"You must show no fear," he warned her. "Especially among the women of the harem. You have to understand that these women are all vying for the attention of a single man, and hate each other. They will do whatever they have to do to destroy a potential rival."

"I think I should rather be at an oar," she told him with a small chuckle, as she attempted to calm herself.

"There is one thing I must insist you do, India," he said. "Under no circumstances say you were eloping with Viscount Twyford. If there is the slightest suspicion that you are no virgin, you could end up being sold in the common slave market, and find yourself in a brothel. You will be safest in the dey's household."

"But what if he gives me to someone else?" India fretted.

"You are still securest in the harem of a wealthy man than in a whorehouse, Cousin, *and* I will be able to find you more easily."

"But poor Adrian," India said piteously. "He will think I have betrayed him, and it will break his heart! I cannot do it, Tom!"

"Adrian will certainly understand that your safety is our main concern," Thomas Southwood told her. "It should be his concern, too, if he truly loves you. Please, India, promise me you will follow my instructions. Eventually I will get us all out of this situation, but you have to trust me, and do as I tell you."

At that moment, Aruj Agha joined them once again. "Bid your cousin farewell, Captain. You realize you will not be able to speak with her again. Quickly! We are ready to depart for the dey's palace."

Tom Southwood hugged India, whispering urgently into her ear as he did so, "Promise me!"

"I'll try," she whispered back, hugging him.

"Come," the janisarry captain said, taking India by the arm and leading her from the deck, down the gangway, and onto the first solid ground she had touched in weeks. She swayed just slightly as she regained her land legs, as the agha called them, helping her into a curtained litter. "Do not remove your veil, my beauty, or attempt to open the curtains once they are drawn," he said sternly.

"It is difficult to breathe," she complained nervously. Where was he taking her? What was going to happen to the others? And Adrian? She had not seen him in several days. Was he all right?

"Lie back against the pillows," he advised her in a kinder tone, seeing her obvious distress, although she made a valiant attempt not to show that she was frightened. "You will find a small embroidered pouch tucked along one side of the litter. In it is a vial of water to assuage your thirst should you need it You will find you can see through the curtains, although no one will be able to get close enough to you to invade your privacy. The town is pretty, and you will enjoy the ride to the dey's palace. It is not a great distance, my beauty." He gave her a small smile, then he drew the litter's curtains closed.

And he had not lied to her, India quickly discovered. She *could* see out!

Aruj Agha was dressed very handsomely this morning, she mused. He wore red silk pantaloons, a green-and-gold-striped shirt with a matching sash about his waist, and a handsome green silk cape lined in red. There was a curved sword hanging from his sash. His boots were of red leather, and upon his head was a small turban with a pearl pendant A rather handsome chestnut gelding was brought forth, and he mounted it easily, observing and directing the unloading of the *Royal Charles* from his perch.

The cargo was packed into mule-drawn carts and put into line behind the agha. India's litter was then moved behind the cargo. Suddenly she saw the English crew coming down the gangway of the corsair galley. They were shackled by their legs, and around the neck of each man was an iron collar from which a chain was fastened to the man before him in the line of prisoners. Only Captain Thomas Southwood was permitted to walk free, ahead of his men, having given his word of honor not to attempt an escape along their route. India's eyes anxiously scanned the shackled men, desperately seeking out Adrian Leigh. She gasped, horrified, to see him first in the line, next to Knox, pale, and treated no better than the common sailors. How could they!

Before she might voice her protest to Aruj Agha, her litter was lifted up by four of the janissaries who had come off the galley. The procession moved off the docks, and onto the narrow, winding streets of the city. Realizing that there was nothing she could do to help Adrian, India took the agha's advice and lay back amid the brightly colored silk pillows in the litter. She could see that the white walls of the buildings were devoid of windows on the street level. Some of the structures had lattice-covered windows on the upper levels, but most did not. Looking into the courtyard entrances she saw tubs and ceramic jars of flowers in a riotous profusion of shapes, sizes, and colors. Sometimes she saw a bubbling fountain. The streets were amazingly clean, and the populace appeared very orderly, going about their daily business without much ado. India quickly realized that the veiled figures were females, but there were actually very few of them. They passed through a large, open market square. There were stalls set up selling all kinds of produce and flowers; meat, poultry, and fish; household goods; fabrics; leather goods; song birds in wooden cages, and live animals. Then she shuddered seeing a block upon which slaves were even now being auctioned off. The people in the market jeered at the captive seamen, but made no other hostile move toward them.

The street they entered on the other side of the market square was slightly steeper, and gently terraced with wide stairs. The houses along it were larger, obviously belonging to a more affluent class of citizen. The street itself began to widen as they moved up it. India could see the dome of the grande mosque, and realized if the dey's palace were just below it, they must be getting closer. The procession entered another square; this one empty of people. There were no buildings on either side of the square; it was walled, and above it was nothing more than cloudless blue sky. The square was paved in blocks of cream and red marble. Ahead of them stood the dey's white marble palace.

They passed beneath a deep, wide entry arch into an open courtyard. Armed guards lined the entry and the courtyard. Their procession moved through another wide archway flanked with heavy wooden doors entering into another courtyard, this one planted, with a tiled fountain in its center. India's litter was set carefully down, and a moment later Aruj Agha opened the curtains and offered her his hand, helping her out. He looked at her a moment, and then nodded as if satisfied.

"You will follow me, my beauty. Do not speak unless the dey gives you his permission to do so. If he questions you, you may answer him. Now, let us go. The time of the dey's audience is almost over."

India looked quickly about her, but her cousin and the other English captives had been already taken away . . . but to where? She couldn't be afraid. She must not be. She genuinely believed her life depended upon her being strong, and so she followed quickly after the janisarry captain. He led her down a wide corridor, and finally into a large, pillared room with an opaque dome through which sunlight filtered softly. The room was crowded, and hot, but she shivered nonetheless. Seated cross-legged on a pillowed dais at the far end of the room from the entry was a man garbed all in white but for a cloth-of-gold sash about his waist. His broad pantaloons were white with wide embroidered bands of gold and pearls, and, most extraordinary, his feet were bare. He wore an open-necked white silk shirt, and she could see a heavy gold chain with a pendant upon his smooth bronze chest. A white satin cape lined in cloth-of-gold was fastened about his neck with a thin gold chain. On his head was a small, low turban, from whose front and center wrapping sprouted an aigrette feather set in a perfectly round diamond.

"Aruj Agha, my lord," the large black slave who was the doorkeeper boomed in stentorian tones.

"Stay here," the janissary commanded her. "When I call you, you may come forward, my beauty." The he hurried up to the foot of the dais, and, falling to his knees, kissed the dey's foot.

"Arise, Aruj Agha. You have returned sooner than I expected. You have had good hunting then, I assume?"

"Indeed, my lord Caynan Reis, I have." The agha scrambled to his feet once again, bowing as he did so.

"What have you brought us?" the dey asked. His face was an oval, and a short, well-barbered black beard fringed his jaw, making a circle about his mouth.

"A fine English round ship, my lord. It is not even a year old, and was meant for the East Indies run, but its captain was breaking it in gently by sailing it between London and Istanbul for the last few months. Its cargo, I regret, is not particularly valuable. Just Portuguese hides, English wool, and tinware, oranges and lemons from Cadiz, and a number of barrels of sherry from Málaga, which we dumped into the sea, remembering the prophet's admonition on wine. Its crew, however, is made up of well-disciplined seamen, quite a cut above the usual scurvy creatures we generally take off these ships. Many, including the captain, have already said they are willing to convert to Islam. and sail beneath the flags of the sultan's government, and El Sinut. *And,* the vessel carried two passengers. A young English milord, who will undoubtedly fetch a respectable ransom, and the captain's cousin, a young noblewoman, said to be an heiress of great wealth. She was being escorted to visit her grandmother in Naples. I am assured she is a virgin, my lord Caynan Reis. She is, I believe, quite a prize."

"Beautiful?" the dey asked. His long fingers toyed with his beard.

"Of course, my lord," the agha replied.

The dey laughed. "First things first," he said. "Bring me the captain of this ship that I may assure myself of his honesty."

Thomas Southwood was escorted in by two janissaries. He first bowed, and then, making obeisance as he had been instructed, touched his forehead to the dey's bare foot. Remaining upon his knees, he straightened his body, and waited.

"Tell me your name, and who your family are," the dey instructed.

"Captain Thomas Southwood, master of the *Royal Charles* out of London, my lord. I am the fourth son of the earl of Lynmouth. The vessel I sailed belonged to the O'Malley-Small Trading Company, in which I have a small share. I am now at your service, my lord."

"You are willing to convert to Islam, and sail for me?"

"Aye, my lord."

"You are quick with your answers, Captain, and I am suspicious of such a cooperative attitude. Is it possible you are considering escape? That you believe you will be given your freedom if you convert and then may flee? I am not such a fool as you may think. You may speak."

"My lord dey, you would know me for a liar if I said I had no thought of escape. Surely every captive dreams of escape. However, once many, many years ago, my grandmother was a captive of Islam. She eventually returned home, and told her children and grandchildren that to suffer for dogma is both foolish, and wasteful of the talents we have been given. That the Christians, the Jews, and the Muslims all worship the same God, no matter the name they call him by. I willingly accept Islam, and I offer to you my services as both a ship's captain and a navigator. It would be a shame if my talents were wasted at an oar, or in the mines, or the fields. I have no wife to return home to, and so I am content for the time being to remain here in El Sinut serving the sultan, as many before me have done. If you will have me, of course, my lord dey. I realize you have the power of life and death over me, but if you will have me, I am your servant."

"You have a facile tongue," the dey remarked. He looked at Aruj Agha, and, speaking in Arabic rather than French, asked, "What think you, my old friend? Is the English captain trustworthy?"

"For the present I believe so, my lord dey. He has certainly been more than candid with you. You could ransom him, of course, if he is indeed the son of a noble."

"Ransoming these people is more trouble than it is worth," the dey replied. "I am giving you my new galley, the *Gazelle,* Aruj Agha. Take this Englishman with you as a navigator. That way you can lock him up when you attack other ships. At least until he proves his loyalty to us. In the meantime, you will have his skill, if indeed he has not lied about that."

"I do not believe so, my lord. He is exactly what you see. No more. My gracious thanks for the *Gazelle.* I shall take her out almost immediately, with your lordship's permission," the agha said. "What will you do with the round ship?"

"I think I shall keep her, and perhaps after your Englishman has proven he can be trusted, he will teach our people how to sail such a vessel. Now, where is this other Englishman of rank?"

The agha signaled, and two janissaries brought Viscount Twyford forward. Adrian Leigh, however, refused to kneel, or even bow, before the dey. Instead, he immediately began a harangue. "I am the heir of the earl of Oxton, sir. I can be ransomed for a handsome sum. Do so immediately that I may be quit of this savage place."

"On your knees, dog!" Aruj Agha roared.

"*What?* Bow to some infidel?" the viscount returned.

"Get on your knees, you damned fool!" Tom Southwood growled. "They will separate your head from your shoulders without a thought!"

Aruj Agha didn't wait another moment. He grabbed Adrian Leigh by his iron collar, and kicked his legs from beneath him, slamming him to the floor, where his aristocratic nose, making hard contact with the marble floor, began to bleed profusely.

The dey watched impassively. Then he said, "Send him to the galleys. I cannot be bothered with the arrogance of this young milord. Perhaps after he has rowed his way across the sea for a few months, he will be more amenable. Put him on the *Gazelle*. Take him away."

"What. . .what is happening?" Adrian Leigh demanded furiously, wiping his nose with his torn sleeve.

"You're going to the galleys for your stupidity," Tom Southwood said dryly.

"I am not being ransomed?" Viscount Twyford's tone was incredulous.

"You speak to the master of El Sinut like he is some stupid servant, and you expect him to ransom you? Jesu preserve you, Viscount. You are an incredible fool," Tom Southwood told him as they were taken from the dey's audience chamber. "And in all the time since we have been captured, you haven't said one damned word about India. Don't you care what happens to her? She has done nothing but fret over your fate, you selfish bastard, but you really don't care, do you?"

"We all know what happens to women in this sort of situation," Adrian Leigh said coldly. "Even if we could all be ransomed, India is surely no longer fit to be my wife. That agha fellow was certainly most solicitous of her, wasn't he? Knox told me he couldn't do enough for the wench. She has undoubtedly saved her own skin by giving herself to him. She's a passionate little bitch, you know."

Tom Southwood's big fist slammed into Adrian Leigh's bruised nose with the speed of lightning, and he actually heard the viscount's nose break. "You miserable bastard!" he roared before their guards pulled him off the viscount, who was once again bleeding from his battered proboscis. "It was nothing more than her fortune, wasn't it?" Tom Southwood said. "But she, poor innocent, wouldn't believe us."

"Of course it was her fortune," Adrian Leigh half moaned. "Why the hell else would a man marry a woman but for her dowry?"

India had watched Adrian and Tom depart the chamber. She had no idea what had happened to them, for she hadn't been able to hear from her place in the rear of the audience chamber, which was now almost empty. Seeing the blood on the viscount's face, she was not just a little frightened. Then she heard Aruj Agha's voice call to her, and he came to lead her up to the foot of the dey's throne. Quickly he removed the long cape she wore, and unveiled her face. India stood silently in her silk shirt and her dark silk skirts. The agha had warned her to keep her eyes lowered. Because she was as yet anxious, and fearful, she was more than willing to follow his instructions. There was not a sound in the hall, it seemed, but her own thundering heart.

The dey arose, and stepped down, moving directly in front of India. Reaching out, he tipped her face up. "Let me see your eyes," he commanded her. His voice was deep and rich, his French exquisite.

She shyly raised her dark lashes, and was startled to see that his own eyes were a deep sapphire blue.

Holding her chin between his thumb and forefinger, the dey gazed directly into her face, and India felt a blush firing her cheeks. "She has eyes like a young lioness," the dey pronounced, speaking to his companions as if she wasn't even there, or worse, didn't understand.

"She is very spirited, my lord dey," Aruj Agha warned.

"*Is she?*" The dey sounded amused. Then he said to India, "Does my captain speak the truth? Are you a thorny English rose?"

"Please, my lord, what has happened to my cousin and Viscount Twyford?" India burst out, unable to help herself.

"She *is* spirited," the dey said, and then he told India, "Your cousin has accepted Islam, and will sail with Aruj Agha. As for that arrogant young milord, I have sent him to the galleys."

The galleys! The words burned into India's brain. It was a death sentence. Adrian would not be able to survive such punishment. She had seen how hard the galley slaves had worked on the agha's ship. And when they had not worked hard enough to suit the overseer, a whip had been applied to their backs to encourage them onward. India shrieked with her fury and her distress. Her eyes went to a dagger in the dey's cloth-of-gold sash. Grabbing at the bejeweled handle, she pulled it out, and stabbed wildly at him with it. "*You have killed Adrian! You have killed him!*" she screamed.

"Allah preserve us!" the agha cried out, and, leaping forward, disarmed India, throwing her to the floor. "My lord, are you seriously injured? Ahhhhh! I shall never forgive myself for having introduced this wretched girl into your presence. My lord! Speak to me!"

The dey, however, was laughing. "*Spirited?* I do not think that begins to describe the wench," he said, rubbing his bruised shoulder. "Do not fear, my good Agha. I am only slightly grazed. Her aim was most dreadful, but she has ripped my cloak." Then he signaled to two of his startled servants.

Immediately they pulled India up, and dragged her across the chamber where they fastened her between two marble pillars, her feet just barely touching the floor. The back of her shirt was ripped away, and her long, dark hair pushed aside. She saw his bare feet by her side.

"You cannot be allowed to attack me without being punished," he said softly. "The lash will be plied so that I do not break the skin on your back and seriously harm you. I will wield the whip myself, and you will receive five lashes. I am being merciful because you are new to our ways, although I am certain that attempted murder in England would be met with a far harsher judgment than that I will mete out to you."

"I do not care what you do to me," India said brokenly. "Your cruelty will kill the viscount."

"Why should you care?" he asked her, his voice curious.

"*Because I love him!*" she half sobbed.

The dey did not answer her. Instead, he moved directly behind her, and India heard the whistle of the whip even before it hit her back. She cried out with the first blow. "*I hate you!*" Behind her the dey smiled grimly, and continued her punishment adding the second. third, fourth, and fifth lashes to her back, but India clamped her lips tightly together and did not cry out again.

When he had finished, the agha said, "I shall take her to the marketplace and sell her, my lord dey."

"No," Caynan Reis said. "I am going to keep her, Aruj Agha."

"But she tried to kill you, my lord! The wench is far too dangerous to keep. I would never forgive myself if she succeeded in a second attempt. No! Let me sell her."

The dey chuckled. "No," he replied. "I enjoy a little danger. She is a virgin, is she not? Well, we all know how passionate virgins can be. She attacked me because she says she loves that arrogant little milord, and she believes I have given him a death sentence. I will turn her foolish heart because it will be a challenge to do so. She may one day become the pride of my harem. Now, let me get a better look at this prize you have brought me, Aruj Agha. Strip her!" he told his servants.

The slaves released India from her confinement between the two pillars. She was half carried, half dragged across the floor to the dais where the dey now stood. The remnants of her shirt and her chemise were pulled away, revealing her bare torso. India swallowed hard knowing that to struggle was futile. This dey would have his way. Her skirts and remaining undergarments were drawn off. One of the slaves knelt, and removed her leather slippers. She was half in shock. She had never felt so naked in her entire life.

Caynan Reis stood silent as India's charms were uncovered. His dark-blue eyes moved slowly over her. Her breasts were round and perhaps a bit small, yet they were incredibly lush. With the proper loving, those little fruits would ripen nicely. Her nipples were like unopened flower buds, all tight and hidden. The triangle of dark curls at the junction of her thighs would be removed, of course, but he could see the mound beneath those curls was plump.

The dey stepped down and stood before her. "Look at me!" he commanded her, and when she did, he reached around her and fondled one of her buttocks. Then his hand smoothed its way down her back. "You have skin like the finest Bursa silk," he told her. He then moved in a leisurely fashion about her. She had beautiful limbs, well shaped and not too thin. Her legs were long, her feet small and slender. He put his arm about her suddenly, and drew her back against his body, cupping one of her breasts in his hand. "Tell me the truth," he whispered in her ear, his fingers caressing her bosom. "Are you truly a virgin?"

India nodded vigorously, at first unable to speak. She was both hot and cold, and had to struggle to remain standing, for her legs felt as if they would give way at any minute. His large hand was splayed across her belly and felt fiery against her skin. She wondered if he could feel her trembling. Finally she was able to speak. "Of course I am a virgin," she gasped. "Why would you think otherwise?"

"Because you have told me you are in love with the milord," the dey answered her.

"I love him, but I am certainly no wanton," India murmured. "And if he had had me, would you set us free?" Oh, God! She wished his hands didn't feel so all-possessing. Every time he caressed her, chills raced up and down her spine.

"No, I would not set you free, although it would displease me to learn that another had traveled the path I have solely reserved for my own pleasure." His lips brushed her ear. "I am going to make love to you," he said softly. "I shall kiss you and caress you until you beg me to relieve you of the burden of your virginity."

"*Never!*" she half whispered vehemently.

"And I shall teach you how to please me." His big hand drew her head to one side, and his mouth branded her throat with kisses. "Tell me your name, my thorny rose."

She couldn't breathe. *She couldn't breathe!* And then she finally managed to say, "India."

"*India,*" he breathed hotly in her ear.

"I am Lady India Anne Lindley, daughter of the duke of Glenkirk . . . I have a brother who is a duke . . . and another brother who is a marquis . . . I am rich and can pay whatever ransom you desire. Ohhh God! *Don't do that!* Please let me go, my lord!"

"There isn't enough gold in the world to buy you from me," the dey told her. Then his fingers teased down her torso, and, pushing his hands between her trembling thighs, he cupped her Venus mound within his palm. "*You belong to me,*" he told her.

India collapsed against him. The touch of his hand in that most secret of places was simply too much for her. With a cry she fainted dead away. The dey caught her in his arms, and calmly handed her limp form to a eunuch. Brushing India's hot cheek with the back of his hand, he smiled to himself. Aruj Agha had been wrong. There had been a valuable cargo on the English ship. and as was his right, the dey claimed this cargo for himself.

"Take her to Baba Hassan," he told the eunuch, "and tell him the girl is to be treated like a princess. I will speak with him later."

The eunuch turned, and exited the audience chamber carrying his burden with extreme gentleness.

"If she kills you, I will not be responsible," Aruj Agha said wryly. "I think she will break you, rather than the other way around."

"We will destroy each other in an excess of passion," the dey answered him. "I have been bored of late. I will no longer be bored. She intrigues me, my friend. She was frightened to death, but she would not admit to it, or even show it by any outward sign. I knew, for I could feel her trembling ever so slightly beneath my touch."

"When she declared she was in love with the milord, I feared I had been misled with regard to her virginity, and I was ashamed to have brought you so poor a gift," the agha said, "but when she fainted at your intimate touch, I knew she was indeed a virgin. I wish you much joy with the girl, my lord dey. Now, I will take my leave of you." Aruj Agha bowed low before his lord.

"The English milord," Caynan Reis said. "Do not kill him, my friend. I want him alive to eventually ransom, but first I think he needs a strong lesson in manners."

"You will ransom him despite the difficulty?" The agha was surprised. "Why?"

"The girl believes I have given him a death sentence. In a few months we will show her that he is still alive, and that I am a merciful man. I will have won her love by then, and so we will ransom him. It amuses me to do this. Now, go and Allah be with you, Aruj Agha. Travel safely, and bring me more treasures to enrich our master the sultan."

The janissary captain departed the dey's audience chamber, and

Caynan Reis dismissed his servants, sitting quietly upon his dais. *Viscount Twyford.* How odd it had been to hear the title that had once come out of his half-brother's mouth. Adrian had, under his mother's tutelage, become an arrogant swine, so filled with himself that he had not even recognized Deverall Leigh, but then, it had been ten years since they had last seen each other. Ten years could be a lifetime, the dey considered.

In that time his half-brother had grown from a snot-nosed brat into a haughty and insolent cad. One of the guards who had escorted Captain Southwood and Adrian from his audience chamber had been a sailor on the ship he had taken from England. That vessel, like the *Royal Charles,* had been captured by corsairs sailing out of El Sinut. The guard, like Deverall Leigh, had accepted Islam, and gained a decent life. Although he rarely heard his native tongue, he had dutifully reported the conversation he overheard between the English captain and Adrian, even as the dey was preparing to punish India for her attack on his person. Captain Southwood's gallant attempt to protect his cousin from scandal undoubtedly came about because the foolish, inexperienced India was attempting to elope with Adrian. He could see his stepmother's greedy hand in it, the dey thought. He doubted the girl's family would have approved any match between his half-brother and India. Not with his stepmother's reputation, and the scandal of Lord Jeffers's murder, for which he had been held responsible.

He simply should have held Adrian in his dungeon until a ransom could have been obtained for his person, although he knew his father was not a rich man. Still, MariElena Leigh would have moved heaven and earth to regain her darling son. The dey smiled grimly. He could imagine her anguish. The little bastard, however, had aggravated him with his arrogance. The order to send him to the galleys was out of his mouth before the dey realized what he was saying. Well, a few months in the galleys wouldn't kill Adrian. It might even make him a better man. After all, the dey of El Sinut had himself been confined in the galleys for almost two years, and he had survived. Surely his half-brother was made of the same stuff.

And when the ransom was finally paid, Caynan Reis decided, he would reveal himself to Adrian. And he would tell him how delicious a prize the beautiful India was, for although his half-brother had now dismissed the girl he had been eloping with, it would certainly madden him to know she was Deverall Leigh's mistress, and would be until he tired of her. Adrian had always been loath to share his toys when he was little. Even when he had tired of them.

His stepmother had taught him one important lesson. Women were expendable, and absolutely not to be trusted. Nonetheless, his revenge would be sweet, and it was little enough for Adrian to suffer. After all, he would go home to England, and one day inherit the title that was rightfully Deverall Leigh's. Whereas Deverall Leigh could never go home because he stood accused of murdering Lord Jeffers. His name was blackened forever, and he knew that his father's heart was broken because of it, for he had been the earl of Oxton's favorite son.

And that was what hurt the dey worst of all. The knowledge that his father had been shamed, and injured because of this. So that a selfish and thoughtless woman's son might supplant him. He wished there was some way he might make his stepmother suffer for all her betrayals, and for the death of an innocent man, but he knew his desire was a futile one. Still, he would think on it. Was it not written that nothing was graven so deeply in stone that it could not be changed?

Chapter

7

India opened her eyes. She was surrounded by pale gold gauze draperies. Gingerly she turned her head. She was lying naked upon a scarlet silk mattress. Beside her was a low table, its top inlaid with blue-and-white mosaic. Atop the table was a crystal goblet half filled with a pale peach-colored liquid. She was so thirsty, but she could hardly move. India moaned softly and instantly a black face appeared in her view. She gasped, trying to cover herself.

"I am Baba Hassan, lady, chief eunuch of the dey's harem. You are thirsty." It was a statement and not a question. The eunuch braced her shoulders in a half-seated position and held the cup to her lips. "Drink it slowly, lady," he advised, apparently impervious to her unclothed state.

The liquid was cool, and fruity, and slid easily down her parched throat. "What is it?" she finally asked him when she had assuaged her thirst. The drink had been sweet, and she could feel the strength coming back into her limbs.

"It is a mixture of fruit juices," he told her, and he lay her back upon the mattress.

"Where am I?" India asked him.

"You are in the harem of the dey, Caynan Reis, may Allah protect and preserve him." Baba Hassan told her. "I have been told you are to be treated gently despite your violent behavior of earlier today." The eunuch's long face wore a disapproving look.

"I did not even wound him," India said defensively.

"You should have not even attempted to do such a thing. It showed an appalling lack of manners," Baba Hassan said sternly. "You are a beautiful maiden, not some wild savage."

"Is our young assassin awake then?" a bell-like voice inquired.

India turned her head, and saw the voice belonged to a very beautiful older woman with silver hair and almond-shaped turquoise-blue eyes. She had a lean body and an elegant carriage, and there was an amused smile upon her unlined face.

"I am Azura, the mistress of the dey's harem," the woman said. "How are you feeling now, my child?"

"Tired," India replied. "Weak. What is the matter with me?"

"A long sea voyage, the distress of being captured by Aruj Agha, fear," Azura said quietly. "And I suspect you are in a little bit of shock having been whipped by the dey. I do not imagine you were ever treated so harshly before, my child, were you?" The older woman's face was genuinely concerned.

"I am a nobleman's daughter, and related to our king. Of course I have never been beaten before," India answered Azura indignantly, and feeling the tears pricking sharply behind her eyelids, she fought to prevent them from overflowing her eyes and displaying her weakness for all to see.

Azura reached out and squeezed India's hand. "Let the tears come, my child. They will be a catharsis for you."

"If I weep you will think me weak," India said stonily. "*I am not weak!* I do not cry before strangers."

"I understand," Azura said calmly, "but when you are alone later, cleanse your sorrow with your tears, my child. Now, are you hungry?"

India nodded.

"Baba Hassan will see you are fed, and then we will take you to the baths," Azura told her. She arose. "I will come back later when you have finished your meal, my child. We will talk."

"Who is she?" India asked the eunuch when Azura had gone. "Is she the dey's wife?"

"Caynan Reis has no wife," Baba Hassan replied. "The lady Azura was the favorite of the former dey. On his deathbed he asked Caynan Reis to protect her and let her live out her days here where she has lived most of her life. Of course he agreed. She keeps order among the women, who are apt to be difficult as all women are," the eunuch concluded. He clapped his hands sharply, and a slave girl appeared with a tray. "Here is your meal, lady," Baba Hassan said.

India sat up slowly, and another slave girl appeared to prop pillows behind her back. Upright, the tray in her lap, India inspected the contents curiously. There was a bowl of yellow grain mixed with pieces of green scallions and bits of chicken, half a round of a flat bread, a small bunch of green grapes, and a thin slice of something pale gold in color. "What is it?" she asked the eunuch.

"Saffroned rice with onion and chicken, the bread and grapes you recognize, and a slice of melon, a sweet fruit," he answered her.

India began to eat using a small silver spoon and her fingers. There was neither a fork nor a knife upon the tray. The rice and chicken were nicely cooked and flavored, the bread still warm, and the melon was absolutely delicious, almost melting in her mouth. "It is all very good," she pronounced as she finished. She washed her hands in a silver ewer the slave girl held out, drying them on a small linen towel provided. The tray was removed.

"We will now go to the baths," Baba Hassan announced.

"But I have no clothes!" India protested.

"You do not need clothing to bathe, and you are certainly in need of bathing," was the tart reply. "You have soft skin, and so are obviously used to washing, but I doubt you could have done so aboard your ship. Why are you so modest, lady? There are only women here."

"You are not a woman," India snapped at him.

"Neither am I a man," he replied dryly, helping her to her feet. "Come along now. The lady Azura will be waiting for us." He pulled back the gauze draperies.

They were in a large room, India now saw. Here and there were other partitions formed by the sheer draperies. Beautiful young women lounged about on low, silk-covered furniture and upon satin-covered pillows. Warm air blew through the latticed windows. There were cages of songbirds hung in the windows. India still felt embarrassed to be so vulnerable among these women, but, remembering her cousin's warning, she grit her teeth and held her head high, ignoring the spiteful remarks spoken in French so she would be certain of understanding them as she passed through the harem.

"Her breasts are too small. Are we certain she is a girl?"

"Dark hair. Ho hum, how common," an overblown blonde said.

"She is soooo hairy."

"Her buttocks are nice enough."

"But the dey is not *that* kind," came the reply, followed by a round of malicious tittering.

"Do you think she's a virgin?" asked another girl.

"She must be. Who would want such a creature?" was the answer.

"She does not look like she will hold much interest for our master once he has taken her maidenhead."

"If he even bothers to before giving her away to some desert sheikeh he wants to believe he is honoring."

There was more laughter among the women of the dey's harem, and India could feel her cheeks flaming. She needed desperately to retaliate so these pampered creatures would not think she was easy prey. She stopped, and, turning about, slowly said with devastating effect, "I wonder which of you I will kill first." Then she continued onward, following behind Baba Hassan with apparent meekness. Behind her there was a sudden, shocked silence.

"You have a fine sense of the dramatic," the eunuch observed wryly as they left the main room of the harem and entered the baths.

"Ahh, here you are." Azura hurried forward, smiling.

"I will leave you in the lady Azura's competent hands while I return to restore order out of the chaos you have created. Half of the ladies will be weeping with fear from your fierce remark." The eunuch departed.

"What on earth did you do?" Azura asked India.

"Those common creatures made unkind remarks about me as I passed through their domain," India replied. "I only considered out loud which one of them I should kill first. Surely they didn't really believe me. I only did it to spite them."

Azura laughed. "You will have frightened them to death," she told India. "You come from a land where the women are free in comparison to the women here. Your women may own land, walk the streets unveiled, in many cases even have a say in choosing their own husbands. Those vapid creatures peopling the dey's harem are incapable of such independence. Their sole reason for being is focused on pleasing Caynan Reis, and any new inhabitant of this harem is considered a threat to be frightened away. You, however, were not in the least intimidated by the ladies of the harem. Indeed, you threatened them with violence, and having heard of your attempt on the dey's life this morning, they fully believe you capable of such an act. It was most naughty of you to terrorize them so." Then she laughed again.

"Where is your homeland?" India suddenly asked Azura.

"I was born in Poitou," Azura said quietly. "Like you, my father was of the noble class, and I, his eldest daughter. I was sent one summer when I was twelve, and a marriage was being arranged for me, to visit relatives near Marseilles. One day, Barbary corsairs stormed ashore, and I was taken, along with my cousins, into captivity. The former dey, Sharif el Mohammed, was my only master. I have lived in this palace for thirty years."

"You had no children?" India couldn't resist being curious.

Azura shook her head. "Sharif el Mohammed had no offspring," she said. "Women. of course, are blamed in such a situation, but my good lord knew better, which is why he never put me aside." She smiled at India. "You are so full of questions, my child, and I must get you bathed. You have never seen baths like these, I will wager."

And indeed India had not. The room into which they entered was constructed of creamy marble. Domed, its pillars were of a pale green marble. In the center of the room was a round pool directly beneath the dome. Around the room were fountains with gold spigots set into the walls, above shell-like indentations in the marble floor. There were marble benches in varying heights set about. The room was warm and damp, and the air was scented with roses. Several slave women hurried forward, bowing politely to the lady Azura.

"Here is the new maiden," Azura said. "You must prepare her properly for our master. She has been aboard ship for many weeks, and is in need of much attention, but unlike many of these girls, she does bathe regularly as you will see by the softness of her skin."

The bath attendants took India in their charge.

"I will remain with you," Azura assured her.

The bath women tsked-tsked over the condition of India's thick, dark curls, admired her golden eyes, and then set to work. She was stood in one of the floor shells and rinsed. A young woman with a small curved silver instrument ran the implement over India's entire body. To her surprise, India saw dirt being scraped off of her skin. She was rinsed again. Next she was washed very thoroughly by two ladies holding large sea sponges filled with a foamy soap. When they had finished, and she had been rinsed off a third time, another woman knelt to examine India's body so closely that India blushed with embarrassment.

"*What is she doing?*" India asked Azura as the woman began to smear a pink paste that smelled of almonds over her legs and Venus mound. "Does she have to touch me so intimately?"

"Our men do not like body hair on a woman," Azura explained as the bath attendant lifted each of India's arms in turn and spread her mixture beneath the upraised arms. "The almond paste will remove the offense. It won't take long, I promise."

While they waited for the depilatory to do its work, India's hair was thoroughly washed, and then toweled almost dry. Azura admired the girl's tresses, for India had hair that curled naturally even to the end of its length, which was about midback. The older woman lifted a handful of the curls admiringly, feeling its texture and thickness.

"It's lovely," she said. "Here in the sultan's realm maidens with golden or flame-colored hair are usually the most valuable, but your marvelous ebony curls are quite wonderful," Azura told the younger woman. "These curls are truly your crowning glory, my child."

The pink paste was washed away, and India found herself feeling shy again as her Venus mound was suddenly so prominently displayed. Azura led her into the bathing pool, which was warm and quite relaxing. India was surprised to see what a fine body the older woman had despite her age.

"When you are feeling relaxed, we shall leave the pool, and the slaves will massage our bodies with sweet oils," Azura explained.

"Do you do this every day?" India asked her.

"Yes," Azura replied. "Bathing is a very social amenity. The poor go to the public baths, the hours being specified for men and for women. There they wash, and exchange gossip and just talk."

"Does the dey heed your words, my lady," India asked. "He must if he entrusts his harem to you. You must tell him that I am a very wealthy girl and can buy my freedom. I must be returned to my family. Since Adrian and I snuck away just as my family was to return home to Scotland, it is just possible that no scandal has arisen from our behavior. If I could just get back home again it would be all right."

Azura was very quiet for a long moment, and then she said, "I will not lie to you, my child. Caynan Reis has not need of your wealth, for he is wealthy beyond all. It is highly unusual for a young and beautiful woman to be ransomed out of Barbary. Once I thought as you did. My heart was broken, and only when I accepted my fate was I able to be happy again. You are not like the little fools peopling his harem. You are clever, and you are intelligent. You can win him over with those qualities if you will but try. I do not believe he has ever loved, which is why it is so easy for him to give his women away when he tires of them, and that is often, for they bore him. I suspect he may have once been betrayed by a woman he was beginning to care for, and so he trusts no woman entirely, not even me. If you displease him enough, he will dispose of you by offering you to someone he wishes to honor, or if you anger him, he will give you to his soldiers to be a barracks whore. He has done it before."

"Has he no heart then?" India asked, a little frightened now.

"Oh, he has a heart," Azura answered the girl, "but it is buried deep within the ice of his soul. Someone must touch him, and melt that ice one day. I think that someone could be you, India."

"I don't know how to make love to a man," India half whispered. "And how can I allow a man I do not even know the freedom of my body?"

"Of course you don't know how to make love," Azura said with a gentle laugh. "You are a virgin, and such knowledge has not yet been imparted to you. Once you have been unburdened of your maidenhead, I will tutor you myself in the arts of love. I have never before done this for any girl, but I believe you can become the dey's true favorite." She patted India's cheek comfortingly. "Come now, and let us have our massage, my child. You will feel ever so much better after it."

They stepped from the warmth of the pool to be dried with thick, fluffy, warm towels such as India had never before seen. Then they lay down upon separate benches, each of which had been padded with a small mattress, and the masseuses began to knead their bodies with fragrant oils, their strong fingers digging deep into muscles, and India finally began to relax. She was being seduced by this delicious luxury, and she knew it, but she didn't really mind at this point in time.

When the masseuses had finished, they arose to be dressed. Azura chose for India a coral-colored silk garment that she called a kaftan. There were wide bands of gold thread embroidery at the wrists of the flowing sleeves, and at the keyhole design of the neckline. Azura now ordered India's curls to be brushed, and a gold band was fit about her forehead. A slave brought Azura a jewel case, and the older woman chose a pair of earbobs, which she carefully fixed in India's earlobes. They were gold, and shaped like stars. Gold bangles were pushed onto both her arms. Then the mistress of the baths personally pared India's finger- and toenails as short as she could without cutting her.

"There, my lady Azura, she is ready," the bath mistress said.

Azura, who had dressed herself in a deep purple-and-silver kaftan turned to look at her charge. "Ahhh, yes, she is lovely," she said. "My compliments, Fatima. As always, your work is perfection."

The bath mistress beamed, well pleased.

"Come, my child," Azura called to India, and she led her back into the main room of the harem.

The other girls were now asleep, lying upon their mattresses within their curtained alcoves.

Azura settled India within her cubicle. "I will return for you when it is time," she said softly.

"*Time for what?*" India said quickly, her nerves tightening again.

"Why, my child, surely you understood that the dey wishes your presence this evening," the harem mistress said. Then she patted India's flushed cheek. "It will be all right, India. You must trust me. I have only your best interests at heart." Then she was gone.

India was horrified. She didn't know this man, nor he her, and yet he would take her to his bed tonight? What kind of a world was she in now? Once again she wished she had obeyed her parents instead of forcing the issue to obtain her own way. She suddenly remembered asking Lady Stewart-Hepburn what it was like to be in a harem. Had it been exciting or awful? Both, her stepgrandmother had replied, but Cat Leslie hadn't been a virgin when she had faced the passions of a powerful Turk. And while it had been exciting to experience the baths with the lady Azura, what lay ahead was too awful to contemplate. Once she had been in the dey's bed, there was no turning back for her. She could never go home again. Never see her parents, or her brothers, or Fortune. The tears came, silent and soundless, for India would allow no one to hear her sorrow, or her pain.

But perhaps there was yet hope. Perhaps the lady Azura would take pity on her despite her honest explanation to India that there was no going back. If Azura pitied her, she would surely speak to the dey. It was India's experience that the rich always wanted more, with few exceptions. Surely this dey was not so wealthy that he couldn't use more wealth. Exhausted, India lay upon her mattress and dozed, praying as she slipped into sleep that the dey might relent and send her home in exchange for a ransom.

Azura had left her charge and gone directly to the dey's apartments. He waved her to a chair, and a servant put a goblet of fresh juice into her hand. Azura sipped the liquid, and then, looking up at the dey, said, "She is terrified, but she will not admit to it, my lord. You must treat this maiden *very* gently."

"You know I am not rough with my women," he replied.

"My lord, Allah has surely sent you this maiden," Azura told him. "She is of your own race, your own class, and if you can but win her over, she would make you a fine wife. She is very beautiful, my lord."

"I had little time to notice," he said mockingly. "I was too busy defending my life from the little wildcat."

Azura laughed. "Her aim was very poor, my lord. She did not even scratch the skin, the physician tells me."

"You like this wench, don't you, Azura? I have never known you to care for one of my women," the dey said.

"Perhaps I am getting old," Azura replied. "This girl could be the daughter I never had, my lord. I barely know her, and yet I like her. There is something about her that touches me. Mayhap it is her courage, for though she is frightened, she conceals it well. When those silly creatures in your harem insulted her this afternoon, she contemplated aloud which one of them she would kill first and set them into hysterics." Azura chuckled. "It was quick witted of her, and most deftly done. They will think long and hard before attacking her again. Yet she responds well to reason and kindness. I have had no difficulty with her at all."

He was thoughtful a moment, and then he said, "So you think I need a wife, do you, my dear Azura? Why?"

"Surely you want sons, my lord. Every man wants sons," she answered him. "Perhaps one day you may go home to your England again, and bring your sons to your father's house."

The dey's face darkened. "I shall never go home again, Azura. How can I with a charge of murder hanging over me? I need no sons for Oxton, nor a proper English wife. What I want is revenge, and I have the means of enacting that revenge. The young man I sentenced to the galleys this morning, the one your India longs for, he is my younger half-brother, now my father's heir. *If he lives long enough for me to ransom him.* He did not recognize me, of course, for ten years have passed since we last saw each other. I should not have recognized him, either, but for his pompous bleating about his importance. Aruj Agha has been told, and will look out for him, but Adrian will row his hands raw for a few months before I inform his dear mother that he is a captive in Barbary. And when she pays his ransom, for MariElena will move heaven and earth to redeem her precious offspring, only then will I reveal myself to my sibling."

"And India?" Azura asked.

"Her very presence here will have ruined her reputation in England," the dey said.

"She tells me that her family was returning home when she ran off with your half-brother, my lord. She believes her reputation could be yet salvaged if she could be ransomed. Take your revenge upon your brother, and send India home to her family. You do not need this particular maiden in your bed," Azura concluded. She had had no intentions of pleading for India until she heard the dey's plans. It disturbed her that he could be so vindictive. True, he was a hard man, for to rule he had no other choice, but this was cruel.

"No," Caynan Reis said implacably. "It is going to give me double pleasure to tell Adrian how delightful a bed partner I found his little betrothed. Of course, being the swine he is, he doesn't want her now. He believes she gave herself to Aruj Agha because the agha was kind to her while she was in his charge. Kindness is a quality with which my half-brother is not familiar. Still, he was never one to share his possessions even when he tired of them. The knowledge that I have had the girl when he has not will enrage him, and give me great satisfaction.

"I also suspect that the girl's family did not approve of him, and so he cajoled the silly creature into running away with him to be married. When they learn he has been ransomed, and she is my captive, I suspect his life will not be worth a great deal anymore. My stepmother will not be able to protect him from the lady India's father and her brothers." Caynan Reis laughed grimly. "I can but imagine her terror and her eventual pain."

"*But what of your father?*" Azura said quietly. "If India's family kill your half-brother, who will follow your father?"

"I know not," the dey replied. "As for my father, he was quick to believe the worst of me, and under the influence of that bitch he married after my own mother died, he disinherited me, I was told. He deserves to have his line die out. How could he believe I was so lacking in honor that I would kill a man over the favors of a well-known court strumpet? That we quarreled over her is true, but neither Lord Jeffers or myself would have killed over such a woman."

"I had not realized before how deep your pain, my lord," Azura said gently.

"The girl, India," Caynan Reis changed the subject. "Do you believe she is really a virgin? If Adrian could convince her to leave her family, perhaps he also convinced her to part with her virtue."

"I cannot answer that question without the physician examining her, my lord," Azura told him truthfully, "but if I were to hazard a guess, I would say absolutely yes. She is a virgin. Her demeanor is modest and quite innocent." She reached out and took his big hand, saying pleadingly, "Promise me, my lord, that you will treat her with kindness."

"Do you know me for a beast?" he demanded curtly, pulling his hand from hers. His blue eyes were indignant.

"You are angry, my lord, but the girl is English," Azura said wisely. "Remember, you yourself believe she was cozened by your half-brother, who probably acted on your stepmother's instructions. She is as much their victim as you once were. Be kind to her, my lord."

"No wonder Sharif Mohammed loved you," Caynan Reis said. "Your heart is too good, Azura, but I will promise you that I shall not harm the girl. Provided, of course, that she does not attempt to harm *me* again," he concluded with a small smile. "I shall make certain I am not wearing any weapons when we meet later this evening."

"Then I shall bring her to you, my lord?"

"I must first bathe, Azura. I have not had the time today before now. Bring her to me in an hour's time, and then you may go to bed. Tell Baba Hassan that I will keep her with me until dawn. He is to come for her then, and escort her back to the harem."

Azura arose, and bowed to the dey. Then she hurried from the room to find the chief eunuch. Baba Hassan was ensconced most comfortably in his own elegant quarters, smoking on a water pipe, when the lady Azura joined him. Wiping the mouth of the pipe, he offered it to her as she seated herself opposite him. Drawing upon the hookah, Azura pulled the water-cooled tobacco into her mouth, and then released it. It was most soothing. Rubbing her essence from the mouth of the pipe, she passed it back to the eunuch.

"I have just come from the dey. He will keep the girl until dawn when you are to escort her back to the harem."

"So," Baba Hassan said with a smile, "you have put your little plan into operation, have you, my old friend?"

"I will not reveal to you what I have heard from his lips this night," Azura told her companion, "but he desperately needs to love, and be loved in return. Of this I am convinced. I believe this girl may be the one to find his heart."

"It is not a good time, Azura, for him to be distracted from the business of governing El Sinut," Baba Hassan said. "I hear whispers on the winds. There is trouble coming."

"What do you hear?" she asked him.

"It is the janissaries again," Baba Hassan said wearily. "They are planning yet another revolt against the Sublime Porte. Their people have been all throughout the empire seeking secret support, attempting to find weaknesses in the vassal states. I am told they will promise the rulers of Barbary autonomy, and freedom from paying tribute to Istanbul, in exchange for their aid."

She did not ask from where he had obtained his information, or if the source was reliable, for Baba Hassan would not have brought it to her attention if it were just idle gossip. Her only question was, "Does the dey know yet?"

The chief eunuch shook his head in the negative. "So far no emissary has come from Istanbul to El Sinut."

"And Aruj Agha?" she questioned him. "Do you think he will be loyal to the sultan or to his fellow janissaries?"

"Aruj Agha has been in El Sinut as long as Caynan Reis has," the eunuch said slowly. "I think he would be loyal to the sultan, but the camaraderie of the corps is strong, and his family has a history of service to it."

"And who would they replace Sultan Murad with, Baba Hassan?"

"The Valide Kiusem had three sons by Sultan Ahmed. Murad has two younger brothers, Ibhrahim and Bayazet."

"But it is the Valide Kiusem who is the true power in Istanbul right now as Sultan Murad is just thirteen," Azura said. "What difference does it make which one of her sons rules if she rules for them?"

"They intend to murder both her and Sultan Murad," Baba Hassan replied. "Then they will put their own people in place, and rule for the next sultan, who will be of their own choosing, and much too young to rule for himself. They might even slaughter the other prince to prevent any rival faction like the Siphatis from springing up. The janissaries are not merciful. Remember young Osman whom they brutally murdered a few years ago, my lady Azura? They have grown very powerful in the last hundred years, and as their strength has increased, so has their influence. They are rapacious in their desire for wealth, and for domination over the empire. If they could rule without a sultan, I truly believe that they would."

"Then perhaps it is a good time for the dey to fall in love, Baba Hassan," the mistress of the harem said thoughtfully. "Right now, his heart is cold, his memories of his family and his homeland bitter. He could act rashly, for what has he to lose? But if he loved the girl, if she bore him a child, then his actions would be wiser, for he would not want to lose this new family to capricious fate, as he lost his old family."

"I cannot fault your instincts in the past, Azura," the eunuch said slowly. "Mayhap you are right now, and perhaps the rumors will come to nothing and the janissaries be content for a time."

"The janissaries are never content," she replied, "but Istanbul is a long way from El Sinut. With luck we will escape the plotting and the inevitable betrayals that will come about from this latest conspiracy."

"I pray to Allah, the most merciful and compassionate, that you are correct, Azura," Baba Hassan answered fervently.

She smiled slightly. "So do I," she said. "Now our main goal is to see that India and Caynan Reis find love together."

"They are two difficult young persons. I suspect dealing with the janissaries may be easier," he told her with a small chuckle.

Chapter

8

India had been dozing. She was feeling very relaxed, and the soft fabric of the kaftan against her skin was soothing. Then, to her annoyance, she was shaken awake, and she heard Azura's voice in her ear.

"Awaken, my child. It is time."

India slowly opened her eyes, rolling back over to ask the older woman, "Time for what, madame?"

"Time for you to go to the dey," came the answer.

She was suddenly awake and completely alert. "*Tonight?* He would really ask for me? After what I did?" Her heart was beginning to pound with anxiety.

Azura gently pulled India from her mattress. "There is nothing for you to be afraid of, my child," she soothed the girl.

"*I am not afraid!*" India protested, but in truth she was. Still, had not Thomas Southwood warned her about appearing frightened? India determined to show no fear no matter what happened.

Azura ignored her protests, drawing a brush through her charge's dark curls, instructing her to rinse her mouth with mint water, and then leading her from the harem into a dimly lit hallway at the end of which were two large arched doors, studded with brass nails and hinged with heavy black iron hinges. Azura pulled the doors open slightly, and said softly, "Go in, my child. He awaits you." Then she gave India a delicate but effective push into the chamber, drawing the doors shut behind her.

The room was softly lit by a large hanging lamp burning scented oil. There was the sound of a tinkling fountain that, India reasoned, was in the gardens she could see beyond the room, past the curved pillars with their pale gauze draperies, that hardly stirred in the warm night air. The floor beneath her feet was tiled. The furnishings were simple but elegant, of polished wood, brass, and tile; some chests, tables, and a single chair with a leather seat.

"*Come here!*"

India started at the curt, commanding voice, and her eyes went to a large dais of carved wood, decorated in gold and silver gilt, which harbored a huge mattress covered in coral and gold-striped silk. The dey, wearing only his white pantaloons, lounged arrogantly upon the mattress. Her eyes widened slightly. She had never seen a man so . . . so . . . unclothed. It was very disconcerting. His chest was smooth and golden. His one garment was worn low on his narrow hips. and cut low to reveal his navel. Without the small turban he had worn in his audience chamber, she could see that he was dark-haired.

"*Come here!*" he repeated.

India shook her head imperceptibly.

Caynan Reis let his eyes examine the girl as she stood, visibly trembling, her back pressed to the door. She was absolutely the most beautiful creature he had ever encountered. The flawless porcelain, ivory skin. He had noted it when he had whipped her earlier. Cleaned up, he could see the prize he had snatched from his brother. He wanted to kiss the full, lush mouth and run his long fingers through her dark, silky curls. He could see she was terrified. Her golden eyes gave her away, but her stance was pure defiance. He slid off the mattress, curious as to how far she would challenge his authority over her.

Seeing him on his feet, coming toward her, India swung about, her hands pushing against the door desperately. She bit her lower lip to keep from crying out as she felt him behind her, his body pressed lightly against hers. She could barely breathe, but she swallowed the cry in her tight and aching throat, standing perfectly still even as she heard his steady breathing next to her. When one of his hands slammed against the door by her head, she jumped in terror.

He laughed softly. "You are afraid," he said, his fingers pulling her dark hair aside, his warm lips kissing the nape of her neck.

"No!" India managed to grate out, her nose just pressing against the heavy oak door between brass nails.

"I will not hurt you," he said, leaning around to nibble upon the delicate lobe of ear. "Ummmm. As I suspected. You are delicious."

She remained silent, although if the truth had been known, a succession of shivers was racing up and down her spine.

"You are a very disobedient little slave," he told her, his fingers playing with her curls.

"I am not a slave," India said fiercely. "I am Lady India Anne Lindley, daughter of the duke of Glenkirk, sister of the marquis of Westleigh, the duke of Lundy, and Lord Leslie of Glenkirk. You have no right to hold me! I am a free-born English woman, and no slave!"

"Your lineage is impressive," he told her softly, "but you speak of what you were, India, and not of who you are now. You are a spoil of war, brought to me by one of my captains, and thus you have become a slave." He pushed his body hard against hers. "It is time you learned your place in this new world you have entered. *You are my slave.* Your sole purpose in life is to please me."

"Never!" The brass nails in the door were pressing against her delicate flesh.

He laughed at her defiance and nipped the back of her neck with sharp teeth. "What other choice do you have?" he mocked.

"I will die," she replied grimly.

"Little fool," he growled low in his throat, "do you think I will allow that to happen quickly? First I would give you to the janissaries in the palace barracks for their pleasure. Do you believe they would accept your feeble refusals? They would strip you naked, holding you down while they took their pleasure of you again and again and again. You would be subjected to every kind of perversion known to man, my innocent little virgin, and when they had finally destroyed your spirit, and your beauty, you would become a common barracks drudge. It would take you some time, several years I suspect, before you would finally die of disease and starvation, India. Is that what you really want?"

The words he spoke were terrifying. "No," she whispered.

"Then you will yield yourself to me," he said quietly.

Again she shook her head. "You may ravish me, my lord, but I will never yield to you. *Ever!*"

"*Ravish?*" He tasted the word with his tongue, greatly offended. "*Ravish?* I want to make love to you, little fool. I want to caress these soft white limbs." His big hand slipped beneath her wide sleeve, and then smoothed down her arm. "I want to love every inch of your body, and kiss that tempting mouth until it is bruised with my kisses." His hands grasped her shoulders. "I want to hear you cry with pleasure when our bodies join and we become one, but I do not want to ravish you."

"The only way you will have me, my lord, is to force me," India said stonily.

He made a sound of annoyance as his hands dropped away from her shoulders. "Little fool," he warned her, "do you not realize that I could have you bound and then take my pleasure of you? You would rejoice when I had finished, for I would have shown you Paradise. No, you do not understand, and I will not coerce a mere girl in order to teach joy to a reluctant maiden. I will not allow you to drive me to such a thing." Grasping her arm, he yanked her away from the door, and then, opening it, half dragged her down the corridor to Azura's private apartments. Entering, he pushed India to the floor, and put a firm foot upon her. "This slave girl," he told the startled Azura, "is unmanageable, my lady. Keep her with you tonight, and then tomorrow Baba Hassan will come and prepare her to serve me as my body slave. I should give her to my janissaries, but I am too soft-hearted, and you know well the reason why; but she will service me in some capacity. If my bed is not to her liking, then there are other ways she may be useful." Lifting his leg, he pushed the shaken girl toward the harem mistress, and then, turning about, departed.

India crouched upon the tile floor trembling.

"*What happened?*" Azura demanded, struggling to keep the anger from her voice. Was this silly little virgin going to spoil all their plans with her stubborn nature? *I will not let her do this,* Azura thought angrily. She roughly pulled India to her feet.

"I refused him," came the expected answer from the pale-faced girl. "I told him he would have to ravish me, but I would not yield myself willingly, *and I will not!*"

Azura shook her head despairingly. "Do you know what might have happened to you?" she cried. "Have you any idea how fortunate you are that he has shown you mercy? This is a fair man, but he is not an easy man. He might have killed you where you stood, and it was his right for you are only a slave now, India. Oh, I don't know what will happen to you! Allah! We must convince him to forgive your outrageous behavior and accept you back in his bed."

"I will not be a whore!" India's voice broke, and, in spite of herself, she began to cry. The dey had terrified her, first with his talk of the janissaries, and then when he had dragged her down the hallway, she had thought surely he was going to carry out his threat. "I want to go home," she sobbed.

"You are home," Azura snapped. "Unless, of course, you continue in your foolish behavior. Allah only knows where you will end up then! Perhaps in some sheikeh's tent out on the desert where your fair skin will be burned leathery as you squat over a campfire cooking your master's supper of couscous and goat." Then, relenting her harshness, she put her arms about the girl to comfort her.

"Won't the dey just ransom me now?" India sniffled.

"No, my child. I have spoken the truth to you when I told you that there is no hope of a ransom for you. You must accept your fate. Now, what is so terrible about becoming the beloved of Caynan Reis? He is handsome, and yet young. If you would give him a child, your position in his household would be assured, particularly if that child was a son. Would this not have been your fate in your own England, India? To marry and have children?"

"You want me to marry the dey?" India was astounded.

"He will take you for his wife if you give him a child," Azura half lied. "That is the way of this world."

"But I am a Christian, and he is an infidel," India pointed out.

"He follows the teachings of Islam, my child," Azura said.

"Mama's father, her real father, not BrocCairn, was a Muslim," India considered thoughtfully.

"We all worship the same God," Azura told her in practical tones. "What difference does it make *how* we worship."

India was thoughtful, and then she asked, "What will happen to me now, my lady? What did the dey mean when he said I was to serve him as his body slave? I do not understand."

"You will be at your master's beck and call around the clock, my child, and you will serve him in all ways except in his bed," Azura explained. "You will have no place in the harem."

"But where will I sleep?" India cried.

"Wherever the dey tells you you may sleep," she replied. "Do not be afraid, India. It is a mild punishment he gave you for the affront to his pride. Perhaps it is better. You will learn to know him." She smiled encouragingly at the girl. "You may sleep here with me tonight upon the divan. Then, in the morning, Baba Hassan will explain your duties to you." She patted India's hand gently. "Lie down now, my child. You look absolutely exhausted, and I can see you are near collapse."

It was barely dawn when Baba Hassan came to awaken India. Both his look and his tone were disapproving. "Get up, girl! Your master must be awakened and bathed."

India scrambled to her feet, casting a desperate look at Azura, but the mistress of the harem ignored her.

"Come along," the head eunuch said, and India quickly followed him. "Now, after you have awakened the dey, girl, you will escort him to the baths, to bathe and dress him, and then you will fetch his breakfast. I will help you this morning, but after today, you must know your duties without me, and carry them out." Baba Hassan pushed open the door to the dey's suite, calling as he did in a low but clear voice, "Awaken, my lord dey. The dawn is breaking, and you have a full schedule." He pulled the naked girl from the dey's side. "Return to the harem, Layla." Then he looked at India. "Gently touch him, girl, and bid him awake."

Gingerly she reached out, and brushed his shoulder with her fingers. "Awaken, my lord," she half whispered.

Caynan Reis rolled over, looking up at her. "She isn't garbed properly," he noted to Baba Hassan.

"She must bathe you, my lord. She will be given her new garments after she has completed her first duties," the eunuch answered his master.

The dey arose. "Let us begin then."

India's eyes widened with surprise and shock. The dey was stark naked. She didn't know where to look, and what made it worse was the slight smile upon his lips that mocked her. First that overripe little creature in his bed! Was she going to be expected to rouse those women every day? Now his nakedness when he certainly knew that she had never seen a naked man in her entire life! Her cheeks burned with her embarrassment.

"The dey has his own private bath," Baba Hassan informed her. He moved across the chamber through another arched door, saying as he went, "Remove your kaftan, girl. You cannot bathe your master dressed. Your garment would be ruined with the water and the steam." They were in the bath's anteroom, and the eunuch swiftly whisked the kaftan over her head, handing it to a waiting slave.

There was no time to protest, or even feel shy. India swallowed hard, not daring to look at Caynan Reis's handsome face, for she knew instinctively that he would be silently taunting her, and she would want to smack his face. She had already learned that attacks on the dey would not be tolerated. She was amazed that her back was free of soreness after the five strokes he had meted out to her yesterday.

"The first thing you must do," the eunuch began, and then he went on to instruct India in the proper method of bathing a man.

"Wield the scraper yourself, Baba Hassan," the dey instructed the eunuch. "I am loath to allow a pointed object in her hand quite yet."

India rinsed Caynan Reis using a silver basin after he had been scraped free of sweat and dirt.

"Very good," the eunuch approved. "Now, continue on as I have instructed you, and when the master is soaking in the heated pool, wash yourself, for it is the only time you will have to do so each day. Then bring our lord to the masseuse, and I will give you your new clothes." Baba Hassan hurried off leaving India alone with the dey.

Caynan Reis sat down upon a marble bench, nodding at India to begin the ablutions. First she washed his dark hair, and when she had rinsed it thoroughly, she toweled it free of water. Then, kneeling, she washed his feet, and lower legs. He stood, and India washed his upper legs, his chest, his belly, hurrying behind him to wash his back, shoulders, buttock, and the back of his legs. Then she rinsed him thoroughly. He had the most beautiful body, she thought, wondering as she did if it were proper for a woman to see a man naked and admire his form. He seemed to be in perfect proportion, lean and hard.

"I am finished, my lord," she said softly.

"I think not," he told her. "You have not yet washed my manhood, India. Remember you are now my body slave, and it is your duty to bathe *all* of me. My manhood is an important part of me."

"Could you not bathe it yourself?" she ventured. My God! He couldn't really want her to wash him *there!*

"Take your cloth. kneel down, and do your duty, India," he said in a not-to-be-argued-with voice.

India gritted her teeth. *I am not going to allow him to bully me,* she thought, kneeling down before him. God! *It* was staring her in the face. Were they all so big? And what was that hanging beneath and behind it? She dipped the cloth into the alabaster jar of thick soap.

"Be gentle," he warned her. "It is tender, and needs a delicate touch. You do not want to injure so fine an instrument as this."

"I'm certain there are better in the world," she retorted, the words out of her mouth before she realized it.

To her relief he laughed. "Possibly," he agreed, "but you must trust me, my little virgin, when I tell you my manhood is a weapon to be reckoned with, and I have had no complaints from my women."

India washed him, and rinsed the potent flesh with warm water. "Your women would not dare complain, my lord. They might be banished from the comfortable idleness of your harem if they did. Now, I believe you are ready for the bathing pool." Turning away from him, she let the dey make his own way into the warm, perfumed water, quickly washing herself while he relaxed. When she had finished, he beckoned her.

"Join me," he said, his look daring her.

India glided down the steps into the water, sighing softly at the luxury of it, and positioning herself opposite him. She said nothing.

"You have the lushest mouth," he told her. "Have you ever been kissed?"

She nodded in the affirmative. His eyes were so blue.

"By your lover, the English milord?"

"He was not my lover, my lord. We were to marry."

"Who else kissed you in an amorous manner?" he demanded.

"No one, my lord. I am not some lightskirt," India replied.

He moved quickly through the water, standing before her, and his lips lightly brushed hers. "Did your milord ever touch you?"

"Once," she whispered. It was really most disconcerting standing here in the warm pool, her body just touching his. "He touched my breasts once." The admission colored her cheeks.

"Like this?" He cupped one of her breasts, his fingers lightly brushing her nipples.

India's eyes closed briefly. "Aye."

"And you liked it," he said softly.

"Please, my lord," India said. Then, pushing him away, for his nearness was most distressing, she exited the pool. "The masseuse awaits, my lord. Please come, and let me dry you."

"In the end," he told her, "you will yield to me, India, but I will be patient with you, for I believe you are a prize worth having." Then he left the bathing room, and she followed slowly, confused.

Baba Hassan was awaiting her. "I have the garment you are to wear in your capacity as the dey's body servant." He handed her a pair of while silk pantaloons with wide bands of gold and silver embroidery at the ankles and about the hips. The pantaloons rode low on her body, baring her navel. The eunuch now stood before her, a small pot and a brush in his hands. Dipping the brush into the pot, he painted each of her nipples carmine red. When he had finished, he said, "You are ready, girl. Go now, and help your master dress for the day."

"Surely there is another garment for me to wear," she gasped, looking down at her bright red nipples.

"This is the costume of a female body slave," the eunuch answered. Then his brown forehead wrinkled. "What am I thinking!" he cried out, and drew from a pocket a beautiful narrow gold collar bejeweled with all manner of gems: diamonds, rubies, emeralds, pearls, sapphires. He fastened it carefully about her throat. "It is not too tight?"

Wordlessly India shook her head, shocked.

"Then go and attend the dey, girl. When he is dressed, and you have escorted him back into his apartment, I shall show you the way to the kitchens. Now go, and stand by your master until the masseuse is finished with her duties."

Caynan Reis was lying upon a pad that had been set on the masseuse's marble bench. He was on his stomach, his head turned to one side, a small sturdily built woman of indeterminate age massaging his buttocks with strong fingers. He opened his eyes and looked lazily at her. "Remain where I can see you," he said, closing his eyes again.

India stood stock-still, her mind awhirl. She could scarcely believe what had happened to her. She was an English noblewoman, not some slave and yet at this moment in time she was a slave girl. She was not the first woman in her family to find herself in such a position. Her grandmother, her great-grandmother, Great-aunt Valentina, even her stepfather's mother had all at one time in their existences been enslaved as she was now enslaved; but they had escaped their captivity, and India intended that she would escape, too. There was only one difference between India and her female relations. The others had not been virgins at the time of their captivity. They had all been married or widowed.

India's golden eyes strayed to the dey's long form. The masseuse was now busily kneading his right leg. It was a shapely leg, she thought, nicely formed, the thigh well muscled, the calf prettily rounded. The foot at the end of the leg below the narrow ankle was lengthy and slender. The masseuse's hands worked the dey's big foot, her thick thumbs pressing up and down the arch, massaging the ball of the foot, pulling each toe slowly and carefully. India watched, fascinated, her eyes following the masseuse's every move, unaware that Caynan Reis was watching her through the slits in his dark-blue eyes.

When the masseuse had finally finished her task, she spoke softly to the dey, and, bowing, withdrew.

"Help me up," he said to India, and when she had aided him to roll over and sit, he casually put his long legs over the table, and stood. "My clothing for the day is in the cedar cabinet there," he told her. "From now on it will be your duty to see that fresh clothing is there for me every morning and every evening. Baba Hassan will tell you my schedule, and if the clothes I need will be for an ordinary day or for an occasion. You cannot sleep as late as you did in the morning, India. In future you must be up long before I am to make your preparations. Do you understand?"

"I am not a fool, my lord. I understand quite well," she replied sharply.

He caught her by the wrist, saying in a hard voice, "If there had been anyone else in the room now when you spoke to me as you did, I should have had to have you beaten again, India. When you address me your voice must be dulcet and amenable, as befits a dutiful female slave. You offended me greatly last night, but I was not unkind. I realized you were frightened finding yourself in what must seem difficult circumstances to an English duke's daughter. You are being given a second chance as my body slave, but I will tolerate neither disobedience nor a sharp tongue from you. If you displease me further, I will give you to my guards to tame."

India opened her mouth to berate him, but remembering her cousin's warning to her, said instead, "Yes, my lord. I apologize."

"If you serve me well, you will find I am not a hard man," he told her, "but I am master of El Sinut, and it is not an easy task. Should I show the slightest weakness, even within the privacy of my household, I should be challenged. I would not serve my master, the sultan, well if I allowed the slightest discord within this vassal state of his. Do you understand, India? I am the dey, not some foolish courtier."

Strangely his words made sense to her. "Yes, my lord, I do understand," she told him. Then, going to the cedar cabinet, she opened it and viewed the garments he would wear today. The white silk shirt was embroidered in gold thread along the neckline. The cuffs of its full sleeves had wide bands that were bejeweled. She brought the shirt to him, slipping it over his head so that it slid over his broad shoulders and chest. There were no laces, and the shirt was open to midchest. India now brought him the white silk pantaloons.

"I can find no drawers," she said nervously.

"I don't wear any," he said softly.

She flushed, uncertain what to do next.

"You must help me on with the pantaloons," he told her, lifting one foot so she could slide the garment over it.

India ground her teeth together to prevent the pithy comment forming in her mind. Kneeling, she pulled the pantaloons over first one foot and then the other. As she stood up again, she drew the silk up his long legs, over his slim hips, finally covering his manhood, which had seemed to grow larger beneath her gaze, from her sight. She pulled the drawstring of the pantaloons together, making a bow and tucking it within the garment, her hand brushing against his flat belly as she did so. Again she flushed, but said in an even voice, "There are two sashes set out, my lord. Which one will you have?"

"Today I shall wear the silver," he told her. "I will show you how to wrap it about my waist," and he demonstrated the method when she had handed him the item in question. Unwinding it, he told her, "Now you do it, India," and when she had, and it was perfect, he complimented her. "Clever girl! You watched carefully."

"Will you take the sleeveless coat lined in the cloth-of-silver then, my lord?" It was a beautiful thing, India thought, the front of the coat embroidered in silver and gold thread, and small sparkling aquamarines and deeper blue tourmalines sewn on it.

"Yes," he said.

"It's so beautiful," India remarked. "Is this coat for an occasion, my lord?"

He shook his dark head. "Nay, India, but today my audience chamber is open to the people of El Sinut as it is one day each week. They come and bring their disputes to me to mediate. As I represent the sultan in Istanbul, it is important that I look a little majestic for them. It does both the people and the sultan I serve honor."

India looked into the cabinet again, bringing out embroidered silk slippers and a small silver turban decorated with a single water-blue aquamarine. "Will you wear these now, my lord?" she asked.

"Bring them with you," he told her. "After I break my fast, I shall finish dressing." Then he turned, and she followed after him back to his apartment where Baba Hassan was waiting.

The brown-skinned eunuch eyed the dey critically. "She has done well, my lord," he finally remarked.

"Yes," the dey replied with a small smile, "she has."

"We shall now go and fetch your meal, my lord. Where will you eat? Inside, or on the terrace?"

"It is still early, and the terrace faces west," the dey said. "I think I may eat there without fear of baking in our hot sun."

The eunuch gestured to India. "Come along, girl," he said impatiently, and she barely had time to set down the slippers and the turban before she had to race after him.

Outside in the hallway India cried out to the eunuch, "Please, Baba Hassan, if you go so quickly, I shall not be able to find my way by myself later."

The eunuch said nothing, but slowed his pace so she might be able to mark her passage alone tomorrow. They entered the kitchens, and he introduced India to Abu, whose domain it was.

"*So this is the girl,*" Abu said meaningfully, looking her up and down. "You are a foolish creature," he noted.

"I have come for the dey's meal," India told him, ignoring the remark. "Will you help me, or must I go back to him, and say you would not?" India replied in a sweetly bland voice. She looked directly at Abu.

"The master was too gentle with you, girl," Abu said sourly.

"It is not my place to criticize the dey," India murmured. "You are bold to speak such words to me, but I shall not repeat your discourtesy to the dey, Abu. Now, what does he eat in the morning upon first arising? I do not know the foods of this place."

Grumbling beneath his onion-scented breath, Abu showed India how to set up the tray she would carry to the dey. "He enjoys a slice of ripe melon," Abu said, cutting a piece and placing it on a blue-and-white porcelain dish. "Yogurt." He ladled a silky white substance from a stone crock into a bowl that matched the dish. "Bread." He placed a small, round, flat loaf on a silver plate. "Honey." He put half a comb on another blue-and-white dish. "And coffee, which the coffee maker will come and make for him. Unless he requests something else, this is what he eats each morning. If there is no melon available, I will give you other fruit for him, for the dey enjoys fruit very much."

"Thank you," India said, picking up the tray and looking to the eunuch.

"Let us see if you were paying attention," Baba Hassan said. "Lead me back to our master's apartment." He was pleased when she was successful, and told her so. "I will go with you later, however, to make certain you remember, for tomorrow you must go alone."

They entered the dey's apartment, and went through to the small tiled terrace that opened onto the garden. India set the tray before the dey, who was seated at a small table. A wizened little man came bearing a brazier, a small pot, a blue-and-white cup and saucer, and other items. He squatted near the dey, emptying some dark-colored beans into a strange vessel, which India quickly discovered was a grinder. Grinding the beans, he heated water upon the brazier and added it to the beans which were now in the pot, which the dey told India was for brewing the coffee.

Caynan Reis ate his meal, and when he had finished, the old coffee maker brought him the aromatic Turkish coffee which had already been heavily sweetened to almost syrupy consistency. He sipped it.

"Clear the table, girl," Baba Hassan whispered to her.

"You may have what I have not eaten," the dey said, and then he ignored her, enjoying his coffee.

"Eat," Baba Hassan advised her. "Unless he tells you otherwise, his leavings are all you will get, girl."

Anger welled up in India, but she quickly swallowed it back. She was not going to allow her pride to overwhelm her good sense. There was still some orange on the melon rind. She nibbled at it, finding it sweet and quite delicious. The silver spoon remained within the bowl of the yogurt, Abu had called it. "What is it?" she asked the eunuch.

"Milk that has been allowed to go sour and congeal," he said.

India put the spoon in her mouth. It was tart, she decided, wrinkling her nose, but it wasn't unpleasant. She finished the bowl. He had left a third of the round loaf. India quickly stuffed it in her mouth, for she could see the dey was almost finished with his coffee. The eunuch handed his master a wet towel to wipe his hands and face with, and then gave it to India.

"Put it on the tray," he said as she wiped her own hands and face. "A maid servant will take the tray. You must now follow the dey as he goes about his business, but first put on his slippers and turban."

The dey sat, and India was forced to kneel as she fitted his silver brocade slippers onto his feet. Rising, she took the turban from Baba Hassan, and placed it upon his dark head.

"Now step back from your master, and bow," the eunuch said. "This indicates to him that you have finished, and he is ready."

India did as he bid her, wondering why once his feet were shod, and the small turban on his head, the dey couldn't figure that all out for himself. She wisely held her tongue, following Caynan Reis from his apartments in the company of the head eunuch. She was suddenly aware once again that her upper body was unclothed, and her bosom visible to anyone who would but look. It was really quite intolerable, but she believed if she gave any more difficulty at this time, she would find herself in worse difficulties than she already was. She was alive, and there was always the possibility of eventual escape.

They entered the audience hall through a small side door. Aruj Agha approached the dey, and with him was Tom Southwood, now in Turkish garb. Tom's eyes flicked over his cousin, shocked, then he quickly looked away. How she longed to speak to him, but she knew she dared not. Baba Hassan led her to the dais, handing her a long-handled fan of peacock feathers. The handle was carved ivory, and the feathers were set in a holder of filigreed gold.

"You will stand here," the eunuch told her, "and slowly fan the dey while the audience is in session. You may stop occasionally to rest, for the day will be hot, but do not allow our master to grow overheated, girl, or I will whip you myself. Do you understand?"

India nodded. Why were they always asking her if she understood or not. She was certainly not feeble-minded. She tilted her head to see if she could hear what Aruj Agha was saying to the dey.

"We will be sailing tomorrow, my lord," the janissary told him.

"The young milord?" Caynan Reis asked.

"Quite shocked to find himself shackled to an oar, my lord, but otherwise unharmed," came the reply.

"See that he remains unharmed. If his manners can be improved, I will consider redeeming him to his family eventually. It seems a shame to lose the ransom." He looked at Tom Southwood. "You look the part," he said dryly. "Are you certain you can fulfill your duties?"

"I can, my lord," the Englishman answered him. "I have taken the name of Osman, in honor of a dear and old friend of my grandmother's who lived in Algiers many, many years ago. He was an astrologer."

Aruj Agha's mouth dropped open. "*Osman the Astrologer? The Osman?*" He turned to the dey. "My lord, he was very famous, and highly respected." Then he looked at Tom Southwood. "Your grandmother really knew Osman? How?"

"It is a long tale, my lord agha, but I shall happily relate it to you on the long nights we are at sea." Then he said to the dey, "My lord Caynan Reis, may I beg a small boon of you before we depart?"

"What is it, Navigator Osman?" the dey replied.

"My cousin . . .?" Tom Southwood murmured.

"Still retains her virtue," the dey said dryly. "I am of a mind to be patient with her and so she serves me as my body slave. She is quite unharmed, and will remain so if she continues to behave."

"Thank you, my lord." Tom Southwood bowed, and then remained silent as the agha and the dey discussed the voyage to come. The English captain glanced a final time at India. She nodded her head just imperceptibly at him, indicating that she had heard and was all right. He looked quickly away from her, and just in time, for the agha was ready to leave.

The two men bowed once again to the dey, and then departed the audience hall. The dey settled himself upon his low throne, and nodded to the head eunuch to order the doors opened. India began to wave the fan over him. The dey's secretary, a small, fussy little man appeared, and handed him a long scroll of parchment which was filled with a great deal of writing, none of which she could read. The doorkeepers flung open the doors, and the hall was suddenly filled with a multitude of people, none of whom were, to India's great relief, interested in ogling her carmine-tipped bared nipples.

Caynan Reis handed his secretary the scroll, and said, "Begin."

"The divorced woman, Fatima, and the merchant, Ali Akbar," the dey's secretary said, and when the two stood before the dey, his secretary told them, "First the woman may speak, and then Ali Akbar."

The woman bowed politely. She was neatly but poorly dressed, and far past the flush of her youth. "My lord, I have come to you for justice. Some thirty years ago when I was fourteen, I became Ali Akbar's first wife. I have given him three sons and a daughter.

In the ensuing years, Ali Akbar took three more wives, which as you know, my lord, is all the wives allowed under the laws of the prophet. In order to take another woman to wife, Ali Akbar has to discard one of us. I am she he cast aside so he might wed with a thirteen-year-old maid who he hopes will restore his lost virility. I will be honest with you, my lord. I am not unhappy to be free of this man. Whatever love that was between us died years ago. However, Ali Akbar has refused to return to me my bridal portion, which, as you know, my lord, is mine under the laws of the prophet. Without it, I am a beggar at the gates. I have no home. I must beseech strangers for my daily bread. Please help me, my lord. I throw myself upon your gracious mercy."

Caynan Reis looked at Ali Akbar. "Is this true?" he asked.

The merchant squirmed beneath the dark gaze. "My lord," he began nervously, "business has been poor of late, and I have other, more important obligations to meet. Fatima could go and live in her daughter's house, but she prefers to shame me by wandering the streets, and importuning all who will listen with her litany of complaints against me."

"Have you returned your former wife's bridal portion?" the dey demanded sternly.

"No, my lord." The merchant shifted uncomfortably.

"Return it this day." The dey looked to the woman, Fatima. "Do you know how much is owed you, lady?"

"Yes, my lord," she said softly.

"You will tell my secretary," he told her. "And you, Ali Akbar, will not argue the price. The lady appears honest to me. And in punishment for your greed, I order you to purchase a house with a garden for the lady Fatima, and two slaves to serve her. She will be permitted to choose the house and the slaves herself. And you, lady, will cease your public complaints against this man in return."

"My lord, you will ruin me!" the merchant cried, and he shook an angry fist at his former wife.

"And," the dey continued, "you will pay a fine to the sultan's coffers of ten gold pieces, and another ten to the chief mullah of El Sinut in penance for your attempt at flouting the laws of the prophet. While the law allows you to discard one wife for another, it also makes provision to protect such a woman. You broke your word when you refused to honor your betrothal agreement. Any further complaint from your mouth, Ali Akbar, will be met with severe punishment."

The merchant was at last cowed, and bowed to the dey before turning abruptly and leaving the audience chamber.

The woman, Fatima, however, fell to her knees, and kissed the dey's slipper. "Thank you, my lord," she said, tears running down her worn face.

"Do not commit your husband's sin of greed when you seek your own shelter, lady," he warned her. "The sword of justice cuts both ways."

"Yes, my lord," she said, scrambling to her feet and backing away from his presence.

India was absolutely fascinated. For a few moments, she had almost forgotten to ply her fan so the dey would not become overheated. She had thought El Sinut a place where women counted for little, but if she understood it correctly, women were protected under the laws of Islam. Caynan Reis had been kind, firm, and very fair in his handling of the matter of the woman, Fatima, and the merchant, Ali Akbar. The other cases brought before Caynan Reis that day were not half as interesting, but he judged them all with utmost equitableness, it seemed to her.

In midafternoon the dey called a halt to the proceedings and dismissed the remaining people from the audience hall. He had heard almost all of the cases on his secretary's scroll, and would hear the others first the following week. He arose, removing his turban and handing it to India. Then he strode from the chamber. Almost flinging her fan at an attending slave, India hurried after him.

"I am hungry," he told her. "Go to the kitchens and fetch me something to eat, India," he said as they entered his apartment.

"Yes, my lord," she said, putting the small turban upon a table. "Is there anything in particular that you desire?"

"Just food," he told her.

"I can find my way," India told Baba Hassan, and she ran out.

"You will need help," Abu told her in a conciliatory tone when she told him that the dey desired food. "He eats his main meal now in midafternoon, and then naps in the heat of the day. I will send several kitchen slaves with you to carry the food."

"What will you give him?" India asked, curious.

"He is not a heavy eater," Abu said. "I will send a roasted chicken, a bowl of saffroned rice with raisins, a dish of olives, some sliced cucumbers in oil, and bread and fruit." As he spoke, he piled the trays with the items he named, signaling several little kitchen maids to take up the trays and handing India a decanter. "This is a lemon sherbet for the dey to slake his thirst. You may carry it, and the silver goblet."

"The dey does not drink wine?" India asked.

"Wine is forbidden by the prophet, although there are some in Barbary who do not obey the prophet." Abu finished darkly.

India thanked the more cooperative cook, and led her party of serving girls back to the dey's apartment. The sun being high now, however, this meal was taken indoors, and when he had finished eating, he again instructed India to eat from his leftovers when she had stripped him of his garments, sponged him with rose water, and helped him to his couch to rest. *This is ridiculous,* she thought to herself, but silently followed Caynan Reis's orders. When he lay, apparently dozing, she crept to the table, and, seating herself, began to eat. Abu was not stingy with the food, and she was quickly satisfied. Afterward she carried the trays, one at a time, back to the kitchen. When she returned to the dey's apartments at last, Baba Hassan was awaiting her.

"The dey will sleep until just before sunset, girl," he told her. "You are permitted to rest also now that your duties are completed."

"Where am I to sleep?" she asked him.

The chief eunuch went to a small cupboard, and drew out a narrow mattress he proceeded to unroll. "This will be yours. You are to place it outside of the dey's bedchamber, and sleep there unless he instructs you otherwise. He will call you when he desires your service. When he arises, you will find a silk kaftan for him in the cedar cabinet. He has no guests this evening."

She was to sleep on a mat outside Caynan Reis's bedchamber door? It was absolutely ridiculous! But at least she was comfortable, India thought. She was not chained to an oar, seated upon a hard wooden bench on Aruj Agha's galley. Silently India spread the mat Baba Hassan had given her before the dey's bedchamber door and lay down upon it. Soundlessly she wept. This was what her pride had brought her to, and if Adrian died, it would surely be all her fault.

Chapter 9

India awoke hot and headachy. Rising, she rolled up her sleeping mat and tucked it back in its cupboard. Then, going to a carafe upon the table, she poured herself a goblet of water. It was warm, but at least it relieved her thirst, and her head began to ache less. Opening the door to the dey's bedchamber, she saw that he still slept, lying quietly upon his aide, his long form just slightly curved. She left the door open to allow the air to circulate, what breeze there was, and walked out into the garden.

It was a walled enclosure, in the center of which was a round tiled fountain with a bronze flower spray in its middle. India sat upon the wide lip of the fountain, for it was cooler there, and the faint mist of the spray was very refreshing. The small, square tiles were sea blue. interspersed with white, and there were pale yellow water lilies in the fountain. Dipping her hand in the water, she startled a fat goldfish, and laughed softly as it skittered away.

The air about her was perfumed with flowers. There were pink damask roses in bloom, and other flowers she recognized. Hollyhocks in white, cream, yellow, and purple stood tall with their fig-shaped leaves at the back of the beds which were edged with blue campanula. There were scarlet martagon lilies in a half-shaded part of the garden, the four-foot stalks holding between eight and ten pendulous flowers, orange-red in color, with their edges turned up like

Turk's caps. In a sunnier area there were yellow Caucasian lilies, sweetly scented and graceful. There were small- to medium-height trees in great blue-and-white porcelain tubs with large trumpet-shaped flowers of pink, red, and yellow, with very prominent yellow stamens with red stigmas that she didn't recognize. Sniffing one, she found they had no fragrance at all, but they were very dramatic and beautiful flowers. There was a greenery with thick leaves she didn't recognize, and cedar trees standing tall and graceful.

She could hear bird song, but could see no birds. There were brightly colored butterflies, and bumblebees wending their way amid the flowers. For a brief moment she could almost imagine she was somewhere else. *Anywhere else but El Sinut.* She started as his hand fell upon her shoulder.

"Do you find my gardens pleasant, India?" the dey asked her.

She jumped to her feet. "Is it all right that I came into it, my lord? Perhaps I should have asked you first." Her golden eyes were wide with her apprehension.

"You are my body slave, and the gardens are available to you as long as your duties are done, India. You do not have to be afraid of me because you came into the garden. Do you like it?" His hand moved away from her shoulder.

"Aye, it is beautiful, and so peaceful. I almost forgot for a moment where I was, my lord," she said candidly.

He smiled faintly. "Do you play chess?" he asked her.

"Aye, I do," she answered him.

"Then fetch me a fresh kaftan from the dressing cupboard, India, and we will play a game here in the garden. I will get the board and the pieces. Do you play well? None of the harem women play well."

"I play very well," she said, and then, "Must you always walk about naked, my lord?" Her cheeks were pink.

He chuckled. "In this heat it is more comfortable, India, but as I respect your modesty, I have asked for a garment. Were you one of my harem women I should not bother, nor would it matter to them. Does not the holy book say that man was created in God's image?"

"I somehow do not think of God as looking as you do, my lord," India told him pithily, and then went to fetch his kaftan.

Behind her he chuckled again. The wench had spirit, and was by far the most interesting female he had come across in years. He knew his chief eunuch, Baba Hassan, and the lady Azura had hopes that he would find a woman he liked enough to wed and have children by. His harem women were kept infertile by means of a special sherbet made for exactly that purpose, for he had made it very clear from the moment he became dey that he wanted no children who others might use against him in a powerful struggle for El Sinut. It was a volatile world in which he lived, and ruled. There were always plots swirling about. Particularly as the central government in Istanbul had not been as strong in recent years as it had been in the past. Still, he might take a wife eventually, but not have children. India had possibilities. She was English, as he was, although at this point in time he had no intention of telling her that. They communicated quite well in French. And she was a nobleman's daughter as he was a nobleman's son.

If she was a trifle overproud she could be gently tamed. Much of her haughtiness stemmed from her youth and inexperience, and, he had not a doubt, fear. She was vulnerable, and he could easily see how Adrian had convinced her to elope with him. Although he knew she would probably never admit it, probably she had already been having second thoughts in the matter, and was not unhappy her English cousin, the captain, had found them out. It saved her the embarrassment of admitting her error in judgment. She would have gone home protesting, but in her heart she would have been relieved the decision had been taken out of her hands. If her family had disliked him before Adrian and India eloped, they would dislike him far more now that their daughter was a captive in Barbary. He chuckled a third time. Particularly if they learned she had gone from the frying pan directly into the flame.

India came running with his kaftan. It was a comfortable cotton garment striped in deep blue and its own natural color. The sleeves were wide, and the neckline open to his navel. Without a word she flung it over his head, yanking it down so quickly he barely had time to fit his arms through the armholes.

"Does my naked form disturb you so much, India, that you must cover it as fast as you can?" he teased her.

"I am not used to such things," she replied. "You have not the chessboard. Tell me where it is and I shall get it."

"It is in the chest in my day room," he told her, smiling. Yes, she has possibilities. She was already learning to treat him with respect before others, while being a bit more at ease with him in private. She was so beautiful, indeed dazzling, with her creamy skin, her dark curls, and those fascinating golden eyes. He had never in his life seen eyes like India's. She would take time to woo and win, although she would never realize he was wooing her. She would come to him, for only if she did could she be truly happy with her decision in having done so. She would be acknowledging a parting from her former life when that day came, and India was certainly not ready yet to do that.

She brought the board with its carved red-and-white marble pieces, and they set it up on a low table upon the terrace, seating themselves upon large pillowsl To his pleasure she played extremely well, almost beating him, and when he said, "Checkmate," she frowned.

"Where did I make my mistake?" she wondered aloud, and it was then he realized that she had indeed been playing to win. It surprised him almost as much as it delighted him. His harem women would have allowed him to win, if indeed they could even play with him. He showed her her error. "I won't do that again," she promised him.

She took the second game, and he the third. The light was now almost gone from the garden, and the night insects were beginning to hum their songs. He had not enjoyed himself so much in years. "Come," he said, rising, and then pulling her to her feet. "Are you hungry? It is my habit to eat only bread and fruit in the evening."

"I will fetch it," she said, and hurried off.

When she returned, he invited her to eat with him in the cool garden. When they had sated themselves with grapes, melon, and warmed flat bread, Baba Hassan appeared.

"I must instruct the girl in preparing your clothing for the morrow, my lord," he said.

"Take her," the dey replied. "I am content with my company."

"Tomorrow," the head eunuch said as he led her off, "the dey must meet with the chief engineer for the city. The great aqueduct that brings fresh water into the town from the mountains is in need of repair. His clothing can be simple." Baba Hassan brought India into a large, enclosed room. About the chamber were silver bars that stretched from one wall to another, and upon the bars were hung hundreds of garments. "These racks," the eunuch said, waving his hand, "are his more elaborate garments. The others have the simpler robes." Bending, he flung open a brass-bound cedar trunk. "You will find his pantaloons, sashes, and shirts in these trunks. The slippers are on the shelves here. The dey's jewelry is kept in a large case in his bedchamber. His taste is simple, you will find."

"How are these things kept clean and fresh?" India asked. "This climate is so warm he must certainly need to change his garments each day, Baba Hassan. Am I expected to do his laundry? Let me warn you I have absolutely no experience in such matters."

The head eunuch chortled. "No, girl, we have laundresses aplenty." He pointed to a large reed basket. "Bring the dey's used garments here each evening when you come to choose the clothing you will put in the cedar cabinet for the following day. This basket is for the discards. A servant will bring them to the laundresses to wash. Now here is the cabinet in which you will place his fresh garments, girl. It opens on two sides, and on the other side you will find the dressing room in the baths. Each evening before you go to bed, choose the proper clothing for the morrow. I will inform you what sort of garments will be needed. Now, let us begin. What would you choose tomorrow for the dey?"

India's careful choices pleased Baba Hassan. The chief engineer of El Sinut, while a valuable civil servant, was not of great importance. "The dey will not need a turban. but where are they kept?" she inquired.

He showed her, and then said, "You are content to serve the dey in this capacity rather than as one of his harem women?"

"I am not content to be here at all," India replied honestly, "but as I am, I prefer being his body servant to being his whore. I only wish it were not necessary for me to be so unclothed."

"Clothing confers status," the eunuch answered her. "You have no status except that which your master gives you, girl."

"What language do you speak here?" India asked him. "I have an ear for languages, as do most of my female relations. I would learn the language of this land. Will you teach me, Baba Hassan?"

Her request surprised him. "We speak the Arabic tongue," he told her. "If the dey gives his permission for you to learn our language, then the lady Azura will teach you. I will inquire tomorrow. For now we will return to the dey's apartments. The final thing I must teach you is how to prepare the love cloths. Our master is a virile man, and requires female companionship every night."

"I know how to prepare love cloths," she said, surprising him once again.

"But you are a virgin," he said, astounded.

"I am," she confirmed, "but my mother was the daughter of the Grande Mughal Akbar. She was raised in India, and when she came to England she brought her servants with her. When I began my monthly flow of blood, Rohana, one of Mama's women, with my mother's permission, taught me how to prepare love cloths. Mama always said that nothing spoiled a man's pleasure more than the unseemly evidence of previous pleasure."

The eunuch nodded. "Your mother was correct, girl, and now I understand why your eyes are almond shaped. Your Mughal blood shows."

They had reached the dey's apartments again, and, leaving her at the door, Baba Hassan said, "Since you know what to do, do it, girl."

India reentered the dey's chambers. In one of the wall cupboards she found a silver ewer. She filled it with water, which she perfumed with rose oil. Next to the basin was a stack of neatly folded linen cloths. Taking a dozen, she brought them with the basin into the dey's bedchamber and set them by the bed. Going back out into the garden, she found Caynan Reis observing the moon. "I have, I believe, completed my duties for the day, my lord. Is there anything I can do for you before I retire to my pallet?"

"Go to the harem, and bring back the woman, Nila," he told her. "She is a blonde, actually the fairest hair of them all; and most voluptuous of form. I wish her company tonight." He looked directly at India, his dark eyes unfathomable.

"I am to fetch your whores for you?" India was outraged.

"You have the choice of fetching them to me, or taking their place," he said coldly. "And do not call them whores, India. They are perfectly respectable harem women, and honored within my house. Do not pass judgment upon that which you do not understand. This is not your England. It is El Sinut. When you have brought Nila to me, you may spread your pallet outside my bedchamber door in case I have need of you in the night. You will not hear me if you are further away."

Turning on her heel, India ran from the room. This was the final humiliation, she thought. First she was forced to walk about half naked all day, the nipples on her breasts painted carmine to draw attention to them, except no one was supposed to look. She had waited on this arrogant dey hand and foot. Bathed him! Fetched his food! Laid out his clothing! Dressed him! And now she was expected to bring his whores to him? It was intolerable, but if she didn't do it, who knew what he would do to her. He was such a complex man. Kind and fair to those whom he judged, yet thoughtless and cruel when he sent poor Adrian to the galleys. She didn't understand this man, but she had quickly learned that he would brook no disobedience.

Finding her way to the harem, she entered, looking about at the women there. They ignored her, for she was not as important as they were, being only the dey's body slave. There were seven women from whom she might choose, and four of them were blond and voluptuous. Then Azura was at her side, murmuring softly, "Which one does he desire?"

"Nila," India answered in a low voice.

"She is the one with the breasts like two soft pillows," Azura told India. "The blonde with the longest hair is Mirmah. Laylu wears her hair always in a thick plait, and the last blonde is Deva. The redhead is Sarai. The tall brunette is Samara. The petite brunette is Leah. Have you enjoyed your day?"

India laughed. "It has been interesting and informative," she told the mistress of the harem.

"Come and see me when you have the time," Azura said. "Now go and fetch the chosen one."

India walked across the main chamber of the harem, stopping before Nila. "The dey desires your presence. You are to follow me," she said in neutral tones. Then she turned, and departed the harem, assuming Nila would follow. The dey's concubine scrambled to her feet and, with a smug look at her companions, hurried after India.

"Do not walk so quickly," Nila complained. "My legs are not as long and gawky as yours are. I am delicate and fine-boned."

India said nothing, but she did slightly increase her speed. Delicate and fine-boned? The girl was a peasant!

"I shall tell the dey of your rudeness," Nila cried.

India stopped, and turned about. "And I shall tell him I overheard you disparaging his manhood when I entered the harem," she told the lush blonde. "Naturally, I was shocked. What did she mean you have the prick of a worm, my lord?"

"You would not dare!" Nila's blue eyes were wide with fear.

"Do not find yourself on my bad side, Nila," India warned her, and then she continued on her way, leading the blonde into the dey's apartments. "I'm certain you know the way from here," she said sweetly.

Nila almost ran past the English girl, and India overheard her trilling as she entered Caynan Reis's bedchamber, "Ohhh, my lord, I have come as quickly as I could!"

"India! Fetch a carafe of sherbet," she heard the dey call. "Why is there none already here? Hurry!"

She slammed from the apartment, and ran through the cool halls to the kitchen. It was empty, but there upon a silver tray was a carafe of fruit sherbet and two small goblets. Picking them up, India hurried back, and slowly entered the bedchamber. The dey and his companion were both naked now. Nila sat between her master's spread legs, and, as he fondled one of her large breasts, she slowly and sensuously sucked the fingers of his other hand, her eyes half closed, her face a mask of open desire. India stopped, not certain where to put the tray.

Nila finished drawing upon the dey's fingers, taking his hand and bringing it down to her Venus mound. The fingers seemed to have a life of their own, stroking her as she began to squirm beneath his attentions. The dey's eyes met India's. He could see the confusion and the surprise upon her beautiful face. She tried to look away, but could not do so, and she flushed with her shame.

"Put the tray by the bed, and then find your pallet," he finally said, taking pity on her.

The hard voice seemed to rouse her from her stupor, and she tripped over her own feet to do his bidding, almost running from the bedchamber to escape the disturbing, yet exciting scene she had just witnessed. Her heart was hammering wildly. Her legs felt weak. Pulling her pallet from the cupboard, she saw a neck roll, and drew it forth, too. She spread her bedding before the dey's bedchamber door, and lay down, but when she closed her eyes, she saw again the dey with his paramour. Her eyes flew open. Why was she so disturbed? she wondered. The dey was not hurting Nila, and, indeed, she was encouraging his attentions. Surely there was nothing wrong if the dey and Nila were content. She closed her eyes again, and dozed, only to be awakened by the sound of a woman moaning deeply. India crept closer to the door, and put her ear against it.

"*Ohhhhh! Ohhhhhhh! Ohhhhhh, my lord, do not stop! I am in Paradise! Oh! Oh! Yessssss!*" Nila's voice cried.

India's eyes were wide with shock, and then she heard the dey groaning. but the sound was one of pleasure.

"I'm not going to stop, you insatiable little bitch," he said. "I'm going to keep on until you are finally satisfied!"

"*Ohhhhh! Ohhhhhh! Yes! Yes! Yes!*" Nila half sobbed.

India curled herself into a ball, her hands over her ears. She might be a virgin, but the audible sounds of lovemaking were obvious. For some reason it disturbed her greatly, and the earlier image of the dey and Nila caressing entered her mind again. *Oh, God, what is happening to me?* she wondered. She tried to picture Adrian Leigh with her in such a manner, but she could not. To her deep distress she found herself taking Nila's place in her mind's eye. It was too horrible to even contemplate. She did not know this man. How could she imagine such intimacy with a man she didn't really know? It was wanton.

The days that followed took on a familiar pattern that mirrored the first day she had begun her service to Caynan Reis, and yet each day was different in its way. She particularly enjoyed the mornings when he would hold public audiences, or when officials or visitors would come to speak with the dey. Only the Europeans and the Jews, seeking the dey's favor, found it difficult not to stare at her naked breasts with their bright red nipples. Oddly, she began to find humor in the situation. The afternoons were hot and long, and very dull. The dey gave permission for Azura to teach India Arabic. It was very difficult having a different alphabet she needed to learn, but it was a challenge, and India always enjoyed a challenge. One afternoon several months after she had come to El Sinut, they finished their lessons, and Azura ordered a cooling sherbet brought with a plate of honey cakes.

"You are doing very well," she praised India. "It took Caynan Reis much longer to master what you have mastered in just these past four months. You have a knack for languages, my child."

"Who is he, Azura? Caynan Reis, I mean. How did a foreigner rise so high in the sultan's service?"

"He was a captive, very much like your own cousin, who now sails with Aruj Agha. He spent almost two years in the galleys, and then one day while his ship was anchored in the harbor, my lord, Sharif el Mohammed, was rowed out to it to see its captain on some small matter of business between them. Caynan had, by that time, proved his worth to the vessel's captain and was no longer chained to an oar. Instead, he served the captain as his steward. Their business over, Sharif el Mohammed left the ship, but as he was getting into his own barge, he fell into the sea. He could not swim, and indeed he was weighed down by his garments. Caynan leapt over the side into the water, and saved the dey, Sharif el Mohammed.

"In gratitude, my own dear lord Sharif freed Caynan and invited him into his service. They became fast friends, and as my lord Sharif began to sicken, Caynan Reis took over more and more of his responsibilities. My lord wrote to Istanbul telling the sultan that he was dying and asking that Caynan Reis succeed him. The sultan agreed. My lord died shortly thereafter, but he was content knowing El Sinut was in safe hands." There were tears in Azura's bright blue eyes.

India reached out instinctively to comfort the woman. "Do not weep, my lady," she said.

Azura laughed weakly. "It has been a long time since the mention of Sharif el Mohammed's name could render me weepy," she said. "He asked Caynan Reis to allow me to remain in the only home I had known since my capture. Caynan Reis is like a son to me. He has been gracious and very kind. Tell me, my child. Are you learning to like him?"

India nodded. "Aye, but not all the time. Sometimes he can be cruel, my lady, although I think he does not mean it."

"You are wise to see that," Azura said. "I do not know what happened to him in his homeland that caused him to leave it, but it hardened his heart, I fear. It will take a very special woman to melt the ice that encases his soul. Perhaps you are that woman. You cannot spend the rest of your days as his body slave. There is so much more you can have, if you will but ask, my child."

"I do not know if I am ready yet, my lady," India admitted.

"Surely you do not think you can be returned to your own land, India? Trust me, my child, it will not happen. Your life is here now."

She thought about Azura's words as she lay tossing upon her pallet that night, attempting to block the cries of the dey's companion from her consciousness. Why did these women all howl so each night when he made love to them, and why did he call out as well? It was a mystery, and not one she was likely to solve unless she would yield herself to Caynan Reis. *Could she?* Was Azura correct? Would she never return to England again? And what if the harem mistress was right? Did she want to live like *this* forever?

She knew his body well enough, India thought, and the sight of it no longer troubled her, or frightened her. She knew her own body equally as well now. The trouble was, she wasn't quite certain what they were supposed to do with their bodies once they were past the caressing and the kissing she had seen between the dey and his women. She remembered once asking her mother about what transpired between a man and a woman. Jasmine had grown thoughtful, and then she had told her eldest daughter that all would be revealed before she married, but it wasn't really seemly that India have such knowledge before then. It might encourage her to experiment, and girls should not experiment with passion before marriage. It was not wise, or safe. And besides, here Jasmine had laughed, it was better that a man believed he was fully in charge of lovemaking, at least at first. But if his bride knew everything, then it would spoil it for him.

India wondered if Azura would enlighten her, and believed she would. She would ask her tomorrow. Azura, she knew, would be very pleased that India was finally showing an interest in the carnal side of her nature.

"*Ahhhhh, my lord, it is too sweet!*" came the cry from the dey's bedchamber.

"Oh, be silent, you silly creature!" India muttered to herself. *I vow,* she thought silently, *that I shall never carry on like those silly women do each night. I think they do it just to please him, and for no other reason. Nothing could be* that *wonderful.* Or could it? And would she be daring enough to soon find out? What if he decided he was no longer interested in her? India wondered nervously. No. Of late she had caught him sending glances her way when he thought she wasn't looking, and when she caught him at it, he had smiled knowingly. Did he suspect her interest? God's boots! How embarrassing!

She finally fell asleep, awakening just at dawn as she had accustomed herself to do. Rising, she stored her pallet and neck roll in the cupboard. Then, opening the dey's bedchamber door, she crept silently into the room, going to the bed and poking at the naked girl curled up next to Caynan Reis. "Samara," she whispered to the long-legged brunette. "Samara, it is time to get up. Go back to the harem."

"Ummmm," Samara murmured sleepily, turning onto her back and opening her eyes. "If I remain, perhaps he will want me again."

India pulled the girl by her arm. *"Get up!"* she snapped. "You know Baba Hassan's rule, and if you do not go back to the harem this minute, I shall go and fetch him! You will be punished."

Samara scrambled to her feet. She was every bit as tall as India. "You are just jealous because the dey does not find you desirable," she said meanly. "You are the lowest of the low. A body slave."

India pushed the naked girl from the room, shoving her kaftan into her hands. "You are mistaken, you overblown Damascus rose. It is I who do not find the dey desirable. I think it will be a long time until you enter his bed again, Samara." She smiled sweetly. "You see, I have my master's complete trust now, and it is I who choose his nightly companion. I do not think I will choose you for a long time."

Samara's lush mouth fell open in shock. "You lie!" she said disbelievingly. *"You lie!"*

India laughed. "Go back to the harem and await your master's next invitation. You will be old and fat before it comes." She thrust Samara out into the corridor and pulled the doors shut on her. "Nasty cow," she muttered to herself. "I'd sleep with him myself before I'd let you go back into his bed again!"

"Would you, India?" The dey stood in his bedchamber door.

"Would I what, my lord?" she asked innocently.

He laughed. "You have a wicked tongue, India, and you bully my women shamelessly. Are you jealous of them?"

"My lord, I may now find myself your slave, but I am a duke's daughter. Your women are of a lower class, and if I did not keep them in line, they would be impossible to tolerate." She pointedly ignored his question. "Come, now, my lord dey, it is time for your bath."

"Yes, my lady," he teased, following her into the baths.

She scrubbed him with great vigor until he finally protested. "Do not be such a bairn," she told him. "Go and soak in the bathing pool."

He stood in the warm, perfumed water up to his neck, watching her as she performed her own ablutions. He had not approached her since that first morning when she had been learning her duties. Now he considered he might attempt her again, and see her reaction. He watched her through half-closed eyes as she rinsed herself with several basins of water, finally putting the silver ewer upon its shelf. Then she stepped down into the pool, positioning herself opposite him as she always did.

"You have no visitors today, my lord," she said.

"I must go over the engineer's plans for the aqueduct repairs," he told her. I wonder if I should not simply have a new aqueduct built for the town rather than repair the old one, which dates to Roman times."

"Why not repair the old one just enough to continue its use while you are having a new aqueduct built, my lord?" India suggested. "That way El Sinut is guaranteed a continuous supply of fresh water. If the original aqueduct is as old as you say, it could give out at any time. Losing it would be a disaster for the city."

"Some would say it has stood this long. Why go to the expense of building a new one?" he told her.

"In the matter of people's welfare, my lord, no government should be penny wise and pound foolish," India replied. "Is not your treasury full? If it is the government's gold, why hoard it? For what other purpose have you collected taxes and tribute if not to make your people's lives comfortable and safe. From what you have told me these past few months, and from what I have overheard, the valide does not want any kind of strife to unsettle her young son's reign. She would have his life peaceful until he comes of age to rule by himself. If El Sinut lost its water supply, the people would turn against the government, and what could Istanbul do to help being so far away? Their solution would be to send troops to put down the revolt. Then they would leave, and the problem would still remain. It is better that you attend to the matter of the aqueduct, my lord dey, and avoid any civil discord," India concluded.

"Your advice is sound," he replied, thinking as he spoke that her intellect was far above that of any woman he had ever known. She had obviously been thinking about the problem for some time now, and she had reasoned well the arguments for and against her conclusions.

She gave him a genuine smile. "Come, my lord dey," she said as she moved up the steps from the pool. "You cannot remain here all day." She held out a large towel for him. "The masseuse awaits you." She wrapped him in a towel, and began to dry him.

Caynan Reis chuckled to himself. He had wanted to attempt a seduction this morning, but she had so fascinated him with her speech regarding the aqueduct, that he had completely forgotten. *She must come to you*, the voice in his head told him.

He had his massage. She dressed him and brought him his morning meal. Then he closeted himself in his library, giving her his permission to do as she chose until it was time for his main meal. The day was overwarm for winter. As he went over the plans brought to him by the city's chief engineer, he could see the wisdom in her words. He sent for the author of the plans and brought up the possibility of building a new aqueduct to replace the old.

"It would be the better strategy, my lord," the engineer told him. "We could indeed do minor repairs on the old system that would hold for several years. A new aqueduct would take us three years to build. You see, we cannot be certain of the damage and wear to the interior of the aqueduct, but a new one would assure us of a supply of fresh water for the next several centuries, my lord."

"The cost?" The dey demanded.

"Not a great deal more than to do serious repairs on the old aqueduct, my lord, which might need more repairs in the future."

"Then we will build a new aqueduct," the dey decided, handing the plans back to the chief engineer. "Start immediately."

Returning to his apartments, the dey found his midday meal already set out for him. His head ached, and the air was unusually heavy for July. Still, his appetite was not affected. When he had finished, he arose, saying to her, "I think it will rain."

"Shall I prepare you for your nap, my lord?" she asked softly.

He nodded. Allah! His desire for her was suddenly eating at him. She removed his garments and sponged him with rose water. He said nothing, but his dark-blue eyes searched her face for some sign that she was weakening toward him. India carefully kept her eyes averted from his. If she looked at him, she would be lost, she feared. She didn't understand the emotions now swirling about inside her.

"Are you well, my lord?" she asked him, seeing his agitation.

"My head aches, India," he told her.

"Sit down, my lord, and let me rub it for you," she suggested.

"Nay," he said, thinking if she touched him again he would explode. "I will rest and it will ease itself," he told her. "Go, and have your lesson with Azura."

"No," India said. "Azura says I have advanced far more than any of her other students in so short a time. I will remain here, my lord, so that if you need me, I may serve you."

"Come and lie with me," he said softly.

She shook her head in the negative.

"Just lie by my side, India. I promise you that nothing will transpire between us. Your presence would comfort me," Caynan Reis said.

"I have not eaten," India said softly, "and I must then return the trays to the kitchen or poor old Abu will be most distressed, my lord."

"When you have finished," he said, "then come to me."

"Are you commanding me, my lord?" India asked him.

"Nay," he replied, and closed his eyes.

India slipped from the bedchamber and ate her meal. Then she carried the trays back to Abu. Returning to the dey's apartments, she warred with herself for several long minutes, and then, entering his bedchamber, she lay down by his side. He did not move, and she was not certain if he was asleep or awake. It had begun to rain, and the sound of the droplets hitting the gravel path and the flora out in the garden was very soothing. Her eyelids grew heavy, and she was soon sleeping.

Caynan Reis took a deep breath, and put an arm about the slumbering girl. She gave a small sigh and curled herself against him. He could scarcely contain himself. She had come to him of her own accord. He let his eyes scan her face. She was dazzlingly beautiful, and she was almost his. He longed to kiss those full, lush lips of hers. To taste the innocent sweetness of her. He balled his hands into fists to prevent himself from touching her further and frightening her away. He knew that other men would consider his attitude toward India ridiculous. If a woman belonged to a man, and he desired her body, she gave it . . . *or he took it.* Yet, from the beginning, he had not been able to force her. Suddenly he realized that he wanted India to want him for himself, and not because he was the dey of El Sinut.

The women in his harem were lovely, and most amenable, but India was correct when she said that they feared him. They did. In their world he held the power of life and death over them. They sought to please him because everything they were, or possessed, was because of Caynan Reis, the dey of El Sinut. While he believed he had tamed India's proud manner a trifle, he had not broken her spirit. She spoke her mind to him, and did not mouth inanities at him. He realized now that he needed more than just willing bodies to pleasure him. He needed a woman who would be his companion, his lover, and who would tell him the truth. *He needed India.* It was as simple as that, but now he had to convince her of it. He couldn't be certain if it would be easy or difficult.

Of late he had seen her looking at him with a questioning look in her marvelous eyes. What was she thinking? Could she ever really love him given the way in which she had come to him? Had they been in England instead of El Sinut, would she have even considered him as a husband? She was seventeen, which was old for a virgin, and she had not chosen a husband, nor had her family chosen one for her. He wondered why. One day he would ask her, he thought.

His head was still aching, though less so when he finally fell into a deep sleep, but when he awoke, his mind was clear. The rain had stopped, and India was gone from his side. Had it all been a dream?

"India!" He called out to her.

"Yes, my lord?" She stood in the open bedchamber door.

"My headache has left me," he said, feeling foolish. He had been like a child for a moment, fearful that she was gone from him.

"I am glad, my lord," she answered him.

He arose, and she slipped a kaftan over him. "Who shall I choose to share my bed tonight, India?" he asked her. "Who shall I choose?"

For a very long moment she was silent, and she pierced him with a look the meaning of which he could not fathom. Then she said in a low voice, "It is not seemly, my lord, that I choose for you. I know you heard my foolish boast this morning to Samara, but it was only to keep the absurd creature in her place."

"Who shall I choose, India?" He repeated the question. He stood directly before her, his hands now resting lightly on her shoulders.

I am losing my reason, she thought. *I cannot!*

"India?"

"Choose me, my lord," she finally said. *"Choose me."*

Chapter 10

He was not entirely certain that he had heard her aright. Reaching out, he cupped her face between his two hands and looked directly into those marvelous eyes of hers. "India?"

"Choose me, my lord," she repeated once again in a soft voice.

"You are certain?" His heart was hammering, and he felt almost weak in his longing for her. This was not simply desire he realized in a blinding burst of cognition. *This was love!*

"I am certain," she replied. "But, oh, my lord! Please be patient with me. You know I am neither incompetent nor witless, but I know very little about passion." Her cheeks flushed with her words.

Caynan Reis bent his dark head, and touched her lips with his. It was a slow kiss, delicate and filled with promise.

When he finally removed his lips from hers, India's hand went instinctively to her mouth, her fingers touching the flesh wonderingly. She hadn't known quite what to expect but certainly not this tenderness. There was something far more to the kiss than she understood, and, seeing the confusion in her eyes, he knew for an absolute certainty her innocence.

"I will teach you passion, India," he told her, his hands leaving her face, his strong arms enfolding her in a warm embrace.

Her cheek lay against his chest. She could feel the beating of his heart beneath the fabric of his kaftan. She trembled, and then angry with herself for what she felt was an unpardonable show of weakness, pulled away from him.

Gently he drew her back, enfolding her once more. His hand sleeked down her dark curls soothingly. "Passion is always confusing in the beginning. Afterward it is merely surprising," he told her.

"I feel foolish," she admitted.

"Do not, my thorny little virgin," he teased her lovingly. "I have never had a virgin in my bed, and I find the prospect an unusual aphrodisiac."

"What should I do?" India asked him.

"Another night I will begin to teach you the things that please me, and Azura will instruct you as well, my precious. Tonight, however, I would simply initiate you into the delights of love."

"Oh."

He felt her stiffen, and, realizing how nervous she must be, he said to her, "Now, India, go and fetch our evening meal. My headache is gone, and I find I am hungry."

She slipped from his arms, and hurried from the room relieved. It wasn't that she wanted to take back her acquiescence. She didn't. But her mood was lightened by the realization that he would not rush her along passion's path. What would *it* be like? she wondered. Would she, too, call out like those silly harem women? She was curious to learn what would make a woman cry with such obvious pleasure. His kiss had been quite wonderful. Much better than Adrian's kisses, and for a moment she felt guilty, but the feeling quickly passed.

She could see now that Adrian had been an utter fool. The dey was not a cruel man, but he absolutely insisted upon being respected, as was his right. If Adrian had behaved better, he probably would have been ransomed by now, and her family would have known where she was. She knew that her parents would have moved heaven and earth to regain her person, but Adrian had not been wise, and while he might eventually escape his captivity, she would never escape hers.

Was that why she was finally assenting to Caynan Reis's desire? To save herself? To make a place for herself in this new world? Or was she intrigued by this man who could be so kind and also so cruel? She wondered if another man would have been so patient as he had been. And what would have happened if she had never decided to yield to him? Reaching the kitchen, she found the evening tray with its decanter of fruit sherbet, the bowl of ripe fruits, and a blue-and-white plate of flat, warm bread. Picking it up, she returned to the dey's apartments.

"I have set up the chessboard," he told her as she set the tray in its accustomed place and then prepared the basin with its love cloths.

She took her place opposite him, and their game began. She had learned much from him about chess, and while India had always been a good opponent, she had become an even better one over the last few months. Tonight, however, she was distracted, and finally, after her third loss in a row, he called a halt to their play.

Reaching out, he took her hand, and raising it to his lips, kissed the fingertips lightly. Unable to help herself, she pressed her fingers along his mouth again. He kissed them again, parting his lips just slightly to suck upon those slender digits. Startled, she pulled her hand away. Then, stretching his arm out, he touched her lips with his own hand. "Do what I did, India," he instructed her softly.

Shyly she took his fingers into her mouth, drawing upon them, timidly at first, and then, unable to help herself, sucking more strongly. Surprised, her eyes widened even as she felt her heart begin to race. Her cheeks felt suddenly hot. There was something so sensual . . . so primitive in what she was doing, and while she forced herself to do so, she didn't really want to stop. She looked at him questioningly as she released his fingers.

The dey caressed her face gently, his knuckles grazing the cheekbone. "Are you hungry?" he asked her.

India nodded nervously, although she really wasn't, but anything to take her mind from the outrageously erotic thoughts now assailing her. She struggled to her feet even as he stood up. Together they moved to the table where the food was laid out. India poured the dey a small silver goblet of sherbet, handing it to him. It was his custom to help himself to the bread and the fruit. Seated opposite each other, they ate in silence for a time. He plucked a small bunch of pale-green grapes from the bowl, and began to pull the individual fruits from their stems with his teeth, slowly, one by one. His eyes met hers. She watched, fascinated, until the action of his strong white teeth and his swirling tongue that snaked out to catch the juice from the grapes made her giddy.

When he had finished, he took a slice of pomegranate, spooned the seeds from it, and, cutting it into pieces, began to feed it to her. She ate several chunks of the tart-sweet fruit, licking the juice from his hand in an action that surprised her. How bold she was becoming, India thought to herself, and blushed at the small smile that briefly touched the corners of his mouth. Could he read her wicked thoughts? She hoped he could not.

Caynan Reis took one of the damp towels that always accompanied his evening meal, and, leaning over, wiped her hands and face before cleaning himself. Then, sitting back in his chair, he said quietly to her, "Disrobe for me, India."

She did not argue. Nudity between them was natural to her now. Standing, India loosened the ties on her pantaloons, and they fell to the floor. Picking the garment up, she laid it across the chair.

"Come here to me now," he said, and when she had moved to stand before him, he took the damp towel and removed the carmine stain from her nipples. "I prefer you as Allah created you," he told her. Rising, he pulled off his kaftan, laying it next to her garment. Then, reaching out, he drew her into the circle of his embrace so that their bodies just touched. "You have no idea, my precious, how much I desire you," he said quietly, "but it is important to me that you are not fearful, India, of what will transpire between us this night. Do you understand?"

She nodded mutely, unable to meet his gaze. It was ridiculous that she felt so suddenly shy, but she did.

"I will not hurt you," he promised her, "and if you become afraid, you will tell me. There is no shame in a virgin being suddenly reluctant, or apprehensive, India. Lovemaking is a joyous pastime, and I would have you gain pleasure from our endeavors."

She nodded again, aware all of a sudden that he was gently

stroking her, his big hand smoothing down her back with a delicate touch. She looked up at him questioningly, and without another word, his mouth covered hers, his lips easing her nervousness, proffering a sweetness such as she had never known. To her surprise she found herself kissing him back, offering herself to him as she certainly never had to Adrian Leigh, and realizing even as she did that she did so willingly. *I want him*, she thought, *and I don't even really know what it is I want of him.*

He took her face between his hands, raining kisses upon it until she truly believed that there wasn't an inch of skin he had missed. "You are so beautiful," he murmured against her lips, alighting upon them again as a bee returning to a flower. He nibbled upon them teasingly, then pressed passionately against her mouth, gently but firmly and wordlessly cajoling her to part her lips. When she did so, he ran the tip of his tongue along the moist flesh, then unexpectedly thrust into her mouth to touch her tongue with his.

India gasped, totally surprised by his action. She wanted to draw back, but the writhing tongue encircling hers was frankly the most sensual feeling she had ever experienced. Hesitantly at first, then more boldly, she fenced with his tongue, feeling her body begin to entertain a strange and sultry heat that, while unfamiliar, was, she decided, in the overall most pleasant. She slipped her arms about his neck, drawing him closer until their bodies were pressed tightly against each other.

For a moment his breath caught in his throat as he felt her breasts pushing against him. She had absolutely no idea the havoc she was wreaking. Had she been any other woman, he would have thrown her to the floor and taken her then and there. Instead, he slowly ended the kiss, loosening her embrace, his hands going to her waist to turn her about so he might reach about, taking her breasts in his two hands. They nestled like two white doves within his cupped palms. He brushed his thumbs lightly across her nipples, smiling to himself as the delicate flesh puckered with her arousal.

India closed her eyes as he fondled her. She sighed, and leaned her head back against his shoulder. She had never felt so cared for in her entire life. She was at ease with this man as she had never been at ease with Adrian Leigh. How could this be? She had loved Adrian. *Loved?* Aye, it was past, she realized, and as she did, she knew that her father had been right. It had just been an infatuation that she had, in her inexperience, stubbornly insisted was more. But it hadn't been more. Yet what was this that she felt for Caynan Reis? And did she feel anything other than curiosity or budding lust? If she didn't feel some emotion toward him, then how could she allow him the liberties he was now taking? *And she had indeed allowed him.* He had not taken advantage of her. Oh, she could not hide behind that old excuse of wanton maidens!

"What is it, India?" His voice sounded softly in her ear, and he then nibbled upon her lobe. "You are distressed. I sense it." His big hands continued to caress her breasts.

"I wonder what sort of creature I am that I enjoy your attentions," she said candidly. "I have been taught that the license I now grant you is an intimacy allowed only between husband and wife, yet I permit you to kiss and touch me in a familiar manner . . . and I feel no guilt. How can that be, unless the high moral character that I have always attributed to myself does not exist and I am little better than a lewd trollop offering her favors in the High Gate."

His hands fell away from her breasts, and, taking her by the shoulders, he turned her about. "Look at me," he said sternly, and, when she raised her eyes to his, he continued. "This is not your England, India. Your parents have raised you well that you hold such a high moral standard up for yourself, but even in England, such standards are not ordinary despite what king and church may proclaim. You must know that, India. Here we do not count it a sin that a man desires a woman. That is why we are allowed up to four wives at one time, and many concubines to please us." He touched her cheek tenderly. "Did it ever occur to you, India, that perhaps you are beginning to care for me, and this is why you feel no shame at our behavior?" His mouth brushed over hers lightly, and his deep blue eyes questioned her gently.

India blushed, and a tremor ran through her slender frame. "I . . . I . . . Oh! I hate this feeling of confusion!" she suddenly cried.

"I told you nothing would be between us unless you wanted it as much as I do," he reminded her, praying silently that she would not elude his passions once again. He was struggling to remain patient.

"But I do want . . . *I do!*" India said softly, and then she hid her head against his chest Why in God's name was she behaving like such a complete ninny? What was the matter with her? Did she care for him?

Allah! he thought. Were all virgins like this? Damn the little witch! She had given her consent, and he would wait no longer. Without a word he swept her up into his arms, gaining his bed, his arms still tightly about her as he collapsed against the pillows.

"*Ohh!*" Her eyes were suddenly wide, and she knew instinctively that there was now no going back. As he slipped her from the comfort of his embrace upon the boldly striped mattress, his look was a look of undisguised passion that even she could recognize, and India thought suddenly of her mother. Had not Jasmine willingly shared herself with Prince Henry Stuart? A liaison that had resulted in her half-brother, Charles Frederick Stuart? *And that had been in England!*

"What are you thinking?" he demanded.

"That your gaze burns me, my lord," she dissembled.

He laughed, and once more kissed her mouth lightly. "If you but knew my thoughts, little virgin, you would burst into flame," he told her. "I cannot ever remember desiring a woman as I desire you, my precious India." He caressed her face with the back of his hand.

"*I am not yet a woman, my lord,*" she half whispered back.

"We will shortly remedy that," he told her, his kisses becoming more ardent as they moved over her face and down the graceful column of her throat, across her chest, and finally to her breasts.

His lips were warm, and seemed to burn her delicate skin wherever they touched. She was acutely aware of everything, her senses suddenly sharpened to every nuance of his passion, even of her own body. Her breasts seemed to be swollen. They almost hurt, and when his mouth closed over a nipple and suckled upon it, a small cry escaped her. "Ahhh, God!" She felt his tongue swirling about the nipple teasingly, and then his teeth gently, very gently, nipped at the sensitive tip. "Ohhhh!" His tongue swiftly laved over the nipple, soothing it, but he hadn't really hurt her at all. When he lifted his dark head, she eagerly guided it to her other nipple so it, too, might know such pleasure.

Then she felt his other hand caressing her belly, moving in teasing little circles over the silky skin. She ached with both pleasure and anticipation for whatever was to come. The hand slipped lower to cover her Venus mound, and India felt her breath catch in her throat. Brushing his fingers over the smooth mound, he ran a single digit down the moist crease separating the fleshy folds. She couldn't breathe, and then the finger pressed itself between the tempting furrow, touching her in a place she hadn't even known existed. India gasped sharply, and the finger began to caress that place. Reaching out, she dug her fingers into his shoulder.

"This is your pleasure place," he murmured, his finger rotating itself about the sensitive nub of flesh. "You can feel it, my precious, can't you? The joy is beginning to stir within you, isn't it?"

"*Yes!*" Dear heaven, this was sweet. She would die with delight, she thought, pressing herself up to meet his hand. She felt as if she were going to burst there, and then indeed she did, the pleasure permeated her entire body like slow, warm wine, oozing through her veins until the delight was as suddenly gone as it had come. "*No!*" she protested.

"There is more," he promised her. "This is just the beginning." Then his finger pushed deeper, finding her passage, exploring her gently. He didn't doubt her maiden state, but he could barely contain his delight at finding her virgin shield fully intact. She was very tight, but already wet, her young body eager for the consummation. He knew he could wait no longer to enjoy her. Withdrawing his hand from her Venus mound, he began to cover her fair body with his, kissing her deeply as he did, his hands lightly pinioning her.

She was completely cognizant of his actions, of the hard length that had been pressing against her, and was even now seeking to possess her. She trembled openly as he tenderly spread her open to his attentions, and he kissed her again. The look on his face was one she could not fathom. There was no lust, only gentleness. "*My lord?*" she whispered, confused, her eyes seeking an answer.

The deep blue eyes looked down at her. "Little fool," he murmured to her. "Have you not yet realized that I love you?" Then without another word he thrust deep inside her, piercing her innocence.

His declaration astounded her even as the sharpness of her defloration briefly pained her. Then, after a moment, he began to move upon her, and India cried out softly at the pleasure she was receiving. She could feel his length, and the breadth of him as he plumbed the secret depths of her. She welcomed him, shyly at first, then more boldly, her arms wrapping about him into an even closer embrace.

"Put your legs about me." He ground the words out into her ear.

She obeyed the command, and then cried out as he plunged deeper into her softness. She had never imagined it would be like this. So wonderful! So intimate! *So indescribable!* She clung to him, her breath coming in hard bursts as he thrust to and fro within her body. Her nails began to claw at him. She couldn't help it. There was a tension building and building within her that needed release. "Ohhhhh, God!" she wailed. "I can bear no more! Ohhh, God, don't stop!" Then it was as if she was almost yanked from her body and flung among the stars. She soared, shuddering, as spasm after spasm wracked her, sending waves of heat and sensation slamming into her, leaving her gasping for breath.

He felt the walls of her sheath contracting and convulsing around his throbbing manhood, and Caynan Reis was astounded. India had been a virgin, and yet her passions were even now bursting, and forcing from him a torrid tribute. With a groan of complete surrender, his love juices filled her, engulfing her secret garden. *I want sons from this woman* was his last conscious thought, and then he rolled away from her lest he crush her, though his arms were still tight about her.

He came to himself at the sound of her soft weeping. "India, what is it? Allah forgive me if I have hurt you! Tell me, my precious." He leaned over her, kissing the tears upon her cheeks.

"I am so happy," she sobbed. "Will it always be like this between us? Will you continue to desire me, or have I lost my allure now that I am no longer a virgin?" She looked up at him, so vulnerable that it almost broke his heart.

"I love you," he told her once again. "Did you think I but said the words to ease your conscience, India, before I took you? I never thought that I should love a woman, but I love you. I will always desire you, little fool. *Always!* I shall make you my wife as quickly as I can do so. You will be the dey's first wife."

"First wife?" She sat up now.

"I am allowed four," he teased her.

"And will you take four?" she demanded, her look angry.

"I think you will be more than enough wife for me, my precious," he laughed. "Allah, I am beginning to desire you again! I would not believe it possible, but I am!"

"And your harem, my lord?" she persisted.

"The dey of El Sinut would be made to look a fool, ruled by his wife, if he did not maintain a harem," he told her. "That is not a matter for us to discuss, India. Now, kiss me sweetly on the lips."

"Will you make love to your harem women?"

He pulled her down beneath him and kissed her hard. "It would seem I will have to, having such a disobedient favorite," he said to her, half laughing. "Am I to deny myself the company of women when you ripen with my children or your link with the moon is broken?"

"Are you so lustful then?" she asked him.

"Aye," he grinned mischievously at her, "I am. Now, fetch the love cloths, for my hunger for you grows as each minute passes."

She pouted, but then slipped from their bed to fetch the basin, and the soft cotton cloths. First. however, she washed herself, startled a moment by the blood smeared upon her thighs, realizing it was the proof of her lost virtue. Then she brought the basin, with its fresh water, and clean cloths to him.

"It is your duty to bathe my member," he told her wickedly.

India eyed his manhood suspiciously. She had, of course, washed him in the baths, but now . . . now it looked somewhat more lethal to her. Soaking the cloth, she wrung it out, and gingerly began her task. When she had finished, and removed the basin and cloths, he called her back to his bed again.

"I want you to caress my love lance," he told her. "Touch it, India. Hold it in your hands. It will not harm you."

She sat facing him, curious to learn more about this part of him that had given her such incredible pleasure. Cautiously she touched his manhood with her fingertips. It was warm, and stirred slightly beneath her touch. She drew her hand back nervously, then gamely reached out again, taking his member into her hand, her fingers closing about him gently. "It seems alive," she said. "I can feel it throbbing." She loosed him, and stroked his manhood with surer fingers now, as if she were petting a favorite pet. To her surprise it began to grow beneath her very eyes, thickening and lengthening, its ruby head sliding from its velvet sleeve. "Ohhh," India breathed softly.

"You see the power you hold over me, my precious," he told her. "I think of you and am excited. You touch me, and I am aroused." Reaching out, he began to caress her breasts again.

"I can encourage your appetites as you do mine," she said, comprehending what he was trying to teach and show her.

He drew her down into his arms, kissing her. "Aye, India. You understand perfectly."

"Make love to me, my lord," she said softly, "and instruct me on how I may make love to you."

"That I will do another time. Tonight is for your delight, my love. For I gain pleasure knowing I have pleasured you." Then his lips took possession of hers once more, and it was heaven, India thought, quickly lost again in the fiery passion he engendered within her, and heedless of the world around her.

Azura, however, had noted there was no call from the dey this night for one of the harem women. When the midnight hour had come, she hurried to the apartment of the chief eunuch, saying as she entered, "He has not sent for a woman, Baba Hassan. Never in all the years he has been dey has a night passed when he didn't desire female company."

"Then the answer must surely be that our reluctant protégé has finally succumbed to our master," the chief eunuch answered the mistress of the harem. "Have you not noticed in the past few weeks the glances he sends her way when she is not looking at him? His patience has been utterly astounding for a mortal man." Baba Hassan arose from his pillows. "Come, Azura. Let us go and see what has happened between them."

"We cannot! It would be a terrible intrusion on the dey's privacy," she answered her companion.

Baba Hassan chuckled, his dark eyes crinkling almost closed with his humor. "Azura, he will never know we have spied on him." He took up a small oil lamp. "Follow me, lady." Walking across the chamber, the chief eunuch reached out to press his hand against the tile border just above his head. Almost immediately a hidden door swung open, revealing a narrow passage. Baba Hassan stepped through the door, followed quickly by Azura. The door swung shut behind them. "Come along," he whispered, and, flabbergasted, she followed behind.

The passage moved this way and that. The air was fetid, but breathable. How was it, Azura wondered, in all the years she had lived in this place, that she had never before known of this secret passage? Several times they came to crossroads, and the eunuch would turn right or left and once he went straight forward, the flame from his little lamp flickering skittishly upon the walls enclosing them. She was beginning to be uncomfortable in this small space. "Are we almost there, Baba Hassan?" she asked him, and, to her surprise, he stopped suddenly. She watched, as, raising the lamp up, he found a small handle, and, silently rotating it, revealed a tiny opening in the wall of the passage before which they now stood.

Baba Hassan turned his head, and said, "Look, Azura, and tell me what you see."

The mistress of the harem peered through the opening. To her astonishment she saw the dey's bedchamber before her. Her eyes went immediately to the bed, and then she smiled. India was in

Caynan Reis's arms, and the dey was making very passionate love to her. And, most important of all in Azura's eyes, India was obviously enjoying her master's attentions. She turned away from her view, saying to Baba Hassan, "It is as you suspected."

The eunuch looked briefly into the room, and then, closing the peephole, led his companion back through the hidden passage to his own apartment again. The two conspirators settled themselves, and the chief eunuch himself brewed the coffee that they shortly drank. As they sat together he said to Azura, "Now we must hope that she has pleased him enough that he will not quickly be bored with her. She must have his child." He looked to the woman seated opposite him. "She has not been given the special sherbet, has she?"

"There was no need for it, as she would not accept his attentions until now," Azura replied. "Unless he orders me to give it to her, I shall certainly not do so." She smiled with her own memories. "He was being so gentle with her, Baba Hassan."

"He is in love with her," the chief eunuch responded dryly.

"Not lust?" Azura replied, surprised.

"No, love," Baba Hassan said. "He is behaving with her the way our late master behaved with you, lady. The girl is fortunate."

"Now let us pray to Allah, the most compassionate, that we have enough time before we are approached by the janissaries," Azura worried. "His heart must be so fully engaged with India that he will act in a wise and prudent manner. Oh, why cannot men be peaceful, Baba Hassan? Why must they always war and plot against one another?"

"It is their nature, lady," the chief eunuch answered her. Then he chuckled almost to himself. "Tomorrow, however, you will find a war brewing in the harem when the other women learn that India has now become a woman, and possibly will be our master's favorite."

Azura frowned, not in the least amused. "Their plotting and planning will rival the janissaries," she grumbled. She arose from her place opposite him. "I had best seek my bed. India will need me come the morning. I will have to protect her from the others.

They were more than well aware that he had not sent for one of them tonight, and were pondering upon it when I shooed them all to their beds. By the morning they will surely have deciphered the puzzle."

"You can control them," the chief eunuch told her.

"Indeed I can," she replied, "but I dislike chaos in our little world, Baba Hassan. I will not, however, hesitate to remove any troublemakers." She hurried from his apartment.

When she had gone, the chief eunuch's face grew serious. The emissary for the janissaries had not yet come to El Sinut, but his contacts in Istanbul had recently advised him that a single agent had been dispatched from the capital to the Barbary States. Only one had been sent to avoid both suspicion and detection. It had been cleverly done. Who knew where he would begin his mission. Would he go first to Algiers, or come to El Sinut? And what disguise would he take? And how would he obtain the dey's ear? Aruj Agha was at sea yet. Baba Hassan sighed. He must be patient. It would all evolve as Allah willed it, but he hated the thought of rebellion.

El Sinut had been peaceful for some time now. The smallest of the Barbary States, it was always in danger of being swallowed up by its bigger, more powerful neighbors. Only a succession of intelligent, strong, and clever deys had kept it independent. That, and the fact that its fleet was larger than its size warranted, and was extremely lucrative for the royal coffers. But a serious rebellion against the sultan was something it had never encountered. Pray Allah, the all merciful, that they could avoid the anarchy when and if it came, the chief eunuch thought to himself.

Chapter 11

"Good morning, my lord. It is time for you to arise. I have brought the morning meal," Baba Hassan said, his smooth brown face impassive.

Caynan Reis rolled onto his back, and his blue eyes opened lazily. "Thank you, Baba Hassan," he said. "Must we get up now?" Propping himself up on an elbow, he leaned over, and kissed India awake.

"It is the general audience today, my lord," the chief eunuch reminded his master. "I could, of course, say you were ill, but that would cause consternation, I fear. Shall I escort you to the bath?"

"That is my task, Baba Hassan," India said, sitting up, and totally unabashed by her complete nudity.

"Your duties have changed, my precious," the dey told her with a smile, and then he kissed the tip of her nose.

"But I enjoy bathing you, my lord Caynan," she told him.

"So be it," he answered, and together they arose from their bed, walking hand in hand from the chamber toward the dey's bath.

A broad smile split the chief eunuch's face. This was very good. They were caught in the throes of love. Then his smile faded as quickly as it had come. But would India cooperate with them to aid the dey in avoiding treason? The English were very independent, but then they were loyal to their monarch, too. Still, the girl was no fool. But if they explained everything carefully to her, she could not fail to see the wisdom in their plan of action and convince the dey of it as well. He hurried off to the harem to speak with Azura.

His associate, however, had her hands full, and when he entered the fountain court of the haremlik. he was immediately surrounded by the dey's women, all chattering at him at once. "*Be silent!*" he thundered at them, and they stepped back, momentarily frightened.

"You see what I must put up with," Azura murmured.

"What has happened to the dey," the dark-haired Samara boldly demanded.

"Oh, Baba Hassan! Please tell us if our master is all right?" the beautiful blond Mirmah pleaded, her blue eyes teary.

"The dey is in excellent health and spirits this morning, ladies," the chief eunuch reassured them.

"But he did not send for one of us last night," the flame-haired Sarai exclaimed. "He always has one of us to warm his bed."

"He was not alone," Baba Hassan replied.

"*The English girl?*" Samara spoke the words with loathing.

"Oh, not the English girl," blond Deva half whispered. "She is so beautiful."

"I will scratch her eyes out!" Samara snarled.

"Attempt it, and you will find yourself in the open slave market within the hour," Azura replied sternly. "How spoiled you have all become! Your duty is to please our master, and if India gives him pleasure, then you should be glad for him. I will not tolerate jealousy in this harem, and neither will Caynan Reis. Resign yourselves to what was meant to be. Or would you prefer to provide entertainment for the janissaries?" She turned away from them, saying, "Come, Baba Hassan, we have business to discuss." Leading him to her own quarters, she asked, "Have you eaten yet? Come, and sit with me. Where is the dey?"

"I awoke them myself," the chief eunuch said. "I brought the morning meal, but India insisted on bathing her lord herself as she has been doing these past several months. Last night I told you that he loved her, but this morning I tell you that she loves him as well. This is just as we hoped, but now, my dear Azura, we must make certain that India follows *our* plan else we all find ourselves in jeopardy from the irrational and foolish behavior of the janissaries."

"I will go to the dey myself, and see what plans he has for India," Azura said. "I am certain that now he will no longer expect her to serve him as a body slave. I shall bring a beautiful kaftan for her to wear today. If she is to become his favorite, then she must have her own apartment, and everything that goes with such an honor. We have been friends since her arrival. Now I shall build upon that friendship. She is an intelligent girl, and can be brought to see reason. If she loves him as you believe, Baba Hassan, she will want to protect him from all harm. Melon?" She offered him a plate, and together they ate their morning meal, all the while planning how to protect the dey and El Sinut from chaos. When they had finished, Azura went to the main wardrobe for the harem and chose an exquisite turquoise-blue silk kaftan, embroidered with gold thread butterflies and creamy pearls, as well as several pale gold veils for India's head, and to shield her beautiful face should she go from the harem today.

Hurrying through the palace, Azura entered the dey's apartments, greeting her lord with a smile and displaying the finery. "I thought, perhaps, my lord, that you would want India garbed somewhat differently today. I have brought these garments for your approval."

"What think you, my precious?" Caynan Reis asked India.

"They are lovely, my lord. If it pleases you, I will wear them, but please let me come with you to the general audience. I love watching you judge and settle disputes. I will be happy to ply my fan today that you not become overheated."

"Nay, you will sit by my throne," he said. "Someone else will ply the fan. Now go and put on your new clothing for me while I speak with Azura," the dey commanded her, and India, taking the garments from the older woman, hurried into the bedchamber. "I want you and Baba Hassan in the audience chamber today, as well as the ladies of the harem. Seat them behind a carved screen so they may see, but not be seen," he told her.

"Is this a special occasion I have somehow overlooked?" Azura asked.

He laughed, and the sound was so happy and carefree that she was surprised, for she had never heard him make such a noise in all the years they had known each other. "I am going to marry her," the dey said. "Do not feign amazement, you lovely creature," he teased Azura. "You and Baba Hassan have dangled her before me since the day she arrived. You wanted this to happen, and while I believed you both mad, it would seem you know me better than I know myself."

"It is a man's nature to want love, and be loved in return, my lord," Azura answered him diffidently.

"Hah!" he chuckled. "You plotted the entire matter."

"My lord." India had come forth from the bedchamber.

Caynan Reis's deep blue eyes widened with approval. "Allah!" he exclaimed. "How exquisite you are, my precious love."

"Then you are pleased?" She smiled happily, then turned to Azura. "Thank you, my lady, for making such a fine choice."

Azura nodded in reply, and then said to the dey, "You will, of course, want the lady India to have her own apartment, my lord?"

"Aye. Have the empty rooms next to mine prepared for her," he instructed the mistress of the harem.

"But, my lord, those rooms are not within the harem," Azura reminded him, a trifle amazed by his instructions.

"The harem is for my concubines," he answered her. "The rooms near me are for my wife. I do not want my bride far from my side. While India will rule my house, and bear my children, you, my dear Azura, will continue to be the mistress of the harem. This is my wish."

"Yes, my lord," the older woman answered him. Allah! He *really* was in love with her. She bowed politely, and backed from the dey's apartments, hurrying to find Baba Hassan so she might tell him of all that had transpired and prepare the harem for their outing. She did not, however, tell her charges of the dey's decision to marry. That must be his little surprise. The concubines would, of course, be distressed by the news, but she would reassure them that their place within the dey's household was a secure one. He would not, for the time being, want their company as frequently as he had in the past, but they would come to accept the new arrangement. Any who caused difficulties would be sold away, and replaced.

While Azura was content that Caynan Reis take a wife and have children, the beautiful India must not be allowed to have such influence over her husband that he perhaps ignore his faithful servants. Eventually there must be a second wife, or at least a favored concubine to engage the dey's interest. India, however, could be the only woman allowed to give the dey sons lest El Sinut be subjected to the same sort of internecine warfare afflicting the Sublime Porte, where the sultan's women warred with each other, ambitious for their sons. It was just this sort of thing that had weakened the empire, leaving it vulnerable to factions like the greedy, power-hungry janissaries, who were even now plotting treason. For now, though, India would serve their purpose while making Caynan Reis the happiest of men, the mistress of the harem concluded.

"Come, ladies," she said, reentering the harem. "You are to dress in your finest garments, and be allowed to sit in the audience hall today, and watch our master in judgment over his subjects."

With cries of pleasure the harem women rushed to find the most flattering clothing that they could; rummaging through their jewel boxes; calling to their personal slaves for their cosmetics and perfumes. Azura oversaw it all, a secret smile upon her beautiful face, watching as Samara chose flame-colored garments, the equally dark-haired Leah, a deep rose. Red-haired Sarai was resplendent in green and gold, and the four blondes exaggerated their delicate coloring in the palest of pastels: pink, sky blue, peach, and apple green. And when the seven women were dressed with matching veils covering their bejeweled hair and their pretty faces, Azura escorted them from the harem to the audience hall.

Before them the chief eunuch went, clearing a path through the waiting populace, all of whom were fascinated to be given even the slightest glimpse of the dey's harem women as they hurried through the corridor, heads bowed, eyes lowered, and heavily veiled. Baba Hassan led the women into the vaulted chamber with its green-and white mottled pillars, and settled them behind a carved wooden screen facing the dey's throne, and set to one side. There, small chairs had been arranged in such a manner that each woman could gain a good view of the proceedings no matter where she was seated.

Samara silently counted the seats. There were but eight. Just enough for the harem, and the lady Azura. She smiled, well pleased. "Obviously the English girl does not merit the privileges we have been given," she announced smugly to her companions. "She cannot have pleased him."

"Remember," Deva remarked archly, "that she is merely his body slave."

"Exactly!" Samara crowed. "Her status remains lowly while ours is a favored one."

"I think she did please him," the blond Laylu replied. *"Look!"*

Azura bit her lip so as not to laugh as the seven pairs of eyes turned toward the dais, where even now Caynan Reis was standing. By his side stood India, her metallic gold veils glittering splendidly in the morning light as the hall grew silent with expectation. The girl's head was lowered just enough to be modest without being servile.

The dey spoke. "Today I bring you good news," he began. "I am the happiest of men, for I have decided to take a wife. I shall ask the chief iman to marry me to this woman before the sun has set this day." He took India's hand, leading her forward, saying, "Behold, she who has brought me the greatest joy I have ever known."

Then, to Azura's surprise, India knelt before the dey, kissing the hem of his bejeweled coat and finally flattening herself at his feet. The hall erupted into cheers even as Caynan Reis raised the girl up, his arm about her protectively. Then he brought her to a small satin stool set on his right hand, and seated her before taking his own throne. Baba Hassan looked toward the carved screen, and Azura knew the look was for her alone. It plainly said what Azura had known all along. India was strong of character. Indeed, she had played this hand beautifully, giving the dey the public respect he must have as the sultan's governor, while cleverly endearing herself to him further. It was obvious that the girl had decided where her fate lay.

"Well, well," Sarai said softly. "I should have never thought resistance was the way to our lord's heart." She shrugged fatalistically.

"Do not despair," Nila murmured. "One wife is always followed by a second. We will have our chance when our lord grows tired of the English girl's waspishness."

"That performance she just put on hardly smacks of pettishness," Samara observed, wiser than the others. "She is clever. Far cleverer than I would have given her credit for, the little bitch!"

"Let us give her a chance," Mirmah said to them, and Leah nodded in agreement. "We do not really know her. Now she will come to live in the harem with us, and it is possible we may become friends. After all, she is to be the master's first wife, and the first wife always has the most influence."

"*Not always*," Samara replied.

Azura held her peace, signaling them to silence now that the audiences had begun. They would find out soon enough that India was not to be housed in the harem with them, which would, of course, cause further jealousy. Samara was an obvious troublemaker, and she would also have to watch Nila and Sarai. Mirmah, however, had possibilities that Azura had never before observed. She would mention them to Baba Hassan, and they would keep Mirmah in mind for a possible second wife. She could prove to be the perfect counterbalance to the strong-willed India. Mirmah was a Circassian, bred for the harem and taught to please a master in a variety of ways.

The dey moved to get through the public audience as quickly as possible without slighting any of his supplicants. The crowds within the hall, however, understood, and some with but simple matters to be adjudicated requested of the chief eunuch that their cases be rescheduled another time so the dey might get on with his own personal business. The hall emptied quickly, for most in the crowds could scarcely wait to get outside into the town and spread the word of the dey's marriage.

When the public audience was finally over, Baba Hassan stepped forward, bowing to his master, and said, "Shall I take the lady India to the women's mosque, my lord, to be prepared for your marriage?"

Caynan Reis nodded, and then spoke quietly to India. "You will submit yourself to a special bath of purification, my precious. Then an iman will ask you several questions. Baba Hassan will translate what you cannot understand, and instruct you on how to answer."

India remembered shreds of stories she had heard from her family, now pushing into her consciousness. "You want me to accept Islam," she said to him.

He nodded. "If you are to be my wife, you must," he told her. "It is customary for all captives to do so in your position."

Words. She would say words. What was in her heart was known only to God, India thought. Her great-grandmother had, in a similar position, accepted Islam. So had her stepfather's great-grandmother. *My own grandfather, whom I never knew, but of whom Mama has always spoken, the great Akbar, believed all religions had value. I do not have to reject Christ,* India considered thoughtfully to herself. Then she looked into his eyes, smiling, and said, "I will do it, my lord, but in return I would have a favor from you."

"Walk with me, my precious love," he said, taking her by the arm, his look telling Baba Hassan to remain where he was. When they were a distance from any who might overhear, he asked her, "What would you have of me, India?"

"I have told you that my mother was the daughter of the great Mughal emperor, Akbar. When she was thirteen she was married to her first husband, a young prince. This prince was a follower of Islam, but while my mother had been raised to respect all faiths, she was, as I am, a baptized Christian. At her request she was also wed, in secret in her own Christian faith. Because he loved her, her prince was willing to acquiesce to her request. Will you do the same for me, my lord? Is there a Christian priest here in El Sinut who would marry us, and keep the secret so as not to endanger you?"

He thought for a long moment, and then said to her, "I am not certain who I can trust within the Christian community, which is very small, India. I promise you, however, that before our first child is born, I will wed you in your own faith. Will you accept my pledge on that, my precious love?"

"I will," she replied, "for I have learned in the months that I have been your body slave that you are a man of honor."

"*Have you?*" He was touched by her words. He had not realized she was observing him so closely. Emboldened, he asked her, "Do you love me just a little, India? Or do you wed me because it is the expedient thing to do?"

"I believe I am beginning to love you, my lord. I know I do not hate you. I realize now that all I have been told since coming to El Sinut is the truth. I will not return to England, and even if I ever did, it would be difficult for me. So is it not prudent for me to accept my fate, and make a happy life for myself?" She smiled shyly at him.

"Yes," he answered her, content for now with her candid answer. Then he led her back to Baba Hassan. "Do what must be done," he told the chief eunuch. "I will go and see the iman."

"We must leave the palace, and go to the women's mosque," Baba Hassan told India. He then gave orders to the slaves about them, and India shortly found herself in a litter once again, leaving the grounds of the palace for the first time since she had arrived in El Sinut five months back.

The women's mosque was a beautiful building of pure white marble. Inside, it was colonnaded with pillars of red-and-white marble holding up horseshoe arches. Baba Hassan put her in the charge of an old woman who took her to the ritual bath already awaiting the bride. It was little different from the harem bath, but India found she was being treated with deep respect by the bath attendants. *It is a little bit like marrying a king,* she thought, realizing that as wife of the dey, she was indeed very much like a queen.

When they had finished bathing, massaging, and perfuming her, they brought her fresh garments: a cream-colored kaftan embroidered with silver and gold threads, and small pearls and diamante. Her dark curls were brushed with fragrant oil and dressed with pearls; a gossamer veil shot through with gold and silver was placed on her head, a matching veil drawn across her face. Soft kid slippers covered in beaten gold were slipped upon her narrow feet.

"You are now ready, my lady," the mosque's bath mistress said. Then she led India back out into a courtyard where Baba Hassan was awaiting.

"Come," the chief eunuch said. "We must now see the iman who presides over the women's mosque. I will translate for you."

She was brought into the company of a white-bearded elderly man. While frail of form, his look was an intelligent and piercing one. Instinctively India bowed to him, and then stood silently, her eyes modestly lowered.

"The dey has chosen a beautiful woman, Baba Hassan," the iman said. "Does she understand why she is here?"

"I do, my lord iman," India said before the eunuch could speak for her. "I have come to accept Islam so my lord Caynan may wed me."

Baba Hassan smiled silently at her carefully spoken Arabic.

The iman nodded. "Had you ever heard of Islam before coming to El Sinut, my daughter? Our faith is an old one, though not quite as ancient as Christianity, and certainly not anywhere near as old as Judaism."

"I knew of Islam, my lord iman," India answered him. "Do we not all worship the same God?"

"Indeed, my daughter, we do. Come, let us sit, and I will tell you of the five pillars of wisdom that are the strength of our faith." They settled themselves upon a low divan, the chief eunuch standing behind them, and the iman continued. "To be a good member of Islam, you must observe our creed in which we demand belief in God, his angels, his books, his prophets, and the last day in which all men will be judged. Our prayer is a simple one. *There is no God but God, and Muhammed is Prophet of God.* Will you say the words for me, my lovely lady?"

"There is no God but God, and Muhammed is the Prophet of God," India spoke clearly. It was such a simple declaration.

"Angels, I know you believe in, having been raised in a Christian country. Our prophets are your prophets. Our holy books are called the Quran. We also recognize the scriptures of Abraham, the Torah of Moses, the Psalms of David, and the Gospels of Jesus Christ, all as revealed by God. The second pillar of wisdom is prayer. We pray five times daily. Upon rising, in early afternoon, in late afternoon, at sunset, and finally at night before retiring. The third pillar is alms giving. Like Christians and Jews we believe in charity toward those less fortunate than ourselves. The fourth pillar requires us to fast in the ninth lunar month, which we call Ramadan. Between sunrise and sunset we refrain from eating, drinking, smoking, and relations with our women. The fifth and final pillar of wisdom requires us to make a pilgrimage to the holy city of Mecca in our lifetime, if we can. These are things upon which our faith is founded, my lady. Will you accept them?"

"I will," India answered him without hesitation.

"Then, my daughter, having now accepted Islam, you are permitted to wed the dey," the old man said to her. "Understand that while it is every man's duty to wed and procreate, marriage in our world is not a religious rite. It is a contract between two people. The dey will settle a bride price upon you which is yours, and yours alone. You must be obedient to his will, and his will alone, my daughter. If at any time he wishes to divorce you, he will say, 'I dismiss thee' thrice. Your bride price would go with you in that event. We do not however, approve of divorce, and discourage men from it."

"What if a woman wishes to divorce her husband, my lord iman?" India asked, curious.

"Such a thing is not permitted," she was told. The iman arose slowly from his seat. "Baba Hassan, you will take the lady now to be wed. The chief iman of El Sinut is awaiting her arrival so he may witness this happy event."

India bid the elderly cleric farewell, and followed after the chief eunuch. The women's mosque was next to the main mosque in the city. They had but to cross a courtyard half shadowed with afternoon sun. He brought her into the building to a small room looking out upon a garden. Azura was awaiting them, along with the dey and the chief iman.

The iman, Abd Allah, was a portly man with a no-nonsense air about him. "Let us begin," he said. "You have settled a bride price upon the girl, my lord, and it is sufficient enough? Good!" He looked at India. "You are willing to marry this man, my lady?"

"I am," India replied softly.

"Excellent!" the iman answered with a smile. "Very well. I will witness you pledging to one another. You may begin, my lord dey."

Caynan Reis took India's hand in his. "Azura will whisper the words to you when it is your turn," he reassured her. Then, with a smile, he spoke his promise to her. "I, Caynan, take you, India, as my lawfully married wife before God, and in front of this company, in accordance with the teachings of the Quran. I promise to do everything to make this marriage an act of obedience to God, to make it a relationship of love, mercy, peace, faithfulness, and cooperation. Let God be my witness, because God is the best of all witnesses. Amen." His deep blue eyes looked directly into her golden ones as he spoke his vows.

India felt her cheeks grow pink. She was being married, and certainly in a manner she had never anticipated, or even expected. For a moment, tears welled up, and she wished her parents and her siblings were here with her. She was not unhappy with her decision, but she missed those she loved best. He squeezed her hand, and she focused upon his handsome face once more, smiling softly through her veil at him as she began to speak her own marriage vows to him.

"I, India, take you, Caynan, as my lawfully married husband before God, and in front of this company, in accordance with the teachings of the Quran. I promise to do everything to make this marriage an act of obedience to God, to make it a relationship of love, mercy, peace, faithfulness, and cooperation. Let God be my witness, because God is the best of all witnesses. Amen."

"It is done then," Abd Allah said with a broad smile. "May I offer you my felicitations, my lord dey. We are pleased to see you take a wife at long last. May the union be fruitful, and may your wife give you many fine sons."

"I will endeavor to see that she does her duty," the dey returned with a broad smile.

"Come," said Azura, taking India by the arm. "We must return to the palace discreetly. The servants have been working all day to prepare your apartments. I think you will be pleased." The two women entered their litter, Baba Hassan walking alongside of them. "And you must visit the haremlik before sunset."

"Why?" India asked her. "I am not going to live there. Those women hated me before I married my lord. How will they feel now? I am content to let them remain in their part of the palace, and I will remain in my part of the palace."

"The dey is not giving up his harem, India," Azura said. "It would be very unrealistic of you to believe he will cleave only to you. His appetite for female flesh is a strong one, and he indulges it daily. There will be times when you are unclean, or with child. You cannot ask him to suppress his desires in those times. It would be unhealthy for his juices to be so pent up. You are now the head of his women, and you must make peace with those silly, foolish creatures for the sake of your husband. His house must be a place of quiet and calm. Now, of the seven, Samara is the most dangerous. Be firm, but fair with her. She will not like you, but it may prevent her from mischief. If it does not, I will have her sold off. Nila is the clever one. She will act to her own advantage, but do not trust her. Mirmah, I believe, can be trusted. She is a gentle creature, and good-natured to a fault. As for the others, they are harmless, though some are sharp-tongued. I have chosen little gifts for you to give them this evening. Each is different, but none more valuable than the other, and they will recognize that."

India sighed deeply. "Very well," she said. "I will follow your advice, my lady Azura. In these matters you know better than I."

Azura laughed. "You are too young to isolate yourself, India. The harem women will be like sisters. Some you will love, others you will probably hate, but you will all manage to get on together."

"You say that with such certainty," India said.

"I have lived in the harem for over thirty years," Azura replied. "You are so fortunate. My lord Sharif made no woman his wife. He feared his enemies too much. While I was his favorite, I had to share his affections with the other women in his harem. It was not always easy for me, but it made him happy that I kept the peace within his house. I never whined at my lord about the other women, which set me apart from them. They were foolish, and were forever pouring a litany of complaints into his ear. My sole efforts were directed toward his comfort, his pleasure. I asked for nothing, and in return received everything. Even though you are the dey's wife now, India, you could benefit from my example," she concluded.

"Was Baba Hassan chief eunuch in lord Sharif's time?" India asked the older woman.

"Nay, the chief eunuch was old Baba Mamood. He died shortly after my lord Sharif. Baba Hassan was my personal servant, and my lord Caynan raised him into his current position on my advice. Baba Hassan and I love Caynan Reis as we would a son. We do whatever we have to do to see to his happiness and his safety," Azura told India.

"Who is he?" India wondered aloud. "I know nothing about him other than he, too, was once a captive. I do not know his nationality, or his station in his former life, or even his age."

"He is twenty-eight," Azura told her. "As for the rest, what does it matter? It has nothing to do with today. You love Caynan Reis, and that is all that should matter to you. Your life is here, and not back there in some other world, in some other time and place."

India nodded. "You are correct, my lady Azura. The past is nothing now. We must live for the present." She sighed. "I only wish that my family might know of my happiness. I hate to think of the pain I have caused them by my precipitous and hasty flight."

"If they knew where you were," Azura said, "they would surely attempt to retrieve you from us. Perhaps in a few years when you have children, you will be allowed to send a message to your mother."

"My grandmother would understand my plight better than anyone else in my family," India said. "She was in a similar position in her youth, and became the fortieth wife of the Grand Mughal Akbar."

"Yet she returned to England?" Azura was puzzled.

"Her family learned where she was, but might have been content except Grandmama's husband, the earl of BrocCairn, was alive. She had thought him dead in a duel, and had gone off to India with her elder brother to meet her parents when she was kidnapped and sent to my grandfather. By the time they found her, and requested her return, Grandmama had had my mother. Her family, of course, did not know that. My grandfather would not allow her to take the baby to England with her, and that is how Mama came to be raised in Akbar's imperial court. My family is not like any others," India finished.

"I should say not!" Azura remarked with a chuckle. "Ahh, we are finally back," she said as the litter was put down with a small bump. "Come, my lady India, and I will show you your new apartments. Then we must go to the harem." She laughed when the bride wrinkled her pretty nose in distaste.

India's new apartments were directly adjacent to her husband's. They would share the garden. There were but two rooms plus a small servant's chamber. The walls were white, the floors squares of large red tile. The day room had a small fountain in its center that was made of yellow-and-white tiles. There were several overstuffed divans with rolled arms, striped in blue and yellow satin; low ebony tables inlaid with tiny squares of multicolored tile; a rectangular cedar table upon which were a silver tray holding a decanter of lemon sherbet as well as a blue-and-white Fezware bowl of fresh fruit. There were large colorful pillows with gold tassels and standing bronze lamps burning fragrant aloes. Lamps of colored glass and warm, polished brass hung from the ceilings. Sheer silken curtains hung in the arches that opened to the garden, the carved screens being pulled aside.

The bedchamber was simple. There was a bed upon a gilt-and-painted dais. The mattress was covered in silver and sea-blue silk. There were more tasseled pillows. Several cedar chests were placed about the room, and upon a lovely table with carved legs was a gold-backed hand mirror and matching brush for her hair. By the bed was a low table upon which rested a silver lamp burning perfumed oils. Carved ivory screens blocked the arches, and were hung with silk curtains.

"Are you pleased?" Azura asked her.

India nodded. "It is all so lovely. Please thank the servants for me, lady. They have done very well. What is in the trunks?"

"Part of your bride price, I suspect. Clothing, jewelry, fragrance. There will be time for you to explore later."

"The harem," India resigned. "Where are their gifts?"

"Baba Hassan will bring them when he knows we are ready," Azura said. "If you go now, you will be able to join your husband all the sooner. Are you not ready again for his kisses and caresses?"

India blushed, nodding. "Let us go then," she replied.

As they entered the harem, the day room grew suddenly silent as seven pairs of eyes fixed themselves upon India.

"Make you obeisance to our master's wife, now head of this household," Azura announced to them. Then her eagle eye observed as the seven women bowed low to India, even Samara.

"I thank you for your greeting," India said in reply. "I have brought you all little tokens to celebrate my marriage today." She turned to the chief eunuch. "Baba Hassan, you know which gift is for which lady. Will you hand the gifts to me? I admit to not choosing them, for I do not know you all well enough yet, but I would have them come from my hand to yours." She smiled.

"Will the harem continue to exist, lady?" demanded Samara boldly. She was not a woman to beat about the bush.

"Whether the harem exists or doesn't exist is not my province. That is in the dey's domain. I am content, however, that you be here, but my husband's house must be free of discord. I will strive to see that it is so, Samara."

Her answer seemed to appease the harem women, and they each stepped forward to receive their gift. The gentle Mirmah set the tone by taking India's two hands in hers, and pressing them to her forehead in a gesture of acceptance and respect. Each of the others followed Mirmah's example, Samara being the last and obviously reluctant. India smiled at each of them, though some more warmly than others as she handed out the gift packets, which were wrapped in silk kerchiefs, and tied with gold ribbons. The ladies cried out, delighted as they opened their gifts, for Baba Hassan had not been stingy in choosing. The women compared the earrings and necklaces, and were all satisfied.

"Will you partake of light refreshments with us, my lady?" Mirmah asked India.

"I will be happy to join you," India replied, noting that Azura had disappeared from the scene.

The women led India to a divan, positioning themselves about her upon cushions as the slaves brought sweet grape sherbet, and a plate with tiny honey cakes and small horns of chopped nuts, and dough filled with raisins, nuts, and honey. There were also sweet dates and juicy figs upon the plate.

"You know I am English," India said as they ate. "I want to know about all of you. Mirmah is Circassian, Azura has told me, but what of the rest?"

"I am French," Nila said. "I am seventeen, and have lived in the dey's harem since I was fifteen. I was a gift to him from the dey of Algiers, who was my first master."

"We are Greek," Laylu said, indicating Deva in her statement. "We came from the same village, and have been enslaved since we were ten. Baba Hassan bought us in the market of El Sinut three years ago."

"I am Venetian," Sarai spoke up. "I come from a family of wealthy merchants. I was on my way to Naples to be married when my vessel was captured. After the corsair captain had taken his pleasure of me, he gave me to the dey, who beheaded him for violating me. Women captives are not supposed to be mistreated."

"I am Moorish," Leah said. "My family was poor, and sold me into slavery so they might survive. I had two masters before I came to the dey's harem last year."

"I am of Syrian birth," Samara said curtly.

India did not press Samara further, for she obviously did not wish to speak on her origins in detail for whatever reason. "It seemed so strange here at first," she said, "but now this is home. Did you all feel that way, too?"

The other girls nodded.

"Most of us were born free," Sarai said. "Being a slave, even a privileged slave, is difficult at first. You have done well to win our lord Caynan's heart and in such a short time, when none of the others of us could do it. He has always been kind, but he merely slakes his lusts upon our bodies. You have gained something more, my lady India, and we are frankly envious of you."

India blushed, not knowing what to say.

"But we are safe and comfortable," Mirmah spoke up, "and we shall all be friends. I was born on a slave farm, and raised to be a harem woman. It is better when the women of the harem get on, my lady India. My first master was Aruj Agha, who purchased me in the great market of Istanbul. One evening when the dey came to Aruj Agha's house for a meal, he saw me, and admired me. Aruj Agha had me delivered to the palace the next morning. I like it here. Aruj Agha had no other women, for he could not afford them. It was lonely waiting for him to return from his voyages. I am glad we have each other, and I am happy that our lord Caynan has found a wife."

Her sweet nature touched India, and, reaching out, she took Mirmah's hand and Sarai's hand in hers, saying, "I agree with Mirmah. We should all be friends, and keep peace in our lord's house. I promise you that I will be a good mistress to you."

"Allah!" Samara exclaimed. "I do not know if it is the cakes or the atmosphere, but I think I am going to be sick from all this sweetness."

India burst out laughing. "You remind me of my sister, Fortune, Samara," she said. "She says exactly what she is thinking, too."

Samara was surprised by India's reaction. She had expected the dey's bride to be offended, but here she was making light of Samara's rudeness. "Did you really take a knife to the dey when you arrived?" she asked India, frankly curious to know if the stories had been only rumor.

"I did," India admitted. "It is fortunate my aim was so poor, as I now love him." she chuckled.

"Allah! You are daring," Samara said with grudging admiration.

"I was not taught to fear," India replied quietly.

"How will you feel if our lord takes a second wife?" Sarai asked India frankly.

"Jealous," India responded candidly, "but I shall have to live with it." She paused. *"If he takes a second wife,"* she concluded.

The other women laughed.

"I suppose it is best to leave everything as it is now," Samara said thoughtfully. "One wife, and a harem. It would appear that we can all get along if we try, and we are content as things are."

The others murmured in agreement, and Azura, watching from behind a screen, was extremely pleased that India had taken her counsel, making her peace with the women of the harem. *She is an intelligent young woman,* the mistress of the harem considered. *She can be influenced if she is approached correctly. El Sinut will be kept safe from the machinations of the janissaries. I am certain of it now.* She turned her attentions back to the young women seated about India and listened with great interest, for they had somehow managed to turn the conversation to matters of a sensual nature.

India, blushing at their teasing, was clever enough to admit that she knew absolutely nothing about lovemaking other than what the dey had introduced her to the previous night. "I am so ignorant," she said. "I know it is audacious of me to ask your help in such matters, but I would please our master."

How ingenious of her, Azura thought admiringly. If nothing else, her very artlessness will win them all over. Even Samara. It is deftly done, particularly calling Caynan Reis our master, and not her husband. By not lording it over them she made herself one of them. It was skillful, and wickedly adroit of India. Azura considered the dey's wife might turn out to be far more than they had anticipated.

The mistress of the harem turned her attention back to the seven women and India, listening with great amusement as they all began talking at once, for each was certain she could teach India how to please the dey better than any of the others. Azura remained to be certain none of the other women misled the bride, but they obviously did not consider it, being far too interested in imparting their own knowledge to her. The older woman shook her head wonderingly. Everything was going even better than she had hoped. Baba Hassan would be equally pleased when she told him. It was simply perfect!

Chapter

12

The chief eunuch bustled into the harem, and, going to India, bowed politely. "My lady, your husband wishes your presence."

India arose at once. "I shall never remember *everything*," she said with a small laugh. "May I come back tomorrow?"

"Yes!" they chorused, and sent her on her way.

"Well," Samara said as the harem doors closed behind the dey's wife. "I have to admit she *is* likable. Or so it would seem. Prepare yourselves for a drought ladies. He will not grow tired of her for some time, and we, fools as we are, are helping her to retain his attentions!"

"She will be with child the sooner," Nila chuckled, "and then the dey will seek us out for his pleasure and amusement."

"Why should she have a child when none of us have?" Leah asked.

"Foolish one," Mirmah told her. "We are fed something in either our food or drink to keep us infertile. It is common practice in the harems of Istanbul. Did none of you know that? The lady India, however, will be given no such cordial. Indeed, she will be fed all manner of delicacies, as will the dey, to encourage them to produce a child. It will be nice to have a baby among us."

"If she does not cease her cheerful, mindless prattle," Samara muttered darkly to Sarai, "I may throttle our little golden bird."

India, meanwhile, followed Baba Hassan back to her own quarters. As they entered the apartment, a young girl came forward, and bowed low.

"On the dey's instructions I have been searching the slave markets these last few weeks, my lady, for a girl who could speak your native tongue and had a modicum of intelligence so you would have someone to serve you in whom you could put your trust," the eunuch said. "I found this wench almost a month ago, and have endeavored to train her properly. If she pleases you, she is yours."

India turned and smiled at the girl. She looked very young, and her gray eyes were quite apprehensive. She was slight of build and had carrot-colored hair that was quite startling in its brightness. "What is your name?" India asked the girl in English.

"Margaret, lady, though I be called Meggie," the girl replied.

"You are English?"

"Nay, lady, I be Scots," Meggie said.

"Ahhh." India smiled. "I thought the accent not quite right. I am the stepdaughter of the duke of Glenkirk, Meggie. I grew up north and west of Aberdeen. Where are you from?"

"Ayr, my lady, where the laddies are braw, and the lassies are bonnie, 'tis said," Meggie told her new mistress.

India turned to Baba Hassan. "The girl will do excellently. You have chosen well, Baba Hassan, but then, I would have expected no less of you. She is not however, English, but a Scot. As I was raised in Scotland, I am comfortable with her. Now, where is the dey?"

"He dines tonight with Aruj Agha, who has this afternoon returned from his voyage. He will come to you afterward, my lady."

"Is my cousin, Osman the Navigator, with Aruj Agha? I would inquire after his health, Baba Hassan," India said.

"I will see, and then bring you word, my lady." He bowed himself from her chambers.

"Come," India said, leading Meggie to a divan. "Tell me how you came to be in El Sinut?"

"My da is a sea captain, my lady," Meggie said. "I was always begging him to take me on a voyage like he did me ma when they was young. So as I was to be married to Ian Murray this coming summer before the clans gather, Da said he would take me to Bordeaux where he was to pick up a cargo of wine. We was attacked in the Bay of Biscay." The girl's eyes grew teary. "Me da was killed right before me eyes, lady. Sliced right through him, they did! Me and the sailors that survived was carried off. I was nae harmed, though. Indeed, they was most careful of my well-being." Then a rush of tears slid down her freckled face. "Now my Ian will marry that smug Flora MacLean, who's always been after him like a cat wi a bird."

"Aye, he probably will, lassie," India said bluntly, "and there is little you can do about it, I fear. Women are rarely, if ever, ransomed from Barbary, and, besides, who would there be to claim you? You are fortunate, Meggie, that the chief eunuch of the dey's household purchased you. You might have been sold to a cruel master or mistress, or, worse, into a brothel. You will be safe with me, and as the dey's first wife, you will have a position of status among the servants."

Meggie wiped her tears with the back of her hand, and, giving a final sniffle, said, "I'll be faithful to ye, my lady, I promise."

"I know you will," India reassured the girl. "Do you know your way to the kitchen?"

"Aye, my lady."

"Then go to Abu, the cook, and tell him that I desire my supper. Bring it back, and I shall eat in the garden. My husband is dining with an old friend."

"Very good, my lady," Meggie said, and hurried off.

Baba Hassan returned to tell India that her cousin was not with Aruj Agha, but had remained aboard their ship. "He has proved himself worthy of trust, my lady, and will soon begin to teach our sailors how to manage his round ship. We have captured two more in the last few months, one from the French, and another from the Dutch. Is the girl satisfactory, my lady? She cannot seem to learn our language, but had enough French that I was able to guide her. She seems willing enough."

"She saw her father killed when their ship was attacked," India told the eunuch. "He was the captain, and she was to be married soon. She is just getting over the shock of it all. If she is not stupid, I'll try to teach her the language. At least enough to get about. She will, I believe, be a good companion for me. Thank you, but tell me, Baba Hassan. You say you purchased her for me over a month ago. I was still the dey's body slave then."

"But you were falling in love with him, my lady, and he with you. I could see it and Azura, too. I knew it to be a matter of time until you succumbed to his passions. You are young, and you are beautiful, and the juices of life flow deep within you. If I had waited until today to seek out a suitable servant for you, I might not have found one for months."

India laughed. "You are a clever man, Baba Hassan. I believe the dey is fortunate to have you looking after his best interests so carefully. I am glad you and Azura are my friends."

"Lady," the chief eunuch said, "I know this is your wedding day, but may I speak with you seriously for a moment?"

India nodded.

"I must ask you to say nothing to your husband about the matter I am bringing to your attention. It is in your husband's best interests, I assure you."

India was intrigued. "I will keep your confidence, Baba Hassan."

"I have many contacts throughout the sultan's realm, my lady. It was brought to my attention several months ago that a plot was afoot in Istanbul to assassinate the sultan and his mother, the valideh. The instigators of this perfidy are the janissaries. Already they have dispatched an agent to the Barbary States. This man will seek to gain the Barbary rulers as allies, promising them freedom to rule without answering to the Sublime Porte, *and* freedom from tribute. It is a generous offer, but I do not believe this plot can prevail. Those who associate themselves with this treason risk death. The janissaries will be forgiven after some punishment. They always are because they are strong. Anyone else involved will not be forgiven, for an example must be made. El Sinut is the smallest of the Barbary States. It is possible we may not be approached, but if we are, Azura and I will need your aid in dissuading the dey from throwing his lot in with the conspirators. Remember, Aruj Agha is his closest friend, and Aruj Agha will be loyal to the corps first even if he disagrees with them. He cannot, will not, betray his fellow janissaries."

"If I were the valideh," India said, "I should punish the janissaries in the Barbary States. They are the least important men in the corps, yet, as janissaries, can be held liable for the betrayals of their fellows in Istanbul without really offending those traitors. I would punish the rulers of the Barbary States, and set men loyal to me in their place. Is that not right, Baba Hassan?"

"That is precisely what the valideh will do, my lady. How astute you are to see it all so quickly and clearly," he told her.

"If my husband is approached," India said, "I will help you and Azura to foil any plots against El Sinut. In the meantime, I will remain silent, for why should Caynan Reis be distressed by that which may not even happen. How will you discourage the agent of the janissaries?"

"If he comes here first, the dey will be advised to tell him to go to the other deys in Tunis, and Algiers, and Morocco, and then return to El Sinut. Caynan Reis will say, as the smallest of the Barbary States, he is the most vulnerable and must be certain the bigger states will involve themselves first before he commits El Sinut. If the agent comes to us last we will simply kill him so he may not return to Istanbul, but we will send his head to the valideh, telling her of the plots to dethrone her son, and that we did not betray the sultan."

"Why not kill him if he comes here first?" India inquired.

"Because if he goes to the others, and they are willing to betray the sultan, and we are not, Caynan Reis looks the better for it. Perhaps the sultan and his mother will reward him in some grand manner, my lady."

"And Aruj Agha? What of him?"

"He will not know until after the agent is disposed of, my lady. We can keep his loyalty and his friendship if we do not ask him to divide those qualities within him," the eunuch answered her.

"I can see that I have much to learn from you, Baba Hassan," India replied quietly.

He bowed low to her, smiling. "I am honored that you think so, my lady India," he responded.

Meggie now returned, struggling beneath the weight of a tray. Staggering across the day room, she placed it with a clunk upon the cedar table. "Abu wasn't certain what would please my lady's palate," she said dryly, "and so he has sent almost everything in the kitchen."

"I will leave you to your meal, my lady," Baba Hassan said, and he withdrew.

India walked over to the table, and began inspecting the foods the cook had sent her. There was chicken, a bowl of what appeared to be lamb stew, saffroned rice, steamed artichokes, a bowl of yogurt with peeled green grapes, flat bread, a honeycomb, a bowl of oranges, figs, a pomegranate and bunch of grapes, and a decanter of fresh sherbet.

"You will eat with me tonight, Meggie," India said.

"Shall I fill your plate, my lady?" the girl asked.

India shook her head. "I will do it," she replied, and cut herself several slices of the roasted chicken, which she lay upon her plate along with some saffroned rice and an artichoke.

When the servant saw her mistress was content, she spooned some of the lamb mixture onto her plate, and tore a piece of the flat bread off the round for herself.

"Is it good?" India asked her.

"Aye! 'Tis certainly flavored better than my mam's," Meggie admitted, "and 'tis true lamb, not mutton, I'm thinking."

India took her spoon, and lifted a chunk of the meat from its gravy. "It is good," she agreed. "Try some chicken. Abu has flavored it with onion and sage, I believe."

The two young women finished off their meal with the yogurt and the fruit. Meggie poured them both some of the tart-sweet sherbet to drink, and when it was consumed, she gathered all the dishes up, and returned them to the kitchen.

When she returned, she asked India, "Where am I to sleep, my lady?"

"That small cubicle is yours," India told her, pointing across the day room. "Make certain there is a pallet for you there, and then come and help me prepare for bed. As my husband is entertaining, I do not imagine he will call for me this evening."

Meggie undressed her mistress, and sponged her with rose water. Then India slid naked beneath the silk coverlet upon her bed, bidding her new servant good night. What a day it had been, she thought! Since this time last night she had lost her virginity, and had gotten married. Now the stories of her female relations' adventures began to surface in her consciousness. She had always listened with but half an ear when they were told. It had been Fortune who had been fascinated by these tales. India had always thought them a little shocking, and perhaps not really true. Just made up adventures to amuse. Now she wasn't certain.

There had been her stepfather's great-great grandmother, Janet Leslie, whose portrait hung in the Great Hall at Glenkirk Castle. She, it was said, had been the favorite wife of a Turkish sultan. And, of course, her own great-grandmother, the fabled Skye O'Malley, who had lived in Algiers as both a wife and a harem slave. And Great-aunt Aidan, who had at one time been wife to a Tartar prince, and held captive in a sultan's harem. And Aunt Valentina, who had been kidnapped, and held in a pasha's harem, the very same pasha who had once enslaved her stepfather's mother, the beautiful Lady Stewart-Hepburn. And, of course, her own grandmother, Velvet Gordon, who had been fortieth wife to the great Mughal ruler, Akbar of India.

It would seem she was following a family tradition, India considered wryly. The only difference was that all those women had eventually been able to make their way home. A tear slid down India's cheek. For the first time since her capture, a great feeling of homesickness overwhelmed her. Until recently, she had not dared to exhibit an ounce of weakness. Now, however, she could not help herself. She wanted desperately to see Mama and Papa, and Fortune and Henry, and the rest of their siblings. Had they cried when news of her capture came? Did they even know? Or had they assumed she had run off with Adrian Leigh, and was now his wife, and would eventually return? Did they even miss her, or had they washed their hands of her, taking Fortune off to Ireland to find her a husband? Fortune, who had thought it very practical that their parents find her a husband. *Will they ever know what happened to me?* India wondered. And she sobbed softly.

Caynan Reis had entered his wife's bedchamber quietly, and now, hearing the sound of her weeping, he hurried to her side. "What is it, my precious?" he asked, joining her upon her bed, and gathering her into his arms. "What has made you sad?"

"I . . .I m-miss m-my family!" India wailed.

"Ahhh," he said, understanding her complaint. He held her close, and smoothed her curls soothingly.

"T-they don't know wh-where I am!"

"Give me a child so no one can steal you away from me, my precious India, and I promise you that you may write to your mother," the dey told her. "I have told you that I love you, and it is the truth. I could not bear it if some misguided parent took you from me."

"I . . . I love you, too!" India told him. "But I want my family to know of, and share in our happiness, my lord Caynan."

"In time," he vowed to her, and then he was kissing her passionately. "You are mine, my beloved, and I shall allow no one to take you back!"

Almost immediately she was swept away by his hungry devotion. All thoughts of her past life disappeared as his burning desire overwhelmed her. She loved, and was loved in return. There could be nothing more wonderful than that! "Ohhh, my lord," she murmured against his lips, "I do adore you!" Her hand caressed his shoulder gently. "I am content to be with you. Let me show you what the harem women taught me this afternoon when I visited them. Tell me if it pleases you."

To his great surprise she slipped from his embrace, and rolled him onto his back. Then she straddled him, and began letting her hands roam across his smooth chest. Shy at first, she grew bolder, taking his nipples between her thumb and forefinger, and rubbing them teasingly. He was about to reach up and take her tempting little breasts in his own hands when she leaned forward, and began kissing his chest, then licked at it seductively with her tongue. Slowly, carefully she moved down his torso, her dark curls brushing his smooth skin seductively. He was scarcely breathing for fear of deferring her progress, wondering how far she would go, and then her hand closed about his manhood.

Her fingers tightened about him briefly while her other hand brushed over his thighs, pushing between them to cup his jewels in the warmth of her palm. India bent lower, astounded by her own daring, but unable to cease her erotic actions. It had all sounded so wicked when the harem ladies elucidated upon it, but now, caught in the throes of her own rising desire, she knew she must continue onward. She squeezed him gently once again. He grew thicker and longer beneath her sensorial ministrations. Her head dropped, and she kissed the ruby-red tip of his manhood, then licked all around it.

He shuddered with the voluptuousness of her behavior, gasping softly as she enveloped him within her mouth and began to suck upon his throbbing member. Tongue and teeth teased at him, causing his whole body to quiver with excitement. Then a single finger reached beneath his pouch, pressing into a spot so sensitive that his whole frame arced with pleasure, and he groaned with sheer delight. "Ohhh, sweet witch, they have taught you well! *Ahhhhhh!* Enough! *Enough!*"

India released him, and looked sloe-eyed upon Caynan Reis. "I do not please you?" she asked innocently.

"You please me, my precious, and you kill me, too, with your skill." He pulled her forward, and, lifting her, said, "Come now and mount me, my beloved. I would encase my weapon within your pleasure sheath."

Now it was India who gasped as she felt him sliding into her eager body. Her eyes closed, her back arched, and instinctively she rode him until his lusts burst within her and she fell forward upon his chest, whimpering with her own pleasure. He maintained the union, gently rolling her onto her back so that it was he who was now the dominant one. His kisses covered her face, and India sighed deeply as she slowly, and most reluctantly, returned to earth.

"I shall reward the ladies who encouraged and developed your skills," he told her, smiling into her eyes.

Now India blushed, realizing what she had done. "I was bold," she said softly, touching his face with her hand.

"Very bold," he agreed affably. "I hope you will continue in your daring, India. I gained great pleasure from it." He slowly kissed her, thinking as he did that she had the most kissable mouth he had ever known. Nibbling upon her lower lip he told her so.

"I like kissing you," she admitted.

"Are my kisses sweeter than your English milord?" he demanded.

"Aye," she told him, realizing as she did that it was the truth. "I did not kiss him a great deal," she admitted candidly, "but I do not believe he had your skill, my lord Caynan."

"Perhaps I shall ransom him," the dey said.

"It would be kind," India agreed. "If he has survived these past months in the galleys, surely that is enough punishment for his rudeness toward you, my lord. His father is old, and sickly, and he is his mother's only child."

"Did you ever meet his parents?" the dey asked her.

India shook her head. "His father remained at his home in the country. He has not left it, I am told, since his elder son killed Lord Jeffers and then fled the country. As for his mother, even poor Adrian admitted the woman was little better than a bawd. He avoided her as much as he could. As I am certain she would have wanted her son's marriage to me to take place, she wisely avoided both my family and me. My parents were taking me back to Scotland to get me away from Adrian when I eloped."

He nuzzled her neck, his kisses sending shivers down her spine. "Did you really intend to wed him, or were you having second thoughts?" he gently pressured India.

It was so hard to think when his body pressed hers so closely and his lips did such delicious things to her senses. "I didn't like running away," she admitted. "It seemed so precipitous, but Papa was so obdurate in his opposition to Adrian. Now, I think, that might have had more to do with encouraging my hasty actions than any love I felt for Adrian. I realized as we traveled that while the adventure was exciting, perhaps we were being dishonest. I should have not allowed Adrian to push me to such an abrupt act. I have only hurt those I love best," India concluded.

"But had you not run away, I should not have made you mine," he murmured softly, his tongue pushing into her ear to tease it.

"No," she whispered. "Ahhhh, my lord, you are growing hard inside me!" She trembled against him. "How can this be?"

"Be quiet, little fool, and let me love you," he growled at her. "You arouse me as no female ever has." He began to move upon her.

Oh, God! This love was so powerful a thing, India thought, as she felt his length begin to slowly piston her afresh. Her eyes closed once more, and her breathing became shallow as he pleasured her a second time. She could actually feel him within her. Hard, and throbbing with heat. If she had only known, India considered muzzily, she never should have resisted him for so long. She felt so safe in his arms. She trusted him entirely, although she didn't understand why. She soared with the waves of hot delight beginning to wash over her as he moved within her fevered body.

"I love you," he whispered into her ear. "You are my precious one; my adorable and adored wife, India. I worship you with my body."

"I love you, my lord Caynan," she murmured back. "I have never known such happiness as I know now in your arms. Give me your son, my dearest lord. *Give me your son!*"

Their deep passion finally overcame them as they fell from the peak together. They tumbled into sleep, limbs tangled, breathing even, she curled against him, his arm protectively over her in a sweetly possessive gesture; and they slept until almost dawn when the dey awoke.

He looked at the girl lying against his chest. *Give me your son,* she had cried out to him in her ardor. Allah, he had emptied himself twice that night into the recesses of her secret garden. He very much wanted to grant her request of him. For the first time in his life he knew he did indeed want children. He had not wanted them with other women, and none of his harem women had ever made such a demand of him. He sighed.

If this had been England he would have offered properly for Lady India Lindley and not rested until she was his wife. Their first son would have been a future earl of Oxton. But this was not England; this was El Sinut, and his first son would be in constant danger from outside forces because his father was the dey. Still, if he could get the sultan to grant him his office in perpetuity, the child would be his heir. He must do the sultan some great service while the boy was yet young, or yet unborn. The valideh was known to dote on her lad and would be generous, Caynan Reis had not a doubt.

It was not such an unusual request. Deyships had been created in the past that continued forever, provided the family was loyal. He smiled in the dusk of predawn. He did not even know if his efforts had made his young wife fruitful. He must continue to labor until she showed the signs of being with child. It was not a difficult assignment.

Caynan Reis suddenly realized he was the happiest of men. A month passed, and then two. Aruj Agha had left the morning following the dey's marriage for another voyage. Now he had returned, and would be in port for some weeks seeing to much-needed repairs on his vessel. His English navigator, Osman, would be working with a crew made up of both Europeans and citizens of El Sinut on his former vessel, teaching the Arabs how to sail and man such a complicated ship. They went no farther than the outer harbor for the present as the Europeans were in a distinct minority aboard the *Royal Charles,* now renamed, the *Sultan Murat.*

"I have never known you to be so content," the janissary captain teased his friend one day as they shared Turkish coffee and the water pipe. "I would not have thought Caynan Reis vulnerable to love."

"All men are susceptible to love," the dey told him with an easy laugh. "Even Aruj Agha. One day you will find the right woman, my friend."

"Once there was a woman I loved," came the surprising admission, "but it was not to be. Besides, in my position, a wife is a liability. In earlier times, in the days of Sultan Selim I and his son, Suleiman, janissaries were not allowed to wed. It was better that way, I think. A man who worries about his wife and offspring is too cautious in battle. Caution does not win victories. Wars are won by those who are unafraid of what they might lose. Those who do not fear death. A man with a wife worries as to her fate if he dies. I am better without a mate."

"Do you not want sons?" the dey asked him.

"I'm certain I've fathered a few in my time, although I cannot be really certain," Aruj Agha said genially.

The chief eunuch entered the chamber, bowing to his master. "There is a visitor from Istanbul to see you, my lord," he said.

"Can it not wait until the general audience tomorrow, Baba Hassan?" Caynan Reis asked.

"I fear not, my lord," the chief eunuch replied.

"I will leave you, my friend," Aruj Agha said.

"Nay," Caynan Reis told him. "You are the captain of the janissaries here in El Sinut. A visitor from Istanbul who would speak privily with me should be heard by you as well. I trust few men as I trust you. Show the man in, Baba Hassan. I will receive him now."

The eunuch bowed, his face offering no emotion. A moment later, he returned with a tall, obviously battled-hardened man with the enormous mustachios of a traditional janissary, who made immediate and respectful obeisance to the dey.

Caynan Reis acknowledged the gesture, and said, "Speak."

"My lord, you have a guest. What I have to say is for your ears alone," his visitor said.

"This is Aruj Agha, captain of the janissaries here. Whatever you have to say to me can be said before him," the dey replied.

"You support the janissaries then, my lord?" came the question.

"I support *all* who wish our lord, Sultan Murat, may he live a thousand years, well, and serve to keep his peace," was the clever reply.

His visitor smiled. "I bring you greetings, my lord dey, from the court of the janissaries. I am Hussein Aga of the corps. The matter I have come to discuss is a delicate one. Do I have your word you will not repeat to any what is spoken here this day?"

Caynan Reis nodded. "Speak," he said.

"My lord, the sultan is young. A mere boy who will not rule for himself for several years to come. We are governed by a woman, the valideh. Such a thing is not to be tolerated. Her influence must be purged from the palace, from the empire."

"And how is this to be done?" the dey asked dryly. "Will you murder this woman, and then rule for the sultan in her place?"

"It is more complex than that, my lord. Sultan Murat loves his mother well. He cannot really be separated from her. It is better that he not rule any longer, but rather be disposed of with his parent."

The dey stroked his chin thoughtfully. "And who would you place upon the throne of the Ottoman, Hussein Aga? One of the poor incompetent elderly princes who has been housed a lifetime in the Cage? The advantage of this sultan is that he has not been in the Cage long enough to be spoiled, or go mad. Who will you put in his stead?"

"There are two younger brothers," was the immediate reply.

"You would have to murder one of those children, too, lest someone else, some other faction, use that boy in yet another revolt," the dey said in practical tones. "I suppose you could kill the next eldest, and place an infant upon the throne, thereby guaranteeing the janissaries a long rule, eh? How old is the youngest? Four? Five?"

"Such matters are for the corps to decide," Hussein Aga said stiffly.

"Why come to me then?" Caynan Reis demanded. "I am the dey of the smallest of the Barbary States. I have no power other than that given me by the sultan, and it does not extend beyond my borders. What do you want of me, Hussein Aga?"

"Your support in this matter," the agent of the janissaries replied. "Give us your loyalty. We will make you autonomous in El Sinut. You will be freed from tribute in perpetuity. Would you not like your son to inherit this little kingdom of yours?"

"I have no son," the dey said quietly.

"But you are a young man, and you could have sons. When El Sinut is yours, you can free your harem women from the draught they are fed to keep them sterile. You might be the patriarch of many in time, my lord dey," Hussein Aga tempted him. Then he smiled, reminding Caynan Reis of a ferret he had possessed as a boy.

"Have you spoken to the deys of the larger states?" Caynan Reis asked his visitor.

"You are the first, my lord," was the response.

Again the dey stroked his elegant, short barbered black beard as if he were giving great consideration to Hussein Aga's words. Then he spoke once again. "As the smallest kingdom, I have more to lose than the others, Hussein Aga. What if I agree to join you in your revolt, and the others do not? Both Algiers and Tunis have been seeking to annex El Sinut for years. I have recently taken a wife. I would not see her widowed and given to another man because I did not show caution. No. I will only consider joining you if the others agree first. If you fail, an example will be made. El Sinut might be considered expendable by Istanbul. I must protect my people. Understand, I care not who rules the empire as long as I am left in peace to do my duty to that ruler and oversee the well-being of El Sinut. I am not saying I will not join you, just that I would be reassured my more powerful and wealthier neighbors will be part of your scheme. When you can bring me that assurance, then I will give you my answer, Hussein Aga. The mouse is wise to look to the cat, eh?" Caynan Reis smiled in friendly fashion.

"I appreciate your candor, my lord dey, and I perfectly understand your position," was the silky reply. "I shall leave tomorrow for Algiers, Tunis, and Morocco."

"But tonight," the dey said genially, "I insist that you be my guest." He clapped his hands, and Baba Hassan was by his side.

"My lord?"

"Have Abu kill a lamb, and make a feast for our noble guest, Baba Hassan." The dey turned to the janissary. "You will stay with us, of course, in the janissary barracks here within the palace walls?"

Hussein Aga bowed his acceptance.

"Aruj Agha, my friend, take our visitor to the baths, and see he is made comfortable. Baba Hassan will provide you with fresh clothing for this evening, and see that your travel-worn garments are cleaned and freshened for your departure tomorrow," Caynan Reis said jovially.

Again the agent from Istanbul bowed. "You are a gracious host, my lord dey. I shall remember it."

The two janissaries left the dey's private chamber escorted by the chief eunuch. Caynan Reis sat alone contemplating what had just transpired. The ever-resourceful Baba Hassan had told him but two days ago of the impending arrival of this agent. The chief eunuch had built up over the years an invaluable network of informants that stretched all the way from El Sinut to Istanbul; from Algiers to Damascus. Whatever was important, Baba Hassan knew in advance. *The eunuch was a man of great talents, and deserved a larger venue, but I am glad he is mine,* Caynan Reis thought.

When he had learned of the plot against the sultan he had spoken of it to India as they lay together, sated with their passion. She had been circumspect in her counsel, advising him to prudence and asking, "Has this young sultan been a bad sultan, my lord?" The dey had told his wife that their boy overlord was ruled by his mother, who so far had proven wise in her judgments and recommendations. The empire was calm and prosperous right now.

"I would avoid committing myself, my lord Caynan," India said. "I think it dangerous, and has any revolt ever executed by the janissaries succeeded? Avoid giving your loyalty to these traitors."

He had agreed with her, and told both Azura and his chief eunuch that he thought his wife very wise for one so young and beautiful.

Now, however, he realized upon consideration that he had been offered an opportunity to gain the right to have his firstborn son inherit El Sinut one day. If he could reveal the plot against the sultan to the valideh before it could be enacted, would not the sultan's mother be grateful? Caynan Reis smiled, well pleased.

Chapter 13

"I do not like Caynan Reis," Hussein Aga said to Aruj Agha as they lounged in the heated bathing pool. He spoke Turkish.

"Why?" the younger janissary captain asked the visitor from Istanbul. "He is a good public servant, and very loyal." He answered his superior in Turkish, the language he had learned as a child, the language of the corps of janissaries.

"He is too clever by far, telling me to go to the other deys and then return to him. I do not trust him. He does not mean to support us. Those who do not support us are our enemies."

Slaves bustled about the two men in the bath, preparing the massage benches for the bathers, bringing heated towels for them.

"It is his way to be cautious," Aruj Agha defended Caynan Reis. "I have known him for ten years now. Not once have I known him to act dishonorably. What you have offered him—freedom from tribute, El Sinut for himself and his heirs—is an irresistible temptation. He has, only several months ago, taken his first wife. He will want the security you offer for his sons, but his is a little state. For years, his larger neighbors have hovered like vultures in the desert, seeking to annex El Sinut for themselves. It makes Caynan Reis a careful man."

"Why in Allah's name would anyone want this remote piece of earth," Hussein Aga demanded scathingly.

"El Sinut has the finest deep-water harbor along the Barbary coast. That is why our tribute to Istanbul has surpassed that of Algiers and Tunis. And beyond the city are date orchards whose harvests exceed any in the region. The dates are plumper and sweeter than others. It is the soil, I am told. And we have salt mines, as well as a famous mineral spring at the Star Oasis where the wealthy from all over the east—even from as far as Damascus—come to be cured," Aruj Agha said.

"I was not aware of how prosperous an area this is," Hussein Aga replied more thoughtfully. "Perhaps you are right, and I am seeing *jiins* where there are none. Certainly your friendship with this petty dey is not to be discounted. I was impressed that he insisted you remain when I asked to speak to him alone. It shows a certain respect for the corps of janissaries."

"He has always worked with us, Hussein Aga, and, frankly, he has been more than generous with the wealth we collect on our voyages. Are you aware that he even sends one ship of tribute to the corps each year, and has since he succeeded the previous dey, Sharif."

"That is why I was sent here first," Hussein Aga said. "It was believed Caynan Reis was a friend to us who could be trusted."

"He can be!" the younger man swore. "I would stake my own life upon it. Certainly you now understand his discretion."

"I will accept your word in this matter," Hussein Aga replied. "I know you for an honorable man. I remember you as a boy in the prince's school, and I know your uncle, who is one of our leaders. But remember, Aruj Agha. If this dey betrays us in any way, it will be your duty to kill him. You do understand that, don't you?"

"I hear, and obey," was the simple reply.

"Good! Good! Now, do you think you can find me a pretty girl to make my evening complete. Surely a young man as yourself knows a number of pretty girls," the older janissary chuckled.

"She will be eagerly waiting for you in your quarters after we have dined with the dey this evening," Aruj Agha said with a smile.

The two men exited the bathing pool to be enveloped in warm towels by the bath slaves. They were dried and massaged, and then dressed in clean clothing. Together they departed the baths to stroll in the palace's public gardens before the evening meal was to be served.

Baba Hassan watched them briefly from his high window, and then turned to receive the mistress of the baths. "You have information for me, Oma?"

"Not I, my lord, but Refet." She drew forward a slight young girl, who had been almost hidden behind the bath mistress.

"Speak then, my child," Baba Hassan said in kindly tones to Refet, who looked half terrified to be in the august presence of the chief eunuch of the dey's palace.

"I am Turkish," the girl began. "The two janissaries spoke in that tongue, for it is their natural language. The older one does not trust the dey because he will not give him an allegiance, but Aruj Agha swore the dey could be trusted, thereby soothing the other man's fears. Nonetheless, the visitor told Aruj Agha that if the dey betrays them, Aruj Agha must kill the dey. He agreed. Then the older man asked for a woman for his bed tonight. That is all, sir."

"Thank you," Baba Hassan said, and dismissed the two from his presence. Then he sat down to consider what he would do. Of course the woman who pleasured their visitor must be carefully chosen. As the dey was little interested in his harem currently, perhaps he would allow two of his own women to entertain the two janissaries. India, of course, could not be part of the evening, but Samara would be happy to be at the dey's side. And sweet Mirmah, who had once belonged to Aruj Agha, would be his again for this night. The passionate flame-haired Sarai would certainly please Hussein Aga. Who knew what information the clever Sarai might extract from this man in the throes of passion.

Baba Hassan arose, and went to his master. The dey was with his wife, and it was obvious they had recently made love. The chief eunuch bowed low, hiding a smile. Then he told the dey what the bath attendant had overheard and the plan he had devised for the evening. "It is better, my lord, that the two women with the janissaries be those we can trust. If, however, you do not choose to share these two women from your own harem, then I shall send for two skilled courtesans from the town who I know are loyal."

Caynan Reis laughed softly, and his eyes twinkled as he said, "Nay, Baba Hassan, my poor ladies have been most neglected of late, as I seem to be otherwise occupied with my beautiful wife. Send my own women, and let Hussein Aga believe I have honored him."

"But why must Samara take my place by my husband's side?" India demanded. "Would it not also do honor to our visitor from Istanbul that the dey's wife ate with him?"

"If this were an ordinary evening, my lady," Baba Hassan told her, "I should not have suggested Samara accompany our lord, but this is a dangerous situation. Outside of the palace, few know your face. It is better for you to be invisible to this man from Istanbul."

"I agree," the dey replied, "especially in light of the news my wife has given me this very afternoon."

"*My lord!*" Baba Hassan's face broke wide with his smile. "Is there to be a child? Ahhhh! This is what we have all prayed for, my lord dey!" He turned to India. "May Allah rain blessings upon you, my lady India! May I tell Azura?"

India laughed happily. "I am not entirely certain, never having had a child, but as the eldest of my mother's children, I believe I recognize the signs. Yes, Baba Hassan, you may tell Azura, and the ladies as well, for it will give them some hope of entertaining my husband again. It might also take the sting from my choosing only three of the seven this evening to entertain the janissaries. If it were I doing the deciding, however, Baba Hassan, I should give this agent of the janissaries two ladies to amuse himself with, for he will surely suspect if only one is sent that she is a spy. Two, though, bespeaks the dey's generosity. I do not believe a fool would have been dispatched upon such a delicate mission. Why not give him Nila as well as Sarai? He will be so overwhelmed with their voluptuous pulchritude, he will not have time to consider anything other than how to gain the most pleasure from those two beauties."

"You plot like a valideh," the chief eunuch said admiringly. "With my lord's permission it shall be done, my lady India."

"Do as my wife suggests," the dey agreed. "Is she not clever, Baba Hassan? What sons I shall have of her!"

"It might just as easily be a daughter," India replied. "My mother had me before my brother, Henry."

"A daughter would please me, too, as long as she is as beautiful as her mother," the dey declared gallantly, and, catching up India's hand, he kissed it passionately. "However, I hope this first child will be a son, my precious, not just for me, but for El Sinut."

"Mama has five sons," India told him with the hint of a smile. Then she said, "You must be prepared for your evening, my lord. A bath, I think, for the day has been hot. If that vixen, Samara, attempts to seduce you, though, I shall have her bow-strung!"

Baba Hassan withdrew chuckling, and made his way to Azura's apartments where he shared the happy news that India was with child.

"Praise Allah!" Azura said, clapping her hands together. Then she smiled at the chief eunuch. "We have been so fortunate, Baba Hassan, haven't we? India is the perfect first wife for Caynan Reis."

"Now, let me tell you the rest," he replied, and went on to explain the decisions that had been made regarding the harem ladies.

"I will instruct Sarai and Nila myself," Azura said when he had finished. "Mirmah will be told only to keep Aruj Agha content. I think she retains a weakness for him yet, despite the fact she has been in the dey's household for several years. As for Samara, you must deal with her yourself. I lose my patience with her, Baba Hassan, *and* she will not be pleased that her evening is to end when the dey withdraws for the night."

"I know how to handle her," the chief eunuch replied with a smile. "As long as her dignity is not trampled, she will obey."

The two janissaries arrived in the dey's dining chamber to be greeted by Mirmah, Nila, Sarai, and Samara, richly appareled in fragrant silks, their faces quite visible beneath diaphanous veils. The dey appeared immediately thereafter, smiling and gracious. He beckoned Samara to his side on the cushions. Aruj Agha, recognizing

Mirmah, who sweetly snuggled against him, realized that these two women were from the dey's own harem, and was surprised.

"I considered that perhaps you would enjoy female company this night, Hussein Aga," the dey said. "These women are from my own household," he confirmed. "The flame-haired beauty on your right is called Sarai. She is extremely skilled in a variety of exotic arts. The golden-haired girl on your left is my own Nila. She is tireless, and will give you exquisite pleasure. My sweet Mirmah is Aruj Agha's companion. He gave her to me several years ago, and I thought he might enjoy her company again."

Hussein Aga was almost speechless. The two women sent to be his companions were a pair of the most luscious and sensual beauties as he had ever seen. Their romantic perfume assailed his nostrils. *Lilies and roses.* Unable to help himself, he ran a finger down Sarai's bare arm. Her skin was like Bursa silk. She smiled seductively at him, showing strong white teeth. Nila, vying for his attention, smiled into his eyes, running a pointed little pink tongue over her full lips. The janissary agent felt suddenly light-headed, and his male member hardened beneath his robes. Were these women spies who would attempt to extract secrets from him? He realized he didn't care, particularly when Sarai pressed a plump breast against his arm. "My lord dey," he finally managed to speak. "You honor me far more than I deserve. I have never known such fine females as these two. They are incomparable!"

"My long friendship with Aruj Agha has always made me favorable toward the corps," the dey said sincerely. "I shall anticipate your return from the other states, Hussein Aga. Enjoy my women. I fear I have ignored them since my recent marriage."

"Indeed you have," Samara said boldly, her red lips pouting. "Has he not, ladies? It is difficult for us to compete with the lady India. She is most beautiful, accomplished, and charming. Even we cannot dislike her. Still, now she is with child and we shall soon have our chance with our good lord again, eh?"

The other women giggled, and nodded eagerly.

"Your wife is to give you a son then?" Aruj Agha smiled warmly at his friend. "Allah has surely blessed you, Caynan." Then he chuckled. "When I think of the first day she arrived in El Sinut! May I tell Hussein Aga the tale? It is a most amusing one."

"Of course," the dey replied, smiling himself with the memory of a fiery and defiant India. As Aruj Agha began to speak, the dey signaled to his servants to begin serving the meal.

There was a wonderful thick soup of lentils, which was accompanied with a hot seasoning of red pepper, salt and garlic; a couscous covered in a spicy sauce filled with vegetables and chunks of beef; a lamb that had been grilled on a spit, as well as three chickens stuffed with almonds, raisins, and rice. There were bowls of purple, black, and green olives in herbed oil, and cucumbers in vinegar. Flat bread, warm from the ovens, was offered the guests. There were bowls of yogurt with peeled green grapes, and a platter with a steamed bass, caught that very morning, lying amid a bed of fennel and carved lemons. Finally a dessert called *khtayef,* consisting of nuts, honey, and sugar in thin layers of pastry was served along with cups of mint tea. A large silver salver of fresh fruit, consisting of green and red grapes, sweet cut pink melons, peaches, apricots, pomegranates, figs, and sugared dates, was set upon the table so the dey's guests might help themselves. There were bowls of shelled almonds and pistachio nuts.

When all but the fruit and nuts had been cleared away, the dey clapped his hands for the entertainment to begin. A snake charmer came with his reed baskets of reptiles. He was followed by a troupe of sensual female dancers, who writhed and twisted themselves in a variety of movements to the high sound of a flute and the deep thump of drums, as they removed veil after veil in a teasing and tantalizing fashion until they were quite naked. Finally a young blind girl was led in, and seated, accompanied by three other women who played upon a rebec, reed pipe, and small drum as the girl sang sweetly passionate love songs.

Caynan Reis watched the janissaries as his women began a subtle seduction of the pair. Sarai's hand had already slipped between the folds of Hussein Aga's robes, and from the look on the man's face, she was as skillful as ever. After the girl had sung for a time, the dey raised his hand, saying, "I believe it is time for me to retire. I will personally see you off in the morning, Hussein Aga. Enjoy your night." Then, arising, Caynan Reis left the dining chamber with Samara, whom he escorted back to the harem. "You did well," he told the girl, kissing her softly upon the lips.

"I am a patient woman, my lord," she told him, dark eyes twinkling.

"Do not let my wife hear you saying things like that," he chuckled, and then brushed her lips a final time. "Sleep well, Samara."

She watched him retreat down the dim corridor, a smile upon her lips. Soon the lady India would grow fat with her child, and the dey would seek the diversion of his harem. She would be favored once again. Baba Hassan had assured her it was bound to happen, and it would. Finally Samara turned away and entered the fountain court.

Caynan Reis had felt her stare as he walked down the long hallway to Baba Hassan's quarters. He needed to speak with his chief eunuch now if his plan was to be put into action. He hurried into the eunuch's apartments. "Baba Hassan," he said without any preamble to his advisor, who was seated upon a divan enjoying his water pipe. "I have a plan that will keep El Sinut from treason, and, give me what I want." He sat down in a chair of carved cedar with a leather seat.

"And what exactly is it that you want, my lord?" the eunuch asked his master, putting down his water pipe, his look attentive and curious.

"The janissaries' plot will fail. They always fail. The Sublime Porte will seek revenge, and it will be more prudent for them to revenge themselves upon the Barbary States than upon those who are truly responsible."

"That is truth, my lord dey," Baba Hassan agreed.

"But what if El Sinut exposed the janissaries' plot before they had an opportunity to enact it?" the dey inquired. "Would not the valideh be grateful? Would she not want to reward her loyal dey of El Sinut? Would she not give him this tiny kingdom in gratitude if he but asked her? Tribute would still be paid, and fealty given to the sultan, but El Sinut would be mine, and my family's forever."

Baba Hassan was silent for several long moments. His look was a thoughtful one. He was obviously considering his master's words very carefully. At last he spoke. "It is dangerous, my lord. Very dangerous. Yet there is danger also in knowing of this plot, and not notifying Istanbul of its existence. While you should make a friend of the sultan and his mother, you will make deadly enemies of the janissaries. We know from the bath attendant, Refet, that Aruj Agha has been ordered to kill you should you betray the corps; and that he has said he would."

"I believe he said it to pacify Hussein Aga," the dey replied. "Our friendship is an old and valued one. Aruj Agha will not kill me."

"My lord, one thing you have never really comprehended about your friend. Aruj Agha's first loyalty is to the corps of janissaries. His grandfather was a janissary, and his uncle is one. He was taken from his family in Bosnia when he was a little boy, and raised in the prince's school in Istanbul. Even at his mother's knee, the lesson of loyalty to the corps was drummed into him. It is a lesson without end. His first ranking was as a gardener in the sultan's palace. The gardeners there are the royal executioners. They are all young men eager to prove their worth, not so much to the sultan, but to the corps, and to their officers. To date, you two have never really been in conflict, but do not ask Aruj Agha to change loyalties, to take your part over that of the corps of janissaries. *He will not do it even if he believes the hierarchy wrong.* You must not ever trust him again if you decide to do this thing."

"What choice do I have, Baba Hassan?" Caynan Reis asked his friend and advisor. "The other states will jump at the opportunity to be free from Istanbul and its tribute. If Hussein Aga returns to me, I must pledge my aid. If I do not, I will be counted their enemy, and they will seek to assassinate me. The Sublime Porte will be only too happy to use me as their scapegoat. El Sinut being small, they can afford to punish us, while the other states are large, and could prove troublesome. I am caught between two fires.

"On the other hand, if I expose the janissaries' plot I have a better chance of remaining alive. I will ask that the sultan remove the janissaries from El Sinut once we are independent. I will form my own guard to protect me. El Sinut will belong to me, and to my sons and my sons' sons. It is worth the risk. Tell me if there is another way, Baba Hassan, that I can keep us all safe."

"There is no other way, my lord. It will be as Allah wills it," the eunuch replied fatalistically.

Caynan Reis nodded wearily. "Now, my old friend, how do we approach the valideh in Istanbul? You will have a way, I am certain."

"We will use two paths, my lord. Our chances will be better at reaching the sultan's mother in time if we do. I have several pigeons, a gift to me from the Agha Kislar of the royal household. Most men in my position hold these birds. We will release three to make their way back to the capital with our message. I shall also send by ship the gift of two young boys to the sultan. They will be accompanied by my most trusted aide, Ali-Ali. He will carry a personal message to the Agha Kislar from me."

"What if he attempts to read your message?" the dey asked.

"The message will be in a code known only to the Agha Kislar, and those to whom he entrusts his messenger birds. It is a good system."

"Why are you sending young boys instead of beautiful girls?" the dey wondered.

"The valideh has encouraged her son in his youth to enjoy the company of boys over girls. That way, no beautiful young creature will arise to challenge the valideh's control over the sultan by either her erotic wiles or by giving the sultan a son of his own. In time, of course, that will change, but our way into favor is through pretty young boys right now, and not pretty young girls."

"How will we know that the sultan has received our warning, Baba Hassan? And will he receive it in time?" Caynan Reis asked.

"We will not know until Ali-Ali returns, my lord. I regret that is the fact of it, but remember, it will take many weeks for Hussein Aga to complete his mission and return to El Sinut. Then he has a voyage to Istanbul. The pigeons I release in two days' time know only to fly to their home in the Yeni Serai. That is how they are trained. They do not forget their way. That is why the Agha Kislar will return the birds to me when Ali-Ali rejoins us, and we will outflank the traitorous janissaries."

"I understand, but why are you waiting two days to send the birds on their way, Baba Hassan? Should they not be sent at first light tomorrow?"

"Because, my lord, Hussein Aga is undoubtedly aware of the Agha Kislar's pigeons. What if he saw one on the wing as he left the palace or the harbor? These pigeons are quite unique. They are white with black-and-white markings and very pink feet, not your ordinary garden-variety bird that one sees upon the roofs of the town, or cadging tidbits in the marketplace. They are recognizable to the knowledgeable, so we will wait until this agent of the janissaries has restarted his journey and is away from El Sinut. We must be extremely cautious in this matter."

"Agreed," the dey said, and then he arose. "Only Azura can know of our plan, Baba Hassan."

"Your wife must know as well," the chief eunuch advised. "She is a clever girl, and will be of use to you if she is aware of all that is going on in this situation."

"But what of the child? Will she not endanger the child?"

"Not knowing is more dangerous, my lord. She is a passionate lady with a great imagination. If she worries, and frets from a position of ignorance, she is more apt to harm her baby. The true knowledge of what is happening will give her courage and strength. After all, my lord, you seek El Sinut for your son, but the child is her son as well. You must not forget that. Women grow irritated, and justly so, when a man behaves as if his son is his alone, and only his doing. Particularly after a wife has carried her child within her own body for almost a year's time."

"How can you have such wisdom, Baba Hassan?" the dey inquired. "There have never been any children in this palace. At least not in my time, or our lord Sharif's time."

"In my youth," the eunuch said, "I served upon the young *ikbal* of a former sultan in the harem of the Yeni Serai itself, my lord. Such a large place, and there were many children, including the daughter of my young mistress. Of course, that was the girl's downfall, and her salvation, having a daughter. But the sultan was no longer interested in her once she was with child, and if the truth be known, she was a pretty but stupid creature. The female infant she birthed was just one of many little girls born to the sultan. My mistress became a troublemaker. She was finally sent with her child to the Eski Serai, the old palace. I was reassigned to accompany the lady Azura to El Sinut, as a gift from the sultan, to his most loyal dey, Sharif. That is how I can tell you about breeding women and their infants," the chief eunuch finished with a deep chuckle. "I have learned much in my fifty years, my lord."

"I must bow to your wisdom," the dey said with a small smile.

Baba Hassan chuckled again. "I am at your service always, my lord dey."

In the morning, Caynan Reis met with Hussein Aga before the agent of the janissaries departed the palace for his ship. "Was your evening a pleasant one, Hussein Aga?" the dey asked his guest pleasantly, noting the older man looked as if he had not slept a great deal.

"Never have I known such a night!" was the enthusiastic reply. "The dey of Algiers will surely not be able to equal your hospitality, nor the dey of Tunis. I shall look forward with much anticipation to my return visit. Both Sarai and Nila are *houriis* without parallel!" He bowed low to the dey.

"I am glad we have been able to offer you a pleasant diversion in your travels," was the smooth reply, and the dey bowed slightly. "May Allah guide you, and give you a safe journey. I shall await your return to El Sinut. Farewell, Hussein Aga."

Dismissed, the janissary exited the room.

"And did you enjoy your companion last night, Aruj Agha?" the dey asked, turning to his friend.

"I did. As always, she is a pleasure to bed, Caynan, but why were you so generous to Hussein Aga? From what he has told me, your two women almost killed him with pleasure. Were you attempting to slay him?"

"Only with kindness so he would not take offense that I did not pledge allegiance to the janissaries' plot against the sultan," was the answer. "How can I unless the others do so first?"

"But you will pledge us fealty if the larger states do?" Aruj Agha probed his friend.

"You know I will do what is best for El Sinut," the dey said sincerely. "Have I not always? And have I not always respected and supported the corps?"

"You have indeed," Aruj Agha said, placated. "That is what I told Hussein Aga in the baths yesterday when he expressed doubts of your loyalty."

The dey clapped his friend upon the back. "We are like two draft animals, harnessed together, my friend," he said. "Between us we have kept El Sinut prosperous and safe. I am a good administrator, but I could not have ruled without your cooperation. May it always be so."

"As Allah wills it," Aruj Agha agreed.

"How go the repairs on your vessel?" the dey inquired.

"Well. We should be able to set sail in another month, and Osman is working very hard to prepare his round ship for service. I believe we shall go out together the first time. I mean to allow him to captain the *Sultan Murat*, but, of course, my troop of janissaries will be aboard."

"It is customary for janissaries to be aboard our ships," the dey said calmly. "I think you wise to take a seasoned captain, and restore him to his rank. My wife will be pleased you do honor to her cousin."

And India was indeed delighted with the news. "Perhaps when we send the janissaries packing," she said, "my cousin will help you form your new guard, my lord. There are many good men from Europe who might welcome such an opportunity."

"You must be more discreet, my precious," he advised. "Nothing has been graven in stone yet, and we must not tip our hand." He sighed. "I regret that I dare not trust Aruj Agha in this matter, but Baba Hassan is right. My friend's loyalty is to the corps of janissaries."

"Perhaps when the time comes, he will see the wisdom in your actions," India attempted to sooth her husband. The dey truly enjoyed this one male friend with whom he hunted in the hills and, until India had come, played chess. It would be lonely for Caynan when Aruj Agha was sent back to Istanbul, but certainly her cousin, Tom Southwood . . . Osman, might take his place. She wished she might see Tom, but now it was no longer possible. At least not until he was admitted to the dey's inner circle as a trusted captain, as well as the relation of the dey's first wife.

Thomas Southwood had heard that the dey had made India his wife. He was relieved she had gotten some common sense, and was protected. He had no doubt that, given the chance, she would want to return to England, and he intended that, when he went, she would go, too. He had promised it to her those many months ago, and how could he justify leaving her behind to the family? Enough of their female relations had been in the same situation as India, and they had returned home. There was no great tra-rah over it. India's fat dowry would erase any number of sins in the eyes of a titled husband. Particularly one in the highlands who would have never heard of El Sinut. He had no doubt both India's grandmother and her mother knew of ways of making what was broken quite whole again. India's husband would have no doubt as to his bride's virginity.

Tom Southwood had been patient. He understood that if he wanted to succeed he had to bide his time. How many poor fools had attempted escape from captivity in the Barbary States and ended up dead? He had counseled those of his crewmen who had remained with him to practice forbearance. They were not ill-treated, and indeed, except for being confined to certain areas, they suffered not at all. "It is a great adventure you will tell your grandchildren in Devon one day," he assured them. "Learn everything you can from the place. Enjoy the women. Enjoy the food. Enjoy the sun, and the warmth. *I will get us back to England!*"

And while he kept their spirits up, he thought carefully of how they would make their escape. To be successful, the planning must be faultless. There was so much involved. He ruminated over and over again on it like a cow with a cud. The lighthouse keepers would have to be incapacitated so they could not raise an alarm. The great chain between the two lighthouses at the harbor's entrance would have to be lowered, and then raised again. Most believed the chain was raised only when an attack on El Sinut was thought to be imminent. Few realized it was raised each night to protect El Sinut from a surprise onslaught. It had been the state's policy as long as anyone could remember that vessels were not welcome in El Sinut's harbor either before sunrise or after sunset.

The hardest thing, however, would involve getting into the palace by stealth to bring India and her servant girl out. Tom Southwood had learned that his cousin's personal servant was a Scottish girl, the daughter of a ship's captain killed when his vessel was taken. Few of that crew had survived, but three had ended up in El Sinut, and one had been wise enough to accept Islam. He had been assigned to "Osman's" crew. It was from this seaman, Captain Southwood had discovered India's serving maid was one of them. She would therefore be rescued as well, but how he was going to do it was a difficult problem.

And Adrian Leigh. He was another problem. There was simply no way they could rescue him, as he was chained to his oar with several other men. To attempt to free Viscount Twyford would endanger their plan, for his shipmates would want to come, too, and then so would all the other galley slaves on Aruj Agha's ship. Many of them were unsavory types, and uncontrollable. They would want to rape and pillage El Sinut before departing. Such rash behavior would destroy any chances they had of making a clean escape. It just couldn't be done, and he hoped that India would not be too distressed over it. They would, of course, notify young Leigh's family as to his whereabouts when they returned to England. It would be up to them to ransom the young man then, but at least they would know where he was.

Slowly and carefully Tom Southwood set everything in place. His men were primed, and ready to go. It was just a matter of time. They had to pick the right time, for he knew they would only get one chance. If they failed, they would be killed. And their deaths would not be easy or pleasant ones. He had seen what had happened to men who attempted to escape their captivity here on the Barbary coast. He did not intend such a death to happen to him, or to any of his men. He would be as patient now that the moment approached as he had been over these past months. Then he would succeed, and they would be home in England within a year of their having been gone.

"Soon," he told his men. "It will be soon. I feel it in my bones. Each one of you knows your task when I give you the word. There can be no mistakes, men."

And then Thomas Southwood saw the perfect opportunity.

Chapter 14

India lay naked in her husband's arms, smiling up at him. "I understand you wanting to hunt, and camp in the hills with Aruj Agha for a few days," she told him sweetly. "I have five brothers, and many uncles and cousins, my lord. Hunting is a man's sport."

He caressed her beautiful breasts lightly, watching with pleasure as her nipples responded. "Did you ever hunt with the men?" he asked her. "I had heard women in your land enjoy the hunt."

"Some do. My mother and my younger sister both enjoyed riding off with my father and brothers to spend a day on the hills or in the forest, but I never really enjoyed such sport." Twisting herself about, she licked the flesh of his belly, then looked up at him seductively. "This is the sport I favor," she murmured.

"You are insatiable," he said, laughing softly and pulling her back into his embrace where he might continue to caress her. She had the loveliest body, and being just newly with child, that body had not yet begun to change. Her belly was yet flat, and her rounded limbs in perfect proportion. The only change he could see was in her breasts, which had become a bit rounder, and the nipples more sensitive. He pulled her about so that she sat upon his thighs, facing him, and, leaning forward, he took one of those nipples into his mouth, his hand holding the breast to which it belonged firmly in his grasp.

Her senses were atingle. Her nipple was like a small stone niblet, yet so sensitive that she could feel most distinctly his tongue encircling it over and over again. And when she thought she could bear no more of his teasing, he pushed her further, suckling hard upon her nipple while he pushed a single finger between her plump nether lips to find her pleasure place. India's head was whirling as her entire being was suddenly focused in a different area. The finger pressed gently, and then began to graze the sentient softness until it stiffened, and she was moaning helplessly as the swells of hot delight began to overwhelm her, sweeping through her body and wracking her with shudders of pleasure.

"You devil!" she half groaned at him. "Do you enjoy torturing me? Cease! Cease! I am close to fainting!"

Laughing, he pushed her onto her back and covered her body with his own, his lips nibbling at her mouth. "Aye, I enjoy torturing you, you exquisite creature." He rubbed himself suggestively against her. "I shall not allow you the upper hand tonight, my precious. I far too much enjoy your cries of satisfaction. His hungry kiss caught her unawares as he pushed his manhood into her trembling body. He filled her full, gently thrusting to and fro. "Do you enjoy this torture, India, my love?" He kissed her again.

She tightened herself about him, pulling her head away from him and demanding boldly, "And do you enjoy *this* torture, my lord?" Her legs wrapped themselves about his torso, squeezing him outwardly every bit as much as she was squeezing him inwardly.

"Ahhhh, bitch! You mean to kill me, do you?"

"Think of me when you are camped in the damp hills, my lord," she taunted him suggestively. "In the dark of night, remember my warmth."

He began to move fiercely upon her. "And you remember my passion as you lay alone in your bed, my precious India," he said, his mouth once more taking hers in an almost cruel kiss.

She could hardly breathe. For a moment it seemed as if his lips were all there were in the world—and it was enough! She could feel the tensions building within her fevered body. Building and building until it burst in a wild frenzy and they collapsed in each other's arms, sated for the moment. India lay against his chest listening as his heartbeat eased slowly from its rapid pulse to a calmer thump. She rubbed her cheek against his skin. It was smooth and damp with his relieved lust. And his fragrance. Warm and musky. She had been surprised to discover that men had their own scent, and his was not unpleasant. Rather, it had become familiar and comforting. "I love you, Caynan," she murmured, kissing his nipple with a sigh.

His arm tightened about her. "I love you," he responded. Ah, yes, he did love her. So much so that he intended keeping his promise to her when he returned from the hunt. He had recently found a Protestant minister in the town, a gentle Lutheran, who had agreed to marry the dey to his first wife and keep the secret of their Christian marriage.

"I understand well, my lord, the need for silence. It would weaken your position should it be known you yielded to a woman's plea. Still, Allah will bless you for it. It is obvious you respect God no matter the way in which he is worshipped." Then the old minister smiled conspiratorially. "I respect God in his many incarnations, too, which is why I am in El Sinut. I am not a man for strict doctrine which gave great distress to my superiors. I was put here to help redeem Protestant captives. It was my bishop's way of keeping me from corrupting the innocent," he concluded with a merry chuckle.

The dey had smiled at the kind old minister. "I appreciate your discretion," he said. "It will make India happy, and it is important to me that she is happy. We will come to you in a few days, for it is easier for me to bring her in secret from the palace than if you were seen within my home. And in return, Pastor Haussler, you will always have access to me in the matter of Protestant captives to be ransomed."

The minister had thanked him profusely, tears in his eyes, and the dey returned to the palace. Aye, they would be wed, as he knew India's parents would want it that way. And there was something else. He intended to tell India that he was English. That he was Deverall Leigh, Adrian's half-brother, and the true heir to the earl of Oxton. He knew this would come as a shock to her, but he also knew that she would believe him when he told her he did not murder Charles Jeffers. That he had been accused unjustly, and, being young, fled, rather than remain to prove his innocence, if indeed he could have proved it. After all, it had been his knife that appeared to have done the deed. A dagger of which he was extremely proud because it had come from his mother's family. A dagger well known to be his prized possession. India would understand. And then he would pay a ransom for Adrian out of his own coffers, and send his half-brother to his uncle in Naples. Whatever the lad did afterward was his business, but he suspected Adrian would not go home to England immediately for fear of the duke of Glenkirk. And finally, when India had delivered their child, he would allow her to write to her parents. He would not let them suffer as his father had been forced to suffer all these years. Looking down on his wife he stroked her dark curls gently as she slept.

When the morning came, she climbed sleepily from her bed to bathe him, a chore she refused to relinquish, saw that he ate a hearty breakfast, and walked with him, properly veiled, into the courtyards to see him off with Aruj Agha. The janissary bowed low to her, and India nodded graciously in his direction.

"Keep my husband safe from danger, *kapitan,*" she said.

"I will, my lady India," he told her with a smile.

Reentering the palace, she was met by Samara, who took her by the hand and said, "Come to the harem. Nila and Sarai are going to tell us how they entertained the visitor from Istanbul. They have saved the tale for just such a time as this so we might all be amused and enlightened, although I doubt there is anything they could tell me that I do not already know," she concluded smugly.

India would have preferred to refuse, for she wanted to be alone but knew to do so would offend. So she allowed Samara to lead her into the fountain court, where the women were already seated awaiting her. Mirmah immediately arose, and called out to India.

"Come, my lady, and sit here." She led India to a comfortable divan, insisting she put her feet up. "I have heard it is good to do so when you are with child," she said.

When the women were finally all settled, and cakes, fruit, and sherbet had been offered, Samara said impatiently, "Well?"

Sarai laughed her smoky laugh. "We all know that a manhood comes in three lengths: the smallest being called *the little fish*, the medium-sized being *the naughty monkey*, and finally the largest being called *the stallion*. Hussein Aga was none of these."

The women gasped with surprise.

"What was he?" Deva finally ventured.

"We nicknamed him the bull," Sarai replied with a wink.

"Never in all my days," Nila told them, "have I seen a manhood so large. This janissary was enormous! As we all know, our lord, the dey, is a stallion, and has a most magnificent weapon. None of us have ever been discontent with him, but Hussein Aga was huge, being both lengthy and thick set."

"And he was as randy as a billy goat," Sarai said. "We disrobed him, and when we had, he was already waving his banner at us!"

The women giggled, even India. She had not thought to enjoy this form of entertainment, but she was amused. "Go on. Go on," she encouraged the two women. "I am the virtual innocent in this room."

The others giggled again, and then Sarai continued.

"He had strong limbs, and a very broad chest. He put an arm around each of us, and walked with us to the bed. We lay him upon his back, and immediately sought to ease his excitement. He assured us, however, that he was a tireless lover. We should both be more than well satisfied by the dawn. We assured him then that he, too, would be quite gratified."

"I, then, began to caress him with my hair," Nila said. "He liked that, but he liked it even better when I took that lengthy rod within my mouth. I practically swallowed him whole, and he began to moan like a boy with his first woman. I would suckle him until he believed he would erupt, and then I would cease, and begin to lick at him. Finally, when he could take no more of such pleasure, I mounted him, absorbing slowly his great length. Allah! He filled me well!"

"He was half mad with lust by then," Sarai took up the tale.

"His eyes were practically bulging from his head." She pouted. "Nila was having all the fun, and so I put my love box over his face, pressing my nether lips against his fleshy mouth, and rubbing. At first he didn't seem able to breathe, but then his tongue poked through, finding my pleasure place. It was a most clever tongue, eager and tireless. My love juices were very copious. He drank them like a man who has been lost in the desert for three days, his pointed tongue going beyond my pleasure place into my sheath, while his hot mouth devoured me. Nila and I entered Paradise at almost the same moment."

"And while she took her own pleasure from Hussein Aga, I rode him hard. His manhood was stiffer than any I have known previously, forcing itself deeper than any man has gone within me. I have never partaken of such fierce lust. I might have been fearful had it not felt so good. Before I closed my eyes and gave myself over to this dark pleasure, I could see his big hands, holding tightly on to Sarai's ivory bottom," Nila told them.

The other women were silent, their eyes wide with fascination.

"*Go on,*" Samara finally managed to croak.

"Nila was weeping with pleasure, but the brute was not satisfied," Sarai told them. "He pushed her off his lance, and rolling me onto my back pistoned me until I was but half conscious. Only then did he explode his seed into me."

"Did you . . ." Leah began.

"Twice more in those moments," Sarai told them.

"You named him well," Laylu told the two women enviously.

"Tell us more," Mirmah demanded. "Did he take either of you as the janissaries are said to do?"

"Each of us," Nila told them, "but only once, for we did not like it, and reminded him we belonged to the dey who did not use us in such a fashion. Still, I have to admit, I found it exciting, yet too perverse."

"I did not," Sarai told them. "He was so big. I was afraid he would hurt me with that huge rod of his."

India looked puzzled. "I don't understand," she said.

"He entered them through their bottomholes," Samara said without any pretensions of delicacy. "Janissaries are raised without the company of women. They are known, when young, to experiment erotically upon one another. Later, of course, they know women, but not as boys. It is unhealthy for a boy, once his jewels have formed and matured, to pen up his juices. There is little harm in what they do."

"I think it is awful!" India said with a shudder.

The other women, but for Samara, nodded. She, however, smiled knowingly. "A woman must do that which pleasures her lord no matter her own tastes. I deny our lord, the dey, *nothing* of my person." It was meanly said.

India was stricken for a moment.

"She but babbles like a brook," Sarai said to the dey's wife, and then she glared at Samara. "Your tongue is so acid that you could engrave brass pots with it. None of us have ever received the dey in such a fashion, and you know it, Samara. Do not distress our mistress."

Samara shrugged, but said nothing else, leaving the inference to lie writhing in India's mind.

"She is a terrible liar," Mirmah whispered. "We know our master every bit as much as she does, and he does not do such things."

"I want to make him happy," India said softly.

"You have," Mirmah replied. "You are to give him a child, and that, Samara will never be able to do. She is bitter. Do not mind her, my lady India."

Mirmah's kind words revived India's spirit, and she said, "Go on with your tale, ladies. I am learning much just listening to you. I shall attempt to put into practice very soon much of what you have told me this day. Some of it sounds very wicked."

"There is nothing wicked in pleasing a man," Deva said. "Particularly if you receive pleasure in return."

The women all nodded, and Sarai and Nila took up their story once again. They spoke of kisses and caresses, of how the janisssary had asked them to make love to each other, and been aroused quickly by the sight, taking them each in turn immediately afterward. He had been as tireless as they had been. Baba Hassan had seen to several basins and love cloths, as well as a decanter of a restorative liquid the trio imbibed throughout the night, until finally, an hour before the dawn, they had all fallen asleep.

"He says he will have us when he returns to El Sinut," Sarai told them with amusement. "I wonder if the dey will be so generous again. He told us he was only giving us to this man in order to placate him temporarily. I do not think he will do it again."

"Aye," Nila agreed. "There is a limit to our master's hospitality."

India remained within the harem to have supper with the ladies, returning to her own apartments in Azura's company later in the evening. Meggie hurried to prepare her mistress for bed.

"She is a good servant," Azura noted as the girl bustled about.

"Baba Hassan chose well," India agreed.

"You are happy?" the older woman said.

"Very happy," India assured her. "Ohh, Azura! I love him! I would not have thought such a thing possible. A year ago I was but a spoiled child, but now I am different because of him. Oh, yes! I am happier than I have ever been in my entire lifetime."

"I am happy to hear you say so, India," Azura answered the dey's young wife. "I will be frank with you, but perhaps you have already suspected it. Baba Hassan, and I somehow knew you were the perfect wife for Caynan Reis, and we strove hard to make you see it, too."

India laughed. "It did occur to me, but only when I realized my love for him, Azura." She flung herself into the older woman's embrace. "He is the son you never had, isn't he?"

"Aye, he is," Azura admitted.

"Mama has always said that one's life is planned even before one is born. No wonder I could not find a husband to suit me in England or Scotland. Caynan Reis was here in El Sinut. If I had not been so silly as to run away with Adrian Leigh, I should have never found my only true love, Azura. How strange life is."

The older woman hugged India, and placed a kiss upon her brow. "Allah who sees all, and knows all, led you to us, my daughter." Then her tone grew brisk, and she released India from her embrace.

"You have had a long day. Let your little servant help you into bed. You carry the heir to El Sinut, and he must be protected. Eh?"

India nodded, smiling contentedly.

The next day passed quietly, but the weather, usually sunny, was overcast, a rarity in October. Storm clouds appeared over the sea in midmorning, and, by late afternoon, had swept into El Sinut with a driving rainstorm and much thunder. The town was virtually deserted, and even the intrepid stall owners in the marketplace had closed down.

"We go tonight," Tom Southwood told his men.

"In this storm, Captain?" Jeremiah James, the second mate, asked.

"They are not used to having such storms in autumn here, and they will all keep to their houses until the morning when it has passed completely. It is the best time, Mr. James. We've sailed in far worse blows than this one. No. It's indeed a perfect time."

"What are we going to do with the El Sinut crewmen, Captain?" Francis Bolton, his first mate, inquired. "In all this planning it is the one thing you haven't told us. If we're going tonight, we need to know now."

"I've thought long and hard on it, Mr. Bolton," Thomas Southwood said. "I considered giving them leave because of this storm, but there is always the chance one or more of them might return to the ship, find it gone, and raise the alarm. I considered killing them, but I don't really want to do that if I can avoid it. Our only option is to capture each of them over the next hour or so, bind and gag them, and throw them in the hole. We will leave them with the lighthouse keepers after we have cleared the harbor. By the time any of them gets loose, or is discovered, we will be well out to sea, and away from El Sinut."

"And her ladyship?" Knox, the steward, queried.

"You, Mr. James, and I will rescue my cousin and her servant from the palace as soon as it gets dark, Knox. Mr. Bolton, you will have charge of the ship until we get back. If we do not return an hour before dawn, leave, sail the *Royal Charles* home to England,

and tell my family what has transpired. At least they will know where lady India is."

"How will you get into the palace, Captain?" Knox asked his master. "We ain't going to just walk in, are we?"

Thomas Southwood laughed. "No, Knox. We aren't going to walk in at all. We're going to climb a wall. I have converted two of our smaller anchors into grapnels. They will aid us in climbing over the dey's palace wall. You, however," the captain told his horrified steward, "will await Mr. James and me on the street side of the wall, and help the ladies when we bring them down."

His three companions looked askance, and so Thomas Southwood continued with a more detailed explanation.

"For months I have been going in and out of the palace, always looking, always studying it for a weakness. The dey's living quarters and his harem are located within an inner court. It would appear that none of its walls is located on an outer avenue. I mentioned this to Aruj Agha, noting it was cleverly done, and similar in design to early English castles. He told me in confidence that the structure was similar to the sultan's palace in Istanbul, but that it did have one small weakness. A far corner in the dey's own private garden, just about three feet of wall space, faced on its far side into a small alley, off a quiet little residential street.

"When I asked why the alley had not been blocked to protect such a vulnerable area, Aruj Agha told me that the wall was fifteen feet high, and always kept free of vines and any other growth that might aid a trespasser. Besides, he said, no one had ever realized what was behind that high wall, and the alley was so remote from the main square of the town that not even the street beggars knew of it. I have walked this city each time we put into port, seeking that little cul-de-sac. I found it only recently."

"Are you certain, Captain, that it is the correct wall?" Mr. Bolton, the first mate, asked him.

"Positive," was the reply. "I went only a few days ago into the hills above the city. When I found a good vista, I sat down and studied the palace. Eventually I found that little susceptible space. I had brought a small glass with me. Then I followed the wall, observing the street niche, letting my eye take note of certain landmarks. When I returned to the town, I went immediately to the alley, and matched what I had marked perfectly. I have the correct location, Mr. Bolton."

"Is Aruj Agha aware of what he told you?" the careful Mr. Bolton persisted. "Ye're sure it ain't no trap yer walking into?"

Thomas Southwood shook his head. " 'Tis no trap, Francis. Aruj Agha is proud of his status not only as the janissary agha in El Sinut, but as the dey's confidant. He is a good soldier, he has a good heart, he is loyal to a fault, but he is prone to bragging about his knowledge and his importance. He did not, I assure you, even realize what he had said, for I was careful not to arouse his suspicions by asking too many questions. Besides, both the dey and the agha are hunting up in the mountains beyond the city. They only left yesterday. Another reason this is the best time for us to make good our escape, and the rescue of my cousin, Lady India."

"Well, Captain," Mr. Bolton said, "you got it figured out just so, it would appear. God help and protect us all this night. I ain't so much worried once we get out to sea, especially with those cannons the janissaries have installed on the ship. We'll be a match for anyone, I'm thinking."

"Particularly if we flys the dey's banner here in the Mediterranean," Mr. James suggested. "Right now, this is a Turkish lake."

"Captain," Knox spoke softly. "Perhaps it might be wise to take yer lady cousin to her grandmother's in Italy rather than expose her to the long voyage home to England. Particularly as there's always the chance we might have to fight a battle or two along the way."

"You might be right, Knox," Thomas Southwood considered. "Aruj Agha will assume we have headed for Gibralter. It will not occur to him that we have gone to Naples. Lady India would be safe with her father's mother. Safer there than on the high seas with us. I think we will do just that. Good man, Knox!"

"Thank you, Captain," the steward said, flushing with pride.

"Time we got about the business of sorting the wheat from the chaff, Captain," Mr. Bolton remarked dryly.

"Aye, 'tis time," Thomas Southwood agreed.

The word was passed swiftly among the English and few Europeans who made up a portion of the crew. The El Sinut men were taken without incident, bound with strong cords, gagged with silk cloths, their eyes blindfolded with dark cloths. Then they were locked in the hole, chained three feet apart along the walls.

"You will be safe as long as you make no attempt to escape," Thomas Southwood told them sternly. "Any man foolish enough to try will be killed immediately. I will not be deterred, and neither will my men." He then left them in the fetid and damp darkness.

On the deck the rain still poured down as the thunder rumbled, interspersed by an occasional flash of lightning that brightened the skies briefly.

"How do we get to your alley, Captain?" Mr. James inquired.

"We'll take the horses assigned to the ship. They're in the dockside stable with only a boy watching over them. I told the stableman he might go home and keep his wife company on this wet night. I said I expected she would be afraid, and he might comfort her. Then I winked at him broadly, and he could hardly wait to go. The boy is too young to ask questions, and has been fed drugged sweets. We'll only take three horses not to arouse any suspicion should someone actually be about in the streets. The women can ride pillion on our return. Let us go now," he said, picking up his cloak and tossing it about his shoulders. He hurried out the door, followed by Mr. James and the faithful Knox, leaving the first mate behind to watch over the ship.

"Good luck, Captain, and Godspeed," Mr. Bolton called softly after the trio.

The stable lad was only a visible lump in a pile of yellow straw, recognizable by his snores, a half-emptied basket of fruit and candies by his side, his face covered with the remains of pink Turkish paste. They saddled the three horses quietly, leading them from the stable and closing the door behind themselves. Mounting their animals, they followed Thomas Southwood as he led them in a circuitous route through the silent and empty streets of El Sinut. The rain continued to pour down as they finally gained the little alley, which indeed, as their captain had said, was practically invisible. They would have ridden right by it had not the captain been with them.

Entering the alley, they dismounted their horses, and Knox took the beasts in his charge as Thomas Southwood and Mr. James took the grapnels from their saddle horns. First one and then the other grapnel was flung upward, each one burying itself tightly by its fluked spikes into the top of the whitewashed wall. Without a word, the two men began to climb the wall, and when they had reached the top, they pulled their ropes up behind them, and dropped them on the wall's far side so they might descend. Almost immediately, they slid away and out of Knox's sight. The ship's steward waited nervously in the rain with the three horses, his heart hammering, starting nervously at a clap of thunder, but, remembering himself, calming the horses while praying beneath his breath.

Dropping into the garden, Thomas Southwood looked about him. He could see the palace on the far side of the area, and lights flickering through the carved screens that were enclosed by delicate arches. Reaching out, he wordlessly touched Mr. James's arm, indicating that his second mate should follow him. Silently the two men slipped along the graveled paths. It was as he had expected. There were no guards in the dey's private enclosure. He stopped, and listened. There was enough light now being emitted from behind the latticed screens for he and Mr. James to see each other. Thomas Southwood put a cautionary finger to his lips, and listened.

"Good night, my lady Azura," he heard India say, and a door closed firmly. "Meggie, run and fetch me my supper. I am ravenous."

"Yes, my lady," was the reply, and again the door opened and closed.

Motioning with his hand for his mate to remain where he was, Thomas Southwood slid a latticed screen softly aside and stepped into the room. "Good evening, India," he said softly.

India recognized his voice, and, stifling her cry, whirled about. "Tom Southwood! Are you mad?" she whispered. "If you are found here you will be killed, and I will have no power to save you!" Her beautiful face betrayed her anxiety for him.

"I have come to rescue you, India," he said. "I promised you I would take you with me when I left El Sinut. I am keeping my promise. We go tonight. I am told your servant is Scotch. We will take her, too."

"No," India said firmly. "I am married now, Tom, and I am content to remain here with my lord. Go now, before you are caught. I wish you good luck. Tell my family that I am happy."

"I am taking you with me, India," he said in a determined tone. "How can I return home to England without you?"

"Tom, try and understand me. *I am happy. I love Caynan Reis. I am his wife.* We went before the iman months ago. I will not desert my husband, and my family would certainly understand. Admittedly it has been an odd courting, but it is a perfect pairing, I swear to you," she told him. "Go now! I dare not ask how you gained entry here."

"You haven't changed at all," he said. "You are still as headstrong and stubborn as you ever were, India. I am not leaving without you. Now, fetch your jewel box if you so desire. We must go as soon as your servant returns. My second mate is waiting outside, and we will escort you to the ship. We must sail immediately while we have the cover of this unexpected storm from the north."

"My lord will come soon, and he will kill you," India lied.

"Caynan Reis is in the mountains with Aruj Agha," he answered. "Do you think I should have been so foolish as to enter this palace when your husband was here? And we could not have taken back the ship if Aruj Agha was among us. *Hurry now!*"

They both heard the footsteps at the same time. India grew pale, but Thomas Southwood stepped behind the carved door even as it opened, and Meggie bustled into the chamber. "I've brought your supper, my lady. Abu thought you would enjoy a nice hot soup tonight."

"Do not scream, Meggie," India said, taking the tray from her and setting it down on her cedar table.

The girl looked puzzled momentarily, and then her eyes widened as Thomas Southwood stepped into her line of vision. "*My lady?*"

"This is my cousin. He says he has come to rescue me, Meggie.

I will not go with him, of course, but if you want to, I will not stop you. I know that you, like me, fret over your mother."

"There's nothing for me back in Scotland but me mam, and she probably thinks I am dead along with me da. It's better left that way, I'm thinking. Ian will hae wed wi Flora MacLean; and she'd make certain I was considered damaged goods. She always hated me because my Ian preferred me to her. Nay, I'll stay wi you, my lady."

"You are both coming with me," Thomas Southwood said, "and I'll have no further argument from either of you."

"If you do not leave now, Tom, I shall scream, and the guards will come," India told him stonily.

"Why can't you listen to reason?" he demanded of her.

"Why can you not believe me when I tell you I love Caynan Reis, and I am content to remain here in El Sinut?" she countered, glaring angrily at him. "Go, Tom! *Go now!*"

He turned away, and then, swinging about, suddenly hit her a blow on the chin, catching her as she collapsed to the floor. "Come on, lassie," he said to the shocked and wide-eyed Meggie as he moved through the open screen.

"Wait, sir! Let me get us cloaks, or we shall be soaked through with this rain, and the mistress catch her death," Meggie pleaded.

"Hurry, lassie," he told her.

Meggie bit her lip as she opened the trunk, drawing out two long, enveloping capes. Should she make a dash for the door, and alert the guards that this man was kidnapping the dey's wife, or should she just take the capes and follow along? This man was her mistress's blood relation. Would her lady thank her if the dey had him beheaded? It was a terrible quandary. Meggie finally decided that she didn't want anyone's death on her conscience. She put one of the capes about her own shoulders, and, bringing the other to where Thomas Southwood stood, she draped it over her unconscious mistress.

"Get a scarf, lassie," he commanded her, and she hurried to comply. "Don't be startled. My second mate is with me, and he'll help you."

She followed him and his companion across the garden to the farthest wall where two thick ropes hung down. There they stopped, and Mr. James, using the silk scarf, tied India's wrists together, and then lifted her up and put her arms about Thomas Southwood's neck.

"She's dead weight, Captain. It will be harder," he said.

"I know, Mr. James, but you heard her resisting me in her usual stubborn fashion. I had no choice but to clip her on the jaw. We could not stay any longer." He grasped the rope, and began to pull himself slowly and with great effort up the wall.

"Put your arms about me neck, lassie," the second mate said. "I can make it up sooner than he can, and we can help him, eh?"

Meggie obeyed him wordlessly, and, before she knew it, the mate was shinnying up the rope like a monkey despite the burden upon his back. He made her sit atop the wall and then, reaching down, helped his captain the final few feet. The ropes were then drawn up and thrown over the street side. The descent was far easier, and Meggie found herself on the ground before she knew it. To her surprise, another man was waiting, holding three horses.

"Is m'lady all right?" he whispered nervously.

"She didn't want to come, the silly wench," Thomas Southwood said. "I had to hit her for her own good to bring her along."

A rumble of thunder sounded above them, and the horses nickered and danced nervously.

"Let's get going," Thomas Southwood said as Mr. James lifted India from his back. He mounted his animal, and, reaching down, took India up upon his horse, cradling her in his arms, drawing her hood up to keep her from getting soaked.

Next to him the other two men had mounted their horses, and Meggie was riding pillion behind Mr. James. They began their return journey to the harbor, reaching it in what seemed like a rather brief time to the young servant girl. The horses were replaced in the stables by the captain and Mr. James, while Knox carried India aboard, followed closely by Meggie. He settled them in the captain's cabin.

"Where are we going, sir?" Meggie ventured.

"Why, home, lassie, God be willing," Knox said. "I have to lock you in until we clears the harbor. Tend to your mistress now. There's water and fruit on the table. I'm sorry we have no wine, but, as you know, they don't hold with spirits here." He closed the door behind him, and Meggie heard the key turn in the lock.

India had been placed upon the captain's bed, and now Meggie hurried to see if her mistress was returning to consciousness. Quickly she untied the lady's bound wrists. She gasped softly, and shook her head in disbelief at the purple bruise forming on India's jaw. "Oh, the brute!" the servant said coldly. "I hope my lady isn't angered at me for not crying out when I had the chance, but I couldn't live wi myself if I had hae the deaths of those three men on my conscience." She shook her head, and, going to the table, poured some water. Raising India up, she gently tried to force a little water down her throat. India coughed, and her golden eyes flew open.

"Meggie!" Her hand went to her jaw. "Ohh, that hurts." Her glance swept the cabin. "Where are we?" she asked her servant.

"Aboard ship, my lady. He hit you, and then carried you from the palace. Ohh, my lady! Had I cried for the guards they would have killed him, and he's your kin. I didn't know what to do!"

"It's all right, Meggie. I'll kill him myself," India said. "Have we left port yet?"

"They're getting under way now despite this storm," was the frightened reply. "That Knox has locked us in, I fear."

"Damnation!" India swore, and attempted to arise, but she fell back with a groan. "Allah! I'm so dizzy." Then her hands went protectively to her flat belly, but everything else seemed all right.

"Give it a few minutes, my lady," Meggie advised, "and then we'll try sitting you up. There ain't nothing we can do now anyhow."

"You must keep my secret, Meggie," India said meaningfully.

The young servant understood, and asked, "Why didn't you tell him, my lady? Then he would have left you in peace."

"I was going to if he continued to persist, but he turned away as if he would go. Then he suddenly pivoted about, and hit me. I did not have the chance," India said. "Now, what am I going to do? We are locked in, and Tom is too busy getting his ship under way. No. I must keep my secret for now. I will think of some way to escape him. I have escaped my family before."

"That Mr. Knox says we are going home to England, my lady," Meggie informed her mistress. "It will be weeks before we see land again. You have no place to escape to, I fear."

"I have learned patience in El Sinut," India said wisely. "When we arrive in London, we shall give my cousin the slip. My parents have shut up the London house, but I can get into Greenwood, and there is no staff there now but the gatekeeper and his wife. We can easily avoid them. I will get a message to my husband telling him where we are. It will all take time, and my child will probably be born before Caynan Reis can come for me, but he will come. I know it! In the meantime, however, I intend to give my cousin Thomas Southwood as difficult a time as possible," India concluded with a wicked chuckle. "The heroic fool treated me as if I was still a child, instead of a woman grown. He will pay for that piece of foolishness."

The ship moved slowly from its dock, edging its way in the choppy waters toward the channel that led between the two lighthouses guarding the harbor. The rain continued to beat down, the thunder booming, the jagged streaks of lightning flashing across the skies. When they had reached the vicinity of the two lighthouses, the sea anchor was thrown out. The longboats were launched, carrying four men each. The boats were rowed quickly to the lighthouses, beached, and then its occupants entered the lighthouses to take the two keeps prisoner, binding, gagging, and blindfolding them exactly as they had the sailors in their vessel's hole. A lantern signal indicated that both keepers were now incapacitated. While the longboats carrying two sailors each made their way back to the ship, the remaining two sailors at each lighthouse began to turn the winch to lower the chain guarding the harbor.

The longboats returned twice to each lighthouse carrying the captive seamen who were marched into the lighthouses only to have their legs rebound and their blindfolds refastened. Each of them was resettled at a distance from the others to prevent any possible contact that might lead to their premature escape. As they knew where they were, they were no longer frightened. The lighthouse doors were locked, and barred from the outside, the *Royal Charles* raised her sea anchor, sailed from the harbor, and once again moored itself, while the occupants of the two longboats moved their crafts to the sea side of the lighthouse islands, raised the harbor chain up to protect the entry, and rowed back to their ship in very choppy seas.

About them the storm continued to rage, the thunder and the lightning even more pronounced now as they hauled anchor a final time, and began to make their way out into the open sea. Leaving command of his regained vessel in Mr. Bolton's hands, Captain Thomas Southwood unlocked the door of his quarters and stepped inside, neatly dodging the pitcher of water his cousin Lady India Lindley hurled at him.

"Idiot! Allah help you when my husband learns what you have done! Aruj Agha will scour the seas for me at my lord's command! And when you are recaptured, Tom Southwood, and they lop your arrogant head from its shoulders, I shall feel not the slightest twinge of guilt!"

"Is this the thanks I get for rescuing you?" he demanded. "You are yet a spoiled child, India."

"I am nineteen, Tom," India told him, suddenly serious. "When my mother was nineteen, she had already had two husbands, two children, and was *enceinte* with a third. My grandmother had birthed my mother, and was about to have my uncle James at nineteen. There isn't a woman in this family who wasn't grown by nineteen. Why do you persist in treating me like a child, Thomas Southwood? I am a married woman, and quite content to be so. Why did you not listen to me when I said I didn't want to come with you? Why did you assume I was some mindless infant who needed your protection? Did I ask for it? Did you ask me if I wanted to be *rescued?* No! You invaded my home, brutalized me, and then carried me off. You are a well-meaning idiot, sir."

"I cannot take you back," he said wearily.

"I know that," she told him. "Do you think I would endanger these men who have planned and struggled to make good their escape? If Aruj Agha catches up with you, there will be no mercy. An example will have to be made. That is their way."

"Do you really love him, India?" he asked her, curious.

"Aye. Have I not said it over and over to you? I am the wife of the dey of El Sinut, and proud to be his wife."

"It wasn't a real marriage," he said, attempting to excuse himself. "It wasn't a Christian marriage, India, and you are a Christian."

"Aye, I am a Christian, but if you knew anything, *really knew*, about Islam, you would understand my marriage is quite valid. Besides, he was seeking a Protestant minister in El Sinut to marry us in my faith, although such a thing would have been done in secret. You were to be our witness, Thomas Southwood."

"He loves you *that* much?" Thomas Southwood was very surprised that Caynan Reis would endanger himself and his position in such a manner. "I think he only told you such a thing to ease your conscience, India. The sultan's dey in El Sinut would never risk a Christian marriage. It could mean his very life."

"He would have done it, and allowed nothing to happen to us. Did you know there is a plot by the janissaries against the young sultan? Their agent came to Caynan Reis, and sought his allegiance. He said he would only give it to them if the deys of Algiers and Tunis agreed. He sent this man on his way, and then sent word to Istanbul to the valideh of the plot. He intended asking the valideh for autonomy for El Sinut as a reward when she offered one, so that our sons would have their own lands," India told her startled cousin. "Do you think I should know these things if I was not my lord's beloved, and trusted by him? Do you think the harem women knew of all of this, Thomas Southwood? But you would *rescue* me, and force me back to Scotland!" She glared at him.

Thomas Southwood had a momentary doubt that perhaps he had not done the right thing in forcing his cousin India aboard his vessel, but he quickly pushed it away. She didn't understand at all. Caynan Reis would have gotten a child or two on her, and then taken a second, possibly even a third and fourth wife. India, he knew, would not have stood for such rivals, and been unhappy. She was better off going back to her family at Glenkirk. Back to the life she knew and understood. They would explain away her year's absence, and find her a husband. She would forget Caynan Reis. Her great wealth would smooth over any difficulties.

He looked directly at her. "It is too dangerous for me to continue on to England with you aboard. We may encounter Barbary corsairs, and have to fight our way out this time, particularly now that we are so well armed. I am taking you to Naples to your grandmother, Lady Stewart-Hepburn. When you return home in a few months' time, it will be said you have been with her all this time."

"And what will be said about poor Adrian Leigh?" India demanded.

"God's boots, India! You don't still care for that arrogant little toad, do you?"

"No, I care nothing for him," India said scathingly. "I love my husband, but Adrian ended up in the galleys because of me. Why didn't you take him with us tonight?"

"I couldn't without involving all the galley slaves on Aruj Agha's ship. For God's sake, India! Your former swain is chained with four other men on a bench. I didn't have the authority to unlock those chains, and if I had attempted to take Adrian off that vessel, there would have been a riot. Our entire escape would have been thwarted. Besides, Adrian Leigh deserves whatever he gets for cajoling you into your rash runaway."

"You really are a bastard, Tom," India said. "If this is to be my cabin while you make your run for Naples, then get out of it! I don't want to see you again. *Ever again!* How easy it is for you to ruin other people's lives, and all for the sake of your damned ship!"

"This damned ship will help to get you home," he said angrily.

"El Sinut is my home now," she replied stonily.

Chapter 15

The morning after their flight from El Sinut dawned clear. The Mediterranean sun shone golden in a cloudless blue sky, and the brisk winds left in the wake of the storm had swung about to the southwest, speeding their progress toward Naples. It would certainly have been discovered by now that the dey's wife and her servant were missing. It would have been ascertained that the English round ship was no longer in the harbor of El Sinut. The chief eunuch, Baba Hassan, would have connected the disappearance of India and Meggie with that of the ship. Particularly if someone finally saw the single grapnel atop the far wall of the dey's private garden. Mr. James had freed, and tossed down to the alley the grapnel by which his captain and India had descended, but having gotten to the ground with Meggie, he had been unable to loose his own grapnel. They had left it. It was unlikely they would be caught before they reached Naples. By the time Caynan Reis and Aruj Agha were sent for, returned to the city, and sailed in pursuit after them, another two days would have gone by.

They sailed on through virtually unoccupied seas that first day, and the next day as well. Finally, on the third morning, they approached Naples. India stood at the rail, enchanted with the muted peach-and-lavender sky. Pearly gray mist hung suspended in the air like sheer, shredded silk. Here and there tiny islands appeared out of the foggy waters. She could just see the small fishing boats in the fog. She heard the call of a church bell over the smooth seas. A gentle breeze puffed at the sails, causing the ship to glide along almost like a fairy vessel. The air was very damp, and warm.

"Well," Tom Southwood said, coming up to stand by her side, "you'll be at your grandmother's in a few hours, India. I want you to stay aboard until I have gone to Lady Stewart-Hepburn's villa and spoken with her. I'm sure she is aware of your disappearance a year ago. She'll send a message to your family posthaste, I have not a doubt. I'll be glad to have you off my hands, quite frankly. You're a very troublesome wench, India."

"And you're a pompous fool, dear cousin," she responded.

"In time you will forgive me, and realize that what I did was for your own good, India," he said gently.

India turned her face to him, her golden eyes almost amber with her irritation. "Go to the devil!" she told him, and then returned to her cabin where Meggie was awaiting her.

"Captain was seeking you, my lady," the girl said.

"He found me," India replied. "I shall be glad to be quit of him. Hopefully Lady Stewart-Hepburn will not be so condescending."

"You do not call her Grandmother?" Meggie asked.

"She is my stepfather's mother, and I only met her in France two years ago. She has lived in Naples for many years now. For my stepfather's sake, I call her Grandmama, but I was never comfortable with it. My Lindley grandparents were dead before my father and mother were wed. The only grandparents I have ever known have been the earl and countess of BrocCairn, Mama's parents, although the earl is also my mother's stepfather. Most of the women in my family have been wed to any number of husbands. We are very long-lived, Meggie."

Knox had brought them a small repast, some flat bread, dates, and a small carafe of fresh water. The two women ate, and then Meggie fetched a basin of water so they might wash. They had no trunks, and were wearing the same garments in which they had left El Sinut. There was not even a comb for their hair, and all of India's precious jewelry had been left behind. At least that, she hoped, would tell her husband that she hadn't departed willingly from his side. *Caynan!* Her heart cried out to him over the many miles now between them. *I love you! Please find me! Please!*

The ship anchored in the Bay of Naples. They had exchanged the banner that flew atop their mast earlier that morning for two flags, one indicating they were an English ship, and the other below it to announce they belonged to the O'Malley-Small Trading Company. Captain Thomas Southwood left his vessel, and was rowed ashore. There he immediately registered his ship with the harbormaster, explaining they had escaped captivity in the Barbary States by stealing back the *Royal Charles.* He requested that a ship's painter be sent out to his vessel to repaint the correct name on its side and stern. Then, asking directions to the Villa del Pesce d'Oro, he rented a horse and made his way to the small estate, outside of the city and on the sea.

It was to this beautiful villa with its gardens that Catriona Leslie had come to marry Francis Stewart-Hepburn. It was from this place that she had been kidnapped, and taken into slavery in the Ottoman Empire. But Francis Stewart-Hepburn would not be denied the great love of his life, and, discovering where his wife had been taken, came to rescue her. He had, as he later told her, crossed three seas and two straits to find her. They had not returned to Villa del Pesce d'Oro, for Lady Stewart-Hepburn had been badly traumatized by her adventure. They had instead gone to another villa in the hills above Rome, Villa Mia.

In the next few years, as the shock of her sojourn had eased and finally faded almost away, they had taken to going to the Neapolitan villa each summer, and remaining into the autumn when they would return to Villa Mia. Lord Bothwell had loved the warmth and the sunshine of Naples. He had been buried there, except for his heart which was taken from his chest upon his death and placed in a carved oak box which was then placed into a decorated silver reliquary, and rested on a table by his wife's bed. It traveled with her. It would be buried with her when she died.

The gates to the villa were opened by a smiling gatekeeper. The door to the house was opened by a craggy-faced Scot in a kilt.

"Aye?" the grizzled fellow growled.

"I am Captain Thomas Southwood, of the O'Malley-Small trading ship, the *Royal Charles*. I should like to see Lady Stewart-Hepburn."

"And what is yer business, Captain?" the doorkeeper demanded.

"My business is private, fellow, and not to be discussed with servants," Thomas Southwood replied stiffly.

"Now dinna get yer breeches in a twist, Captain," the Scot said, "but nae one gets into this house wiout my knowing their business. I promised my lord on his deathbed that I would watch over her ladyship, and 'twas nae a promise made lightly."

"I am a son of the earl of Lynmouth, uncle to the duchess of Glenkirk," Thomas Southwood answered. " 'Tis family business I have come about. Now, are you satisfied, and will you let me in?"

"Aye, come in then, and I'll take ye to her ladyship," the Scot said calmly. He turned, and led the way into a bright salon overlooking the colorful gardens of the villa, now a riot of bloom. "Captain Thomas Southwood, m'lady," he announced.

Catriona Stewart-Hepburn had been sitting at an embroidery frame by the open windows. She arose now, and he saw she had the same elegance that his late grandmother had possessed.

"My lady," he said, bowing over the outstretched hand.

"*Southwood.* Are you related to the earl of Lynmouth, sir?" she asked him.

"Robert Southwood is my father," he replied.

"How kind of you to visit me," she told him. "I do not often have visitors from the north. Do you bring messages from my family?"

"I've brought your granddaughter, Lady India Lindley," he announced, smiling at the look of astonishment that crossed her face.

"*India!* Oh, thank God! Jemmie and Jasmine have been so worried! Where did you find her? Is she all right? Where did she disappear to?" She sat down heavily, waving him into a chair.

"India will tell you everything you need to know in detail, my lady, but I will tell you briefly. Almost a year ago, Adrian Leigh,

Viscount Twyford, convinced India to elope with him. Neither my cousin, Jasmine, nor her husband, approved of this young man. With great foresight India had him book them passage out of England upon one of our ships, and she came aboard disguised. Her masquerade was fortunately discovered, and I took her in my charge immediately, putting her rash young swain into custody. Shortly afterward we were taken into captivity by a Barbary corsair. I advised my crew to accept Islam, which most of them did, thus avoiding service in the galleys. We were brought to El Sinut, and led before its dey, Caynan Reis.

"Because ours was the first round ship they had ever captured, and because I had accepted Islam, I was first sent back out to sea with the janissary agha of El Sinut as his navigator. When it was at last decided that I could be trusted, I was assigned the task of teaching the dey's seamen how to sail my ship. I planned our escape for months, and at last three nights ago I accomplished our flight, rescuing India so she might go with me, along with the little Scots lass who is her servant."

Catriona Stewart-Hepburn knew the answer to the question she now asked. "What happened to India when you arrived in El Sinut?"

"The dey fancied her, and she was taken into his harem," was the answer, as she had expected.

"Ahhh, the poor child," Lady Stewart-Hepburn said, remembering her own sensual captivity, and the trauma she suffered for several years after her husband rescued her. "How is she, sir? When may I see her?"

"She's mad as hell, madame, for she fancies herself in love with the dey. I had to knock her unconscious to get her to safety. As to seeing her, I would very much appreciate it if you would take the troublesome wench off my hands, and see to the task of getting her back to Scotland or England, and into her parents' charge again."

"She is aboard your vessel?"

"Aye, madame, she is," he answered.

"I shall send my Conall down to the harbor to fetch them," Lady Stewart-Hepburn said. "Does she have much luggage?"

"Madame, I carried her unconscious over a fifteen-foot-high wall in the clothing she wore," Thomas Southwood said.

"Where was the dey?"

"Hunting in the mountains with the janissary agha, or I should have never attempted such an escape," he replied honestly.

"Stay with me for a few days," the older woman said. "Both you and your men could surely use the rest after your great adventure."

"I thank you, madame, but we must put to sea again as soon as possible, and direct our efforts to getting home to England."

"If you sail west, Captain, you certainly risk being recaptured again," she said in very practical tones. "I think if I were planning to foil my enemy, I should remain in Naples for a few days, take on a cargo, and sail east to Istanbul. By the time you return west again, the dey and his minions will have tired of the chase, and you will have a profit for your trouble." She smiled at him, and her leaf-green eyes twinkled.

"Your legend, madame, does not do you justice," he said.

"Please," she said, "would you go to the door, and tell Conall to fetch Lady India and her servant from your ship. He is standing on the other side of the panel attempting to hear what is being said, but his hearing is not as good as it once was, I fear."

The door snapped open, and the Scotsman said in glowering tones, "I hear well enough, my lady. Ye need nae insult me, and me so faithful to ye. What is yer ship called, Captain?"

"The *Royal Charles*, but right now it's got itself a Turkish name on her sides and stern in those wiggly scroll-like lines they call letters. The harbormaster can tell you where we're moored, and arrange for my longboat to take you out to fetch my cousin. I thank you, Conall."

The kilted Scotsman stamped from the room even as his mistress was pouring two exquisite crystal goblets of deep red wine. She handed Thomas Southwood one of the goblets. "Wine, sir?"

The captain took the liquid gratefully, eyed its beautiful ruby color, and sniffed its fragrant bouquet. A look of delight passed over his face. " 'Tis Archambault wine, madame! From my grandmother's family estates in France. God! I have dreamed of this wine all those long months in captivity while I quenched my thirst with water, mint tea, sweet sherbets, and that damnably thick Turkish coffee." He took a sip, and then another, and then drank the entire goblet down before her eyes. "Ahhhh, that was good! Do you know, when they captured my ship, they threw an entire cargo of sherry overboard?"

She refilled his glass, laughing.

"All those barrels floating in the sea," he said mournfully, and began to sip at his goblet once again.

Conall More-Leslie fetched his mistress's carriage and driver. Then, mounting his horse, he led the way to the harbor, instructing old Giovanni to wait for him. "I hae two ladies to bring back to the madonna," he told the coachman. "They are aboard a ship in the harbor."

He was rowed out to the *Royal Charles*, and, approaching it, saw a painter already hung over the side of the vessel upon a rickety scaffolding, painting out the Turkish squiggles, preparatory to restoring the ship's proper name. He clambered up the ladder hanging over the vessel's side and onto the deck, introducing himself to Mr. Bolton.

"I'll fetch her ladyship, and Meggie," the first mate said, "and glad I'll be to see the last of them. Women on a ship's bad luck, and we've had nothing but bad luck since her ladyship came aboard."

Conall More-Leslie nodded as if in agreement, but he thought the first mate a damned fool to believe such superstitious nonsense. His look was quizzical when India and Meggie appeared before him. Both were attired in foreign garb, and they were barefoot. Then he bowed to India. "I am Conall More-Leslie, your grandmother's majordomo. I hae been sent to bring you to her, my lady. And the wee lassie, too."

"Let us go then," India said briskly. "How the hell do we get off this damned boat?"

"Ye'll hae to climb down the ladder over the side, my lady. I'll go first, and then yer serving girl, and then ye," he told her. "Mr. Bolton, will ye help the ladies, please."

"Aye, and glad I am to do it," the first mate said enthusiastically.

"Good-bye, Knox!" India called. "Thank you for everything."

To her surprise, both India and Meggie navigated the rope ladder in their bare feet without incident. Safe within the longboat, they looked toward the shore. Shortly afterward they found themselves settled in a large, comfortable coach, riding through the streets of a noisy city. The smells were ferocious. India grew dizzy with it all, and leaned back against the upholstered seat.

"How can my stomach be so unsettled on such little food?" she wondered aloud.

"We're getting used to being back on the shore again, m'lady," said Meggie. "And perhaps the wee one is hungry for some nourishment. Ohh, I could use a bowl of Abu's good soup now, I could!"

"Lady Stewart-Hepburn will take care of us, Meggie. Although I barely know her, I can tell you she is a woman of uncommon good sense."

The city was left behind, and they traveled along a rural road by the sea. Finally the carriage turned into the gates of the Villa del Pesce d'Oro, the horses trotting smartly up the graveled drive, finally stopping before the beautiful double doors of the mansion. A servant ran to open the carriage door and lower the steps, offering India his hand. She stepped out, and immediately through the open doors of the villa she saw Catriona Stewart-Hepburn.

The older woman held out her arms to India, who felt compelled to fly into them and be well hugged. "I said you'd cause a scandal if they did not marry you off," Lady Stewart-Hepburn said dryly. "And here you are safely back from your adventures. Jemmie will be so relieved. Come into the house, my dear. You look exhausted, and will want a bath, some food, a rest, and fresh clothing. Is this your servant? Weren't you a lucky lass, child. Had you not been my granddaughter's maid, you might not have had the opportunity to go home to Scotland again."

"Yes, m'lady," Meggie said, dropping a curtsey to this beautiful woman who didn't look old enough to be anyone's grandmother.

"Come along now," Lady Stewart-Hepburn said, and led them into the cool of her villa, then into her salon where Captain Southwood awaited.

"Ah, you are here, Cousin," he said pleasantly.

"Get out of my sight," India said coldly. "If it hadn't been for you, I should be with my husband now. I will never forgive you, Tom!"

"What is this?" the older woman said, looking between the two antagonists. "You told me the dey fancied India, not that she was his wife, Thomas Southwood!"

"How could an English noblewoman be married to an infidel?" he demanded angrily.

"Because the iman made it so, you arrogant bastard!" India almost shouted at him. Then she rounded on her stepgrandmother. "He would not listen, madame. He struck me a blow that rendered me unconscious, and then kidnapped me from my home." She stuck out her jaw, and pointed with her finger to the faint purple bruise. "Caynan will be frantic, madame. You must return me to him!"

"He will replace you with another girl from his harem," her cousin said cruelly. "One wench is pretty much alike to these fellows."

With a shriek India flew at him, clawing at his face. "Bastard! Bastard!" she screamed. "I would kill you if I could!"

Conall More-Leslie leapt forward, and pulled the furious girl away from her victim. "Easy now, lassie. Dinna slay the man for doing what he thought was right."

"*He wouldn't listen!*" India shouted once more. Her heart was pounding with her burning anger. She couldn't believe the murderous fury Thomas Southwood had engendered in her. She had never been this angry in all her life.

The captain touched his face, looking slightly horror-struck at the scarlet stains on his fingertips. "You've blooded me," he said incredulously. "You've actually drawn blood, you damned wildcat!"

"I would tear your heart out with my teeth if I could," she responded darkly, her eyes blazing violent rage.

Instinctively he stepped back, shocked by the look.

"I think it is best my granddaughter be taken to her room now," Lady Stewart-Hepburn said quietly. "I will send my own women, Susan and May, to help her." She put her arms about a resisting

India. "We will solve this problem together, India, I promise you." Then she sent her off with Conall and Meggie.

When they had gone, she turned to Thomas Southwood. "Perhaps you should have listened to her, sir. She is extremely distraught. It is not the attitude of a woman taken from a man who was holding her in bondage. If the dey of El Sinut took her for his wife, then she is his wife. I understand your family loyalty, but what do you think awaits her back in Scotland?"

"They'll find a husband for her," he said sullenly. "She's rich enough, madame, that her wealth will cover her sins."

"Oh, dear," Catriona Stewart-Hepburn said softly. "You are having second thoughts, aren't you, my dear? Well, the deed is done. You will have to get on with your life, and I shall have to straighten out this unfortunate muddle. You will remain in Naples for a few days? And you will take my advice to take on a cargo and sail to Istanbul? If the dey of El Sinut catches you now, I truly fear for you, sir. Go back to your ship, and return for dinner. We eat in the evening here. My son Ian will be coming. You will like each other. Like you, he has yet to settle down," she laughed. "Before you go, however, allow me to attend to those scratches." She peered at his face. "They are not deep. Your handsome face will not be scarred."

"I never realized what a troublesome witch India was," he grumbled. "Your son has obviously had his hands full raising her."

"My son adores her, and she him. I think that may have been the difficulty for India in choosing a husband. No one could quite measure up to Jemmie. And then the charming Viscount Twyford came along. Rather than being supportive, Jemmie was jealous. Although from what I have been told, the young man was really quite unsuitable for an heiress of India's social standing; my son might have handled the situation a bit more tactfully. Sometimes he reminds me very much of his father, Patrick Leslie. Patrick was always quite heedless of the consequences when he wanted his own way," Lady Stewart-Hepburn said. Then, reaching out, she tugged at the tapestried bell pull, and moments later a maidservant appeared. "*Acqua e uno bacile,*" she said.

"*Sì, madonna,*" the girl said with a curtsey.

"You speak Italian?"

His older companion laughed. "I have lived in Naples and Rome for over twenty-five years, Captain. Although some of my servants are Scots, most of them are local people. It was necessary that I gain a good command of the tongue. It's a beautiful language; very lyrical and romantic, unlike my own Celtic tongue."

The basin and water were brought, and Lady Stewart-Hepburn quickly cleaned the blood from Thomas Southwood's face. When she had finished, she sent him on his way and hurried upstairs to see how India was faring. She found her in a tub of scented water being tended by Meggie. Her own two serving women, Susan and May, were nearby, seeing to fresh clothing for their guest and preparing her bed.

"I have instructed Captain Southwood to return to his ship, but he will be back for dinner," she told India.

"I cannot bear his company, madame. Please understand," India said.

"You do not call me Grandmama as you did in France," Lady Stewart-Hepburn said.

"I only met you for the first time there. I do not think of you as my grandmother," India answered her honestly.

"Then you must call me Cat," the older woman said. "I was baptized Catriona Mairi, but I was always Cat to my friends and family. I hope we are at least friends, my child."

"Oh, yes!" India said, favoring Cat with a smile. She arose from her tub, and Meggie wrapped her in a warm towel, seating her mistress upon a small chair and drying her wet hair as the two women continued their talk.

"You must forgive poor young Southwood," Cat said. "He was only doing what he thought was right."

"Like all men, he didn't listen, or if he did, he didn't hear," India said. "I have to get back to El Sinut!"

"You are certain you want to return?" The leaf-green eyes scanned the younger woman's face.

"*Yes!*" India said. "Ohh, Cat! I love him, and he loves me! I have never been happier than I was with Caynan Reis. We had so many plans. I told my cousin that I was glad to remain. I asked him to carry a message to my parents for me, but no! With his misguided sense of honor, and family loyalty, he had to steal me away. I cannot forgive him the pain he has caused me and my husband."

"I understand," she said. "I truly do, India. When I was separated from my lord Bothwell, I thought I should die. I could actually feel my heart cracking with my misery. The first thing we must do is send a message to your husband in El Sinut that you are safe, *and* we will say nothing to your cousin about our decisions. As long as you are certain, I shall not keep you from the man you love, even if the rest of the whole world disapproves!"

India burst into tears. "Ohh, thank you!" she sobbed.

"I shall excuse you from dinner tonight," Cat said. "You have had an exhausting voyage. Your cousin will be here for a short time, and before he goes, you will reconcile with him. He need not know the reason why, but you will do it to please me, India, since I have agreed to help you."

"Ohh, yes, Cat! I will!" India sobbed.

"May . . ." Lady Stewart-Hepburn called to her serving woman. "Go to the kitchens and fetch some of Anna's hot soup, a piece of fresh focaccia, some fruit and wine, for Lady Lindley. She must eat, and then I want her put to bed." She turned to Meggie. "What is your name, lassie? I am told you are one of us. Where do you come from?"

"I'm Meggie, your ladyship, and I'm from Ayr," was the answer.

"Go with May then, Meggie, and remain to eat something. Anna will see you are well fed. Then come back to watch over your mistress. There is a nice trundle beneath this bed which Susan will see has fresh bedding and linens for you. You look fair worn, child."

"Thank you, your ladyship," Meggie said, curtseying. "Mistress?"

"Go, Meggie. I will be fine," India said. She was now quite dry in the warm air, as was her dark hair.

Cat's other serving woman, Susan, came now with a soft silk nightgown which she slipped over India's body. "There, my lady.

There's nothing like a nice bath and fresh clothes to make a body feel better."

"You're a Scot," India noted.

"Lord bless you, m'lady, aye, and we are. May and me is sisters. We hae been wi our mistress for longer than I care to remember. Conall is our uncle. We came from Glenkirk wi Mistress Cat many years ago."

"Do you ever long for home?" India wondered.

"Not really," Susan said honestly. "The climate here and in Rome is really far better than in our dear old Scotland. Come along now, m'lady, and get into bed."

India was glad to climb into a comfortable bed. She was certain she would fall asleep before May returned with her meal, but she didn't. The two serving women bustled about her, tucking a napkin beneath her chin, settling the tray, and then sitting by her side as she ate. They were full of stories of their mistress and her early adventures. India found herself laughing at the story of how Cat was in labor with India's stepfather, yet would still not marry his father until Patrick Leslie returned property of hers that her father had wrongly included as part of her dowry, instead of allowing it to remain in her hands.

"Did she get it back?" India asked, her mouth full of bread and delicious cheese.

"Aye," Susan said, "and then her waters broke even as she said her vows to her husband."

"She had spirit," India remarked, rather fascinated by these new glimpses of Cat.

"She still does," Susan replied, "even if our life is not quite so exciting as it once was."

When India had finished her meal, and drunk down a goblet of wonderful red wine, the two servants took the tray and left her to rest. She wasn't certain she could sleep now, or that she would sleep well, but she slipped into a slumber that lasted until early the next morning, when she awoke to find Meggie snoring happily upon the trundle. India lay quietly in her bed, listening to the sounds of early dawn. The air coming through the long windows that led onto her balcony was sweet with the scent of flowers. Only the early chatter of the birds broke the silence. It was all very lovely, but she missed El Sinut. Cat had said they would send a message to Caynan Reis, but how? That was something that had to be settled today. Surely Cat was not attempting to gull her.

But the older woman was very serious in her attempt to reunite India with Caynan Reis. She had sent Conall to the harbor that very morning to find a ship that would travel across the Mediterranean and stop at El Sinut. There were none. Finally Conall found a fishing boat willing to make the passage and take a message to the dey.

"But can he be trusted?" India asked the highlander, who had brought his information to his mistress while India was breaking her fast with Lady Stewart-Hepburn.

"The man says he fishes, but he and his crew smuggle a little, too," Conall said. "Their little felluca goes back and forth between Tunis, El Sinut, and Naples wiout any difficulty. They pay protection to both ports, and half the men aboard are Arab. They can get there, get your message delivered, and they can get back."

"And they will do it?" Cat asked her majordomo.

"Aye, they will. I've promised them an extraordinary amount of coin, half before they go, half when they get back. And, I've hinted they are doing the dey of El Sinut a great service for which they will receive an additional reward when they return to Naples wi his answer. Greed is a powerful spur," he finished dryly.

"They will go today?" India demanded.

"As soon as I put your message in their hands, my lady, they will depart the port," he told her.

Cat supplied the parchment and pen, and India immediately sat down to write to her husband. She told him of how her cousin had invaded their private garden by coming over that tiny piece of the wall that was vulnerable to the outside world. How he had rendered her unconscious and carried her off, forcing Meggie to go, too. That she was now in Naples at the villa of her stepfather's mother, Lady Stewart-Hepburn, who had agreed she must return to her husband, but because of the constant strife between the Barbary States and

Christian Europe, the women did not know how this end might be accomplished. She wrote that she loved him, and was desperate to be back in his arms again.

The waterproof parchment was then folded and sealed. Then it was placed into a leather envelope, and sealed again. Conall More-Leslie returned to the harbor, giving the leather carrier into the hands of one Captain Pietro, along with a pouch of coins. The captain weighed the pouch in his palm, his look thoughtful and assessing.

" 'Tis all there," Conall told him. "When you get to El Sinut, go to the dey's palace, and ask for the chief eunuch, Baba Hassan. Tell him the leather envelope contains a message from his mistress, and is to be given to the dey immediately. Then do exactly what this man tells you to do, and when it is permitted, you will return to Naples with any answer, coming to the Villa del Pesce d'Oro to deliver that reply and collect the rest of your reward. As I have told you, the dey will instruct us to pay you additional for your service, so do not fail us, Captain Pietro."

"This is no plot against Naples, is it?" the captain asked.

Conall shook his head, rather amazed to find this smuggler was a patriotic man. "It is a private matter," he said. "Nothing more."

The captain nodded. "*Bene,*" he said.

Knowing her messenger was on his way back to El Sinut softened India's stance somewhat toward Thomas Southwood, but she was not entirely mollified, and wouldn't be until a message of reassurance came from her husband. Still, she sat at the table that evening with Cat, her handsome son Ian, and Thomas Southwood. It was Ian Stewart-Hepburn who kindled his mother's emotions, and took the attention completely from India by announcing his intentions to go with Thomas Southwood.

"What on earth for?" Cat demanded.

"Because, my dear mama, it is time I made something of myself and my life. I am thirty-three years of age, and I have spent much of my time in idle pursuits. I cannot continue to be a wastrel."

"But what will you do on Tom's ship?" Cat asked, somewhat

confused. "You are not a sailor, Ian, nor can you be one at your age."

"But I can be a merchant-trader, Mama," he told her. "I've bought a cargo of fine olive oil, and I've sent to my saddle maker in Firenze for a dozen of his best saddles. I intend shipping them on the *Royal Charles*, and finding a market for them in Istanbul. Then I shall buy something there, perhaps silk, and return to Naples."

"Ian! You are the son of the earl of Bothwell," Cat said. "What can you be thinking that you would go into trade?"

"Aye, I am the youngest son of Francis Stewart-Hepburn, once the earl of Bothwell, cousin to the royal Stuarts, but my father was outlawed, and driven from Scotland. Everything was taken from him. They even tried to take you from him, Mama. There is no title, or estates, to inherit, and if there were, Margaret Douglas's sons would have long ago laid claim to them, for she was his first wife, and her children take precedence over we youngest three, who were born when you were wed to the earl of Glenkirk. Until our father claimed us, we were thought to be Leslies, Mama.

"I am my father's son, Mama. I cannot live my life in idleness and boredom. I cannot return to Scotland, for there is nothing there for me, and I should be considered Bothwell's bastard, and scorned. I need to make a life for myself. I have been astoundingly well educated, and I have spent several years enjoying myself while I played. Now I need to move onward. Your generous allowance allows me to attempt this venture. I think I shall be good at it. I like the business of business. Perhaps if I make a small success of this, I shall even take a wife at long last. I know that would please you, eh, Mama?"

For a moment she stared at this man who looked so much like his father, with his blue eyes and auburn hair. She wondered what Francis would have thought of his youngest son's desire to go into business. The world was changing, she realized, and those who did not change with it would certainly be doomed to extinction. Francis would have agreed with that sentiment. He, himself, had been a man born ahead of his time. At least their son wanted to make something of himself, and he had some Leslie blood in his veins through her, for Cat's mother had been a Leslie. The Leslies had always been fascinated with trading, and the wealth it brought them. "I'm surprised," she admitted candidly to him, "but if this is what you want, Ian, then I cannot deny you. But make a success of it, damn it! Trade carefully, and be clever, and get your own vessel as soon as you can. That's where the money is, my son. In owning your own ship, and not having to pay someone else to ship your goods."

"Exactly, madame," Thomas Southwood said. "The *Royal Charles* is mine, which is why I was so anxious to regain her custody."

"Would you consider selling a third share in her, sir?" Cat asked the surprised young man. She turned to Ian. "It would be my gift to you, which would allow you not only the profits from your own cargo, but a third profit from the ship itself." She looked back to Thomas Southwood. "The third share I buy for Ian will ease the loss of the cargo you carried when you were captured last year. I know you sail under the banner of the O'Malley-Small Trading Company, but do they own any share of the *Royal Charles?*"

Tom Southwood shook his head. "She's all mine, madame," he said. "Several of my relations have their own vessels now, but we still sail under our family's banner for a number of reasons."

"I understand," Cat said, "but will you sell me a third share?"

"Aye," he consented, "I will, madame. The price you agree upon will indeed ease my loss, and allow me to pay my men a small stipend, for they lost, too, by our sojourn to El Sinut."

India had been fascinated by the conversation, but now as the talk turned to concluding the bargain, her mind wandered. How far had her message traveled? How would her husband retrieve her safely? What would her family think of all of this? She was hesitant to write to them just now for fear they might somehow manage to prevent her from returning to El Sinut. She knew it was a silly fear, for they were so far away in Scotland, or perhaps England, at this point in time. Still, she might err on the side of caution, and wait.

Several weeks went by during which the *Royal Charles* was restored to her full glory, but the cannon installed by the janissaries remained aboard. Thomas Southwood had decided that the loss of some cargo space was worth the ability to defend his ship. Finally, one sunny morning, he and Ian came to bid the ladies a farewell, the vessel being fully loaded, and ready to set sail for Istanbul.

"When do you plan to send India home?" the captain asked Lady Stewart-Hepburn. "Have you written to your son yet?"

"There has been no time with all your excitement, and Ian's plans," Cat said ingenuously. "I shall, of course, write to Jemmie and Jasmine soon. I enjoy India's company, and think I may take her with me to my villa outside Rome for the winter. Next spring is time enough for her to return home." She smiled at him.

"I leave the matter in your hands, madame. I have done my duty in rescuing my cousin from Barbary. My conscience is clear," Tom replied with a smile of his own. He kissed her hand, then turned to India. "I am happy to see you are returning to reason, Cousin."

"Go to hell," India told him, smiling brightly.

He laughed. "I think you will be too old by the time you return to Scotland for a husband. Perhaps it will suit you to live out your life without a man. I wish you good fortune."

"Farewell, Thomas Southwood. Go safely," India said, and turned away to bid Ian Stewart-Hepburn an adieu. "I hope your venture will succeed. Listen to Tom. He is knowledgeable, if pig-headed."

Ian chuckled. "Godspeed, India," he said with a wink.

For a moment, she looked a bit puzzled, and then India realized that Ian knew of her plans. She laughed aloud, then said, "I thank you, Ian. You may look like your father, but you are your mother's son as well, I think." Then she kissed him on the cheek.

Several days later, Captain Pietro appeared at the Villa del Pesce d'Oro. He was shown into the salon where the two women awaited him. He tried hard not to gape at the exquisite furnishings and the two beauties, only coming to his senses when Conall poked him roughly.

"Well, man, what news do you bring?" Conall demanded.

The smuggler drew the leather envelope from his shirt, and handed it to Conall. "We could not deliver it, signore."

"*Why?*" The single word snapped from India's mouth.

"There is a rebellion in El Sinut, madonna. The city was half aflame, the people alternating between fleeing into the hills and rioting. The janissaries were attempting to restore order. It was impossible to even get near the palace. Besides, the dey has been killed by the janissaries. He was, it appears, disloyal, or so the rumor being bruited about said. I am sorry, madonna."

India never heard him. She had already crumpled to the floor.

Part III

SCOTLAND AND ENGLAND, 1627–1628

Chapter 16

"Never, madame, did I expect to ever see you standing in this hall again," the duke of Glenkirk said to Lady Stewart-Hepburn. "Welcome home, Mother. *Welcome home!*"

"Thank you, Jemmie." Cat let her eye wander. Little had changed in all the years she had been gone. Her great-grandmother, Janet Leslie, still commanded the hall from her portrait above one of the two large fireplaces. *God's boots,* she thought. *Did Mam ever face the problems I now face, and must solve?* Cat doubted it.

"Where is India?" he asked her.

"She is with her mother, Jemmie. They need to talk," Cat replied. "India has suffered greatly."

"Come and sit by the fire, madame," he invited her, leading her by the hand to a comfortable chair. He signaled a servant to bring them refreshment. "India deserves to suffer for her disobedience," James Leslie said harshly. "I suppose haeing had his way wi her, that young English fop deserted her. I always thought it was India's wealth that attracted him, nae just what was between her legs. I suppose when he discovered only her mother and I could release that wealth to her, he departed. Still, either way she's ruined herself, and I'll nae forgie her for it!"

"God's blood, Jemmie, you've become narrow and pompous in your old age. While it is true that India eloped with young Leigh, she was wise enough to do so on an O'Malley-Small vessel. She went aboard disguised as an old lady being escorted by her nephew to Naples. Fortunately, the captain was your wife's cousin, Thomas Southwood. Her ruse was quickly discovered, and India was taken into his custody while her equally foolish swain was confined to his cabin. The only intimacy between them were a few stolen kisses.

"Unfortunately, the ship was taken by Barbary corsairs out of the state of El Sinut. When he saw they would be captured, Tom Southwood advised his men to accept Islam and avoid the galleys. He did so himself, and was eventually able to steal back his own ship. Young Leigh, however, offended the dey of El Sinut, and is still today in captivity and chained to an oar. We don't even know if he is yet alive."

"And my daughter? What happened to India?" the duke asked.

"The dey was attracted to her, and took her into his harem. He fell in love with her, and made her his first wife. She was very much in love with him, but Tom Southwood kidnapped her when he and his men escaped El Sinut. He would not listen to her when she tried to tell him she was content and happy. He brought her to me in Naples. When I heard the story, I, of course, planned to send her home to her husband, but then we received word there had been some sort of civil unrest in El Sinut, and that the dey was killed trying to put it down. She has been inconsolable ever since. That was why I decided to bring her home, instead of keeping her with me in Rome this winter. India needs her family now more than she has ever needed them, Jemmie."

"We told all our neighbors that she hae remained in England, and that she was visiting her relations in France and Italy," he said slowly. "I doubt anyone in England knew of her foolishness since we hae planned to leave London, and hae already taken our leave of the court just before she ran away. This misadventure in Barbary can be covered up if we are clever and careful. She is close to twenty, but I believe I can still obtain a good husband for her. Her wealth will be the key to her salvation."

"Jemmie, there are things you don't know," Cat told her son.

"Do not be in such a hurry to find India a husband. She is not able to face such a prospect right now. Be patient with her."

"Madame, I hae surely been more than patient wi India, but my patience is at an end," the duke of Glenkirk said irritably. "There are several possibilities, and I'll hae the wench wed before Twelfth Night. Then she is nae my responsibility any longer, and whatever mischief she may get into 'twill nae be my problem. 'Twill be her husband's problem. I love her dearly, Mother. Every bit as much as I love the sons and daughters of my own blood, but India is a wild wench. I canna hae her disrupting my household. Jasmine would nae go to Ireland to find a husband for Fortune when India disappeared, and she, poor lassie, is eager to wed, and be gone to her own home. Nay, India must be wed as soon as possible, madame."

"And what man will have me, my lord, *in my condition?*" India said as she came into the hall. She walked directly up to her stepfather.

James Leslie's dark-green eyes grew almost black with his anger as he saw her rounding belly. "Jesu!" he swore angrily. "Whose bastard do ye carry, mistress?"

"How dare you speak to me in that manner," India said in cold, even tones. "I carry the son my husband and I joyously created. This child is all I have left of my lord, Caynan Reis. I had a husband, Papa. I will have no other. No man will ever take *his* place."

The duke of Glenkirk was speechless for a long moment.

"You have seen your mother?" Cat asked quietly.

"Aye, and I have told her all," India said. "She understands, and says I am welcome home. I have told her I do not intend to stay after the baby is born, but rather will purchase a house near my brother's seat at Cadby. I prefer English winters to highland winters."

James Leslie finally found his voice again. "And what will you tell people about your bairn, mistress? Who will ye say his sire was? Some infidel who took you into his harem? The child is a bastard, India, plain and simple. You will nae find a husband wi that bairn about yer neck like a millstone."

"I was wed to Caynan Reis," India said wearily.

"In a Christian church? By a Christian minister or priest?" he demanded furiously. His temples were throbbing as they had not throbbed in many months. He loved her. He had raised her, but she was the most irritating female he had ever known in his entire life.

"We were married by the grand iman of El Sinut," India said, "but my husband promised me a Christian marriage when we could find a Protestant minister who would be discreet."

"Why did the minister need to be discreet?" the duke shouted.

"Because for an Islamic ruler to wed in a Christian marriage ceremony would be a cause of strife. My lord was the sultan's governor in El Sinut," India explained. "God's blood, Papa, Mama's first husband, Prince Javid Khan, married her secretly in a Christian rite."

"The bairn will be thought a bastard, India," the duke said.

"As my mother was said to be a bastard?" India countered.

"Your mother was a royal Mughal princess," he replied. "She was raised by her father in India. Your grandfather, Akbar, was wise enough to know that if your grandmother Velvet had brought her daughter home with her to England, the bairn would hae been considered bastard-born. When your mother came to England, she was full grown, and none but your aunt Sybilla dared to question her birth, and she only because she fancied herself in love wi me, and was jealous of your mother, whom I preferred."

"I am a wealthy woman, Papa. I do not need another husband. I do not care what anyone may think of my son's parentage. If I find England unwelcoming, then I shall go to France or Italy," India told them.

"I think we should end this discussion for now," Cat said. "My granddaughter and I have had a long trip, Jemmie. Besides, I have another matter of great importance to discuss with you. India, my child, return to your mother while I talk with my son."

India bent to kiss Cat's cheek, and then she hurried off.

"You like her," James Leslie said.

"I do. She is honest, and loyal. Give her time, Jemmie, but now to that other matter. As you know, Bothwell is buried at the foot of our garden in Naples. However, his heart is in a silver reliquary that I have carried with me since his death. I have brought it home to bury in Scotland. The spot will be unmarked as will our future grave here. Grant me this request, and I shall never ask anything of you again," Cat finished.

James Leslie shook his head. "You nae ere asked anything of me, madame, ye always give wi yer whole heart. My father was a fool to ever let ye go."

"Nay," Cat said. "Do not criticize Patrick, for ours was a match made by our families when I was barely out of nappies, and he a young man. He was as set in his ways as you are, my son, and I was as wild as a highland pony. I loved him well until he betrayed me by allowing the king to victimize me, but the truth is, and we both know it, Jemmie, Francis Stewart-Hepburn was the great love of my life. Both of us would have gone to our graves never admitting that had your father not been so mindless and jealous in the matter of the king. Patrick Leslie was not foolish. He was simply stubborn, and every bit as wild and proud-hearted as I was, though he would not admit to it."

"We will make a place for ye both," the duke of Glenkirk said.

"Only you, Conall, and I shall know the truth," Cat told her son with a small smile.

"When do you want to do it?" he inquired.

"As soon as possible. I want to return to Rome before travel becomes utterly impossible with the winter weather. I only came to bring Francis home to Scotland, and India back to you," she told him frankly. "I'll sail from Aberdeen before Christmas."

"Remain the winter," he pleaded with her.

She shook her head. "I cannot take the weather anymore, Jemmie. I am no girl, but an old lady of sixty-five years. Rome is a milder climate, and better for me now."

" 'Tis a bad time to be on the sea," he noted.

"There is always that fair time in December before winter sets in," Cat said quietly. "I shall be in Calais in a shorter time than if I had to travel overland down through England to Dover. I shall visit your sister and Jean-Claude a brief time, and then go on to

Marseilles, through Monaco, San Lorenzo, and Genova, and down the boot through Firenze and on to Rome. I have friends in Monaco, Genova, and Firenze. It will be an easy trip. We came that way, but only stopped each night to rest my horses, which are awaiting my return with my coach and coachman in Calais."

"How did you get from Aberdeen?" he asked her, surprised, for he had assumed she had traveled with her own equipage.

"The Kira bankers arranged everything," she told him. "They always do for me."

True to her word, Catriona Hay Leslie Stewart-Hepburn stayed only a brief time with her son and his family at Glenkirk. There was barely time to gather her family, but learning she was with Jemmie, they all came: her other sons, Colin and Robert; her daughters, Bess, Amanda, and Morag; all Patrick Leslie's children. She hadn't seen them in so long, and while they were her children, they were virtually strangers to her. And the grandchildren. There were so many grandchildren. Her brothers and their families came, and again there was the feeling of strangeness. They had always been good-hearted, rough highlanders. She had been the odd one. But still, there was that feeling of *clan* amongst them all, and she wept to see them go.

There was nothing Cat could do to ease the anger and the estrangement between her son and India. Even her daughter-in-law, Jasmine, was at a loss. It made no difference to James Leslie that both his mother and his wife counseled patience to each side. Jemmie was angry, and India was angry. A collision between these two strong wills was inevitable.

"Why would she nae listen to me?" the duke asked his wife for the hundredth time. "Did I nae tell her that Viscount Twyford was not suitable? Look now what her willfulness has cost her!"

"She is a widow having a child." Jasmine attempted to put a simple face on the problem. She looked at her husband's hands in hers, and looked into his face. "Jemmie, in El Sinut she was legally, and lawfully wed. *And she was loved.*"

"By whom?" he demanded. "Some handsome renegade, nameless and of unknown origins," the duke despaired, pulling his hands from hers. "Jasmine, we canna allow her to go off on her own to raise her bairn. There will always be questions. How do we answer those questions? What man will take the lass to wife wiout the answers? We hae said she was in England, in France, and finally wi my mother in Italy. That she hae come home wi Mother is to the good. It gives substance to that lie, but there is nae way we can explain India's big belly, or the bairn she will hae in the spring. I canna let our lass ruin her life, and I will nae!"

"Then what are we to do?" the duchess of Glenkirk demanded of her husband.

"She must go up to A-Cuil where she will nae be seen once her condition becomes too obvious, and that will be soon. We will make some excuse for her absence. That she is in Edinburgh, perhaps, visiting family. When the bairn is born we will foster it out to some cotter's wife. Nae at Glenkirk, but perhaps at Sithean or Greyhaven. India is nae to be told where the bairn is. If the birth is hard, we will tell her that the bairn died, and that will be an end of it. Then we will seek a match for her. It is the only solution."

"Ahh, Jemmie," his wife said, "you make it all sound so simple, but there are factors you have not considered. How do we explain the loss of India's maidenhead to this new husband? And how will you get my daughter to give up her child so easily? My father drugged my mother so that he might take her from me, and she never forgot it. India loved her husband. She will never let you take her child from her!"

"She will hae nae choice, Jasmine," he said.

"If you do this thing, I will never forgive you!" the duchess of Glenkirk threatened her husband angrily.

"I do what is best for India," he countered. "If ye hae let me make a match for her in the first place, instead of allowing the lass to run wild, we would hae nae of this trouble, Jasmine. Now I will do what I know is best for our daughter!"

"What am I to do?" Jasmine despaired to her mother-in-law.

"Do not allow this situation to divide your house," Cat advised wisely. "I know you love your daughter, but you and Jemmie love one another, too. India has made her own fate, and now must deal with it herself. You cannot protect her forever, my dear."

"You agree with Jemmie?"

"Nay, I do not, but I know my son well enough, and so should you, Jasmine. You surely understand you cannot push him in a direction he does not choose to go. To get him where you will have him, you must draw him first down this path, and then the other, until you reach the destination that you wanted all along, and he is none the wiser." She laughed. "He is as stubborn as I was in my youth, and as heedless of the consequences of his actions as was his father, God assoil his soul. Jemmie is not an easy man, Jasmine. I know that, and so do you. Do not let your daughter and her problem blind you to the fact that you love your husband. India will recover from her broken heart sooner than later, marry and leave you and Jemmie. You do not want an estrangement between yourselves when that time comes."

"But India's child. What will become of that child if it is fostered out, and we do not know where?" Cat fretted.

"Just make certain you know where the bairn is," Cat said. "Do what you must, but learn where that child is. Then visit the cotter's wife who has it, and make certain she knows of your interest in the child and its well-being. It is the best you can do. Later you can educate it if it is a lad, and even tell of its heritage. If it is a lass, then educate her and see she has a respectable match one day. But *never* allow Jemmie to know of your interest, or your involvement."

"And India?"

"Tell her only one day when she is happy again so that her broken heart may be completely mended," Cat replied.

"I wish you would stay with us," Jasmine said, teary-eyed.

Her mother-in-law laughed heartily. "Nay, my dear, I far prefer the quiet life I now lead in Rome and Naples. I am not used to all this agitation, aggravation, and uproar any longer. Adventures aplenty I had in my youth, but now I simply enjoy sitting in my gardens, or watching the sea, or dining with friends, or reading and writing letters from family and friends. India is your problem, and while I was happy to help where I could, I shall be delighted to depart for Aberdeen tomorrow, and then home to Villa Mia, which with luck I shall reach by February." She patted Jasmine's hand comfortingly. "You are a clever woman, Jasmine, but you have allowed your mind to stifle here in the safety of Glenkirk. Use your wits to help India now!"

Lady Stewart-Hepburn departed the following morning, her coach rumbling over the drawbridge of the castle and down the hill to the high road. Ten days later, a message arrived from Calais to say her voyage had been uneventful, and she would write from her daughter's château outside of Paris before she departed for Rome.

The weather was getting colder, and the rains icy and more frequent. One morning as India lay abed, her father came to her. They had managed to exist without shouting at each other in the time since Cat's departure, but neither spoke to each other unless it was necessary.

"Are ye well?" he asked her gruffly.

"Well enough," she replied.

"You're leaving Glenkirk, India," he told her. "I'll hae no gossip about yer big belly, and if ye remain any longer, we'll nae be able to disguise it. Ye hae to go."

To his surprise, she agreed, saying, "Aye. If Fortune is to have a decent husband, there can be no scandal about me."

"I'm glad ye understand," he said, relaxing his stern attitude just a little. "I'm happy to see ye thinking of yer sister before yerself, India. I'm nae angry wi ye anymore, lassie, but I must do what is best for ye now." He reached out to pat her hand, noting it was cold.

"Where am I to go, Papa?" she queried him. "To Edinburgh wi Great-uncle Adam and his Fiona? Or to Queen's Malvern? None come there now except in the summertime when my brother is in residence."

"Ye're going up to A-Cuil, India. Meggie will go wi ye, and Red Hugh's younger brother, Diarmid," the duke of Glenkirk told India.

"I'll freeze to death in that place!" India said. "Are you attempting to kill me then, Papa?"

"The house is stone," he said, "and there's a good fireplace in the main room, and yer bedchamber as well. Ye'll nae freeze, but ye'll be isolated, and yer shame well concealed. Nae one will know of the bairn. Diarmid will light a signal fire when yer time hae come, and yer mother will come to ye then."

"What will happen to my child?" India asked bluntly.

"We'll worry about the bairn when it's safely born," he soothed her, then put an arm about her. "Lassie, lassie, I just want to protect ye. Ye're my daughter, and I hae only wanted what's best for ye."

India suddenly began to cry. "Ohh, Papa, I am so unhappy! *I loved him, Papa!* I loved Caynan Reis! I should be in El Sinut, in the palace with Baba Hassan and the lady Azura, happily sharing the joy of our child with us." She looked up at him. "Papa, I don't even know what has happened to him! They said he was killed in the rebellion. What has happened to the ladies of the harem? To Baba Hassan and Azura? I should have been with them! If I had been, then maybe this would not have happened. Azura always said I was the stable influence in Caynan Reis's life."

The arm about her tightened, and then the duke said, "If ye hae been wi them, India, ye might hae been killed, or, worse, shipped off to some other man's harem, or sold on the block. Thank God ye are home safe wi yer mother and me than wi that rebel!"

"You don't understand, Papa! My husband was not a traitor," she explained, her face tear-streaked. "The janissaries were plotting against the sultan, and it was my husband who warned the valideh, and her son of the plot. He took a great chance, but he did it for us and our children. The valideh was certain to reward him for his loyalty, and he was going to ask for autonomy for El Sinut. The people of El Sinut would not have revolted. They were a peaceful, contented, and prosperous people. It is surely the janissaries who have killed my husband!"

"And there is nothing ye can do about it, lassie," he told her. "The man is gone, God help him, but ye're alive. I cannot weep for a man I dinna know, who took my daughter from me and got her wi bairn. I must protect ye, India. Tomorrow the weather will be fair, as it always is after two days of gray and rain. Ye'll go up to A-Cuil then, lassie. Dinna fret, for ye'll hae all the comforts ye want. I'll nae hae my lass uncomfortable, India. I just want ye where there will be nae gossip."

"Yes, Papa." What else could she say? India thought sadly. She would be twenty in the summer, but had had only a small control over her personal fortune before she fled England with Adrian Leigh. Now she had not even that. They had made certain she had no access to her wealth, but for pin money, and she would not now until she married. Where could she and Meggie go without funds? She was trapped, and for the time being forced to cooperate with her parents. Let them think she was doing it willingly. And when they were lulled into believing her complacent, she would take her son, and find a safe haven where no one would care about her or her child. Eventually they would have to relent. There had to be someplace in this world where she could go. She would sell her jewelry to give them a new start. There had to be someplace where she could raise Caynan Reis's son in safety.

The duke of Glenkirk kissed his daughter's forehead. "I am glad ye're being reasonable, sweeting. I know ye've had a terrible misadventure, but dinna fret, sweeting. Papa will make it all right for ye just as I always hae done, eh?"

God's boots, India thought, as he left her, *does he really still think of me as a child?* Certainly he saw the woman she was, or did he? James Leslie had been a wonderful father. He loved all his wife's children. The three she had had by her second husband, Rowan Lindley; the son she had had by Prince Henry Stuart; the sons she had given him. He loved them so well that not one of them but India had left the comfort of their family.

Since her departure, however, her brother, Henry, the marquis of Westleigh, had made the decision to live at his seat at Cadby in England, but the rest of them were still at home. Papa might complain about Fortune's not being able to go to her estates in Ireland and seek a husband, and he might blame India's disappearance for it, but he didn't really seem too enthusiastic about sending Fortune off next summer. James Leslie was a patriarch, and he obviously enjoyed having his children about him.

But he would not welcome his first grandchild, India knew. What he meant to do with her child she had no idea, but she would have time to make her escape once the baby was born. Mama would protect them, she was certain. For now she knew she needed rest, and the security of knowing that she would be safe and well cared for while she carried Caynan Reis's son.

Who was he? she wondered not for the first time. While she had been with him, it hadn't mattered at all, for he was Caynan Reis, the dey of El Sinut. But he had been someone else before he had been Caynan Reis, and now she desperately wished she knew who that someone was. She wanted a name for her child who would never know his father.

The next day dawned bright and cold, as James Leslie had predicted. The small caravan was prepared by midmorning, and ready to depart. India had decided to accept the comfort of a cart as opposed to riding her horse. A baggage wagon was ladened high, as was another wagon with enough provisions to last them the winter. Jasmine was very teary, for she didn't approve of sending her daughter into the mountains to the family's hunting lodge. A-Cuil was small, she knew, for she had spent time there herself, but it was far more isolated than Jasmine would have wished. What happened if India's child decided to come in a snowstorm? How could she get to her daughter?

"Please, Jemmie, don't send her to A-Cuil," she begged her husband at the last minute.

"Mama, it's all right," India said. "I am quite content to go. Meggie will be with me, and Diarmid will do the heavy work, such as cutting us wood for our fire and hunting for our game. I won't be the cause of spoiling Fortune's chances in the marriage market. My situation is rather unique," she finished with a wry smile.

"The lass hae more sense than ye do, darling Jasmine," her husband chided his weeping wife.

"And I'm going, too," Fortune announced suddenly.

"You most certainly are not!" Jasmine snapped.

"Aye, I am, Mama," Fortune declared with a toss of her red head. "Come, Mama, we are very isolated here at Glenkirk. Who will know if I am here at Glenkirk, or in Edinburgh, or wherever? I want to be with India. I lost my sister once, and I'll not lose her again."

"There!" Jasmine cried to her husband. "Are you satisfied now, Jemmie? I will lose both my girls because of your stubbornness and excessive pride."

He knew better than to argue with her. He knew better than to argue with Fortune. "Go along, Diarmid, and take yer party of ladies up the ben." He looked to his second daughter. "Dinna come down the ben alone, lassie. If ye go, ye stay. Would ye miss Christmas and Twelfth Night at Glenkirk? 'Twill be yer last if I let ye go off to Ireland next year."

"I've enjoyed many a Christmas and Twelfth Night at Glenkirk, Papa," Fortune said quietly. "Now I would be with my sister, for I believe she needs me more than you do." Then Fortune climbed upon the large gray gelding she favored, and followed after India's little train.

Jasmine swallowed back her tears, saying to her husband, "Does she know what you intend doing with her child, Jemmie?"

"Nay," he said. "There was nae need to distress her. Ye saw. She was almost herself again. I dinna want to spoil it."

"Aye," Jasmine agreed. "You were wise not to do so." She looked after her two eldest daughters, and thought she heard India laugh as Fortune caught up with the cart.

"Is Mama still weeping?" the younger asked her elder sibling as the gelding danced dangerously near the wheels of the vehicle.

"No, she stopped," India replied. "What made you come with me?" she asked Fortune. "Have you ever been to A-Cuil? It's tiny, old-fashioned, and dull, not to mention very small. We'll probably end up killing each other."

"I'd rather be with you than stuck at Glenkirk all winter," Fortune responded. "You can tell me all about your adventures, and what it's like to be loved by a man. I have that ahead of me next summer."

"If Papa lets you go," India said.

"Mama won't let him stop us this time," Fortune replied. "So you noticed it, too; how suddenly he does not want to let his *lasses* go away." She laughed. "Poor Papa. He really does love us all, doesn't he? But by this time next year, you and I will have husbands. Henry is already settled at Cadby, and the king has written to Papa that after this winter, Charlie must become part of the court and take his rightful place at Queen's Malvern as the duke of Lundy should. He'll just have to be content with Patrick, Adam and Duncan.

India laughed in response to her sister's question. "I don't know, but I think it will be up to us to help her escape, Fortune."

"It's so good to hear you laugh again," Fortune said.

"There hasn't been a great deal to laugh about lately," India answered. "But soon I will have my son, and then I will be happy."

"Beware," Fortune warned India. "Papa means to take the bairn from you. Mama is trying to change his mind in the matter."

"Mama will succeed, but in the event she does not," India said, "Papa will find a deadly enemy in me, for I shall not allow my child to be taken from me, Fortune. This is Caynan Reis's son, and I will protect him, as will the spirit of his father. We will let nothing happen to our son, and James Leslie be damned if he should attempt to harm my child!" India said fiercely.

"You have changed," Fortune said softly.

"Aye," India agreed. "I have become a hard enemy to any who would threaten me or mine."

Chapter 17

A-Cuil had come into the possession of the Leslies of Glenkirk through the current duke's mother, Lady Stewart-Hepburn. It had belonged to Cat's paternal grandmother, Jean Gordon Hay, who had given it to Cat. Its value was in its isolated beauty, and the mountain forest that belonged to it. It had been used as a hunting lodge by several generations of Gordons, Hays, and Leslies, and always kept ready for visitors. Once in the not-too-distant past, Jemmie and Jasmine had hidden themselves there to escape a rival for Jasmine's affections.

The small lodge itself was set upon a cliff that commanded a spectacular view of Glenkirk Castle, Sithean Castle, and Greyhaven, Cat's girlhood home, as well as several small lochs far below. The forest surrounded the lodge and its stables. It was beautiful, wild, and totally isolated. Built of stone with a slate roof, it was virtually undetectable nestled on its cliff, the endless sky spread out above it.

While knowing of its existence, neither India nor Fortune had ever been to A-Cuil. The well-marked trail from Glenkirk Castle grew fainter and fainter as they climbed into the hills, and finally up the steep ben. Several times the cart tilted so precariously that India thought it would tip over, casting her down onto the gorse and rocks. At one point, the forest was so deep that the sun scarcely penetrated to the forest floor. Up and up their little train climbed until finally they entered out into a sunny clearing where the lodge and its stables were set neatly awaiting them.

"God's boots!" Fortune swore. "It is small, isn't it?"

"You can go back with the provisions cart," India said.

Fortune shook her head. "Nay. 'Twill be an adventure, and, besides, the forest looks like good hunting. I've hunted with Diarmid More-Leslie before. Between us we'll keep in fresh meat."

India's cart came to a halt, and she exited the vehicle as Fortune slid from her horse's back. "Let's go inside," India said. "I want to see the living quarters."

Within the lodge was charming, but, as they had been warned, of insignificant proportions. On the main floor there were but two rooms. The smaller of the two served as a kitchen area with its tiny pantry. The larger room with its big fireplace and wall oven would be where they spent most of their time, and where they would cook their food, for the little kitchen had no hearth. The furnishings were simple, although over the years, a few more comfortable pieces had been added than were originally there. There was a small trestle and two chairs in the kitchen.

"Jesu," India grumbled, " 'tis colder than a witch's tit in January in here. Diarmid," she shouted, "bring some wood! We're freezing to death in here! Meggie, go and help him."

"Yes, my lady," Meggie said, running outside where she would have sworn it was far warmer than inside the damp lodge.

"Let's see what's upstairs," Fortune said, and began to climb the narrow flight of stairs followed by her elder sister.

At the top of the stairs they found a single bedchamber, and entered it. On the door wall was a fireplace. To the left was a bank of casement windows overlooking part of the valley view, and the forest. To the right was a single round window. It was not a large room, but it comfortably held several pieces of furniture. Opposite the door was a good-sized canopied and curtained bed. At its foot was a carved clothes chest. There was a little table beneath the round window, and a tapestried chair by the fireplace. There was a pier glass on the bit of wall to the left of the door. On the floor were several thick sheepskins.

"Everything is clean, even the windows," India noted. "Papa must have been planning this since I returned to Glenkirk." She turned and slowly descended into the main room of the lodge. "Even here, everything is dusted and swept. But it really is small. When I think of my palace in El Sinut . . . why, my personal apartments were larger than this by far, weren't they, Meggie?"

"Your day room was bigger than this," Meggie said frankly. "This is nae more than a wee mousie's hold, my lady, but more folk hae lived in smaller places, I can tell you. We'll manage."

Diarmid had brought the wood, and there was already a fire started in the large fireplace. "I'll begin a fire in the bedchamber, my lady," he told India.

"Put enough wood in there for the night," she told him. "I don't want to be frozen in the morning."

The carters from Glenkirk unloaded the provisions, and, directed by Meggie, brought them into the lodge where the serving woman put them away. There was flour for baking, salt, and spices. Bundles of herbs were hung from the kitchen's rafters. Several barrels of wine, ale, and apples were stored in the larder along with a large wheel of cheese and two whole hams. Two milk cows had climbed the ben tied to the back of the cart. They were now led into their barn. A coop holding half a dozen chickens and a rooster were uncrated in the yard. A haunch of beef and one of venison were hung in the larder next to the ham. There was even a block of sugar, and a small barrel filled with honeycombs. There was a large fat tomcat to keep the rodent population down, a small collie, and a deer hound for company, protection, and hunting.

"Last chance to go back to Glenkirk," India said to Fortune as the carts began their return journey. It was past the noon hour, and the sun would set in another two hours.

"I'm starving," Fortune said, ignoring the invitation. "What's for dinner?"

"I'll see what's in the basket," Meggie said. "Cook was kind enough to send something along so we would nae hae to fuss today." She bustled into the kitchen.

"What a treasure," Fortune noted to her sister. "You were fortunate to find each other. She isn't any older than we are, is she? What luck she didn't decide to return to Ayr, India."

"I don't think she would have left my service," India replied, "but when Papa inquired discreetly for her, we found her mother had died suddenly, even before Meggie was captured, and her father killed. Her betrothed, of course, had done exactly as she had anticipated, and wed with his second choice, Meggie's rival. There was nothing for her to go back to, Fortune."

Supper was a roasted capon, a rabbit pie reheated in the brick fireplace oven, bread, cheese, and apples. India insisted that Diarmid eat with them at the trestle, dragging two more little chairs from the common room so they might all sit.

"You must go back down to Glenkirk tomorrow," she told him, "and tell Papa we need carrots, onions, and leeks. We cannot live the winter on just meat, bread, and cheese."

"Aye, m'lady, but I dinna know why not. 'Tis good food," the clansman said. "Still, the duke hae told me to humor ye, and so I'll go for ye. As long as the weather is good, I can fetch up whatever takes yer fancy. Will there be anything else while I'm about it?"

"Pears. They'll keep in the cold," India said.

"And conserves," Fortune added. "And perhaps some jam. I like jam on my bread."

"Check in the kitchen, Meggie," India told her servant, "and see if there is anything else you'll need."

The clansman nodded, and, having finished his meal, took his leave of the women, saying, "I'll leave the collie wi ye. Bar the doors both front and back, m'lady. I'll be sleeping in the stable loft. There's a wee room there."

"Will you be warm enough?" India fretted.

"Aye, the room is tight, and I hae the dog for warmth," he told her with a small smile. Then he was gone out the door, which Meggie shut, and firmly barred.

The three young women slept in the upstairs bedchamber, India and Fortune sharing the big bed, Meggie on the trundle pulled from beneath the bed. The collie lay down at the head of the stairs, as if guarding them until sleep finally claimed her, too.

The following day dawned clear. After a meal of oat cakes and ale, Diarmid More-Leslie went down the ben to Glenkirk to fetch the required items. Meggie began to put her kitchen in order while India and Fortune explored the nooks and crannies of the lodge, discovering an old oak tub in a kitchen recess, and some woman's clothing in a small trunk in the upstairs hall.

"Do you think they were Mama's?" India wondered aloud.

"Nay," Fortune said, admiring the doeskin jerkin with the silver-and-horn buttons she had just pulled out. "Mama wasn't as long-waisted, and the style is old-fashioned. Besides, Mama never wore such a garment in her entire life. She is far more elegant." Fortune tried on the jerkin. "I think it may have belonged to Papa's mother. They say she hid herself up here to avoid marrying her first husband. I think I'll keep it. I like hunting clothes."

"It suits you," India said, smiling at her younger sister. Then she caught her breath suddenly.

"What is it?" Fortune said, seeing a strange look come over her sister's beautiful face.

"*He moved!*" India half whispered. "The baby moved within me, Fortune!" Then she burst into tears as she sat down upon the top step of the staircase. "Damn! Damn! Damn!" she swore softly. "My bairn is alive within me, and his father will never know him. It isn't fair, Fortune! It just isn't fair!"

"You have hardly spoken of him since you came home," Fortune said, sitting down next to her older sister and putting an arm about her. "Did you love him very much, India? What was he like? Was he handsome?"

India sniffled, wiping her nose on her sleeve. "Aye, he was handsome. He was tall, and had hair like a raven's wing, and the bluest eyes you have ever seen. His nose was straight, and his jaw firm, and his mouth . . ." She paused a moment, then continued. "His mouth was the most deliciously kissable mouth in all the world."

"What's it like being kissed?" Fortune asked.

"Wonderful," India replied. "I cannot explain it. Someday you will kiss the man you love, and you will understand, Fortune."

"I suppose so," Fortune replied matter-of-factly.

Their days took on a comfortable cadence. By virtue of their social status, India and Fortune had never really done a great deal for themselves. Now, however, they arose each morning, and, after dressing, Fortune went down to the barn to gather eggs from their hens and drive the cows into the small pasture on sunny days. Until it snowed, the cows could forage, but once the winter set in, they would be confined to the barn. It became India's task to set the table for meals and gather up the clothing that would need laundering, but neither of the other two girls wanted India overtaxed for the sake of her child.

Some days Fortune rode off into the forest with Diarmid to hunt for small game. India and Meggie walked in the forest and high meadows most early afternoons. And Meggie cooked and cleaned and did the laundry. The sisters, however, kept the bedchamber neat and dusted. Each morning they shook out their featherbed as Meggie taught them, and then drew the bed clothes back over it smoothly and neatly. Neither had ever done such simple tasks, but it helped to fill the lonely hours. Fortune had requested her lute be sent up from Glenkirk, and on many evenings she played for them, and they sang the old songs of unrequited love, great battles, heroes, and kings. Diarmid had his pipes, and was easily encouraged to play.

Like his brother, Red Hugh, he was a big man of few words, but practical and kindly. His hair was a nut brown, and his eyes an amber hue. He wore a short beard with his hair drawn back, secured by a leather thong. He was popular with the ladies, the sisters knew, but he had never married. The winter would be lonelier for him than for his three female charges, who at least had each other. While deferential to the duke's two daughters, Diarmid had struck up a budding friendship with Meggie. Up before the first light each dawn, he had the fireplaces blazing and water brought into the kitchen even before Meggie came down to put the bread dough that had been rising all night in the oven to bake. While he spoke little to India and Fortune, Meggie could get him talking, and even bring a rosy flush to the big man's cheeks.

"You've made a conquest," India teased her maid servant.

"Hummph," Meggie replied, but she smiled.

Just before Christmas it snowed. They awoke to find the white flakes swirling about the lodge. Diarmid found a Yule log for them in the nearby forest, and dragged it into the little house on Christmas Eve, setting it in the fireplace where it burned merrily for almost two days. They took turns telling the Christmas story, and sang Yule songs. They lit a fire outside on the cliff top on Twelfth Night, and watched as the other fires sprang up for as far as the eye could see, vying to identify the Glenkirk fire first.

Now the winter set in hard. India insisted that Diarmid sleep before the common room fire at night rather than in his stabletop loft. It was just too cold. Even the cows, horses, and poultry were brought into a small shed attached to the lodge on the kitchen side. It was warmer for them there than the stables. The lodge took on an earthy smell, but it did not bother either India or Fortune. Survival was more important.

By February, the days were beginning to grow longer again, but the weather remained cold and snowy. By March, the snow came less frequently, more often than not mixing with the rain. India's belly was now enormous, and she waddled when she walked, but she never complained. Instead, she would lie upon her bed, her hand protectively cradling her stomach, a dreamy expression upon her face as she wondered what her child would look like. It would be a boy, of course. Her instinct told her that. What would she call him? She knew that Caynan Reis had been a European by birth, but that was all she knew. His origins, and his name remained a mystery to her. If she had known his name, she would have named her child after his father, but she hadn't a clue.

Finally, she decided. "I shall call him Rowan after our own father," India told her younger sister one rainy March afternoon.

"Rowan *what?*" Fortune asked frankly.

"He'll have to have my name, as I don't know his father's," India replied just as frankly. "Rowan Lindley. I like it!"

"And what will you do after Rowan Lindley is born? You don't still mean to go off by yourself with your child, India, do you?" Fortune was beginning to worry about her sister.

"It is what I want to do," India replied calmly. "I will not bring shame upon you, and ruin your chances of marriage because of my adventures."

"God's blood!" Fortune swore. "Do you think I care what people may say? I am Lady Fortune Lindley, daughter of the late marquis of Westleigh, an heiress in my own right, and anyone who does not love my family—*all my family*—can go to the devil. Think about it, India. Our heritage is greater than anyone's. Our grandfather was a great ruler of a great land. Our great-grandmother bested a mighty queen, and lived to tell the tale. What a woman she was, Madame Skye! We are women who make our own rules in life, and then live by them. We are not mealymouthed, pious little kirk-goers who live dully, and sin in the shadows. We live as we please, do as we please, and the devil take any who would dare to criticize us!"

India burst out laughing. "Do you know how much I missed you when I was away, Fortune?"

"Well," Fortune replied. "I am your sister!" Then she jumped up. "It isn't raining hard. Get your cloak, and let's go for a walk."

"Take your boots off before you come into this house then," Meggie warned them. "I'll nae hae you two tracking mud all over my clean floors!" She glared at them sternly.

"Come with us," India begged.

"I'm nae a duck, my lady," Meggie said, "and besides I hae to start the dinner. Rabbit stew."

"*Again?*" the sisters chorused.

"Be glad spring is here," Meggie said sharply. " 'Twill be the last of the carrots and onions you see in that stew tonight, and lucky we are to hae it. Almost everything is gone, and only that Diarmid trapped the rabbit this morning, we'd be haeing bread and toasted cheese."

The sisters walked through the forest to a high meadow. The light rain stopped, and the sun peeped out now and again from behind the thinning clouds.

When they returned to the lodge, Meggie's stew was bubbling in the pot, and it smelled wonderful. India slowly climbed the narrow little staircase to the bedchamber to lie down, for she was tired and her back hurt. She awoke to a piercing pain.

"*Meggie! Fortune!*" she called, struggling to sit up.

Hearing her call, the two girls raced up the stairs, and into the bedchamber. One look told them that India was probably about to have her child early.

"Do you know what to do?" Fortune asked Meggie.

Meggie swallowed hard, saying, "I think so. I was there when my mother birthed her last child. We'll need hot water, clean clothes, and, for God's sake, send Diarmid down to Glenkirk to tell the duchess. She'll want to come and be with my lady India. This could take hours."

Fortune flew from the room, dashed down the stairs, filled the cauldron with water, and set it to boil. Then out into the stable yard she ran, calling to Diarmid as she went. The big man took one look at the girl, and knew the reason for her fright and excitement.

"Get yer horse, Mistress Fortune, and ride to fetch yer mam and yer da. Ye're no use here, I can see. I'll be more help to Meggie than ye will, lassie, meaning no offense to ye."

Fortune didn't argue with the big man. She knew he was being kind, and, more important, speaking the truth. "I've put a kettle on to boil, and there's a stack of clean cloths we prepared for this occasion in the cupboard in the fireplace wall, Diarmid."

He nodded, and walked toward the lodge as she hurried into the stable to saddle her gray. It was a two-hour ride to Glenkirk, but she would make it before sunset. Still Mama would be coming up the ben in the darkness, but come she would. Fortune tightened the cinch on the gray, and clambered onto his back, riding him right out the stable doors and onto the track that led down the ben toward Glenkirk.

India's labor was hard, but very, very short. She sweated, and she swore blue oaths that turned Meggie's face bright red, and set Diarmid to chuckling as he encouraged her onward.

"Ohh, m'lady, dinna let the bairn hear such words, and him just coming new into the world," Meggie pleaded with her mistress.

"Bloody hell!" India snarled. "It hurts, damn it! Why won't the little wretch be born? Ahhhhh! *Merde! Merde! Merde!*"

"Ye're doing fine, lassie," Diarmid said quietly. "Now, when ye feel the pain again, gie us a hard push to help the wee laddie along."

India nodded.

"I dinna think you should be here," Meggie fretted.

"He stays!" India snapped. "He obviously knows more about this than you do. Besides, I suspect there's nothing I have that Diarmid hasn't already seen. Ooooooooh!"

"Push, lassie! Push! Ah, there's a good lass," Diarmid said calmly in the very same tone India had heard him use with the collie. "And here's his wee head, dark as a raven's wing, it is. Gie us another push, lassie." And when India complied, he said, "he's half born now," and, bending, he opened the infant's mouth and pulled a clot of mucus out of it.

The baby took a breath, and began to wail.

"Ohhhh! Ohhh! Ohhhh!" India cried, and, feeling herself swept by another spasm, she pushed hard again, and felt the baby sliding fully from her body. "Is he all right? Let me see him!" she cried out to them.

Meggie had caught the child in a linen cloth as it was born. She wrapped it about the baby, and lay him on his mother's belly. "Here he is, my lady," she said, tears in her eyes.

India cradled her son for a long moment. He did have black hair, and the blue eyes that looked up at her were the eyes of Caynan Reis. Tears slipped down her face as she looked at this miracle their love for each other had wrought. The baby had stopped crying now. "Rowan Lindley is your name, my son," she whispered to him.

"Gie me back the laddie, my lady," Diarmid said. "I must cut the cord, and ye must let Meggie finish what ye hae started. Ye dinna need me here now." He took the child, neatly cutting and knotting the cord. Then, without another word, he left the bedchamber.

"Thank you, Diarmid More-Leslie!" India called after him.

Meggie now wiped the baby free of the birthing blood with warmed oil and wine. Then she swaddled the infant, giving him back to India, who pushed the afterbirth from her body into the basin Meggie held. Setting the ewer aside, the servant took the child again, and set him in his cradle by India's side. Then she helped her mistress up, bathed her, gave her a fresh shift, settled her in the chair by the fire, and changed the linens on the bed. Finally she helped India back into the bed, returning the baby to her to cuddle. Then, gathering up all the debris of the birthing process, she said, "I'll leave you wi the bairn, m'lady. I'll come back shortly wi a nice hot posset to nourish you, and put wee Master Rowan in his cradle then."

India lay quietly cuddling her newborn son. He was everything Caynan Reis would have wanted. Beautiful and strong of limb. She searched his small face for some sign of his father, but only the blue eyes reminded her of her husband. The little baby face was entirely unfamiliar, but the look he suddenly gave her was direct and fierce. "We will do fine, you and I, Rowan, son of Caynan Reis," she told him. The infant closed his eyes, and was immediately asleep, safe in the comfort of his mother's arms. Looking through the window, India could see a magnificent sunset.

She was half dozing when Meggie returned, bringing with her a mixture of herbs, eggs, and rich red wine. The servant took the baby and set him in his cradle which she moved to the warmth of the fireplace. India drank down the nourishment, and, handing the goblet back to Meggie, fell asleep. Meggie tiptoed from the room, and back down the stairs to join Diarmid in the common room.

"I'll get us some supper," she said. "My lady and the bairn are sleeping. 'Tis been a long day. Do you think the duke and duchess will come tonight, Diarmid?"

"Aye," he answered her. "The duchess will be anxious over her eldest lass. They'll come. Mistress Fortune will hae reached Glenkirk long since, I'm thinking. 'Tis only sunset now, and the twilight will last a bit longer. They'll come wi torches up the ben. The dogs will let us know when they approach."

She served them up plates of rabbit stew, bread, and cheese. They toasted Rowan Lindley in the last of the brown October ale. He helped her with the washing up, and then together they sat companionably by the fire, talking low.

It was dark when the dogs began to bark. Diarmid arose, and, going to the lodge's door, opened it. He could see the flickering of the torches through the trees as the duke's party came out of the forest and into the clearing.

James Leslie, duke of Glenkirk, pushed his horse forward, stopping by Diarmid More-Leslie's side and asking, "Is the bairn born yet?" He dismounted.

"Several hours ago, my lord. A laddie, strong and sweet," was the reply.

Jasmine dismounted her stallion. "Is my daughter all right?"

"Very well, my lady. She's sleeping. Come into the house. Meggie can tell ye more," the clansman told his duchess.

"See to the men," the duke commanded him, and, taking his wife's arm, entered the lodge.

Meggie bobbed a curtsey. "My lord. My lady."

Jasmine smiled at the serving girl, and then hurried up the stairs to the bedchamber. Entering it, she saw India, sleeping soundly. She looked into the cradle and smiled. The baby was absolutely beautiful.

"Mama?" India suddenly called to her mother.

"Sweeting, he is a lovely lad," Jasmine said softly.

"His name is Rowan," India murmured, then fell back to sleep.

Jasmine's heart contracted painfully. Her daughter had named this infant after her own true father. She doubted India could remember anything of Rowan Lindley, but she had chosen to name her child after him. The duchess of Glenkirk went back downstairs again.

"How is our lass?" Jemmie asked his wife.

"Sleeping, though she woke a moment. She has called her son Rowan. He is a beautiful boy," Jasmine told her husband.

"You know what must be done," the duke said stonily, his handsome face set.

"Jemmie, in the name of God I beg you not to do this thing. India will never forgive you. Is that what you want? For your daughter to hate you for the rest of her life?" Jasmine pleaded with her husband.

"Jasmine, we hae no other choice. We hae discussed this all winter long. There is nae other way if India's reputation is to be salvaged. We hae had a good offer for the girl, and I've taken it, but she canna go to her husband wi her bastard."

"My grandson is no more a bastard than I was, James Leslie," Jasmine said angrily.

"But her marriage to this infidel, and this child, are nae easily explained," the duke said. "India will be wed as soon as we can manage it. The earl is willing to do it by proxy, and then she will be gone down into England before the summer hae come in, Jasmine." His tone softened. "Do ye remember the time that A-Cuil was our refuge?"

"Do not attempt to wheedle me, Jemmie," his wife said harshly.

Meggie was totally confused, but rather than tax herself with the meaning of the conversation between the duke and the duchess, she brought them wine instead. They thanked her, and then the duke told his daughter's serving woman to go upstairs and remain with her mistress for the night. He and his wife would remain here.

The baby was beginning to whimper when Meggie entered the room. India was instantly awake, and Meggie brought her child to her to be put to the breast. The infant nursed until he fell asleep, and Meggie returned him to his cradle.

Twice more before the dawn, the boy was fed at his mother's breast, India speaking softly to her son, gently touching his soft downy dark hair.

The sun was just beginning to peep through the bedchamber windows when the duke of Glenkirk entered the chamber. India awoke as her father reached into the cradle and, taking the baby out, made to leave the room.

"Give me my son," India said, frightened, and Meggie, sleeping by the fire, awoke, and looked from her mistress to the duke.

"Ye hae nae bairn, India," the duke said, and departed, his booted footsteps echoing as he went down the stairs.

India scrambled from her bed, and after him. *"Give me my son!"* she shrieked. "If you hurt him, I shall kill you, Papa! *Give me my son!"*

The duke of Glenkirk handed the baby, now awake and crying, to Diarmid More-Leslie. "Ye know what to do," he said.

The clansman took the swaddled infant, and exited the lodge through the front door.

Weakened, India lurched down the stairs, screaming, *"Bring him back! Bring my son back!"* She fell the last few steps, but, struggling to her feet, tried to follow after her child.

The duke shut the door, and, blocking it with his large body, said to her, " 'Tis for the best, lovey. Ye're to be wed in a few weeks' time. The lad will be taken care of, I promise ye." He reached out for her.

India shrank back, her eyes wild. "Get away from me, you bastard! *Get away! I want my son! I want my son!"* She flung herself at him, and tried to claw him aside.

"There, there, lassie, 'twill be all right," he promised her, and caught the hands that would beat at him in her effort to follow Diarmid and her child. "Jasmine!" he called to his wife. "Come and take yer daughter back to her room. She will need her rest now if she is to recover and be wed on time."

Jasmine glared at her husband. She had never known Jemmie to be such an insensitive clod. She tried to cradle her daughter, but India flung her mother away.

"How could you let him do this, madame?" the distraught girl sobbed. "How could you allow him to take my son? *I will never forgive you. I will never forgive either of you!*" Then she collapsed to the floor, sobbing bitterly.

Chapter 18

She was cold. Cold as ice. The fire Caynan Reis had roused in her had been extinguished when they had kidnapped her son, Rowan. She felt nothing but emptiness, and for a time did not care if she lived, or died. It made no difference. None of it made any difference. Her eyes, once an unusual gold, were now dulled amber. She spoke only when spoken to, and then her answers were monosyllabic, or as brief as she could make them. She wept more often than not. The day her breasts finally dried up of their milk she was completely inconsolable, and attempted to fling herself from the battlements of Glenkirk Castle.

The duke of Glenkirk was furious and frantic by turns. He had done what he truly believed was best for his beloved stepdaughter, yet she would not see it. India was no longer in the first flush of her youth. The marriage offer he had received from England had been the answer to his prayers. India would have the noble husband she deserved, and none but a sworn-to-secrecy few would be the wiser of her misadventures. Her intended had agreed to all the conditions laid down by the Leslies of Glenkirk in order to protect their daughter and her personal wealth. The large dowry had already been paid, but here it was the beginning of May, and the bride was nowheres fit to travel south to her new lord. Indeed, she grew thinner and paler with every passing day. A large-eyed, dark-haired wraith whose only show of spirit was the look of hatred she fastened on her parents whenever they came into her view.

"I tried to stop him," Jasmine attempted to explain to her eldest child as she sat with her one afternoon, trying to reach her. "For the first time in all our marriage, I could not reason with him, India. I am attempting to find out where they have taken your son. When I do, I swear to you that the lad will lack for nothing!"

"Except his mother," India responded bitterly. "How could you, madame? You of all people, who was forcibly taken from her own natural mother. How could you rob me of the only thing I had left of Caynan Reis? At least my grandmother had the comfort of knowing that you were with your father, and your foster mother was her dear friend, Rugaiya Begum. I have no such comfort. My lawful husband is dead in an uprising, our son is stolen from me, and I am to be sent as wife to some stranger. *I want my child returned to me!*" She had not spoken so much, or so very passionately, since they had brought her back to Glenkirk from A-Cuil.

"I do not know where Rowan is," Jasmine repeated. "I am trying to find out, India, but I am not capable of miracles. Jemmie has been most adamant in this matter. As for your betrothed husband, you have little time left to dissemble on the subject. Your marriage has been arranged, and you will go to England as soon as you can travel. No later than the end of the month, your father says." She caught her daughter's hands in hers, and looked into those dreadful, dead eyes India now possessed. "It is a good match, India, and he agreed to all our terms. Considering your age, we are very lucky."

"I was content to take my child, find my own home, and live a quiet, discreet life, madame," India replied. She was ready at last to voice her anger.

"How would you have explained Rowan?" her mother asked.

"Why would I have to explain my son?" India snapped. "Did not my great-grandmother return from Algiers *enceinte?* And who dared to challenge her story of a Spanish merchant who had been her husband? Aunt Willow was accepted to polite society. She even served the old queen as a maid of honor, and married quite well, too. Why was I not believed? Why was my son ripped from my breast just hours after his birth and hidden away as if he was something shameful?"

"There has never, *ever* been any question regarding my aunt's parentage," Jasmine said defensively.

India snorted derisively. "I suppose it was a *simpler* time," she said mockingly. "It would have been better if I had lived then rather than now. Then I should have my child with me."

"I am doing my best," Jasmine wearily told her daughter.

"Your best is not good enough, madame," India answered her coldly. "You should have prevented your husband from kidnapping my son."

"India, your father did what he thought was right to protect you!" Jasmine cried.

"James Leslie is *not* my father, madame. Rowan Lindley was my father. As for you, you may have given me life, but I should have been better off being raised by a she-wolf as by you. You, who played the strumpet before the whole court with Prince Henry and bore his bastard openly and proudly. You, who kept the child of that liaison, yet, I, who was lawfully wed to my husband, has been robbed of our child. Now you want me to marry a husband of your choosing, and go off to England as if everything is perfect so the bloody Leslies of Glenkirk, and their overproud duke, will not be put to scorn and shame. Well, madame, I shall indeed go, and do your bidding, but for one reason, and one reason alone. *To get away from you and James Leslie.* You will never be welcome in my home. I never want to see either of you again once I have departed this place!"

Jasmine staggered back as if her daughter had physically assaulted her. India's words, cold, hard, unforgiving, battered her. Her chest felt tight, and she could barely breathe with the pain.

"Who is he?" India demanded.

"*What?*" Jasmine croaked the single word.

"Neither you, nor your husband have bothered to tell me who this paragon is that I am to wed," India said. "Who is he?"

"The earl of Oxton," Jasmine began, only to be interrupted by a screech from her outraged daughter.

"*The earl of Oxton?* Adrian's father? He is a dying man, and he has a wife!" India shrilled.

"Adrian's father is dead. He died some months ago," Jasmine murmured. "His second wife, the Italian woman, was returned to her family by the current earl, Lord Deverall Leigh."

"Adrian's *brother? The murderer?* Really, madame, this is too much, even for you and your husband to have done!" India was outraged to her very core. They would marry her to a murderer?

"Lord Leigh has been cleared of all the charges concerning Lord Jeffers's death," Jasmine began hesitantly, waiting for India to shriek again, and when she didn't, continued hurriedly. "He returned to England several months ago with the information that exonerated him, and the king gave him a pardon. He was reunited with his father, who died shortly thereafter. The dowager countess was then sent to Italy, banished by royal command from ever entering England again. Lord Leigh saw you at court when you were a child. He inquired regarding your marital status, and when he learned you were not wed, offered for you. It is an ideal arrangement, India. Despite the royal pardon, he is slightly tarnished by the matter that threatened his good name for so long. Respectable families will not consider him as a son-in-law. As for you, while there is no firm ground upon which you may be charged with misbehavior publicly, there are too many suspicious, and enough wagging tongues who remember your less-than-discreet conduct regarding Adrian Leigh, which renders you equally difficult to match no matter your vast wealth and excellent connections," Jasmine concluded.

"You would not let me marry Adrian, but you will allow me to marry his wastrel half-brother? I am confused," India said sarcastically.

"The earls of Oxton are a reputable family," Jasmine explained, ignoring her daughter's caustic tone. "Deverall Leigh's mother was Susanne Deverall, daughter of the marquise of Whitley, another eminent family. The unfortunate Adrian had a foreign mother of less-than-distinguished lineage. According to Lady Stewart-Hepburn, the di Carlo family in Naples were merchant-traders less than two generations ago."

"Both the Leslies and the O'Malley family are in trade," India said. "What makes us any different from the di Carlos?"

"Really, India," Jasmine answered her daughter, surprised. "Our families were noble first, and merchant-traders only because we enjoy it, and the gold that flows into our coffers from our endeavors. Had the di Carlos not helped some duke avoid a scandal, they could not have climbed as high as they did, and they have come no further. Had not their daughter's youth and beauty captivated the late Lord Charles Leigh, who knows what would have happened to her. As it was, she was no better than a whore in her behavior, which undoubtedly drove poor Lord Charles to his death. His eldest son, however, is a very suitable match for you. He is, I am told, a pleasant-looking man, whose youthful exuberance has been long since tempered by his adventures."

"It matters not," India said stonily.

"He wants children," Jasmine said softly.

"Do you think another man's child will make me forget my firstborn?" India replied icily. "Did Grandmother really ever forget you, madame? How many tears did she weep in hidden silence? I will weep far more not even knowing the fate of my son."

"I will find him, I swear it!" Jasmine promised her daughter.

The dead eyes flicked over the older woman. "I expect a trousseau, madame, and *all* my possessions, jewels, plate, linens, furs, whatever is mine I will take with me, for I shall never return here again."

"You shall have everything, everything you want, dearest," Jasmine said. "You are an heiress in your own right, and the duke of Glenkirk's stepdaughter. We will not allow you to go to your husband in a beggarly fashion."

"I wish to leave the thirtieth of May. I shall go to Queen's Malvern first. Where is Oxton Court, madame?" India asked.

"Not far from Queen's Malvern, but not in Worcester, in Gloscester," Jasmine told her daughter. "The estate is very lovely and rural, I am informed. I believe you will like it there."

"It matters not if I do, or nay," India replied. "It will be my home until I die and am reunited with my beloved Caynan Reis."

"If you die," Jasmine said pithily, "then what will become of young Rowan Lindley? Will you not live on the hope of finding your little son one day, India? Perhaps if the earl of Oxton is a kind man, and you win his favor, the child can come and live with you. Do not, I beg you, tell your stepfather that I said that! He would be angry with me for even thinking it, and then I would have no chance of finding your son for you, my daughter."

"Do you think it possible?" India asked, her voice hopeful for the first time.

"If you gain your husband's love and trust, it might be possible," Jasmine encouraged her daughter.

"I must tell him immediately, else he wonder why I am not a virgin," India said. "I am certain that the duke has not even considered my predicament in that matter. How am I to explain such a thing if I have never been wed? He will think me a wanton, but your husband did not think of that, did he? All he considered was a good offer and a chance to rid his conscience of my presence!"

Jasmine had no answer to her daughter's accusation, for the truth of the matter was, India was absolutely correct. James Leslie had been so delighted by a decent offer for India that he had snatched at it like a drowning man at a straw. When she had brought up the fact of India's womanly condition, her husband, in one of his maddeningly rare bouts of Scots logic, had suggested ways to give India the appearance of virginity, and Jasmine should see to them. The duchess of Glenkirk had swallowed back her humorous retort, because she could see her Jemmie was deadly serious, and that he wanted this match for India.

"I think," she said carefully, "that you might tell the earl of Oxton that you contracted a marriage while abroad, but that your bridegroom died shortly thereafter. There are ways of restoring the tightness of your love sheath, India, and I would advise we consider them. There is no reason you should not like your husband. Mayhap you will come to love him. As you are aware of the pleasures a man and a woman's bodies can give each other, you will surely want to give the earl sweet enjoyment. It cannot help but win him over so that he will want to please you *in all matters,* even that of little Rowan."

"And when do I explain *that* to my new husband?" India asked, half sarcastically, half warily.

"Only when you have gained his full respect and confidence," her mother advised. "India, wherever your son is, he is safe. Jemmie may be a hard man, but he has never been deliberately cruel. The child is unharmed, and well cared for by some cotter's wife, delighted to have the extra income. This woman knows she must take good guardianship of her ward else she lose the silver paid her and be severely punished. Remember, the duke's own man brought her the child. I have told you, and you cannot say I ever broke a promise to you, that I will find your Rowan. Then I will begin to make personal visits to him, impressing upon his caretaker the importance of this child, his health and his happiness. While I am doing that, it is up to you to make your husband love you, or, at the very least, want to please you enough so you may ask to have little Rowan brought to you."

"I shall tell the earl *before* we wed that I have a son," India said stubbornly. "I cannot be happy without my child, and I cannot marry this man unless he agrees to allow me to have Rowan with me."

"India, in God's name," the duchess of Glenkirk pleaded with her daughter, "wait before you inform Lord Leigh of your child! If you ruin this proposed marriage, where will you be? Jemmie will lock you up in Glenkirk's highest tower, and you will never see your child again. He will make certain of that. If you are clever, you can gain everything your heart desires. Do not spite yourself, and your son, simply to gain a moment's revenge on your stepfather."

India was silent for what seemed a very long time to her mother. Then, at last, she said, "You are correct, madame. I would be very foolish indeed should I act in haste. Now, tell me, when is my marriage to be celebrated, and where?"

"Here, at Glenkirk, by proxy, prior to your departure," Jasmine answered. "The earl has left the choice of a proxy to you."

"Since neither Henry nor Charlie are here, I think the best choice would be my brother, Patrick Leslie," India said. "It will be good practice for him when he weds one day. Patrick and my younger brothers seem to know little of the niceties of polite society, although I know you strive hard with them, madame. Still, they persist in being wild Scots. Fix the day for the thirtieth of May, at dawn, and then I shall depart immediately thereafter for England. Will the earl send an escort for me?"

"You will be escorted as far as the border by Glenkirk men, and the earl's men will meet you there," the duchess told her daughter.

"I am taking Meggie with me, and Diarmid More-Leslie would come, too. He and Meggie have asked my permission to wed. I have given it. They will marry immediately after I have been wed. It is far more practical that they travel as man and wife."

Jasmine nodded, agreeing with her daughter. "Your father . . . *stepfather*, must give his permission to Diarmid," she said.

"Surely he can have no objection," India replied.

"Oh, I am sure he does not," Jasmine replied quickly lest India fly into a temper again.

"We haven't a great deal of time, madame. We should begin my trousseau immediately," India announced. "And I will want a full accounting of my possessions as well. Nothing of mine is to remain at Glenkirk."

"I am giving you the Stars of Kashmir as a wedding gift," Jasmine said softly. "You are my eldest child, and my first daughter. When your first daughter weds one day, see that you give the jewels to her. They are to remain in the female line. Jamal Khan's father gave them to his mother, and he gave them to me. Now I give them to you, India."

"Mama!" India was overwhelmed. "Surely you do not want to part with the Stars of Kashmir now, do you?"

Jasmine laughed. "I always meant them for you," she said. "Besides, we live simply here at Glenkirk. I have no occasion to wear them anymore, and they simply lay alone in their case. You will enjoy them, I am sure. Perhaps the earl will take you to court, and you can dazzle everyone there with them."

"It would be amusing to visit court as the countess of Oxton,"

India remarked. "I hope, however, this earl prefers the country. I will not leave the raising of my children to others."

Jasmine nodded in agreement.

The next day, seamstresses arrived from the local villages to prepare the trousseau India would be taking with her to England. She stood patiently, being measured, and pinned. She chose the finest and richest fabrics in the castle storerooms: jewel-toned velvets, and rich brocades, and silks. The farthingale was no longer fashionable. Skirts were flowing. Numerous under-petticoats were required to support the gown skirts. These were made of fine lace-trimmed cotton, and soft white flannel. The skirt petticoats, which topped the under-petticoats, were of silk and brocade. There were chemises perfumed, and plain but for a lace frill at the neck. The necklines were cut low with a short V opening in front where it was tied with silk ribbons. The large, balloon sleeves of the chemises were finished with lace ruffles. India also insisted upon a dozen pairs of calescons, or silk drawers, and a matching number of half-shirts. She had at least two dozen nightgowns, all lavishly trimmed with lace.

"There shall be nothing left in the storerooms for my trousseau," Fortune complained, watching enviously as the bejeweled bodices and matching skirts, the fur-trimmed capes and newly made leather boots and shoes with silver buckles piled up. The bodices had beautiful buttons of precious stones, as well as ivory and bone. There were combs with pearls around the arch, lawn handkerchiefs trimmed in lace, muffs of fur, and luxurious fabrics, beautiful fans, and painted masques.

The duchess had gathered all the jewelry that had been given to her by her second husband, Rowan Lindley, the marquis of Westleigh. The pieces that belonged to the Lindley family she put aside for the bride her son, Henry, the current marquis, would choose one day. The jewels that Rowan had given her, she divided equally between their two daughters, India and Fortune. Dark-haired India favored the sapphires and rubies. Flame-haired Fortune preferred the emeralds and diamonds.

There were other things that belonged to India as well. Large carved chests of embroidered linens, featherbeds, pillows, and bed coverings, with matching draperies. There were silver candlesticks, and candelabra, as well as ornate silver salt cellars. There were decorated cups of both silver and gold, Florentine forks, table knives with bone handles, and silver spoons. Porcelain bowls, plates, and matching cups. Silver bowls. All were gathered and packed carefully. The days flew by with a rapidity that even surprised India.

"She will nae forgie me, darling Jasmine, will she?" the duke sadly said to his wife.

Jasmine shook her head. "Nay, Jemmie, she will not forgive you, and you cannot blame her that she does not. Do you think a husband can make up for the loss of her firstborn son?" The duchess of Glenkirk touched her husband's face with a gentle hand. "I love you, Jemmie Leslie, but I agree with my daughter. You have been monstrously unkind. Even I don't know where our grandson is. It would be better if I knew, so I might make certain that he is well cared for, my lord. A man's eye is never as keen as a woman's in matters like this. I should know if the cottage was truly clean, and if the woman into whose hands you have put our grandson is really kind-hearted, or an abusive slattern. India says the laddie was born in true wedlock, and I believe her. Our grandson cannot be raised nameless, or of little account, Jemmie."

He nodded. He did not tell her but he had been to see the child several times now. His grandson was safe, but in a remote area of the estate lands. The cotter's wife thought his interest in the lad stemmed from the fact that the duke was his father. She treated the child kindly, envisioning an even greater reward one day. It was not necessary that James Leslie enlighten her otherwise. Rowan was a bright wee bairn, his blue eyes darting about at every sound, a thatch of black hair upon his tiny head. "When India is safe away in England," James Leslie said to his wife, "I will tell ye where the bairn is. I know ye well, darling Jasmine, and ye'll nae be satisfied until ye can see him again for yourself." He caught the hand that caressed his cheek, and kissed it.

The duchess smiled at him. "I am satisfied then," she replied, and later when she was alone with her daughter, she told India of his words. "Let it set your heart and mind at ease now, my daughter," she said gently to India. "Jemmie is feeling guilty, for he knows I thoroughly disapprove of his actions, but he will not relent until he sees you happy again, and wed. You must make an effort, India, for all our sakes, especially wee Rowan's."

"I will," India promised her mother. "More than anything, I want my son back again!"

Two wedding gowns had been made for India. She would wear the simpler one at her proxy wedding. The bodice of the rose-colored silk gown had a square neckline, and the bride wore a wired lace collar about her slender throat. The opening of the skirt was decorated with an embroidered golden braid trim. The skirt petticoat was silver and gold tissue. The puffed sleeves were decorated with cloth-of-gold bows to match the trim. About her neck, below the lace collar, India wore a single strand of fat pearls with matching ear bobs. Her hair was dressed in a simple chignon on the nape of her neck. On her feet she wore rose-colored silk slippers.

Her half-brother was dressed in his blue-and-green kilt, his white shirt trimmed with lace on the sleeves, silver buttons on his sleeveless velvet doublet. Patrick, with his father's dark hair and his mother's turquoise-colored eyes, proudly escorted India to the altar, where the Anglican minister awaited them. He made the responses required of him as the earl of Oxton's representative in a clear, loud voice. India's voice was less sure. The memory of her marriage day to Caynan Reis flooded her senses so painfully that she almost wept, and was unable to speak for a moment.

When it was finally over, she stood motionless, receiving the congratulations of her family, and wondering why they bothered tendering their good wishes when they knew she had been forced to the altar. Wordlessly she witnessed the marriage of her two servants, Meggie and Diarmid, a happier event for her as she knew the two were in love. The formalities over, they repaired to the Great Hall to break their fast.

The duke of Glenkirk toasted his stepdaughter. "May ye be

happy always, and may ye hae healthy sons." He lifted his goblet to her, and then drank it down.

India glared, outraged, at him. Then she lifted her goblet. "To my son, Rowan, wherever he may be," she said softly.

James Leslie's eyes darkened with anger, but then he laughed. "Ye're nae my problem any longer," he said honestly. "Eat yer meal, India, and then Godspeed to ye, lassie."

Jasmine squeezed her daughter's hand beneath the highboard, silently begging India not to quarrel with James Leslie. The younger woman squeezed back her reassurance as the wedding breakfast of poached eggs in heavy cream and Marsala wine was served, along with baked apples flavored with cinnamon, freshly baked bread still warm from the ovens, newly churned sweet butter, thick slices of ham, and thin slices of salmon simmered in white wine with dill. There was a honeycomb for the sweet tooth. Ale, cider, and wine were served to drink.

India gazed about the table; her eyes lighting upon her siblings. Henry and Charlie were in England. She would see them soon enough. Her half-brothers, Patrick, Adam, and Duncan, now eleven, ten, and seven, she would probably see rarely, if ever again. Patrick, of course, would one day be the second duke of Glenkirk. The younger two would have to marry heiresses. *We'll never really know each other*, India thought sadly. *How lucky Fortune and I were to have each other!*

Fortune. Beautiful, practical, yet impulsive Fortune. What did fate have in store for her? MacGuire's Ford, its castle and lands in Ireland, were, of course, her marriage portion, but Ireland was such a disturbed land. Still, her parents had always spoken of seeking a husband for Fortune in Ireland. Her sister wasn't getting any younger. She would be seventeen in July. But who on earth was there in Ireland who might make a suitable husband for Fortune? She looked at her sister. Fortune gazed up at that moment, and smiled encouragingly at her. Whatever was meant for Fortune, she obviously had no fear of it. *I envy her*, India thought, and how Fortune would mock and tease her if she ever knew *that*, India considered with a wry smile.

"Now that you have married me off, madame," India said to her mother, "I expect Fortune will be next, eh? What have you in mind for my sister? As you have obtained an earl for me, certainly you must do as well for her."

"I don't care who he is as long as he has a brain in his head and a good heart," Fortune replied, laughing. "I don't need some man's title to make me presentable. I have my own title."

"We plan a visit to MacGuire's Ford this summer," Jasmine said. "We will not be coming to Queen's Malvern. I have been in correspondence with Rory MacGuire, our estate manager. As Fortune is the heiress to those lands, the folk are very interested in meeting her, as they have not seen her since she was an infant."

"I remember when Fortune was baptized," India said. "It was in the church at MacGuire's Ford. I remember telling Great-grandfather Adam that I had wanted a pony, not a baby sister. A black pony! Who baptized Fortune, madame?"

"My cousin, Cullen Butler," the duchess replied.

"A Papist?" Fortune looked shocked. "I was baptized by a Papist, Mama? Why was I never told?"

Jasmine spoke quietly. "You certainly know how I feel regarding religion, Fortune. I hold to the old queen's maxim that there is but one Lord Jesus Christ, and the rest is all trifles. My father held to such thought, allowing all faiths to be practiced in his kingdom. It is outrageous arrogance for any one faith in God to believe it is the be-all and end-all of religion. That all other faiths are wrong. Did not our Lord Christ Himself say that in His Father's house were many mansions? Surely He did not lie. And if there are many mansions, then there must be many paths leading to the doors of those mansions in God's kingdom. Aye, you were baptized in what is referred to as the old faith. Your godparents are a good lady named Bride Duffy, who is the most respected woman in the village, and Rory MacGuire, our estate manager. Before the English took away his lands, and gave them to me, Rory was the lord of Erne Rock Castle. He has cared for your lands with honest diligence. I am very grateful to him, as you should be. The descendants of Nighthawk and Nightbird are the most sought-after horses in both England

and Europe. Rory MacGuire has made you a rich woman, Fortune. Remember it well. As for your baptism by a *Papist*, it is a valid one, even in England."

Fortune flushed. "I think I am going to have a great deal to learn about Ireland, Mama. I hope Master MacGuire will help me so I do not offend the people I must care for; but tell me this: How is it that there has been peace on my lands all these years?"

"Because both the poor beleaguered Catholics and our Protestant tenants have been taught to respect one another. Each has a church. The village elders are equally divided, and we keep our people as isolated as possible from the rest of the area so they will not be contaminated by the hate generated by the political and religious factions. Anyone unhappy with our rule is free to leave and go elsewhere," the duchess of Glenkirk said. "I will not have our lands in constant turmoil. It is unproductive and wasteful. That dreadful hate was responsible for your father's death. I will *never* forget that."

"I do not know if I can keep such order," Fortune said nervously.

"You are the lady of Erne Rock Castle," her mother told her. "With Rory MacGuire's aid, and the right husband, MacGuire's Ford will continue to flourish." She now turned to India. "It is time for you to change your gown, daughter, and leave us. You have a long trip ahead of you, and the sooner you are on your way, the better."

India arose from the highboard, and departed the hall. She found her bedchamber virtually bare, and quite sparse, for all her belongings, had, in accordance with her instructions, been packed. The baggage train that would accompany her was large.

Meggie helped her from her gown. "Shall I pack it?" she asked.

"Nay, leave it. I do not want it," India said. "I would give it to you, but I don't ever want to see it again to remind me of this day."

" 'Tis too grand for me," Meggie said cheerfully. "And, besides, when and where would I wear it? I laid out yer riding clothes. I thought you would prefer to be a-horse as to being in a closed carriage."

India nodded in agreement. She pulled on the doeskin breeches and stout woolen socks. Her leather boots were more comfortable than the slippers she had worn. A white shirt, and doeskin jerkin with silver-edged horn buttons completed her outfit, along with the small green velvet cap with a single eagle feather she clapped upon her head. She took the perfumed leather gloves Meggie handed her, and then stopped a moment to look about the room. Meggie discreetly withdrew.

While India was still furious with her stepfather, she did have mixed feelings about departing Glenkirk. It had been her home for many years. She had come as a child with Henry, Fortune, and Charlie. They had all grown up here, chasing through the hallways, playing hide-and-seek in the largely unused tower rooms. She had been happy here. Glenkirk had been her refuge, but she would now forever associate it with the loss of her son, Rowan. For that she could thank her stepfather. In one brutal act he had wiped away all those happy years. No. She would never forgive James Leslie.

Without a backward glance India swept from the room, hurrying downstairs and out into the courtyard of the castle. She bid the servants she had known since childhood a gracious farewell, accepting their good wishes for her happiness. She kissed her youngest brothers, Adam and Duncan, but Patrick, the eldest of the Leslies, thrust out his hand at her. Brushing it aside, India hugged him hard. "Don't be in such a hurry to grow up, Paddy," she whispered. "It's hard to be grown, as you'll find out one day too soon, I fear."

"Dinna saw at yer horse's mouth," he replied, squirming out of her grasp. "Yer too impatient with the beastie, India, and its puir mouth is sensitive. Will ye remember now?"

"Aye," she said, ruffling his dark head. Her glance swung to her stepfather. She nodded curtly at the duke of Glenkirk. "Farewell, sir," she said coldly, and then turned to her mother. "Remember your promises to me, madame. I shall send a message when I have arrived at Queen's Malvern, and afterward at Oxton Court."

Jasmine put her arms about her eldest child. "You were born from a deep and great love, India. I have tried, whatever you may think, to be a good mother to you. I do love you." She kissed her daughter's smooth cheek. "May the God of us all guard and guide you, India. May that God keep you safe, my child."

"I love you too, Mama," India replied, feeling the tears pricking behind her eyelids. While she was angry at James Leslie, the anger she had felt toward her mother had dried up over these past few weeks. She kissed her mother back, and then India turned, mounting the horse that Diarmid held for her. "Farewell," she said, raising her hand to them, and then she moved off through the portcullis and over the drawbridge of the castle onto the road south.

She was surrounded by over a hundred Glenkirk men-at-arms who would accompany her to the border with England. There was a large and comfortable traveling coach, should she choose to ride in it with Meggie, who now sat alone within the vehicle, and a great train of fifteen baggage carts holding all her possessions, as well as a dozen fine horses that were part of her dowry. India sat straight in her saddle, her eyes forward, taking in the familiar landscape. In her heart, however, she could not help but wonder where amid those green hills her son was now hidden. She would find him. Whatever the cost she would find her son. *Caynan Reis's son.* No stranger would raise or claim her blood. Rowan was out there amid the bens, or in some hidden glen, and she would find him. Her intentions resolute, the newly married countess of Oxton turned her horse south for England.

Chapter 19

Deverall Leigh, earl of Oxton, had spent the morning riding across his estates. After eleven years on the Barbary coast, he couldn't get enough of the wonderful green of England. His lands, set in a verdant valley between the rivers Severn and Avon, were both beautiful and fertile. The meadows were filled with sheep. His vast orchards of apples and pears, for which the region was famed, were even now at peak bloom. There were lush green pastures awaiting the arrival of the horses his bride would bring him, and with which he intended to begin breeding race horses.

His bride. Lady India Anne Lindley, daughter of a duke, sister to a marquis and a duke. A conniving, deceitful little bitch who had swooned in his arms and sworn she loved him. But she hadn't. She had taken the first opportunity presented to her to flee El Sinut with his child in her belly—if indeed there had been a child, and that was not just another lie to lull him into trusting her. God only knew he had learned early that women could not be trusted, and yet he had allowed the golden-eyed vixen the opportunity to dig her claws deep into his heart; and once she had him, she had wantonly flung him aside.

He well remembered his return from the mountains with Aruj Agha. The town was in an uproar for two nights before a group of English captives had taken back their round ship and sailed out of

El Sinut. It had been cleverly executed, a well-thought-out workmanlike plan that had given the English many hours' advantage. It wasn't worth going after them. It was unlikely he would find them in the vast sea. He chalked the loss up to fate. Then he learned that India had disappeared on the same night. As it had been her relation, Captain Southwood, who had made good the escape, it was obvious where she was. He was both devastated and furious by turns.

"She was kidnapped, my lord," Baba Hassan insisted, and Azura strongly agreed with him.

"She loves you, Caynan Reis," the older woman said. "She was so happy about your coming child. She would not have left you of her own free will. She was taken. You must go after her, my dear lord!"

"A part of the garden wall was not secured," Baba Hassan continued on. "We did not realize it, my lord. I hold myself completely responsible. They came over the wall using grapnels and stout ropes. Only when we discovered the lady India missing did we search the garden and find the evidence. One grapnel and rope remained, and so it is obvious that there were two of them. When the second man slid down into the street, it was impossible to release his grapnel from the top of the wall, and so it was left behind. The marks of the second grapnel were plainly visible in the top of the wall. Both your wife and her servant were stolen away. They could not leave the girl behind, and since she was one of their own, they would, of course, take her, too, rather than kill her."

"Why did India not scream?" the dey demanded angrily. "Surely she could have cried out and alerted the guards."

"She would not have wanted to endanger her blood kin, my lord. I am certain that was her reasoning. She is a woman, and soft of heart. And then, too, there was that terrible storm that night. It is doubtful if she had cried out that anyone would have heard her call," the eunuch replied logically. "We must find her, my lord!"

"She had the advantage over her captors," Caynan Reis persisted. "They could not have gotten her over that damned wall, nor the servant girl, either, if she had not gone willingly. She has betrayed me, the false bitch!"

"What if the two women were rendered unconscious?" Azura suggested.

"Both of them?" the dey scoffed. "It would be difficult enough climbing that wall alone, or with someone on your back, but with a dead weight, I think it improbable. Nay, my good Azura. India was always determined to escape El Sinut, though she learned to hide her true thoughts from us. She has betrayed me. She has betrayed you who were her friends. She is no better than other women, whatever we may have previously thought."

"Improbable, but not impossible," Baba Hassan persisted. "Those hooks on the grapnels were dug deep into the wall, my lord."

"Proving what? That each rope held two people? That we already know, my good friend. I know you do not like to admit that we have all erred in our judgment, but we have. She bedazzled us with her beauty and charm, and then deceived us. I do not wish to hear her name ever again, Baba Hassan. Do you understand me?"

"But what of the child?" Azura cried out to him.

"I suspect she cozened us there, too," the dey replied sadly.

"Nay, never!" Azura said boldly. *"Not India!"*

He sent them away. His heart was broken. He had loved her. Nay, he loved her yet, despite her behavior. If she walked into his chamber this moment he would forgive her. And as for the child, he might deny it to ease his own heart, but he could not believe that she would have lied to him about *that.* There was no way she could have been privy to her duplicitous cousin's plans until the moment the captain appeared in her apartments to help her escape. If she had lied about the child, what excuses could she have made when there was no child?

The earl of Oxton turned his horse toward home as his thoughts moved on to the events that had brought him back to England. Knowing of his interest in the young English milord, Aruj Agha had, shortly after their return from the mountains, brought the dey word that the young man had a serious fever, and was in the slaves' hospital by the harbor.

"The physician does not think he will live," the janissary told the dey.

"Allah!" the dey swore. "I must go to him. I meant to ransom him long since, but in my happiness I completely forgot. Perhaps if he has the hope of going home, he will rally himself. Now my joy is ashes, and the same woman who brought me such misery can also be said to be responsible for Adrian's demise."

"*Adrian?*" Aruj Agha was both fascinated and mystified. "Is that his name? And how do you know it, my lord?"

"He is my younger half-brother," Caynan Reis admitted. "I believe that he and his mother are responsible for my having had to flee England. I took India to my bed originally to spite him. He did not recognize me, of course, when we met in my audience chamber. He was still only a boy when I left my homeland, and I did not wear a beard. I meant to tell him after I took his betrothed for my own. I thought to hurt him as he had hurt me, but then things did not go as I had planned. I decided I would release him from the galleys, and hold him here in El Sinut until the ransom had been paid. Then I would reveal myself to him, and tell him how happy I was with my beautiful English wife, who might have been his wife. Both he and his greedy mother would have been quite piqued to learn that not only had I taken a ransom from them, but an heiress as well. But in my happiness I forgot about him! Now you tell me he is dying? I must go to him at once! He is my father's son, too, and my brother, for all he and his mother have done to harm me."

The aga brought the dey to the slave hospital. Caynan Reis stood by the younger man's pallet gazing down upon him. Gone was the soft and foppish arrogant milord. A lean, hard-muscled young man lay flushed and quiet upon the straw mattress. The dey's blue eyes filled with tears as he remembered the little brother he had taught to ride. He sat heavily when a stool was brought for him, waving everyone else from his presence.

"Adrian," he said quietly. "Open your eyes, Adrian. We must

talk together, you and I." The English words felt strange on his tongue.

Adrian Leigh's purple-shadowed eyelids fluttered open, then closed, and then open again. "Who are you?" he asked softly.

"Your brother, Deverall Leigh," was the reply.

Adrian Leigh stared hard, and then hot tears rolled down his gaunt cheeks. "Forgive me, Dev!" he said.

"Forgive you? I should be asking your forgiveness for having so cruelly condemned you to the galleys, little brother, but I was still angry at what your mother had done to me."

"You knew?"

"I knew what poor old Rogers babbled to me that night," Deverall Leigh told his brother. "That Jeffers was to be killed, and I would be held responsible. That I must flee, or die on the gallows. One way or another I was to go else I stand in your way. MariElena was quite determined that you succeed our father as earl of Oxton. Of course, with my usual stubbornness, I waited hidden to see what would happen, but when I heard of Jeffers's death, and that my dagger had been found in his chest, I boarded the first ship I could."

"How came you here?" Adrian asked, curious, and then he coughed.

The dey of El Sinut held a cup to his brother's lips, feeding him cool water, and when the fit had subsided, laid him back on his pallet. "My ship, like yours, was bound for the Mediterranean. Like yours, it was captured, and I began my service in the galleys. When I proved trustworthy, however, I was released because I accepted Islam. I served the captain of the vessel as secretary because of all the languages I speak. One day we were anchored in the harbor here when the dey Sharif came out in his barge to speak with my captain. A freak wave overturned the barge, and all were cast into the sea. I dove overboard, and saved the dey Sharif. In gratitude he freed me, and took me into his service. We were close, he and I, and he formally adopted me as his son, and asked the sultan in Istanbul if I might succeed him as he was ill and wished to retire. Permission was given, and that is how I became the dey of El Sinut, little brother."

"I am dying," Adrian Leigh said softly.

"We will heal you," the dey replied. "You will not go back to the galleys, but rather home to England."

Adrian Leigh shook his head slowly. "Nay, I shall never see England again. I must right the wrong that my mother and I perpetrated upon you all those years back, Dev!" He coughed again, but manfully regained control of himself despite his weakened state. "I need someone to write it all down, Dev, and then I will sign my name to it. Father has suffered greatly since your departure. You must succeed him as it was always meant to be. You are Viscount Twyford, not I."

"I am the dey of El Sinut, Adrian. It suits me. You are going to get well, and return to England," the dey replied.

"*No!*" Adrian cried out weakly but desperately. "I must clear your good name, and you must go home again! Can you tell me that your heart is really not in England, but in this hot and sandy land? Please, I beg of you, fetch someone to write down my tale so I may go to my God with a clear conscience. Do not let me die with this stain on my immortal soul, Dev!"

"I will send for your secretary," said Aruj Agha, who had not gone and had been privy to all that had been said.

The dey nodded, and took his brother's hand in his to comfort him. "Go," was all he said.

When the scribe finally arrived, and was seated cross-legged, pen and parchment at the ready, the dey asked him if he could transcribe what was said in the English language. The scribe nodded.

"I can, my lord, as well as French and Italian, too."

Adrian Leigh began to speak in a low and halting voice. He told how he had, at his mother's instructions, stolen into his brother's chamber and taken the Deverall dagger, so prized by his sibling, because it had belonged to his mother's family. He told how Mari-Elena had become Lord Jeffers's mistress for a brief time in order to gain his trust. Of how she had killed him by putting a mixture of finely ground glass and hair into his wine. Of how when he was dead, she had instructed her child to push the dagger into her lover's chest so it would be thought he had died at the hand of his rival for Lady Clinton's favors. The dey's secretary wrote on, his wrinkled face impassive, his only acknowledgment of the tale the occasional raising of his iron-gray eyebrows. Adrian continued that by making her son wield the dagger, his mother had hoped to bind him to her forever. It had disturbed him to see his father's pain over the charge that Deverall Leigh had murdered another man, and he had felt great personal guilt for his father's decline.

Growing up, he had gone to court, escaping his mother's constant company. He had caroused with new friends, and had a fine time. Then he had met India Lindley. She was beautiful. She was wealthy, and she was innocent of men. At first it had been a game to see if he might seduce her, succeeding where others had failed. Then it had dawned on him that this beautiful girl might actually make him a good wife, and that her wealth would give him the power over his mother that he had never had. India, he learned, had never been courted. He courted her with charm and passion, yet he could not convince her to go against her family. She was extremely close to them.

Finally his mother, hearing of his attempts with India, had hurried up to London with the perfect solution. He had followed her advice, and convinced India to elope with him to his uncle's home in Naples. Actually, it had been her father's unqualified disapproval, and plans to return India immediately to Scotland, that had done the trick. But the captain of the vessel upon which they had sailed discovered the ruse they had used to travel safely, and separated them. Then they had been captured. "My arrogance is responsible for my plight," Adrian Leigh finished, "but I cannot go to my grave without clearing the name of my elder brother, Deverall Leigh, Viscount Twyford. He is innocent of the murder of Lord Charles Jeffers; and my mother, the countess of Oxton, and I, are the guilty parties. May God have mercy on us."

"You are finished, sir?" the dey's secretary politely inquired.

"I am," came the now very weak reply. "Let me put my signature to this document before I will not be able to do it."

They held him up, placing a quill in his hand, and Adrian Leigh grasped it with his last bit of strength, and signed his name in a legible hand. Finished, he dropped the pen, and slumped back into his brother's arms. There he lay, until several hours later he finally breathed his last. His body was wrapped in a white shroud, and quickly buried lest the heat decay it. It was placed in the small Christian cemetery outside the walls of the city. The kindly old Protestant minister who was to have married the dey and India came to pray over Adrian Leigh's body. Seeing the dey's open grief, he asked no questions.

The dey of El Sinut now shut himself off from his household, mourning his loss alone. In his hands he held the parchment that would clear him of the charges of murder in England, yet he didn't care. He fell into a deep depression from which he could not seem to rouse himself. He had lost the woman he loved, and the brother he had loved, too. Nothing mattered any longer. Then fate stepped in, forcing his hand, compelling him to make a decision.

Two troupes of janissaries crossed his borders. One from Algiers, and the other from Tunis. They marched toward the city, and their intent was plainly hostile. Baba Hassan's spies brought him the information he needed to save Caynan Reis, but only with scant time to spare. The chief eunuch hurried to inform his master.

"It is you they seek, my lord. The order has been given to assassinate you because you have betrayed them to the sultan. In Istanbul the rebellion has been squelched, although there has been fighting in both Algiers and Tunis, for they have not yet received the word that the rebellion is over. So, my lord, you have been targeted for death."

"Who gave the order?" the dey asked.

"The chief of the janissaries, my lord. The sultan will look the other way. Your death is a small price to pay. He has managed to keep his throne. If the janissaries want revenge on the man who saved that throne, he cares not, nor does his mother," Baba Hassan said. "You must leave El Sinut, my lord, before they may kill you."

"No. I will fight them," Caynan Reis said.

"With what?" Baba Hassan demanded. "You have no army. You have a troupe of janissaries to protect El Sinut. They will not go against their brothers. They will turn their backs on you, my lord, while the others slaughter you. You have the means to return to your own land. Allah has given you this good fortune just when you needed it. Go back to England, my lord. Find India and your child, and *live!* If you will not do it for yourself, then do it for Azura and me. We have loved you as if you were our own son. And what of your blood kin? If you do not return to England, he has no heir to his family name and lands, my lord. Will you throw your life away when you have been given the chance to regain what you once believed lost?"

"What of you and Azura? What of the ladies of the harem?" the dey asked him. "I cannot leave you to suffer for me."

"I have managed this palace for more years than I care to admit," said the eunuch. "And the lady Azura, too. We will be safe, as will the ladies of the harem. I suspect that Aruj Agha will hold sway here in El Sinut in your place, my lord Caynan Reis, for many years to come."

He had made up his mind in an instant. "I will go," he said. Why shouldn't he? Baba Hassan was right. His father needed him, and he had several scores to settle in England. The first with his deceitful stepmother, and the second with Lady India Anne Lindley. He followed the chief eunuch to the lady Azura's apartment.

She knew the moment they entered that the decision had been made. Going to a cabinet, Azura drew out a beautiful white wool cloak lined in green silk. "This is for you, my lord dey. The green lining is a false one. Behind the silk, and between another layer of silk, is a small fortune in gold coins, each sewn into a separate pocket. The hems of your cloak are filled with precious stones. Not just the bottom hem, but beneath the gold braid edging as well. It is little enough for your service to El Sinut, my lord. We wish it might be more." She set the floor-length cape about his broad shoulders, coming around to fasten the gold frog closures that he saw were diamond studded.

The dey took her into his arms, and kissed her forehead. "I will never forget you, my lady Azura," he said. "If I sent for you one day, would you not come, and run my home as you have done this palace? You, and Baba Hassan together?"

She smiled up at him. "My lord, I have lived too long in Barbary to ever be content anywhere else, but I thank you for the offer."

"I, also," Baba Hassan replied. There was a small awkward silence, and then the eunuch said, "Come, my lord. I must get you out of the palace before it is too late. You can already hear the fighting in the streets, for the janissaries have been looting, and causing general havoc along their way. We have a small felluca for you in the harbor. I have chosen several young European captives to escape with you. Naples is your best bet, and the easiest port to make from here."

The dey kissed Azura's hands, and then, turning, he followed Baba Hassan from her apartment. The eunuch led him through the small dark corridors he had never known existed. They saw no one as they passed. Finally they exited the palace, crossing a small courtyard, and going out through a little door in the walls. They hurried down several narrow, twisting streets until finally the dey could see the waters of the harbor sparkling in the late-afternoon sunlight and smell the salty tang of the sea. He quickened his step.

As they moved onto a slightly larger thoroughfare, they were startled by a young janissary who stepped into their path. Before Caynan Reis might draw his sword, the janissary slashed at him, his blade slicing down the dey's handsome face from the corner of his left eye to the left corner of his mouth. The injured man's hand went automatically to his face even as Aruj Agha came behind the younger janissary and ran him through. The assassin crumpled heavily to the ground, quite dead.

"A young Turk who would make a name for himself, but one cannot gain honor in the corps through a dishonorable act, my lord dey." He handed his friend a handkerchief to staunch the flow of blood.

"Take care of Baba Hassan, Azura and the harem ladies," Caynan Reis said to his friend.

"I will," came the reply, and then Aruj Agha turned away, disappearing into an alley. "Allah go with you," he said as he went.

"Let me see," Baba Hassan said worriedly, and examined the wound. "You will have a scar, my lord, but it is not life threatening," he pronounced. "Come. There is the felluca. You must clear the harbor before sunset else the chain be raised against you."

Three young men were waiting for them. They were Italian, and Baba Hassan gave each of them a small bag containing a gold coin and five silver coins. "Get this man safely to Naples, and each of you will be given another gold coin by my agent, who will meet your vessel to make certain your passenger is safe. You have been given your freedom for this purpose. Fail me, and I will know. You shall be punished wherever you attempt to hide."

The three men nodded.

"Thank you, Baba Hassan," the dey said quietly and with deeper meaning. He stepped down into the felluca.

The chief eunuch nodded. "Allah go with you, my lord Leigh," he said quietly, and, turning away, disappeared into the maze of streets.

They had departed immediately, clearing the harbor. He had had no difficulty from his companions, and three days later they had reached Naples. At the docks a well-dressed man had been waiting their arrival, and paid off the three sailors.

"The felluca is yours," he told them, and then turned to Deverall Leigh. "My lord Leigh, I am Cesare Kira. You are to come with me, please. We will go to my father's banking house in the ghetto where you will want to make your deposit, and then we will arrange for your transportation back to England."

Deverall Leigh had followed the young man, and been taken to Benjamino Kira. The elder Kira had taken the cloak from his guest and handed it to his daughter, who had removed the false lining with its gold-filled pockets, handing the coins to her father who piled them up upon his counting table. When she had finished, Benjamino Kira counted the coins, and weighed the gold. Then he nodded to his daughter, who slit the hems of the long garment individually and spilled out its jeweled contents onto her father's table. When she had finally finished, she sat down and began to repair the cloak so he might wear it again.

"I do not need a double lining in the cape, mistress," he said to the girl. "If it would please you, please keep the silk."

Her face lit in a sweet smile. "Thank you, my lord, I will." She then bent her head to sew the hem.

"You are generous," Benjamino Kira said. "It is a fine piece of Bursa silk you have given my daughter. It will make her a wedding gown, eh, Soshanna?" He smiled at the girl's blush, and turned back to Lord Leigh. "Baba Hassan has sent you with quite a fortune, my lord," he noted. "What do you intend to do with it, and how may we help you?"

"I am the heir to the earl of Oxton," he had explained. "How much of my story do you know, Signore Kira?"

"I know you have been the dey of El Sinut for nine years, my lord, and left because of the rebellion by the janissaries that caused your life to be in danger."

"It was my warning of that rebellion that saved the young sultan. In thanks, he threw me to his enemies. I had no choice but to leave. Now I will go home to England to clear my name of a crime I did not commit. I carry the proof of my innocence with me." He withdrew the rolled parchment from his shirt. "I hope to gain a royal pardon with this. Then I will marry, and lead the life I was meant to lead."

The banker nodded. "Fate has an odd way of manipulating us about," he said dryly. "Now, however, we must plan for your trip. With your permission, my lord, I shall make the arrangements, and see that your gold and jewels are transported safely to London."

Deverall Leigh had traveled to Paris in the company of a train of merchants. There he had been taken in hand by the banker, Henri Kira, and sent on to Calais. He crossed to Dover, and was met by Master Jonathan Kira, who escorted him up to London to his father, James Kira.

"Your trip was a pleasant one, I hope, my lord," the English banker said. "I have taken the liberty of inquiring as to your father's health. The earl is frail, but in no immediate danger. I have also taken the liberty of putting a watch upon the countess so that we can be certain she remains in Glocestershire while you complete your business here." He indicated a small chest upon the table, and, opening it, said, "Your gemstones, my lord. Will you ascertain that they are all here?"

Deverall Leigh, somewhat amazed by the efficiency of the Kiras, took out the inventory slip that he had prepared in Naples and checked it over. "Everything is here," he said finally. "The gold is on deposit, I take it, Master Kira."

"It is, my lord," said the banker with a smile. "Now, then, you will need a private audience with King Charles, will you not?"

"I will," he had replied.

"It will be arranged. The duke of Buckingham's family does business with this house." He looked into the still-opened jewel chest and plucked a large, round diamond forth. "Set in gold, a nice gift for the king, don't you think?" he said. "And a crucifix of gold, rubies, and pearls for the queen, I believe will be quite suitable."

"I shall leave it all in your obviously capable hands," Deverall Leigh replied. "Where am I to stay, Master Kira, and how long must I remain in London? As you can imagine, I am anxious to see my father."

"It will take a few days, my lord, to arrange an audience with the king for you. It would be better if you remained here as my guest. I do not want you out wandering the streets where you might be seen until you have been pardoned by the king and are free to do so without danger of arrest."

He had been grateful to the Kiras, and gladly accepted their hospitality. He was well treated. Several days later, he was presented with a new suit of black velvet, the doublet of which had an exquisite fallen lace collar. Each leg of his knee breeches had a wide silver ribbon garter with a black-and-silver bow. His doublet was trimmed with silver buttons, and the fine cambric of his shirt shone through the slashes on the puffed sleeves. White silk stockings were worn below where his breeches ended, and his black leather shoes sported silver rosettes. He had silver lace trimming his white leather gloves. His hair was short, and contrary to the fashion, he wore no beard or mustache. One side of his face was perfect in profile, but the scar running from his eye to his mouth on the left side of his visage gave him a menacing yet tragic appearance.

He rode to Whitehall Palace in a coach provided him by his hosts. He was met by a gentleman of the court in debt to the Kiras, a member of the duke of Buckingham's family, who took him to a private apartment. He was told to wait. Shortly afterward the king arrived. He listened to Deverall Leigh's tale, and accepted the confession that Adrian Leigh had dictated before his death. Charles Stuart read the parchment, and then he arose, requesting that his guest remain until he returned. There was wine, and there were biscuits to be had.

Deverall Leigh waited. He poured himself a half a goblet of wine, but ignored the biscuits. He paced back and forth for a time, and finally sat by the fire wondering what the king's decision would be. Would he accept Adrian's confession, or would he hang Deverall Leigh? It had begun to rain outside. He watched the droplets running down the leaded pane windows as the fire crackled noisily. Finally the door to the privy chamber opened, and the king reappeared. Deverall Leigh jumped to his feet, bowing low.

Charles Stuart's mouth twitched, but his mouth was serious when he spoke. "I have spoken with my counselors, *Viscount*," he began. "We are agreed that the confession you have brought us is genuine. Given your stepmother's reputation, it is entirely possible that it happened just as your unfortunate younger brother has dictated. We regret his death, of course. It has also been noted that while you might have been considered an impetuous youth, you were never known to be violent. Nor were you considered dull-witted, and given Lady Clinton's notoriety, it is considered unthinkable that you would have killed another man for her favors, which were so readily available to all. We understand your fright at the incident, and your belief that it was necessary to flee England given the fact that the alleged murder weapon belonged to you. Ground glass and hair. It is an interesting choice."

"It is a method that was developed in Naples," Deverall Leigh said.

"Ahhh, yes," the king replied. "And, of course, your stepmother comes from Naples. It would have never been considered, my lord. Perhaps you were wise, indeed, to flee England; and you have certainly had your share of adventures. I imagine you will find life in Glocestershire quite dull after all you have been through. You will want to marry, of course."

"Yes, Your Majesty, *if I am pardoned,*" Deverall Leigh responded.

"If you are pardoned? God's blood! Did I not say it? No! I did not say it, or you would not have asked. Aye! You are fully pardoned, Viscount Twyford. My secretary is even now drawing up the papers for you so you will have no difficulty with the local sheriff. Now, is there some pretty lady who has been awaiting you all these years?"

"No, my lord. In my youth, I fear, I was far too interested in sowing wild oats than seeking out a respectable woman to wed. Now, however, I must begin my search. When I was at court years ago, I saw a pretty little maid who would, of course, be grown and of an age to wed, if she has not already wed. Her name is Lady India Anne Lindley."

"You aim high, my lord," the king said. "Lady Lindley is my nephew's half-sister, and a considerable heiress. Still, it is my recollection that she was quite flighty, and could not decide upon a husband. I believe her family took her back to Scotland. I have not heard, however, that she is married. My nephew would have said so if she were. He lives here at court with us now. She must be at least twenty. I would seek a younger wife if I were you."

"I will take Your Majesty's advice under consideration," Deverall said in a noncommittal tone. Then he reached into his doublet, and drew forth two velvet bags. "I have brought this for Your Majesty," he said, proffering the royal purple velvet bag, "and this for Her Majesty." He handed the second bag, this one of white velvet, to the king.

Charles Stuart plucked the round diamond which had been set in gold with three carved gold plumes behind it, and designed as a pin, from its bag. He held it up, admiring it, and then pinned it to his doublet. "A fine piece, my lord," he approved. Then he drew forth the queen's gift, and a small chuckle escaped him. "For a man who has been away from England for a time, you understand my wife better than I do, sir. She will indeed esteem your gift." He slid the pearl-and-ruby crucifix on its gold chain back into the white velvet bag.

The king's secretary had come in then with his pardon. He was given the rolled parchment with its royal seals and dismissed.

"You are free to go home now, my lord. Godspeed," were the king's last words to him.

He left London that day, and a week later, beheld Oxton Court for the first time in eleven years. His father wept upon seeing him and learning of his pardon for the crime he had not committed. His stepmother wept upon learning of Adrian's death, but afterward she came to his room and attempted to seduce him as she had of old. He spurned her, telling her what he had not told his father. That the king knew the truth of Lord Jeffers's murder, and if anything happened to him, she would be hung. MariElena Leigh was not a particularly intelligent woman. This man was not the easily gulled boy she remembered. This man was a dangerous creature, and she was afraid for the first time in her life. From that moment on, she went out of her way to avoid him, and when their paths did cross, she was deferential toward him.

His father died a month later, worn out but content that his favorite son was free to assume the duties of the next earl of Oxton. His stepmother was now terrified as to what would happen to her. She learned her fate in short order. A royal messenger arrived with an edict of banishment. MariElena di Carlo Leigh would be sent back to her family in Naples, and never allowed to set foot in England again.

"You will have a yearly allowance, madame, paid to the banking house of Benjamino Kira, upon which you may draw. The deposits will be made quarterly," Deverall Leigh told his stepmother coldly. "Be glad I have not killed you for what you have done to my family. My father might have lived many more years, and my unfortunate brother, too, had it not been for your behavior. You may take your clothing, and any jewelry that my father gave you, but not family pieces." And he had searched her luggage prior to her departure with her wizened one-eyed servant woman who had originally come with her from Naples. Because she was dishonest by nature, he had removed not only several valuable family pieces from amid her possessions but also a pair of silver-and-gold candlesticks given his family by King Henry VIII. Sophia, the serving woman, had muttered curses at him under her breath. He then sent the two on their way to London, where they were put on a vessel bound for Naples by an escort from the Kira bank, who personally watched as the ship sailed down the Thames with the dowager countess of Oxton aboard.

Now it was Deverall Leigh turned his attention to the matter of that faithless bitch, India Lindley. He approached her father by his intermediaries, and was quite surprised to have his offer of marriage quickly accepted. In turn, he easily agreed to their conditions that India's wealth remain in India's hands, and she continue to manage it as she saw fit. The dowry was twice what he expected, and just to see how far he might push his future in-laws, he had requested a breeding stallion and eleven mares from their horse farms in either Ireland or Queen's Malvern. His request was accepted, the contracts signed, the dowry delivered, and the proxy marriage celebrated. His bride had left her home in Scotland several weeks ago, and was expected any time at Oxton Court.

Deverall Leigh rode into his stableyard, and dismounted his horse. Soon he would have her in his power again, and she would regret that she ever played him false. Of course she would not recognize him, for Deverall Leigh, smooth-shaven and scarred, with his clipped English accent, was not Caynan Reis, with his elegant beard and soft French accent. No. She would not know him, for he was an entirely different man now. A man who knew better than to trust, or love any woman. He would not be patient this time. He would bring Lady India Anne Lindley to heel like any bitch in his kennels. And he would never again give her the opportunity to betray him. He would kill her first. *After he learned what she had done with their child.*

Chapter

20

When India's train reached the designated spot on the Scots and English border where they were to meet the earl of Oxton's men, they found twenty men-at-arms. The earl's captain took one look at the bride's party, and shook his head.

"I can't be responsible for such a great muck," he said frankly. His eye scanned the baggage carts. "Fifteen! What the hell is the lass bringing to Oxton Court?"

"Watch yer mouth," Red Hugh, the duke's captain, warned the Englishman. "Her ladyship is a great heiress, and nae some wee creature of little worth. Yer master's a lucky man to hae our mistress as his countess. I expect like most men he dinna realize a bride coming to her husband packs everything she owns, and my mistress owns a great deal, as ye can see," he finished with a small chuckle.

"And horses, too!" the earl's man said.

"How safe is the road to Oxton?" Red Hugh demanded.

"Safe as any nowadays," the Englishman replied.

Red Hugh grunted thoughtfully. Finally he said, "We canna allow ye to attempt to take her ladyship to Oxton wi so small a force. I'll send some of my men home, and the rest of us will go wi ye as far as Queen's Malvern in Worcester, where her ladyship means to rest a few days before greeting her new husband."

"I'd be damned grateful for your company," the earl's man said, relieved. "Fifteen baggage carts, and all those horses is far more than I was expecting. I thought a coach, and perhaps one cart."

Red Hugh, Diarmid's uncle, sent twenty of the Glenkirk men back home to the duke, explaining the dilemma faced by the English escort. He knew that James Leslie would have expected him to do just what he did. The bridal party moved down into England, traveling at a good pace, but not so quickly that the carts could not keep up with the riders.

When they had at last reached Queen's Malvern, India sent the baggage carts and horses on to Oxton, but stopped in her brother's house to rest from her journey. She was delighted to find her sixteen-year-old sibling, the duke of Lundy, in residence. Brother and sister greeted each other warmly, hugging.

"Why aren't you at court?" India asked.

Charles Frederick Stuart rolled his eyes dramatically. "I couldn't take a moment more of it, India. The queen and Buckingham squabble over the king's attention and favor like two children. I don't know which of them is worse. I asked my uncle's permission to come home to Queen's Malvern to see my estates, although there is really nothing to see. They are all well taken care of, and I have nothing to do but hunt with Henry, and visit with him over at Cadby. Still, it is a pleasant change from court, where I am stalked constantly by ambitious mamas, forever thrusting their nubile daughters at me. I am too young to marry, as I keep telling them, but all those damned women see is my royal connections, my dukedom, and my fortune. It is really quite annoying, sister. When the right time comes, I shall pick my own bride."

India laughed, and, seating herself in a chair next to the fire, stretched her legs out. "How tragic for you to be so handsome, rich, and sought after, Charlie."

"Am I handsome, do y'think?" he asked her ingenuously.

"Very handsome," she replied.

"They say I look like my sire," he told her proudly.

India looked closely at her younger brother. "Aye, you do," she agreed. "I remember Prince Henry well. He was always so kind to us. It was sad when he died shortly after you were born."

"I would have liked to know him, but of course if he had lived, he couldn't have married Mama anyway, being old King James's heir, and Mama's bloodline not quite up to royal snuff."

"Mama was a royal Mughal princess," India said defensively. "Her father's family is just as old, and their blood as blue as that of the Royal Stuarts."

"Aye," Charlie responded affably, "but the Mughal Empire ain't England."

His sister laughed. "Aye, you're right," she told him.

He poured them goblets of wine, and they sat together for a time. "Tell me about this earl you've married?" he said.

"I know nothing about him really," India said. "He made an offer, and the duke of Glenkirk snapped at it like a hungry trout to a fly. He was quite eager to rid himself of me, Charlie."

"Tell me what happened?" the duke of Lundy asked his sister. "You disappeared for a time, and while Mama said you were first here and then there, I think it not the truth. And you are angry at Papa. Why, India? You were always his especial pet. What has happened to change all that? Tell me. I will keep your secrets, sister."

She told him everything in detail. Her attempted elopement. Her capture. Her resistance to Caynan Reis that grew slowly into a deep love for the dey of El Sinut. How their cousin had kidnapped her, and how she had learned of her husband's untimely death. She told of her return home, and the duke's decision to hide her away at A-Cuil, and his taking her son from her after Rowan was born. "I will never forgive him, Charlie. Considering the history of this family, how could he have done such a thing?"

"And then he jumped at the earl of Oxton's marriage offer," the young duke said. He shook his head. "I wish I could tell you something of the man, India, but other than the gossip surrounding Deverall Leigh's flight from England, and sudden return last year, I know nothing. He keeps to himself."

"It doesn't really matter," India said. "He is now my husband. The only way I could escape Glenkirk was to marry, and this man seemed as good a choice as any. His reputation is lightly tarnished, and so certainly he cannot mind if mine is, too."

"You may remain at Queen's Malvern as long as you like," her brother said to her. "I am happy for your company."

"Just a few days so I am well rested and able to cope with whatever I must face at Oxton," India told him.

Henry Lindley, the nineteen-year-old marquis of Westleigh, arrived the following morning. "I've come to stay until we escort India to her new husband at Oxton," he announced, kissing his sister soundly on both cheeks. "You've grown thin, lovey. Tell me what has happened."

They sat together in the family hall at Queen's Malvern eating baked apples and clotted cream while India told Henry what she had told Charlie the evening before. Her brother listened, his handsome face impassive but for his eyes, which mirrored his emotions.

"You've had a hard time of it," he said when she had finally concluded her tale. "I agree that our stepfather was harsh, but I can also understand his fear that you not be considered marriageable after such an adventure. Times have changed since our great-grandmother and her contemporaries' day. The Puritans are gaining power. They would call you a fallen woman, and make your life and your son's a misery, India," he concluded with a small smile. He was a very handsome young man with his father's tawny hair matching his Van Dyke mustache, and their mother's turquoise blue eyes.

"I might have known you would take *his* side," India said, half angry.

Henry Lindley shook his head. "I take no one's side, sister. As a man, however, I understand the duke's difficulty. If the truth had been known, both you and the child would have been ostracized. Your son ain't no royal Stuart, after all, and Mama barely got away with it herself, but that Prince Henry's parents were soft-hearted." Reaching out, he patted her hand. "Set your mind to making a new start, lovey, and mayhap you will get your child back if this husband you've taken falls in love with you, which he is bound to do if you will but smile and half try."

"And just when do you plan to take a wife, brother dear?" India cooed at him.

The marquis of Westleigh rolled his eyes. "God's blood, lovey. I ain't ready to settle down yet. Charlie and I have a few more oats to sow," he chuckled.

"You've been to court?" India was surprised.

"The winters are dull at Cadby," the marquis pronounced. "Aye, I spent the winter at court, and what a time of it it was. The parliament and the king constantly fighting over the muck-up that's been made in the war with Spain, and the fact that parliament don't think enough has been done to help the French Protestants. I sat in Lords a few times, and what I've heard was enough to keep me down here in the country in the future. Charles Stuart is a good man, but a terrible king, I regret to say."

The duke of Lundy nodded. "I fear for my uncle," he said. "It isn't just those who hate Buckingham, India, it's the fanatics as well. The king likes the Anglican service in church. He is accused of advancing and elevating the high churchmen, whom the Puritans call *Arminians*, over those churchmen who they prefer."

"What's the difference?" India asked him. "Church is church."

"Nay, Sister, not in the minds of those men. The high churchmen believe in free will rather than predestination to achieve salvation. They hold to a more Catholic ritual and rites in the church service. Their sermons are mightily long, and they are given to impromptu prayers. For the Puritans everything must be plain and hard, and just so. God's mercy extends only to those who do exactly what *they* say must be done. Ritual and rite are forbidden. It's all quite ridiculous on both sides."

"And then there was the Petition of Rights that was drawn up," the duke of Lundy said. "Lords concurred. We disapprove of forced loans to the royal treasury, which are never repaid. We dislike having the king's soldiers billeted in our homes without reimbursement, and we are against arrest and imprisonment without just cause. The king accepted the petition, but it is unlikely he'll abide by it. He dissolved the parliament when it threatened to impeach Buckingham for the mess in Spain. That's when Henry and me excused ourselves, and came home."

"There's going to be trouble sooner or later," Henry Lindley said darkly, "and I'd just as soon be safe at home when it comes."

For the next few days, India and her brothers forgot that they were grown now, and romped happily together. They hunted and fished. They rowed on the lake. They sat in the gardens of Queen's Malvern talking. They knew it would never be this way again for them. They voiced their sadness over the fact Fortune was not with them, and wondered what would happen to her in the next few months.

"She'll not accept any man she doesn't want," Henry said wisely, and his siblings agreed.

Finally they could delay no longer. It was less than a day's ride over to Oxton Court, and India knew she had to go. A dozen Glenkirk men would escort her before Red Hugh took his troupe north again into Scotland. Charlie Stuart and Henry Lindley rode with their sister. Diarmid and Meggie had gone on ahead the day before to tell the earl of Oxton that his bride would be arriving.

The respite from her travels had done India good. Her brother's servants had fed her and cosseted her for almost a week. Her eyes had lost their lackluster look, and sparkled golden again. She wore a rich blue silk riding outfit, trimmed lavishly in lace, and in cream-and-gold braid. Topping her dark curls was a blue velvet cap with two soft white plumes. She rode astride as she was accustomed to doing, but her full, long skirts were draped modestly to prevent any show of leg above her leather boots.

They left the hour after sunrise, stopping at a small inn to rest themselves and their horses at the midday hour. They reached Oxton Court in early afternoon. Red Hugh had sent a rider on ahead to warn the earl of their impending arrival. On the hill above Oxton, India looked down into the valley where the house was set. It was very beautiful. Her new home was of weathered old brick, the four wings built about a quadrangle. Sheep grazed placidly in the green meadows. She could see her horses browsing contentedly in the verdant pastures. A splash of color on one side of the house indicated gardens. It was a large and lovely old house with a slate roof that obviously had been built around the same time as Queen's Malvern. A small village with a church was clustered at the far end of the valley. India and her party began their descent.

The road wound through lush orchards, whose trees were already heavy with half-grown apples and pears. It was all very peaceful, and a wonderful place to raise children, India thought. *Please God,* she prayed. *Let the earl be a kind man who will allow me to bring my son to live here. I will be a good wife to him, I promise. Just let me regain my wee Rowan again. He is all I have left of Caynan Reis.*

They drew nearer to the house, and suddenly, from the courtyard, a man came walking, stopping just past the archway into the quadrangle. She strained to see his face, but the sun was in her eyes. All she could tell was that he was formally dressed in black to greet her. India shivered. What if they did not like each other? What if they could not come to some sort of arrangement? The horses stopped before the man, and, reaching up, he lifted India from her mount. She gazed shyly up at him, and was terrified by what she saw. A long scar ran from his left eye to the left corner of his mouth, and his blue eyes were icy. Unable to help herself, she shivered.

Her brothers had quickly dismounted, and Henry, stepping forward, held out his hand to the earl of Oxton. "I am Henry Lindley, sir, the marquis of Westleigh," he said. Then he drew his younger sibling forward. "And this is my brother, Charles Frederick Stuart, the duke of Lundy. We have brought our sister, Lady India, your bride, home to you, my lord."

Deverall Leigh shook hands with both young men. "I thank you, my lords," he said. "Will you stay the night with us?" He offered India his arm, and began to escort her through the archway into the courtyard.

"Thank you, my lord," Henry spoke for them both, "but we must return to Queen's Malvern so I may go home to Cadby tomorrow."

"You will take a cup of wine with us, though, gentlemen," the earl said. "Oxton Court is known for its hospitality, and I would not want it said I sent my bride's brothers on their way without refreshment."

"Thank you, my lord, we will," Henry replied.

"Ohhh, how lovely!" India exclaimed, her eyes sweeping about the quadrangle, which was lavishly planted with roses, and other flowers of all kinds. There was also a large fountain with a spray of water cooling the courtyard.

"You enjoy gardens, madame?" the earl asked her.

"Oh, yes!" India said, and she forced herself to smile up into that harsh face.

"I am glad then, for the house, and its gardens are yours to do with as you will," the earl responded politely.

They entered the house, and he brought them into the Great Hall, a room of soaring arches from which hung multicolored silk banners that had obviously once been carried into battle. The tall curvilinear windows that lined the hall allowed the golden afternoon light to pour into the room. At one end was a great stone fireplace flanked by lions. The highboard was set to one side of the fireplace, and at the other end of the room was a minstrel's gallery. Servants hurried forth with goblets of wine for all. They smiled shyly at India, who smiled back. The talk revolved about the earl's fine orchards, and he promised to send his two brothers-in-law baskets of both apples and pears after the harvest. India remained silent until the time came for her two brothers to depart.

"I wish you didn't have to go," she murmured softly, her eyes filling with tears.

"Make your peace quickly with the man," Henry said softly as he hugged her. "The scar is a bit frightening, but he doesn't seem a bad fellow." He kissed her on both cheeks. "I'm at Cadby if you need me," he concluded.

Charlie hugged her, too. "Behave yourself, my lady," he teased her with a grin, brushing a tear from her cheek that had, despite her best efforts, slipped from her eye.

"The pot calling the kettle black," she half laughed, kissing him and then swatting at him fondly.

"We're both near," Charlie responded softly, "if you need us, big sister."

And they were gone with her husband, who escorted her brothers from the hall and the house. India stood alone, not knowing what to do, or where to go. The earl had virtually ignored her since her arrival, and she could feel her temper rising. His greeting was hardly a warm one, and he had not spoken more than a dozen words to her. Then she caught herself. Perhaps he, too, was feeling the strain of this situation; meeting his wife for the very first time, wondering if they would like each other. Women were the softer sex, and it was up to her to put him at ease with her so she might be at ease with him.

When Deverall Leigh entered the hall again, India smiled at him. "I am happy to be here at last, my lord," she said pleasantly.

"You are very beautiful," he responded, "but I suppose you have been told that by many men."

"Not really so many if you count my brothers, my uncles, and all the rest of my male kin," India replied with another smile.

"When the king pardoned me, he advised me to seek a younger wife. How old are you, madame?" the earl said.

"I was twenty on the twenty-third of June," India told him. "Why did you not follow the king's advice?"

"Because I wanted you," he told her. "Why is it you were not wed before this, madame? It is said that you are flighty, and yet you chose a man you have never seen to marry. Why is that?"

India felt her temper rising again, but she swallowed it back. He was certainly being candid with her, and so she would be as honest with him. *At least to a point.* "I did not choose you, my lord. My *stepfather,* the duke of Glenkirk, chose you. I had refused all other offers that had come to me because they did not suit me. And for your information, I have been married before. A liaison I contracted in Europe when I was with my grandmother. He died, and I will not discuss it further. My stepfather chose you because it was the only offer he had received since my return. He was quite insistent that I be married again before there were no offers at all. Your family is suitable, and since your reputation is somewhat tarnished, the duke thought us an ideal match."

"Indeed," he said softly. God's blood, she was forthright with him, the little bitch; but then, she had always been. His eyes could not get enough of her, for he had always thought her the most beautiful woman he had ever seen. "Frankly, I am relieved you are not a virgin, madame," he told her. "Virgins are always most difficult to deal with, and I have not the patience. Would you like to see your apartments now? Your servants are awaiting you. We shall have to find something to do for Diarmid, however. What is his position?"

"He is my bodyguard," India replied sweetly.

He almost laughed, but refrained from his open amusement. "You will have no need for a bodyguard at Oxton Court, madame," the earl told her, "but as he is your maidservant's husband, you will find him a suitable place in the household. Come!" And, taking her gloved hand in his, he led her from the Great Hall, up the wide staircase, to her new apartments in the south wing of the house.

Meggie curtsied as they entered the room, and then ran forward to take her mistress's gloves, and cap. "Welcome home, my lady!" she said with a smile. " 'Tis so very lovely here, and his lordship has given us our own room for me and Diarmid!"

"I am glad you are content with the arrangement, Meggie," India said to her beaming servant. "Diarmid," she said to Meggie's husband, who was standing respectfully waiting to greet her, "can you write and do your numbers?"

"Aye, my lady, I can," he responded.

"Then you shall be steward of my personal household as the earl assures me I do not need a bodyguard at Oxton," India replied. She turned to her husband. "Does that not solve the problem, my lord?"

"Indeed, madame, quite neatly. You are quick-witted, I am pleased to note. I hope you will pass the trait on to our children." He saw the shadow pass quickly over her face. So quickly that had he not been looking directly at her he would have missed it. "Is everything all right, madame?" he queried her.

"Of course, my lord," she said swiftly.

So the mention of children disturbed her. False bitch! What had she done with their child? And that quick admission of a marriage to a husband dead that she would not discuss. Was he supposed to believe her so distraught with grief that she could not speak of it? Oh, she would pay for her perfidy, he promised himself silently. Then he said to her, "Will you dine with me tonight, madame? A wedding supper of sorts, one might say, after the minister blesses our union."

"Of course," she answered him, but she had longed to refuse. When he had spoken of children, she had wanted to weep with her pain over her son, but how could she have explained such behavior.

"I will leave you then to rest from your ride," he said, bowing politely and withdrawing from her apartments.

She noted that he went through a small door in the wall, and not out into the hallway. She looked about the salon in which they were standing. It was a lovely room with light wood paneling decorated with gold trim. The large fireplace was flanked with standing angels. The draperies on the window were of a light-blue velvet trimmed with gold braid. The furniture was well polished, the upholstery and floral tapestry fresh, and bright. The floors were covered with Turkey carpets. There were silver candlesticks, and bowls of rose potpourri.

"Ain't it grand?" Meggie declared.

"It is as nice as my own family's houses," India agreed.

"Come see the bedchamber!" Meggie enthused, hurrying to open the door. Diarmid remained discreetly in the salon.

India had to admit she liked her new bedchamber very much. The draperies were her favorite shade of rose velvet, as were the matching bed hangings. The bed itself had an eight-foot headboard of linenfold paneling, and the carved canopy extended on all four sides of the bed. The pillars holding up the canopy were carved with leaves and vines. The bed was made with her own scented linens, featherbed, and pillows. On each side of the bed was a table, and upon each table a silver nightstick and tiny snuffer. The fireplace opposite the bed was flanked on either side with delicate stone deer, a doe and a buck. The andirons were well-polished brass. By the fireplace a comfortable chair had been set, and next to it, a candlestand. A cushioned window seat was built into the large box window to the right of the bed. On the opposite wall was a small refectory table and two straight chairs. The rest of the furniture was the usual carved chests. On the table was a bowl of roses.

"It's lovely," India finally spoke, "and you have put everything away, bless you, Meggie."

"Everything? Nay, not by any means, my lady. Diarmid and me will be busy unpacking those baggage carts for days," the maidservant said. "Let me take your gown now. You'll want a bit of a liedown before supper, I'm thinking."

"I want a bath," India asked. "I cannot change from my riding clothes into another dress smelling of horses."

"There's many that does," Meggie observed. "I've never known such a one for washing as yerself, my lady."

"I'd rather smell of flowers than stink of my own sweat," India replied. "Water is good for the skin. It keeps it soft, and you want to keep that wild highlander of yours by your side, don't you, Meggie. I saw some pretty little faces in the hall below."

"And let one of them try to make free with my husband," Meggie said, glowering, "and I'll snatch the trollop bald!"

India laughed, and then she sobered, realizing that she had felt the very same way about Caynan Reis. She very much doubted if she would feel that strongly about Deverall Leigh. Still, she was married to him, and would have to make the best of it, especially if she was to regain her son, Rowan. She had already begun by telling him she had been previously married. He had not, thank God, asked if she had had any children. She was not ready to share that with him. He might very well be glad she had not brought her child, not wanting another man's son in his house to raise. *No. I must gain his favor and trust before I mention my child to this man*, she thought with surety. *He does not look sympathetic, or easily led.*

She had a leisurely bath, and then napped for a short time. Awakening, she allowed Meggie to dress her in cream-colored silk brocade trimmed in lace, the gown prepared for the church ceremony here at Oxton. It was to take place this evening in the estate church. The earl had said that he wanted the official formalities celebrated immediately. Meggie affixed the Stars of Kashmir about her neck, and slipped the ear bobs into her ears. India touched them wonderingly. What history they held!

She descended the staircase to find him awaiting her. "The church is but a short walk," he said, handing her a nosegay of sweet white flowers and offering her his arm.

Outside, the sun was setting to the west over the Malvern Hills. To the east, the moon was rising. It was very still, and only the faintest breeze ruffled her curls.

The little stone church was filled with the servants, including Meggie and Diarmid. It was softly lit with beeswax candles. The minister greeted them, and announced to the assembled that, as the earl of Oxton and his bride had accepted the proxy marriage celebrated at Glenkirk on the thirtieth day of May, in the year of our Lord sixteen hundred and twenty-eight, they were legally and lawfully wed. Now, tonight, on this eighteenth day of July, he would give the blessing in God's name, on behalf of His Majesty, the king. The couple knelt, and the minister intoned, " 'Those whom God hath joined together, let no man rent asunder. In the name of the Father, and of the Son, and of the Holy Ghost. Amen.' "

"Amen!" the congregation replied.

"Now, my lord," the minister said, his eyes twinkling, "you are quite free to kiss your bride."

India's eyes widened as his lips brushed her coolly. *Kiss?* She hadn't thought of kissing. *And lovemaking!* Oh, my God! In her anger and her eagerness to escape Glenkirk, she had put from her head these more intimate matters. About her, the assembled cheered, and the earl led her from the church.

"You are surprised I kissed you," he said as they walked back to the house.

"It was hardly a kiss, my lord," she replied. "More like a butterfly brushing my lips."

"Passion should be a private matter between a man and his wife, madame," he said reprovingly. "I could hardly avoid the formality when the Reverend Master Barton was encouraging me to it so publicly, and in such a loud voice. We would have disappointed the servants."

"If I asked for a respite from your company tonight so I might recover from my journey, would we disappoint the servants?" she asked him boldly.

"You would disappoint me," he told her. "Besides, you had several days in your brothers' company at Queen's Malvern to regain your strength, madame."

"I am not ready yet for a man in my bed," India said frankly.

"Why?"

She stumbled, but he caught her up before she might fall. "I don't know really. I just know I am not."

"Obviously, your experience with men is slight," he said quietly, "but I am ready to have a wife in my bed, madame, *and you are that wife.* You are merely shy, which speaks well of your character. I am no monster." *And I cannot wait to have you in my arms again, you false bitch,* he thought to himself. *You will yield yourself to me whether you will or no. I have spent months dreaming of this night, and you will not deny me, India. You will never deny me again!*

It had all gone as he had expected so far. She had not recognized the earl of Oxton as the dey of El Sinut. Why should she? The earl of Oxton had short, dark hair, a rather sinister scar marking his face, and was clean-shaven, which gave his high cheekbones and jaw a totally different look. He spoke English. The dey of El Sinut had had a close-cropped dark black beard that fringed his jaw and encircled itself sensuously about his mouth and chin. His skin was bronzed from the hot sun. He spoke French to her in a soft voice, the voice of a lover in the language of love. But when he made love to her tonight, it would not be as the dey of El Sinut had made love to her, all sweetness and passion. It would be as the earl of Oxton would make love to his wife.

He was yet angry with her. How could she have left him after declaring her love for him? When she was ripening with their child? Adrian had given him the answer when he had said India's loyalty to her family was greater than any other loyalty. If he had not been forced to flee El Sinut himself, he might have never found her again. *And where was their child?* He would, of course, have to reveal himself to her eventually if he was to regain custody of his child, but for the moment, he intended taking his revenge upon her. He could not believe her so insensitive that she would have left the child in danger of any kind. There was time. And did he have a son or a daughter?

They ate dinner in the little family hall. There were but the two of them. There were raw oysters brought to the earl which he swallowed with relish, his eyes making deliberate contact with hers at one point, and she blushed to her dismay. There was a small roast of beef; a duck stuffed with fruit and rice in a sauce of wine and plums; a lovely broiled trout set upon a bed of braised lettuce, surrounded by carved lemons, an extravagance; a bowl of tiny new peas, and another of little carrots; fresh bread, sweet butter, and half a wheel of hard, sharp cheese.

He watched her nibbling unenthusiastically at a slice of beef, a spoonful of carrots, some bread. "You are not hungry?" he asked.

"It is all very good, and well prepared," India quickly said, sipping upon her second goblet of rich red wine. "My appetite has been poor of late, I fear, my lord. Food upon the road is often not of the best quality, even at the finest inns."

"When you have finished, then," he told her, "you may go to your chamber and prepare yourself for me, madame."

She practically leapt from her place, and, curtseying to him, fled the hall.

He smiled wolfishly watching her go. India was not a woman to admit to fear, but she was afraid, and he knew it.

She could feel his eyes, those cold blue eyes, boring into her back as she went. God's blood! What kind of a man was he to insist on bedding her immediately? True, they were man and wife, but they had met but a few hours ago. They knew virtually nothing about each other. Then, in a flash, she understood. If the marriage were consummated, she could not demand an annulment. After all, had she not told him quite bluntly that marriage to him had not been her choice? He, of course, would want to take no chances with losing her dowry, or a rich wife who controlled her own wealth but could undoubtedly be cozened into parting with some, or all of it. Men! They were so obvious. He was no different from the rest, but then, she had not expected that he would be.

She was no virgin to be terrified of a man's love lance. As for her husband, he would probably assert his rights in a brusque and perfunctory manner, then return to his own bedchamber. She wasn't the first woman to be in such a position, nor would she be the last. It would have been nice if they might have gotten to know each other a bit before coupling, but so be it.

"You looked so lovely in that candlelit church, m'lady," Meggie said, taking the Stars of Kashmir from her mistress and replacing them in their case. "I've laid out a lovely nightdress for you." She bustled about, taking India's garments, shaking and brushing them, and putting them neatly away. "The earl seems a pleasant gentleman."

"Aye," she said.

" 'Tis a terrible scar he wears on his face, poor man," Meggie noted. "I wonder how he got it. He don't seem the type of gentleman to get into a brawl. Mayhap it were an accident."

India took the soft flannel cloth that had been laid out, and sponged herself off with the warm, scented water Meggie had put in a silver ewer. Then she scrubbed her teeth with the cloth, rinsing her mouth with minted water. She slipped behind the painted screen in the corner of her dressing room, and, sitting on her commode, relieved herself, washing herself afterwards. Finally she pulled off her chemise, and Meggie slipped the rose-colored nightdress lavishly edged in lace over her head.

"Find your own bed now, Meggie," India said quietly, and, taking up her silver hairbrush, she sat on the edge of her bed, brushing her long, dark curls, as, with a curtsey, Meggie hurried out the bedchamber door. India smiled after her. Meggie was obviously finding married life with Diarmid a pleasant thing. She looked about the room again, admiring the serenity and order of it. The fireplace burned brightly, and but for the two candles on the nightstand there was no other light. Meggie had drawn the draperies closed. The room was comfortably warm, and she could smell the heady scent of the roses from the bowl on the table.

A small door in the paneled wall opened, and the earl stepped through into the room. To her complete surprise, he was naked. "Remove your nightdress," he said quietly as the door behind him closed. "Unless you are suffering your woman's cycle, are greatly advanced with child, or I tell you I will not be visiting your bed, you will always sleep naked, India, as do I. Do you understand me?" Then he stood watching as she removed her garment, nodding in answer to his question. "Good," he said. His eyes swept over her. "You have a beautiful body, madame."

She was nonplussed. She certainly hadn't expected him to behave in such a manner. It was very disconcerting.

Reaching out, he put his hands about her waist and turned her, drawing her back against his hard body. A single hand clamped over her right breast. His lips touched her shoulder, scattering a row of kisses across the warm flesh, even as his fingers crushed and marked the skin of her full breast.

She couldn't breathe. Her chest felt tight. His actions were not what she had anticipated at all. She could sense the lust beneath his careful deeds. He frankly frightened her. He was obviously dangerous. He was her husband, and she was at his mercy. India struggled against her own fright. She knew she must not show any fear with this man, but when he pushed a finger between her lips and into her mouth, she could not prevent a gasp of surprise.

"*Lick it!*" The two words were snapped into her ear sharply.

After a moment's hesitation, her tongue reached out and touched the finger. Slowly she encircled the digit several times. It was long and thick, and very suggestive of another member of his body.

"*Suck it!*" His hand opened, then slipped beneath her breast, cupping it. His thumb began to rub against her nipple.

India could feel her heart hammering in her ears. She drew on the finger within her mouth over and over again while his hand fondled her breast hungrily, and her nipples puckered like frosted flower buds.

The hand moved from her breast finally, sliding down her torso, caressing her Venus mound. Pushing through the folds of her nether lips, he found her pleasure place and began to stroke it with his fingertip. "What a sweet wanton you are," he whispered in her ear. "You are already wet with your desire. You want to be fucked, don't you, madame?" He pulled his finger from her mouth so she might speak.

"You are my husband," India replied in a shaking voice.

He laughed, and it was a dark sound. "Little whore," he murmured. "You would want to be fucked even if I weren't your husband, wouldn't you?" The finger playing with her pleasure place was obtaining the proper results, and she squirmed her bottom against his groin, desperate to reach that honied place where the tensions in her loins would dissolve in a burst of hot sweetness.

In that moment she hated him, for she was fully aware that he knew what he was withholding from her. The knowledge gave her a moment of strength, and she pulled away from him, whirling about to face those cold eyes. "How dare you speak to me in such a manner, my lord? I am your wife, and not some servant girl to be insulted!"

He moved quickly, one arm wrapping itself about her, the other hand tangling into her dark hair. His mouth found hers in a long, hard, deep kiss that left her once again breathless. Shoving her down onto the bed, he flung himself atop her, his hands spreading her open. Without a word, he entered her body with strong thrusts of his hips, pushing deeply even as she attempted to unhorse him, spitting her rage and swearing fiercely at him.

But it was too late. He had prepared her well, and while India wanted desperately to deny him, her body welcomed him eagerly. She was hot and wet. Her tight sheath encased him. They groaned in unison as their linked bodies pleasured each other. She clawed at his broad back. He caught her hands and pinioned them over her head, struggling to propel himself deeper.

"Put your legs about me, you eager little bitch," he growled into her ear, and without hesitation, she did, using her wrapped limbs to lever herself forward and sink her teeth into his shoulder. He yelped, but continued pistoning her.

She couldn't . . . she couldn't fight him any longer. She fell back gasping like a fish out of water, drawing great gulps of air into her lungs even as she felt herself shoved up to the heights of a frenzy of heated passion that burst over her and then receded, leaving her weakened, and helpless. "Ohh, God!" she sobbed as release flooded her very being. "Ohh, I hate you for this!" And she shuddered with the final spasms of her defeat.

He lay atop her for some minutes, his heart hammering, his breathing rough. It had been so long. So long since he had known the pleasure of her body, and the sweet fulfillment that only she could give him. He wanted to wrap his arms about her. Tell her the truth. But he couldn't because he couldn't trust her. She was a hot-blooded and deceitful little bitch. No better than his step-mother had been. She would yield her body to gain her own way. He rolled off India, and arose from the bed. "Good night, madame," he said, and returned through the door in the wall from which he had come.

India lay astounded. She was battered, and probably bruised. Every bit of her ached, and yet she felt quite relaxed and shamefully satisfied. He had called her a wanton, a little whore. He had almost made her feel like one. The single kiss he had given her had been a fiercely passionate one. Her fingers touched her mouth. His lips had triggered a reminiscence that she could not quite pull up from her memories. She began to cry softly, not even understanding why she was weeping.

He had behaved like a complete bastard, and she had not expected it at all. A quick assertion of his marital rights and nothing more was what she had assumed. That this cold, stern man was capable of such heated passion astonished her. India crawled beneath the down coverlet, curling herself into a tight knot. She realized that she was trembling, and the tears were hot on her face. What had she done in agreeing to this marriage, and what other surprises had her husband in store for her? She wanted to be loved. Loved by a man who no longer existed, and not by Deverall Leigh, the earl of Oxton. *Were it not for my baby,* she thought, *I should just as soon be dead.*

He heard her weeping, and every instinct made him want to go to her, but he would not. She wept, the deceitful bitch, only because he had been rough with her, but God help him, she had inflamed his senses. The touch of her skin, the familiar scent of her. They had all conspired to drive him to madness. She would probably hate him in the morning, but he didn't care. Why should he care about how she felt? She had deceived him and then deserted him. He didn't know if he could ever forgive her, but he didn't care. He was going to fill her belly again with his seed, and this time he would not let her steal this child away.

Chapter

21

India awoke the following morning still feeling as if she had been in a battle. She could see a thin ribbon of light through the crack between the two draperies. She listened carefully but heard nothing, and so she quickly arose and slipped her nightdress back on before Meggie could find her without it. It had been the oddest wedding night that anyone could imagine, she decided, climbing back into her warm bed. He had, she concluded, been neither cruel or brutal, just simply very determined in his approach to her. Still, she could see she was going to have to teach him better bedchamber manners. While he had been careful to see she obtained her share of passion, she realized upon reflection, he had forced it from her, rather than coaxing it. He obviously knew little about making love to a woman, and that was going to have to change, India concluded.

She did not see her husband until evening when they met at the highboard for their meal. She had spent her day helping Meggie and Diarmid to unpack her belongings. She told him so, and then inquired about his day and activities.

"I oversee my estates," he told her. "I am not a man for court now that I have the responsibilities of Oxton. We support ourselves here through our flocks and our orchards. Perhaps you noticed the fruit ripening as you arrived yesterday. With your dower horses, I hope to breed racing animals, madame. Are the horses Irish stock?"

"Yes," she answered, "they are. The Irish lands were given to my mother on her eighteenth birthday by my father, the marquis of Westleigh. Her estate manager is the former owner of the land. He chose a fine stallion, Nightsong, and the mares personally. Now the estate will be turned over to my younger sister, Fortune, for her dowry."

"I am grateful to you for the stallion and the breeding stock," the earl said to his wife. "Now, madame, I have something to discuss with you. The servants in this house are all old, and have been in service here since my late father's youth. It is past time that they were retired to their cottages on the estate, and most wish to go. It will be your responsibility to staff the household. Can you do it?"

"With the help of the present staff, yes, I can," India said, flattered that he was vesting this decision in her. "Diarmid More-Leslie will become the majordomo of the household. I will ask Dover to teach him his duties before he retires. Will that meet with your approval, my lord? It is your home first, and I would not offend you in any manner."

The barest ghost of a smile touched his mouth for just a brief moment. "If you will but consult me before any final decisions are made, madame, that will suit me well," he said.

They ate the rest of the meal in silence. Then India arose to excuse herself. "It is my custom to take a bath before I retire each night," she said softly. "Will you be joining me later, my lord?"

"Aye," he said, and nothing more.

She curtsied, and went to her apartments. He was such an odd man, she thought. Meggie had her bath ready. Undressed, she climbed into the warm, scented tub and washed herself, being careful to pin her curls atop her head. When she was dry, and in her nightdress, Meggie and Diarmid together emptied the tub and stored it away before bidding her a pleasant night. When they had gone, India arose, removed her gown, and laid it carefully upon a chair before climbing back into her bed and snuggling beneath the down coverlet.

The curtains were drawn once again. The firelight lit the room. Meggie had forgotten to light the tapers on either side of the bed, but India didn't mind. She dozed half seated against her pillow, awakening when she heard the sharp click of the door in the paneling. As the previous night, the earl entered her bedchamber naked, but this time she had a small opportunity to observe him. He was well made, she could see, with no deformities. There was a dark mat of hair upon his broad chest that extended into a narrow treasure trail leading to his groin. His masculine parts were also extremely well made, she noted, large and healthy.

Lifting the coverlet, he climbed into bed beside her. "I am pleased to see that you followed my instructions," he told her.

"Asking me to be naked in my bed for your attentions is hardly an onerous order, my lord husband," India answered him.

"Lay back," he said, throwing the bedcoverings aside. "I wish to examine you in more detail, madame. I did not have the opportunity last night to do so. I would see what Glenkirk has sent me."

"Like one of my mares," she mocked him sharply.

"Precisely, madame," he told her, and took up her hand.

"Our situation is intimate, sir," she replied. "Will you not call me by my given name, and permit me to call you by your name? In public, formality is required, I understand, but surely not here in my bed." He was kissing each of her fingertips, having examined her hand in great detail.

He put one of her fingers in his mouth, and began to suck on it slowly, drawing on the finger deeply, his tongue working its way about the slim digit. His other hand slid between her thighs, and began to play with her sex. When she was wet with her arousal, he took his finger and pushed it into her mouth, and, without being asked, she began to suck upon it. "That is how you taste," he said softly. He sucked harder on her finger.

Her eyes were wide with shock, but her blood was pulsing with excitement. This cold and correct husband of hers was the most sensual man she had ever encountered. Even her beloved Caynan Reis had not been so strongly animalistic. India shivered, and pulled the finger from her mouth.

"Are you cold, India?" he asked her solicitously, drawing her finger from his mouth and kissing the palm of her hand ardently.

"Why do you taunt me, Deverall?" she whispered.

"I am attempting to make up for my crude behavior of last night," he said innocently. "I am trying to make love to you, India, but perhaps you preferred being thrown on your back and roughly fucked." Leaning over, he nuzzled her ear. "Do you like being taken *that* way?"

"*No!*" she managed to husk out as his tongue made circles in the shell of her ear.

"I imagine you thought I had no manners suitable for a lady's chamber," he almost purred at her.

"Aye," she quickly answered, "I did!"

"Then let me prove otherwise to you, India," he said, pressing her back into her pillows and kissing her, his lips warm and firm against her own.

To her surprise, the kiss was a tender one, but then it began to deepen, and his tongue was pushing into her mouth to meet with hers. She trembled. *His mouth. The kisses he kissed her.* Why did they touch a chord somewhere within her? She wanted to weep again.

He was startled to feel the wetness on her cheeks, the salty tears against his mouth. Why was she crying? He knew instinctively not to question her. Instead, he took her face between his two hands and kissed the tears from it, pretending he believed her emotions stemmed from his passion toward her. "Do not weep, India," he said. "I will never be rough with you again," he said. "Would you prefer if I left you now?"

"I want to be a good wife to you," she half sobbed. Ohh, God's blood, she was behaving like a perfect ninny!

He took her declaration to mean that he was to stay. He let his kisses move down her throat and across her chest. She murmured, and calmed. He kissed her breasts gently, and then he took a nipple into his mouth, suckling upon it, gently at first, and then harder.

Her fingers dug into his shoulder as his mouth worked her. She remembered once telling Caynan Reis that she wondered what manner of woman she was to enjoy his attentions so avidly when such pleasure should be reserved for a husband and wife. This man, his dark head lowered to her bosom, was her husband, yet he was making her feel like a perfect wanton. She did not truly know him, and yet his attentions were arousing her to a frenzy. She murmured, and caressed his hair.

Bitch, he thought. *Wanton bitch!* She responded to his attentions eagerly, although she struggled to hide her feelings. How quickly she had forgotten Caynan Reis. Now she murmured, and moaned with her rising arousal as he stroked and petted her. He could have killed her did he not love her so damned much. He began to kiss her again, his lips wandering across her torso. Her belly was sweetly rounded, and he licked the quivering flesh, causing her to cry out softly with her pleasure. She needed to be punished, he thought irrationally. Spreading her, he drew her slender legs with their silken thighs over his shoulders, and, sitting back upon his haunches, he drew her to him.

India shrieked her surprise as his mouth made contact with the most intimate part of her. He gripped her buttocks firmly in his two big hands, and his head buried itself in her sweetness, his lips mashing themselves against her nether lips, his tongue running up and down her slit before pushing through to find her pleasure place. Her head spun with her rising passion, and she panted like an animal. "*Deverall! Dev!* Oh, God, my lord, you are killing me!" The first wave crashed into her. She could feel his teeth, gently, oh so very gently, nibbling on her flesh. She cried out, shuddering violently. The second wave raised her up. His flickering tongue teased, and teased, and teased at her sensitivity, and then plunged as deeply as it could into her sheath. "Oh, God! Oh, God! Oh, God!" she cried. Then he released her but a moment before pressing his body against hers and plunging into her. She screamed her pleasure as the third wave flung her down, and down, and down.

He thrust again and again into the hot, honied sheath welcoming him. There had never been a woman like India, and there would never be one like her no matter she was a lying and deceitful little bitch. He could feel himself swelling, then breaking, his love juices flooding her womb. He lifted his dark head a moment to kiss her lips, and saw that she was practically insensible with his passion. He brushed his mouth across hers, whispering softly, "*Je t'aime seulement, ma bijou! Seulement toi, India. Ma femme precieuse. Seulement toi!*"

In her half-conscious state she heard *his* voice. "*Mon seigneur Caynan*, she whispered, "*Je t'aime aussi. Ahh, retournez-moi! C'est un rêve.*" Then she fell into an exhausted sleep.

I love you also. Return to me. This is a dream. Her soft words slammed into him with violent force. What did she mean by such words? She had deserted him. *Or had she?* Both Baba Hassan and Azura had insisted India would not leave him willingly, yet he had thought otherwise. During most of her time with him she had been defiant, and eager to be free. When she had disappeared, he had assumed that she had been but feigning her love for him and run off with her cousin.

Why had he even thought such a thing? Because in his heart he had not trusted her. He had never trusted women since the time his stepmother had seduced him, and then laughingly rejected him when another lover took her fancy. She had made a man of him, MariElena told him, but he quickly realized she had done it in order to have a wedge to drive between him and his father. Worse, he was bitterly ashamed of having betrayed his sire. Then she had warned him mockingly that he must never trust a woman again. He had taken her advice to heart.

But suddenly he was beset by his own doubts that he might have been wrong about India. What if she had indeed been kidnapped by her cousin, the sea captain? What if she had not gone willingly, and been forced to return to her family in Scotland? He had renounced her as dey of El Sinut. If his rule had not been overthrown, and he returned to England, what would have become of her? The duke of Glenkirk would obviously have accepted any decent offer for her, believing he was doing the right thing by his stepdaughter. *But what of their child?* Had she had the baby, and what had become of it?

Deverall Leigh arose from the bed, and returned to his own bedchamber. He slipped his nightshirt over his long, lean body, and began pacing the room. How was he to reveal himself to India? How could he face her having believed her so unworthy of his trust?

He knew India. She was going to be furious. Had she not once taken his own dagger to him in a rage? And this situation was much, much worse. He needed time to think. He would shut himself off from her for a few days and try to decide how to get himself out of this disastrous mess he had so easily gotten himself into thanks to his overweening pride.

India did not see her husband for several days. He sent word the following morning that he must ride out across his estates for the next few days. She was free to pursue her own interests. After the furious passion of the previous evening, India was relieved. This strange, intense man was a puzzle she needed time to solve. She began the task of replacing the servants, and having them trained by their predecessors, who were eager to now retire. Dover, who had been the majordomo, was full of advice and local information. He liked Diarmid, telling him he had worried about who would replace him.

"Ain't none here with the polish and snap as is needed in such a position," he said. "I followed poor old Rogers because I had been his assistant in London. After the earl was accused of murder, we never went back to London. Oh, young Master Adrian did, but the family never did. The folk hereabouts likes you. You'll do fine."

Diarmid laughed. "I'm flattered that you think so," he said to the old man, "but I'm naught but a highland lad. I'll need all the help ye can give me, Dover."

" 'Taint the experience, laddie," Dover told the Scotsman. " 'Tis the bearing and the attitude, and you have both," he said wisely.

The only one of the servants refusing to retire was Mrs. Cranston, the cook. "I only replaced Mrs. Dover when she died some eight years ago," she told India. "I'm years younger than the rest of them as you can plainly see, m'lady, and I'm not ready to be put out to pasture yet!" She stood before her young mistress, hands upon her ample hips, her white cap bobbing vigorously, her plump cheeks red with the constant heat of her kitchens.

"Do you need any more help?" India asked her.

"Well," Mrs. Cranston allowed, "most of them is young, and

suits me fine, but if I might have a pot boy, and one more lass to scrub, I'd be most grateful, yer ladyship."

"Have you anyone in mind?" India asked cleverly.

"Well, yer ladyship, I do. 'Tis a young niece and nephew of mine that I would place in your service. They're honest children, and will do their work well, for they've had obedience beaten into them by my sister, their mother."

"His lordship must make the final decision, Mrs. Cranston, but I believe he will concur that your niece and nephew are suitable. Bring them into the house. They will have their wages at Michaelmas, and be given room and board. What are their ages?"

"The lad is nine, and the lass eleven, your ladyship," Mrs. Cranston replied, smiling broadly, "and I thank you kindly."

To India's surprise, her husband did not arrive back home for some five days. Entering the house, he noted many new faces smiling at him. At the evening meal India told him of all the changes she had made, with his permission, of course. He approved it all, and India sent immediate word to the staff as she retired to her apartments to await her husband's coming. She bathed, and, dismissing Meggie, climbed into her bed.

When he entered her chamber, she was surprised to find he was wearing a white silk nightshirt. "We must talk," he said quietly, and began to pace back and forth about the room.

"About what?" she asked him, wondering what it was she might have done to displease this strange man.

"Tell me about your first husband," he said bluntly.

Her heart leapt in her chest. What could he possibly have heard? Had Adrian somehow returned, and exposed her adventures to his elder brother? "What do you wish to know?" she ventured nervously.

"You said he died." Deverall Leigh was looking directly at her.

"Yes," India answered. Her fingers clutched at the coverlet.

"*How?*"

"There was a rebellion in his country," she answered him. "He was killed." Her chest felt tight, and she could feel tears coming.

"How do you know he was killed?" the earl persisted.

"*How?*" What did this man want from her? She swallowed back her tears.

"Yes. How?"

"I was with my grandmother, Lady Stewart-Hepburn, in Naples. She was arranging for my return to my husband when word came of the rebellion, and that my husband had been killed in it. I never returned back to my husband's lands again. Lady Stewart-Hepburn returned with me to Glenkirk. I was content to buy myself a house here in England, and live quietly the rest of my days, but my stepfather would not have it. I told you it was he who insisted that I remarry. I did so to escape him, and to regain control of my own wealth. Nevertheless, my lord, I shall endeavor to be a good wife to you in all ways. We need not be enemies."

She had thought him dead. But that did not solve the problem of how she got to Naples, although he was certain it was in the ship stolen by Thomas Southwood. He pressed her further. "Just who was this man to whom you were wed, India? What was his name?"

India closed her eyes a moment to regain her composure. Then, looking directly at him, she said, "My husband's name was Caynan Reis, and he was the dey of the Barbary State of El Sinut. Are you content now, my lord? I was a captive, and I was made the dey's wife because we fell in love with each other! Are you horrified? Will you divorce me now that you have discovered that I was the beloved of an infidel?"

"How did a dey's wife get to Naples?" he demanded. "Is it not unusual for a woman of the harem to be allowed to travel so far?"

"What does it matter how I got to Naples?" India cried. "Why do you pursue this matter, my lord? Why should you care?"

He ceased his pacing, and sat down upon the bed next to her. Taking her face between his two hands, he said to her, "*Regardez-moi, India.* Look at me!" The blue eyes softened. "Do you not recognize Caynan Reis in Deverall Leigh? The beard is gone, and I have a scar, but can you not see me, my love?"

Her eyes widened in shock. *His mouth! His kisses!* That was what had been niggling at her all this time. "You bastard!" she hissed venomously at him, pulling away from his hands, leaping naked from the other side of the bed. "You bloody bastard! How could you have done this to me? And you say you love me? *I will kill you!*" Reaching for the nearest object at hand, she flung the bowl of roses at him.

" 'Tis I who should kill you," he shouted back at her, ducking, "but not before I find out what you did with my child!"

"*Your child? Your child!*" she shrieked. "Is that what this has been all about? *Your child?*" Grabbing up her silver hairbrush, she hurled it at him. "Why could you not have come to Glenkirk to reclaim me? Do you know what I have suffered over you, *my lord?*" Her eyes cast about for another object to throw at him, but the room was virtually empty of such trinkets. She bared her teeth at him, moving about the bed toward him. Then she launched herself at him, fists pummeling him, nails seeking out his eyes.

He would have laughed at this naked fury if the situation had not been so serious, but now he realized if he did not calm her anger, and indeed his, nothing would be resolved between them. He caught her hands in his, and, forcing them to her sides, wrapped her in his embrace. "India, India," he pleaded. "There is some terrible misunderstanding between us, and we must rectify it. Stop struggling, you little wildcat, and tell me how you got to Naples? It was with Tom Southwood, wasn't it?"

She squirmed against him, pulling half free of his grasp. "I can say nothing if you persist in smothering me," she snarled at him.

He loosened his grip slightly, but not enough so she might do him a mischief. "How did you get to Naples?" he repeated.

"That fool of a cousin of mine learned of a small section of wall that surrounded your garden that opened onto a narrow public street. He had wheedled the information out of Aruj Agha by means of flattery. He came with one of his men the night of the terrible storm. I told him I loved you. That I was content to remain in El Sinut. I tried to reason with him. I might have cried out, if indeed the guards could have even heard me over all the thunder that night, but he was my cousin. I did not want to be responsible for his death. It meant nothing to me that he chose to escape El Sinut just as long as he left me in peace, but no, Tom would not listen.

He assaulted me, knocking me unconscious, hauled me over that damned wall, and dumped me in Naples. Meggie came, too, rather than be left behind.

"Once we were in Naples I told Lady Stewart-Hepburn the truth, that I loved you, and was with child. I had never had a chance to tell my cousin that I was *enceinte*. Cat, that is what I call my stepgrandmother, agreed that I should go back, but then we heard about the rebellion, and were told that the dey had been killed. When I learned that, I nearly died myself. Cat brought me back to Scotland, but when Glenkirk learned of my condition, he banished me to the family's hunting lodge in the mountains with Meggie and Diarmid. My sister, Fortune, insisted on coming with me, and there we remained until Rowan was born."

"*Rowan?*" He stared down into her face.

"*Our son.* I named him after my father," she said softly.

"Where is he?" Deverall Leigh demanded.

"I do not know," India replied, her eyes filling with tears.

"*You do not know?* Madame, what have you done with my son?" he shouted at her angrily.

"I have done nothing. Glenkirk took the lad from me shortly after his birth, and hid him away. He would never say where," India told him, her chin quivering with her emotions. "But none of this would have happened if you had come to Glenkirk to reclaim me instead of playing this perverted game with me! Why, my lord? Why have you done this to me? *Why?*" she sobbed.

"Because I am a fool," he said sadly. "I thought you had deserted me, India, had willingly gone off with Captain Southwood. Baba Hassan, and Azura defended you, but I would not listen." He told her of his stepmother, and why he had been unable to trust women.

India sighed sadly. Then she asked him, "But how is it you were able to return to England, and how on earth did you get that scar on your face, Deverall?"

"Adrian is responsible for my return. He caught a fever, and I revealed myself to him. When I did, he told me that it had been a plot of my stepmother's to kill Lord Jeffers, and blame me so he might inherit. MariElena did the deed herself with poison. Then she implicated my brother, who was still a child, by having him place the knife in a dead man's chest. Adrian dictated a confession, and signed it. I kept it for myself, and had no intention of returning to England; but the janissaries had learned of my warning to the sultan, which had put an end to their plans to overthrow him and his mother. They sent troops from Algiers and Tunis to invade El Sinut, and the sultan looked the other way. I was to be sacrificed to their revenge. Fortunately, Baba Hassan learned of it just in time, and arranged for my flight. On our way to the harbor I was surprised by a young janissary eager to make a reputation. The scar is from his cowardly blow. Fortunately for me Aruj Agha was nearby. He killed the assailant, and I was able to make good my escape."

"But what of the others in the palace?" India asked.

"Aruj Agha promised to see they were taken care of, and as he has been appointed the new dey, according to my sources, I think we can both rest assured that they are safe," the earl told his wife. Then his arms tightened about her again. "Do you know how much I love you, India?"

"But you do not trust me, my lord, and I do not know if I can forgive you that," she said quietly.

"I will never mistrust you again," he vowed, and, tipping her face up to his, he sealed his words with a kiss.

"*Diarmid!*" India suddenly cried, breaking away from her husband. "Diarmid will know where Rowan is, for it was he who took the baby away at my stepfather's request."

"Glenkirk would not harm the lad?"

"No," India said firmly. "His only purpose in taking him was to make certain I appeared respectable to you. One reason I mentioned my *first* husband was that I hoped to gain your respect, and perhaps even your love eventually. Then I would have told you of the child, and asked to bring him here to raise with our other children. My mother swore she would learn where the child was hidden, and make certain Rowan was all right. I did not desert our son willingly, Deverall, and I did what I could to find him. At Glenkirk, however, it is very different from here in England. No one will oppose the duke. Their loyalty is strong. Many are bound by family ties of one sort or another. I did my best for Rowan, and now I long to hold him in my arms!"

"In the morning we will question Diarmid, madame," he said. "Then we shall go north together to regain custody of our child," he promised her, smiling for the first time.

"Send Diarmid ahead," she told him. "They plan to go to Ireland this summer to seek a husband for Fortune. If we do not get word to them before they have gone, no one will help us. It is probably already too late, I fear." And her eyes filled with tears again.

"Diarmid's loyalty must be to Oxton now," the earl said quietly. "He will tell us, and then we shall fetch our son ourselves, India. This I promise you, my beloved. We do not need Glenkirk's permission. And I will always trust you from now on, my darling. Look what my foolishness has almost cost us both."

"And my foolishness, too," she admitted graciously. "We must make a memorial for Adrian. Poor boy. Had he not eloped with me he would still be alive today."

"Had he not attempted to elope with you," he corrected her, "we should have never found each other, and I should not have been so bedazzled by my love for you that I came across two seas to be reunited with you, my beautiful first wife."

"Your beautiful *only* wife," she said, laughing up at him. "You had best get used to me, Deverall Leigh, for you shall never have another wife!" Then Lady India Anne Lindley-Leigh kissed her husband passionately, and Deverall Leigh, earl of Oxton, knew that she spoke the absolute truth.

Epilogue

OXTON, SUMMER 1629

"I am forgiven then?" the duke of Glenkirk asked India.

"Deverall has convinced me it is the right thing to do, my lord," she replied.

"But you are still angry at me," he said. "I know you were born of Rowan Lindley's seed, India, but I am the father who loved and raised you after his death. You and Fortune are every bit my daughter as any born to me. What I did was not out of unkindness, or cruelty. I did what I thought was best for my daughter. Please, poppet, it has been the worst year of my life believing you hated me, and would hate me forever."

"If Deverall had not turned out to be the dey of El Sinut," India said, "I might have lost Rowan. I cannot help but wonder what Rowan Lindley might have done in this situation. You did not trust me, my lord. Would he have? You did not listen. Would he have? I know it has turned out all right, but if Deverall had not been Caynan Reis . . ." she sighed.

"I know," he replied, "but my grandson was safe, India. Flora More is a good woman, and took good care of Rowan."

"It is true, she did," the duchess of Glenkirk said, coming to stand by her husband's side. "Besides, India, you were parted from your son but five and a half months, not five years. Deverall was

Caynan, and you regained your child. Stop dwelling on what might have been, and be glad for what is," her mother said sensibly.

The ice that had been encasing India's heart suddenly cracked as she looked at her son toddling about the gardens, his nurse in pursuit. Rowan Leigh, the future earl of Oxton, was a sturdy little boy with his father's dark hair and deep blue eyes. At seventeen months of age he was a happy little boy who would never have any memory of his few months in a highland cottage. Her mother was right. The worst hadn't happened.

"Will you promise me never to doubt any of your children again, *Papa?*" India asked him.

"I swear it!" the duke of Glenkirk said fervently, kissing his daughter's hand.

"I shall hold you to it when Fortune finally goes in search of a husband," the countess of Oxton warned her father. The infant at her bosom murmured impatiently, and, laughing, India switched her daughter to her other breast. "Adrianna is such a little piglet," she said, gazing adoringly down at her week-old daughter.

"And every bit as beautiful as her mama," Deverall Leigh said, coming to stand by his wife's side. Then he smiled at his mother-in-law. "I believe, Jasmine, that your granddaughter has your turquoise eyes, although I am told it is too soon for me to tell. Still, I see that unique shading in Adrianna's eyes." He touched his daughter's tiny dark head with a gentle finger.

"Let us hope she leads a quieter life than we have led," the duchess of Glenkirk said dryly.

"The great-great-granddaughter of Skye O'Malley?" James Leslie said with a chuckle. "I think not, madame. I think not! Adventure seems to be in the blood of this family's women. Heaven only knows what hazards and risks this pretty wench will take when she is grown."

"She might turn out to be like Great-aunt Willow," India said. Then she saw the twinkle in her husband's eyes, and, hearing the unrestrained laughter bubbling up in her parents' throats, the countess of Oxton was forced to concur. "You are right, Papa. You are doubtlessly right. *Not the great-great-granddaughter of Skye O'Malley!*"